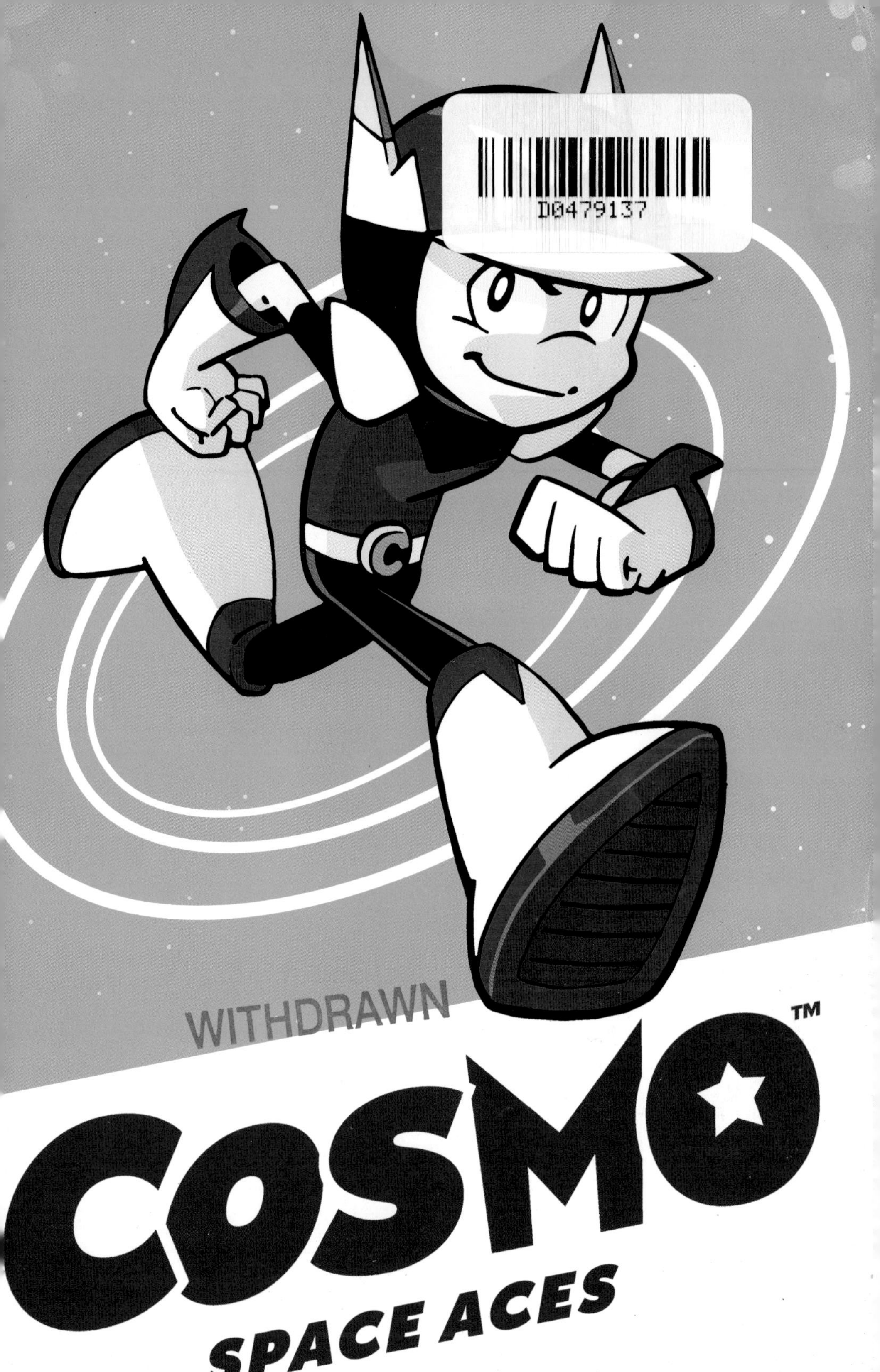

COSMO™

SPACE ACES

STORY BY
IAN FLYNN

LETTERING BY
JACK MORELLI

COLORS BY
MATT HERMS

EDITOR-IN-CHIEF
VICTOR GORELICK

PUBLISHER
JON GOLDWATER

ART BY
TRACY YARDLEY
Chapters 1-4, Chap. 5 (p. 1-8, 10-11, 18-20)

EVAN STANLEY
Chap. 5 (p. 9, 12-17)

MAURO FONSECA
Chap. 5 GAME SPRITES

EDITORS
VINCENT LOVALLO
AND ALEX SEGURA

ASSOCIATE EDITOR
STEPHEN OSWALD

ASSISTANT EDITOR
JAMIE LEE ROTANTE

COSMO™

ADVENTURE AWAITS...

The original Cosmo the Merry Martian series was printed way back in 1958. A lot of things have changed since then: our understanding of our Solar System, our understanding of each other, our collective sense of humor, and more. But one underlying element remained eternal: Cosmo was weird, and that was fantastic.

Jump ahead sixty years and Cosmo's crew launches once again. Cosmo's still our brave leader, but he's a bit more thoughtful this time. Astra's the pilot now, and we see what drives Orbi. Prof. Thimk is out and Dr. Medulla is in (but is there a relation?) The Queen of Venus is looking far less human, and far more threatening. But things are still wonderfully weird–and limitless!

Here you'll read about the Cosmo crew's adventures on the Moon, but what about the queendom of Venus? The vegetable people of Saturn? The eternal golf course that is the Kuiper Belt? Our Solar System is a treasure trove of alien worlds that can be spun in all sorts of wacky ways. And the galaxy beyond? The universe? Every star, every comet, and every lump of space rock out there has something fun going on. I really hope that, one day, we'll be able to take you there.

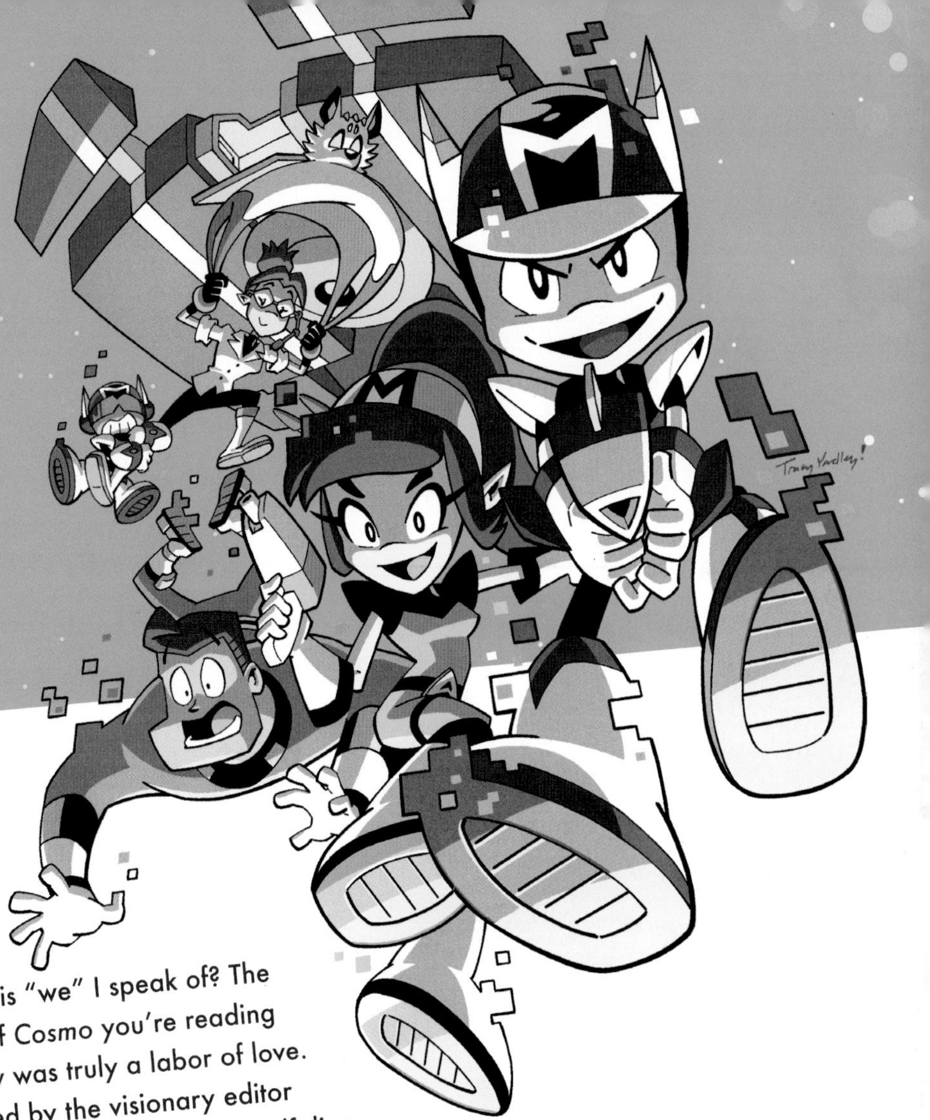
Tracy Yardley!

Who is this "we" I speak of? The volume of Cosmo you're reading right now was truly a labor of love. Captained by the visionary editor Vincent Lovallo, he steered myself, line masters Tracy Yardley and Evan Stanley, color maestro Matt Herms and veteran letterer Jack Morelli through a project to take your grandfather's space hero and update him for readers today. I couldn't have served with a better crew.

Whether you're joining us for the first time, or picking this up to complete your Cosmo collection–welcome! It's been a delight helping to bring Cosmo's adventures to you, and I hope you enjoy the ride.

See you, Space Cowboy

IAN FLYNN

CHAPTER 1 • SPACE ACES

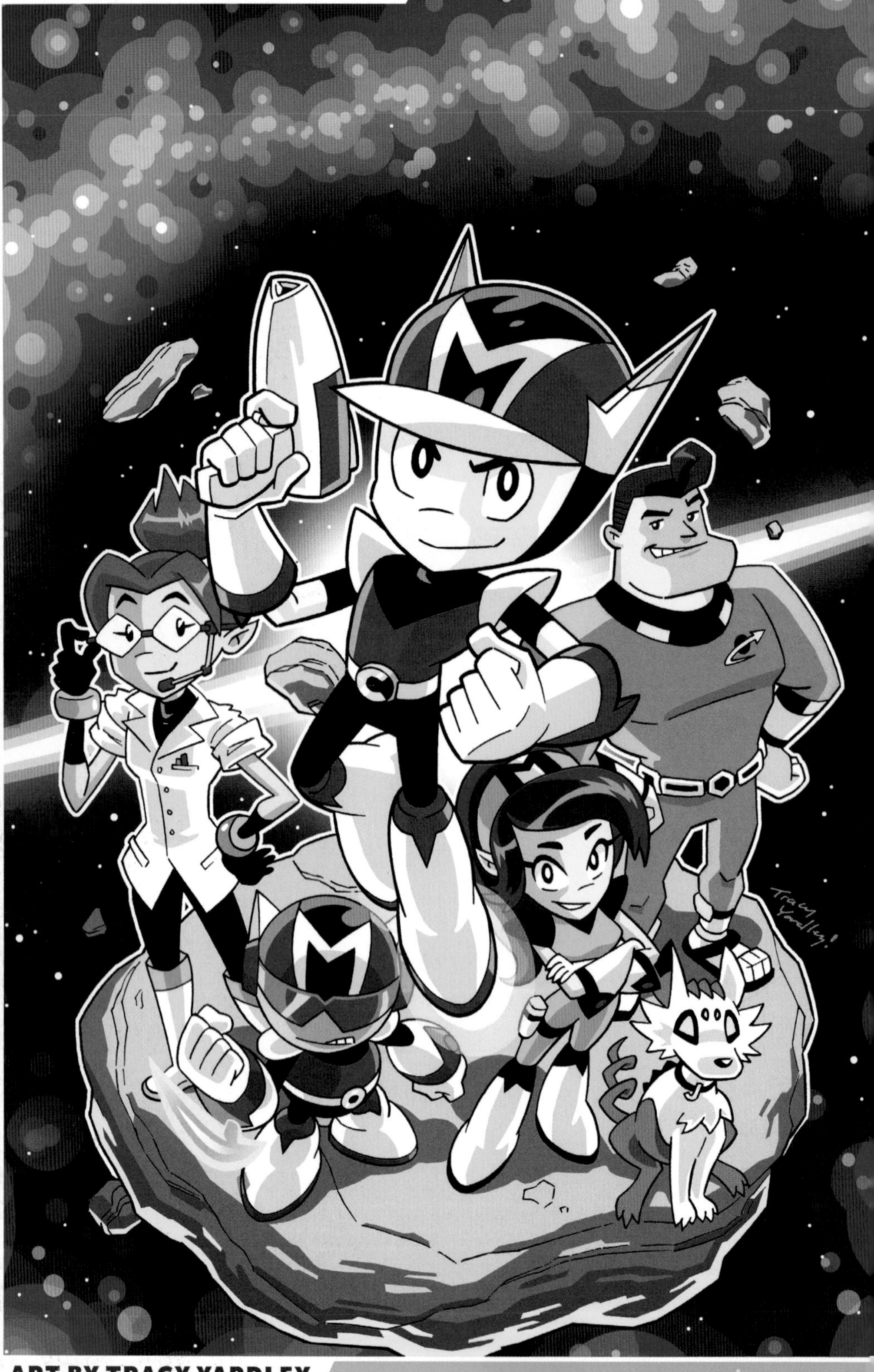
Tracy Yardley!

ART BY TRACY YARDLEY

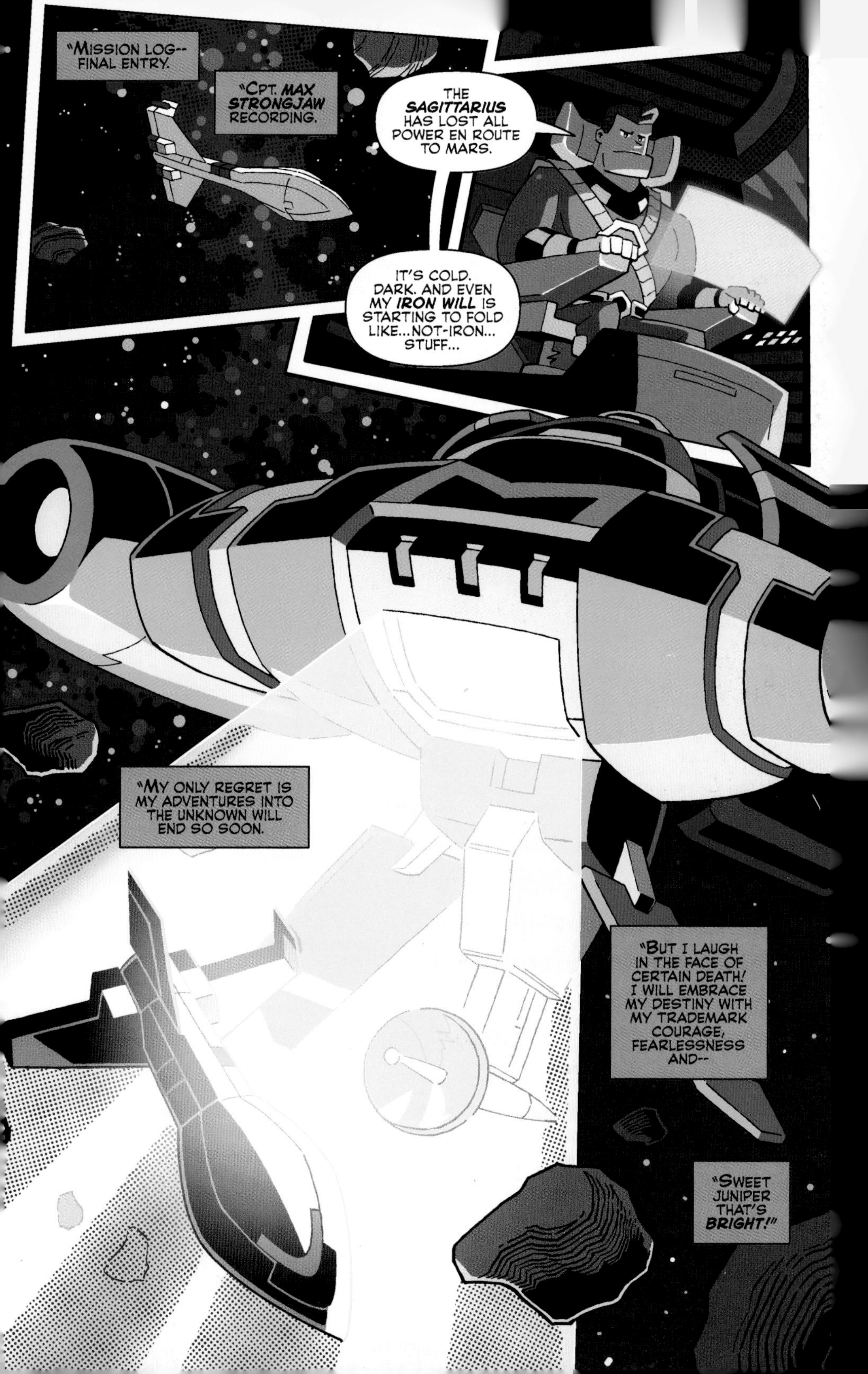
"Mission log--
final entry.
"Cpt. Max Strongjaw recording.
The Sagittarius has lost all power en route to Mars.
It's cold. Dark. And even my iron will is starting to fold like...not-iron... stuff...
"My only regret is my adventures into the unknown will end so soon.
"But I laugh in the face of certain death! I will embrace my destiny with my trademark courage, fearlessness and--
"Sweet juniper that's bright!"

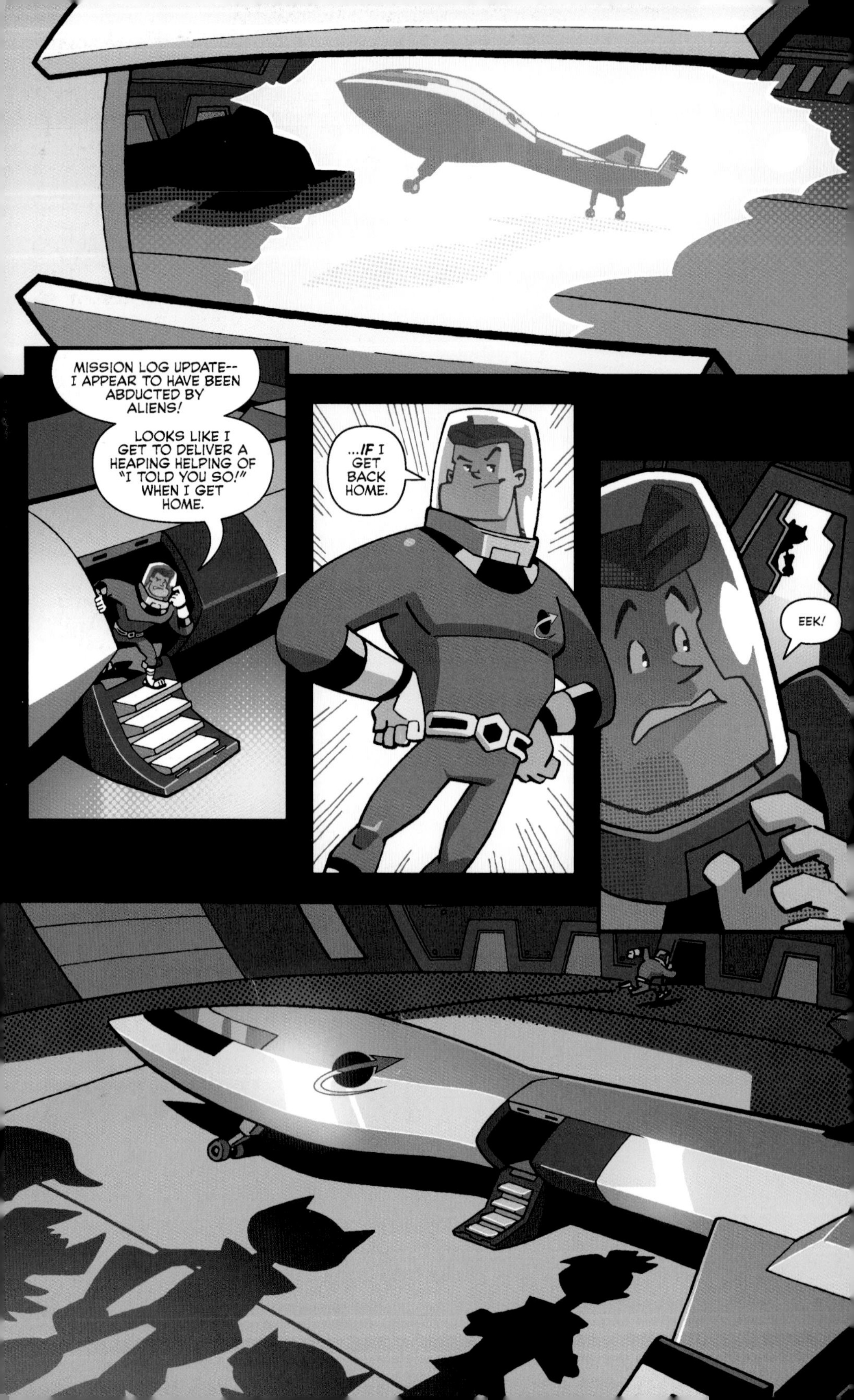
MISSION LOG UPDATE-- I APPEAR TO HAVE BEEN ABDUCTED BY ALIENS!
LOOKS LIKE I GET TO DELIVER A HEAPING HELPING OF "I TOLD YOU SO!" WHEN I GET HOME.
...IF I GET BACK HOME.
EEK!

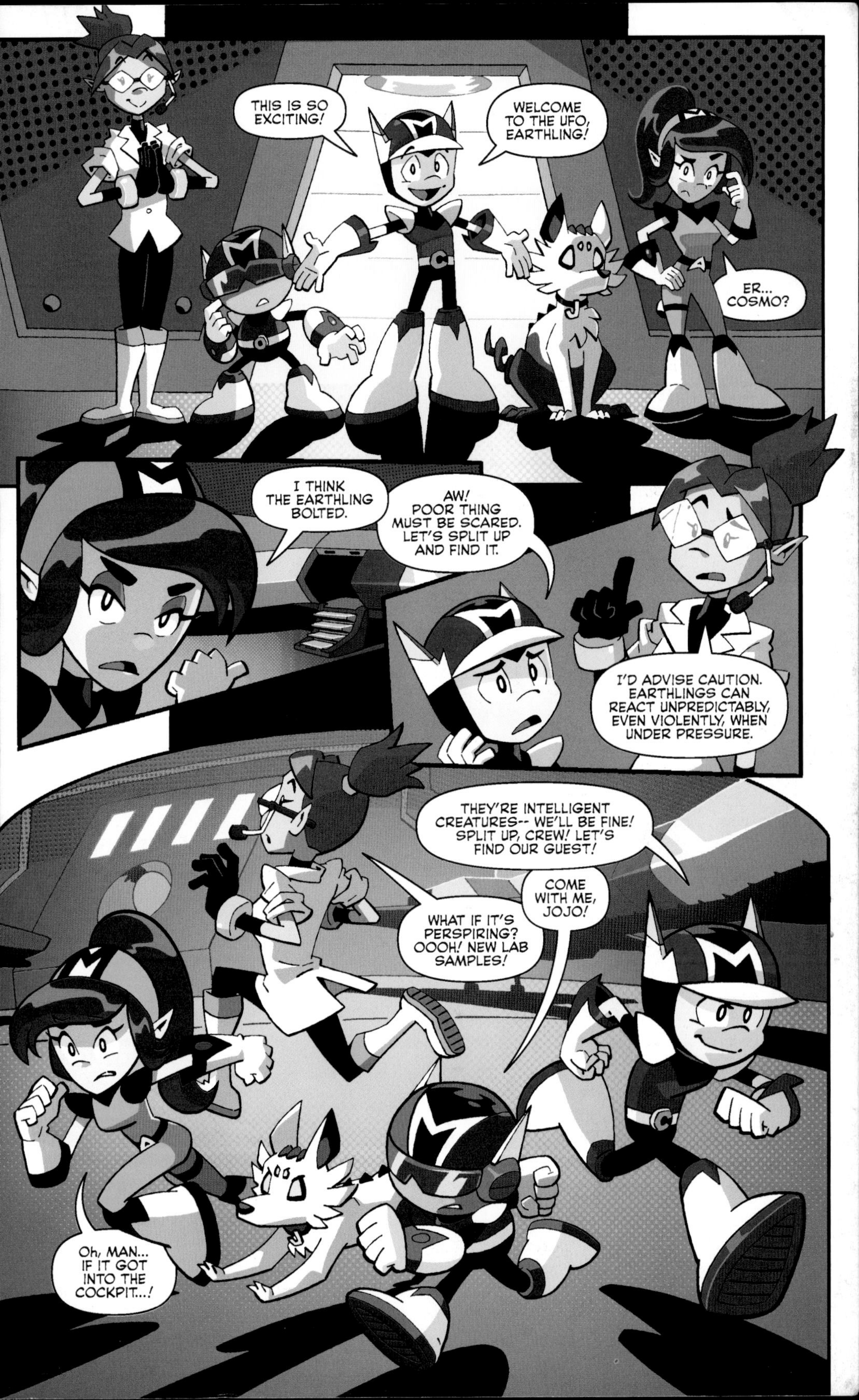
THIS IS SO EXCITING!
WELCOME TO THE UFO, EARTHLING!
ER... COSMO?
I THINK THE EARTHLING BOLTED.
AW! POOR THING MUST BE SCARED. LET'S SPLIT UP AND FIND IT.
I'D ADVISE CAUTION. EARTHLINGS CAN REACT UNPREDICTABLY, EVEN VIOLENTLY, WHEN UNDER PRESSURE.
THEY'RE INTELLIGENT CREATURES-- WE'LL BE FINE! SPLIT UP, CREW! LET'S FIND OUR GUEST!
COME WITH ME, JOJO!
WHAT IF IT'S PERSPIRING? OOOH! NEW LAB SAMPLES!
Oh, MAN... IF IT GOT INTO THE COCKPIT...!

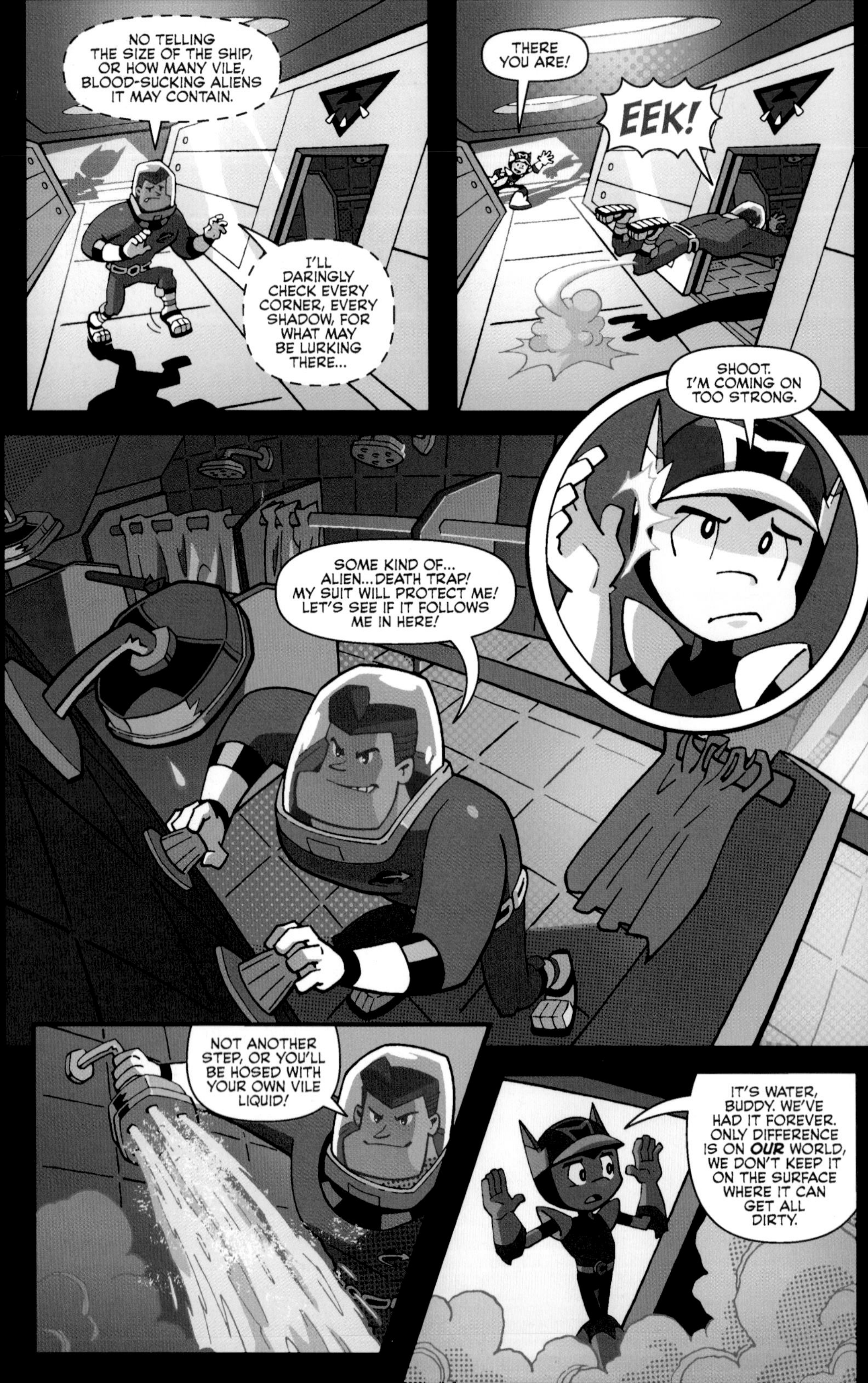
NO TELLING THE SIZE OF THE SHIP, OR HOW MANY VILE, BLOOD-SUCKING ALIENS IT MAY CONTAIN.
I'LL DARINGLY CHECK EVERY CORNER, EVERY SHADOW, FOR WHAT MAY BE LURKING THERE...
THERE YOU ARE!
EEK!
SHOOT. I'M COMING ON TOO STRONG.
SOME KIND OF... ALIEN...DEATH TRAP! MY SUIT WILL PROTECT ME! LET'S SEE IF IT FOLLOWS ME IN HERE!
NOT ANOTHER STEP, OR YOU'LL BE HOSED WITH YOUR OWN VILE LIQUID!
IT'S WATER, BUDDY. WE'VE HAD IT FOREVER. ONLY DIFFERENCE IS ON OUR WORLD, WE DON'T KEEP IT ON THE SURFACE WHERE IT CAN GET ALL DIRTY.

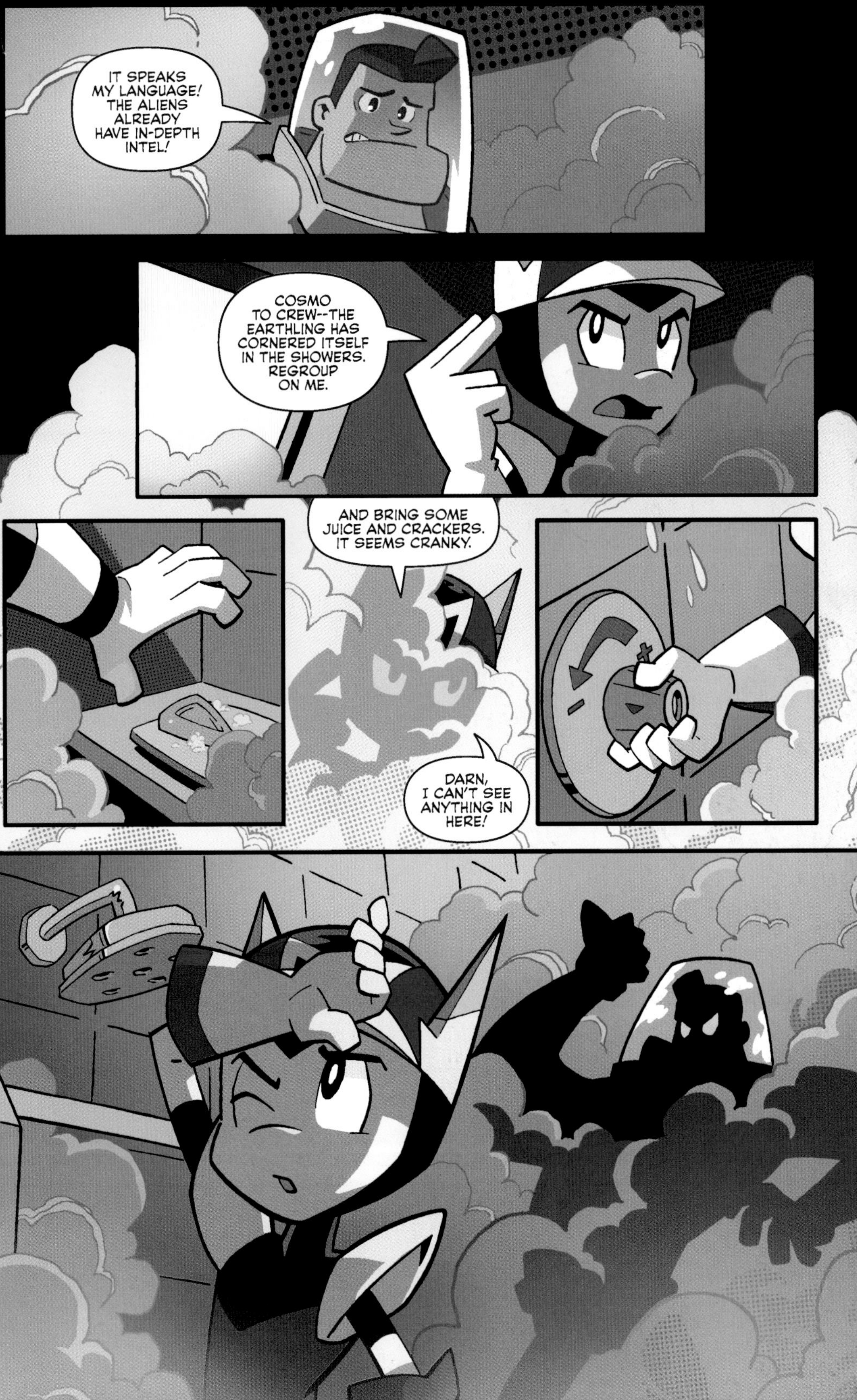
IT SPEAKS MY LANGUAGE! THE ALIENS ALREADY HAVE IN-DEPTH INTEL!
COSMO TO CREW--THE EARTHLING HAS CORNERED ITSELF IN THE SHOWERS. REGROUP ON ME.
AND BRING SOME JUICE AND CRACKERS. IT SEEMS CRANKY.
DARN, I CAN'T SEE ANYTHING IN HERE!

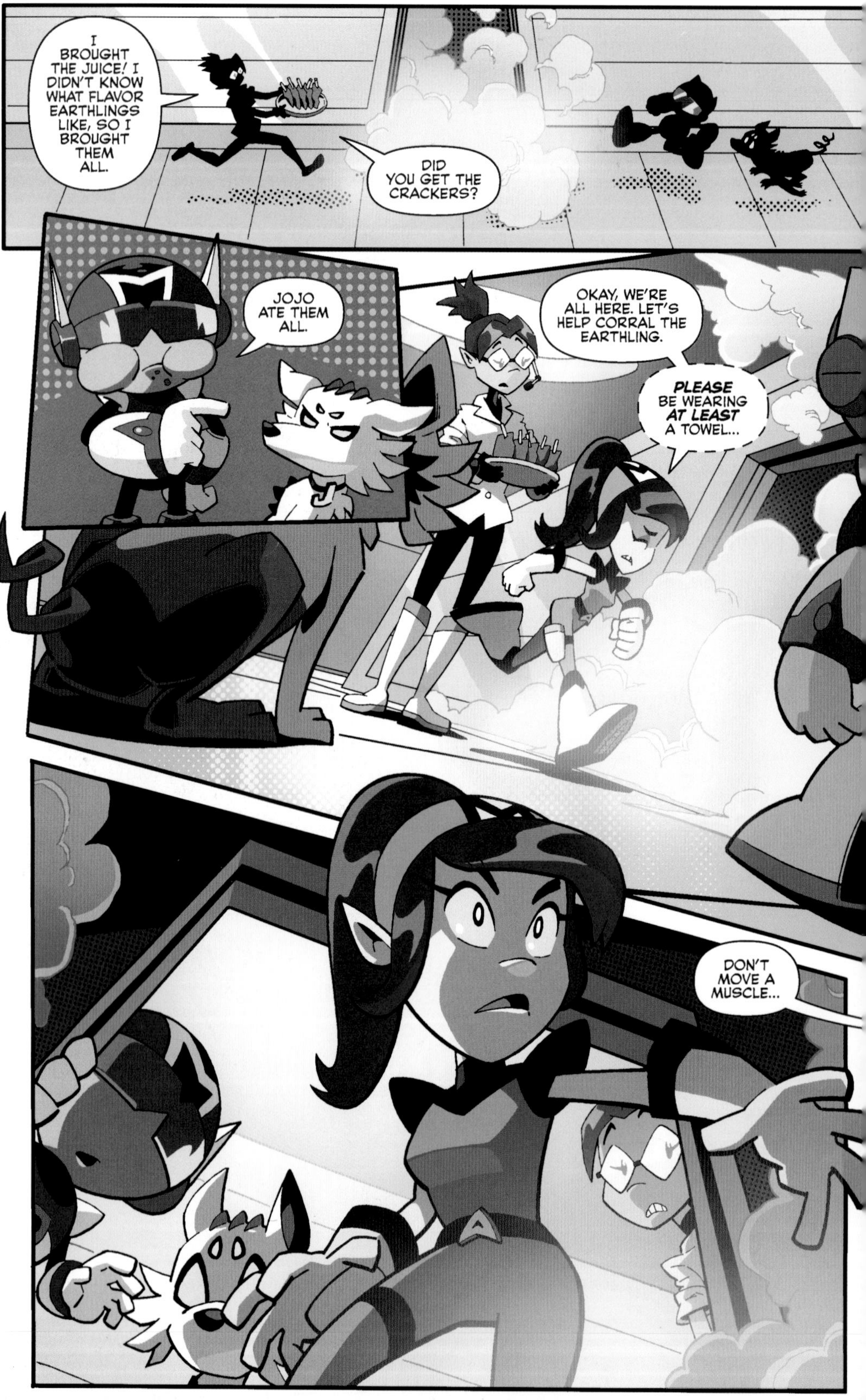
I BROUGHT THE JUICE! I DIDN'T KNOW WHAT FLAVOR EARTHLINGS LIKE, SO I BROUGHT THEM ALL.
DID YOU GET THE CRACKERS?
JOJO ATE THEM ALL.
OKAY, WE'RE ALL HERE. LET'S HELP CORRAL THE EARTHLING.
PLEASE BE WEARING AT LEAST A TOWEL...
DON'T MOVE A MUSCLE...

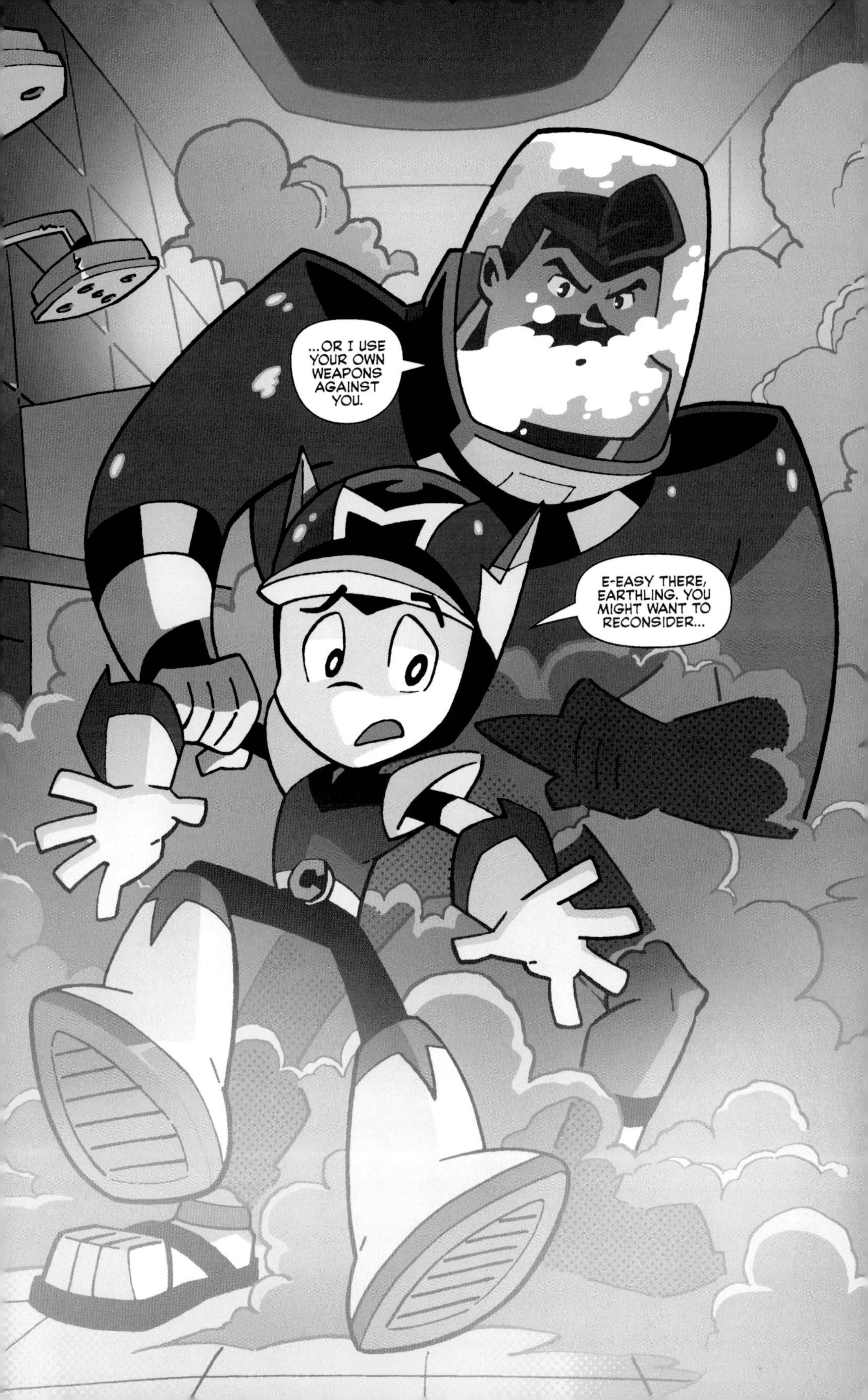
...OR I USE YOUR OWN WEAPONS AGAINST YOU.
E-EASY THERE, EARTHLING. YOU MIGHT WANT TO RECONSIDER...

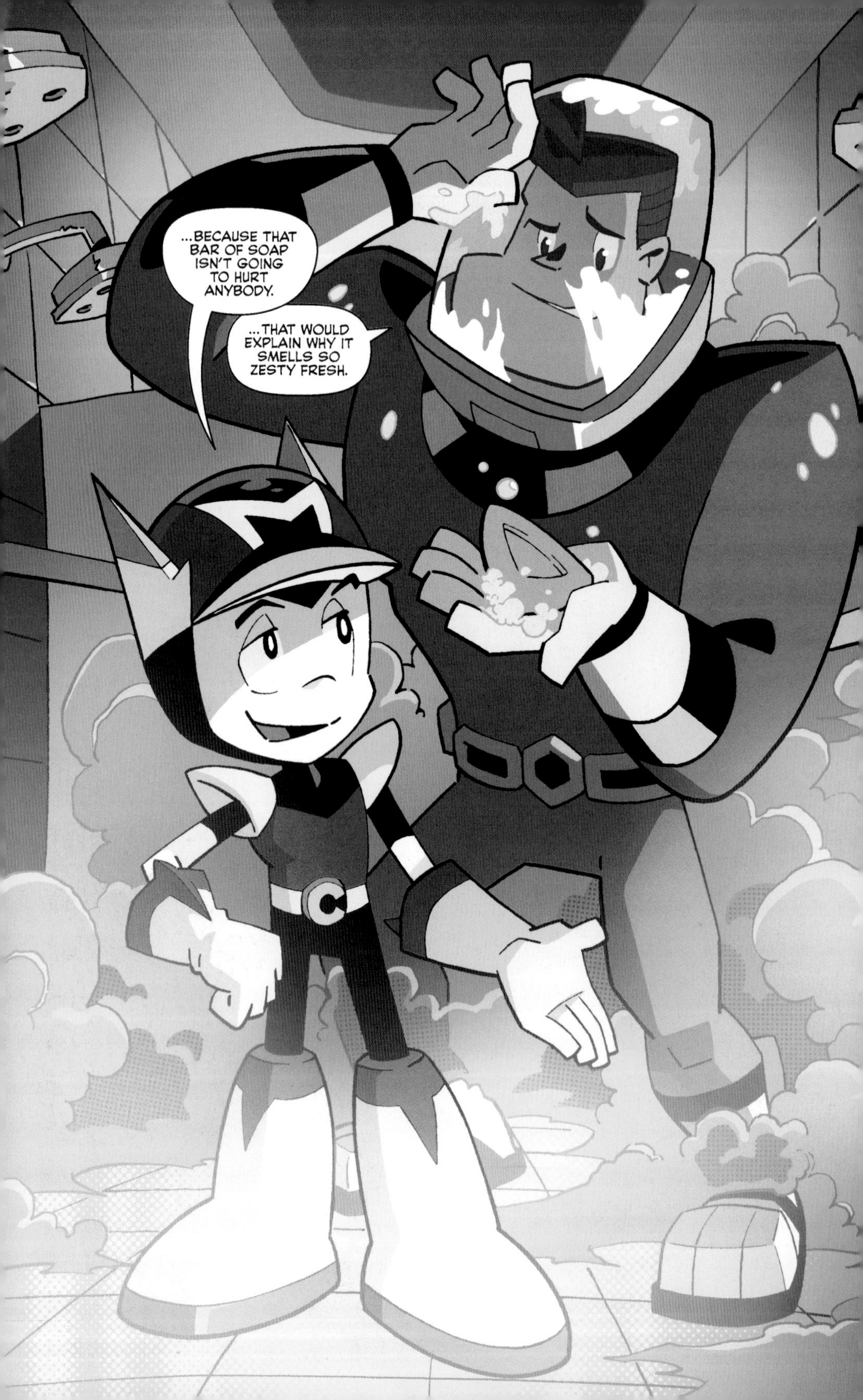
...BECAUSE THAT BAR OF SOAP ISN'T GOING TO HURT ANYBODY.
...THAT WOULD EXPLAIN WHY IT SMELLS SO ZESTY FRESH.

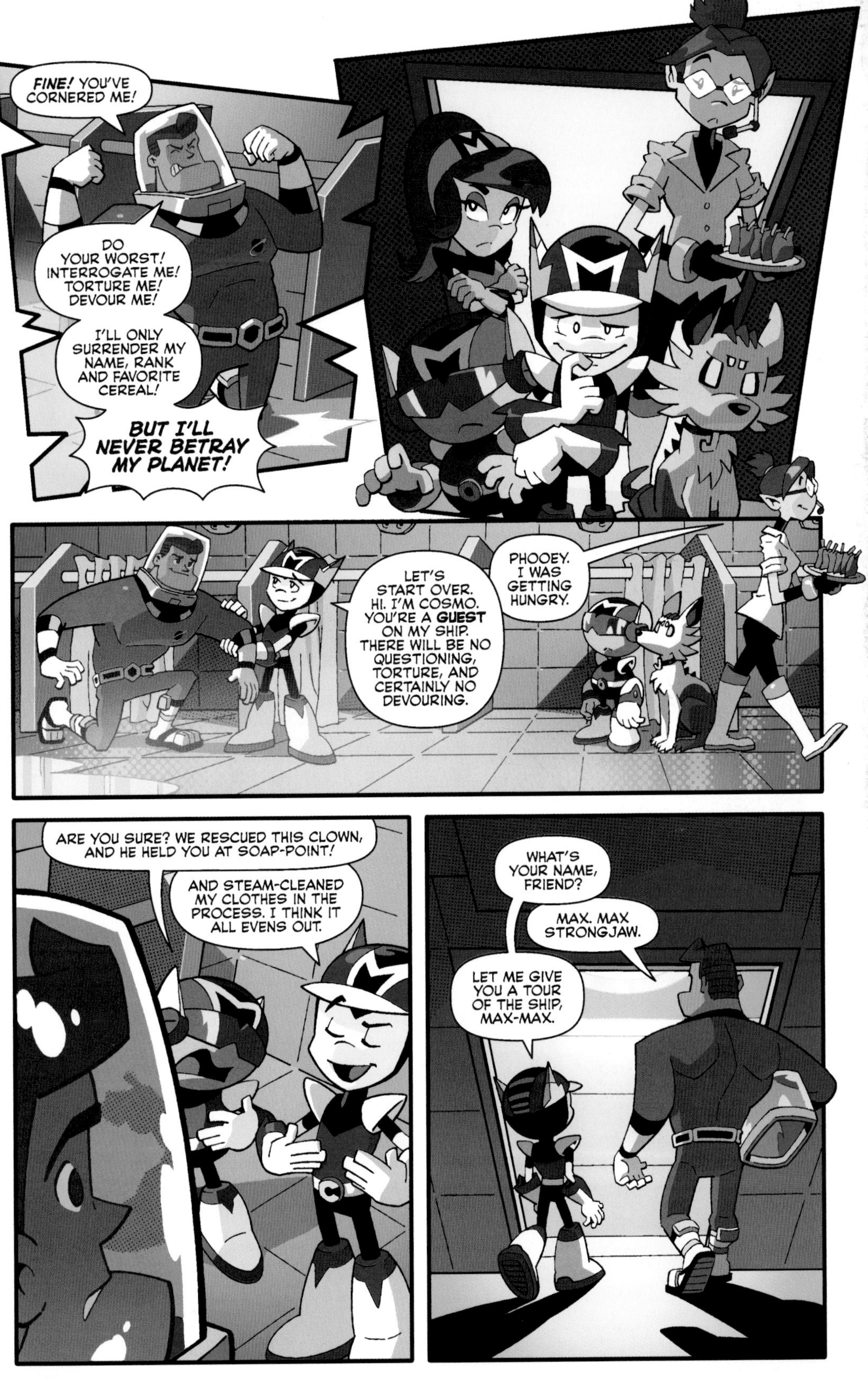

FINE! YOU'VE CORNERED ME!
DO YOUR WORST! INTERROGATE ME! TORTURE ME! DEVOUR ME!
I'LL ONLY SURRENDER MY NAME, RANK AND FAVORITE CEREAL!
BUT I'LL NEVER BETRAY MY PLANET!
LET'S START OVER. HI. I'M COSMO. YOU'RE A GUEST ON MY SHIP. THERE WILL BE NO QUESTIONING, TORTURE, AND CERTAINLY NO DEVOURING.
PHOOEY. I WAS GETTING HUNGRY.
ARE YOU SURE? WE RESCUED THIS CLOWN, AND HE HELD YOU AT SOAP-POINT!
AND STEAM-CLEANED MY CLOTHES IN THE PROCESS. I THINK IT ALL EVENS OUT.
WHAT'S YOUR NAME, FRIEND?
MAX. MAX STRONGJAW.
LET ME GIVE YOU A TOUR OF THE SHIP, MAX-MAX.

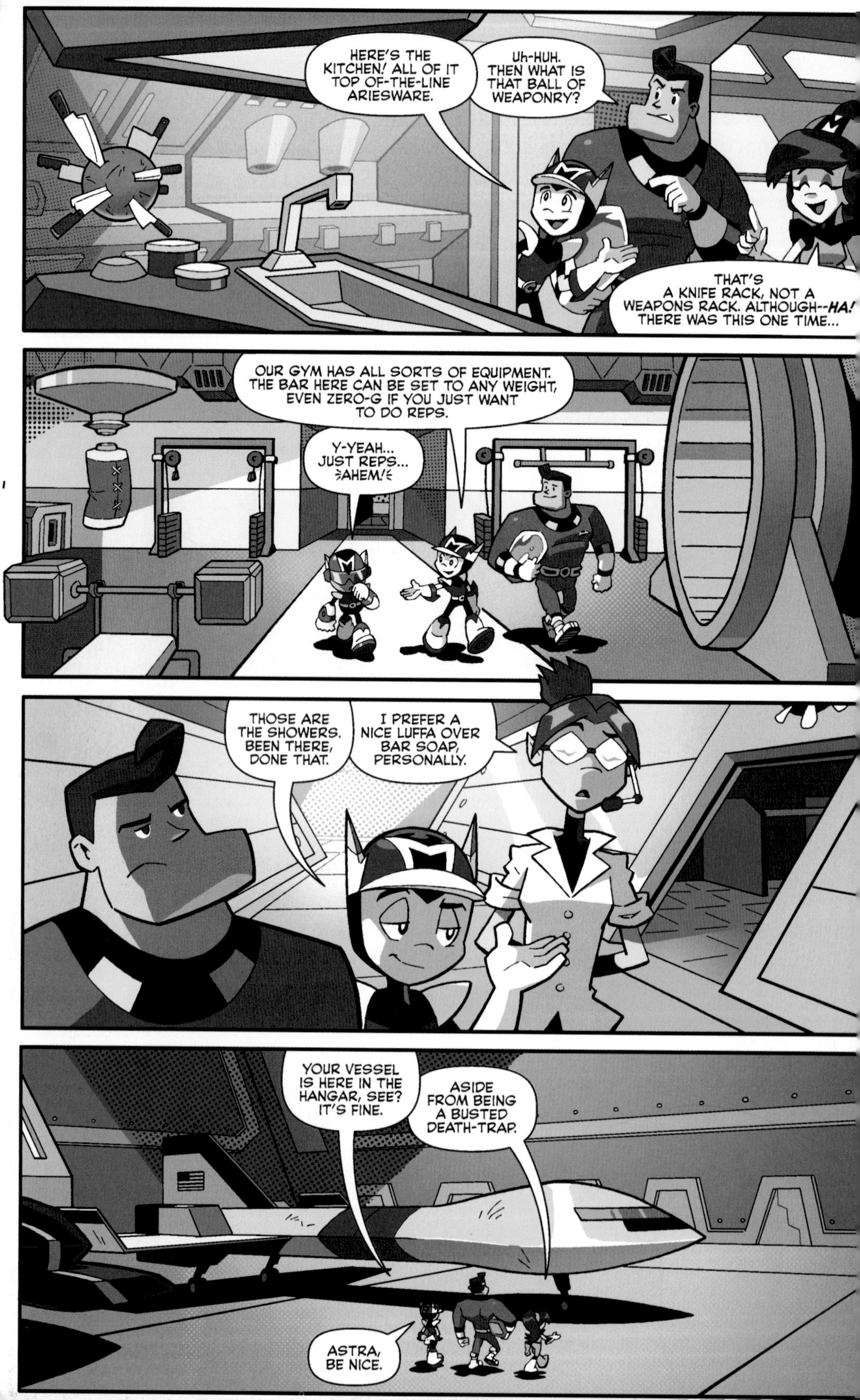
HERE'S THE KITCHEN! ALL OF IT TOP OF-THE-LINE ARIESWARE.
UH-HUH. THEN WHAT IS THAT BALL OF WEAPONRY?
THAT'S A KNIFE RACK, NOT A WEAPONS RACK. ALTHOUGH--HA! THERE WAS THIS ONE TIME...
OUR GYM HAS ALL SORTS OF EQUIPMENT. THE BAR HERE CAN BE SET TO ANY WEIGHT, EVEN ZERO-G IF YOU JUST WANT TO DO REPS.
Y-YEAH... JUST REPS... AHEM!
THOSE ARE THE SHOWERS. BEEN THERE, DONE THAT.
I PREFER A NICE LUFFA OVER BAR SOAP, PERSONALLY.
YOUR VESSEL IS HERE IN THE HANGAR, SEE? IT'S FINE.
ASIDE FROM BEING A BUSTED DEATH-TRAP.
ASTRA, BE NICE.

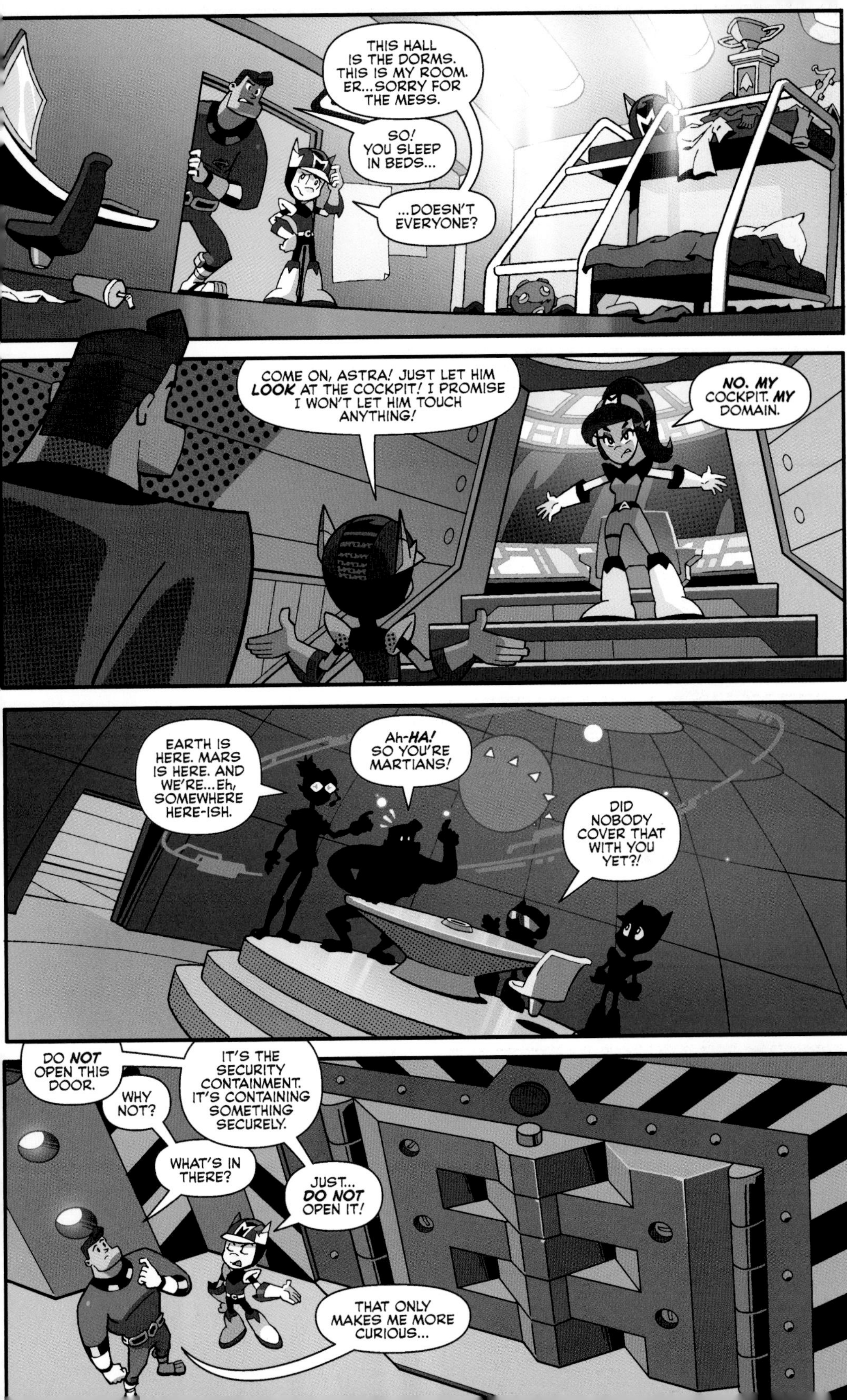
THIS HALL IS THE DORMS. THIS IS MY ROOM. ER...SORRY FOR THE MESS.
SO! YOU SLEEP IN BEDS...
...DOESN'T EVERYONE?
COME ON, ASTRA! JUST LET HIM LOOK AT THE COCKPIT! I PROMISE I WON'T LET HIM TOUCH ANYTHING!
NO. MY COCKPIT. MY DOMAIN.
EARTH IS HERE. MARS IS HERE. AND WE'RE...Eh, SOMEWHERE HERE-ISH.
Ah-HA! SO YOU'RE MARTIANS!
DID NOBODY COVER THAT WITH YOU YET?!
DO NOT OPEN THIS DOOR.
WHY NOT?
IT'S THE SECURITY CONTAINMENT. IT'S CONTAINING SOMETHING SECURELY.
WHAT'S IN THERE?
JUST... DO NOT OPEN IT!
THAT ONLY MAKES ME MORE CURIOUS...

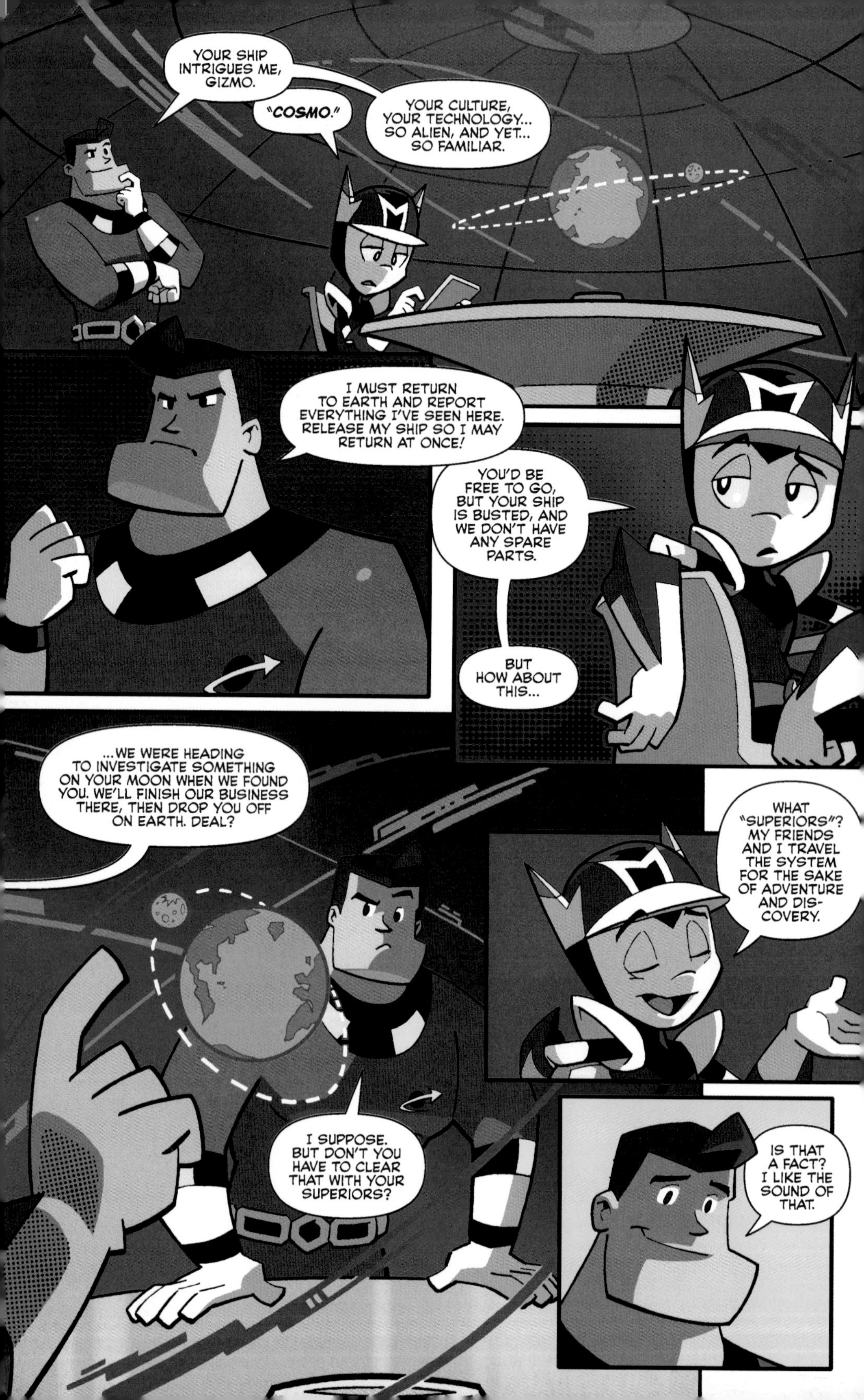
YOUR SHIP INTRIGUES ME, GIZMO.
"COSMO."
YOUR CULTURE, YOUR TECHNOLOGY... SO ALIEN, AND YET... SO FAMILIAR.
I MUST RETURN TO EARTH AND REPORT EVERYTHING I'VE SEEN HERE. RELEASE MY SHIP SO I MAY RETURN AT ONCE!
YOU'D BE FREE TO GO, BUT YOUR SHIP IS BUSTED, AND WE DON'T HAVE ANY SPARE PARTS.
BUT HOW ABOUT THIS...
...WE WERE HEADING TO INVESTIGATE SOMETHING ON YOUR MOON WHEN WE FOUND YOU. WE'LL FINISH OUR BUSINESS THERE, THEN DROP YOU OFF ON EARTH. DEAL?
I SUPPOSE. BUT DON'T YOU HAVE TO CLEAR THAT WITH YOUR SUPERIORS?
WHAT "SUPERIORS"? MY FRIENDS AND I TRAVEL THE SYSTEM FOR THE SAKE OF ADVENTURE AND DIS-COVERY.
IS THAT A FACT? I LIKE THE SOUND OF THAT.

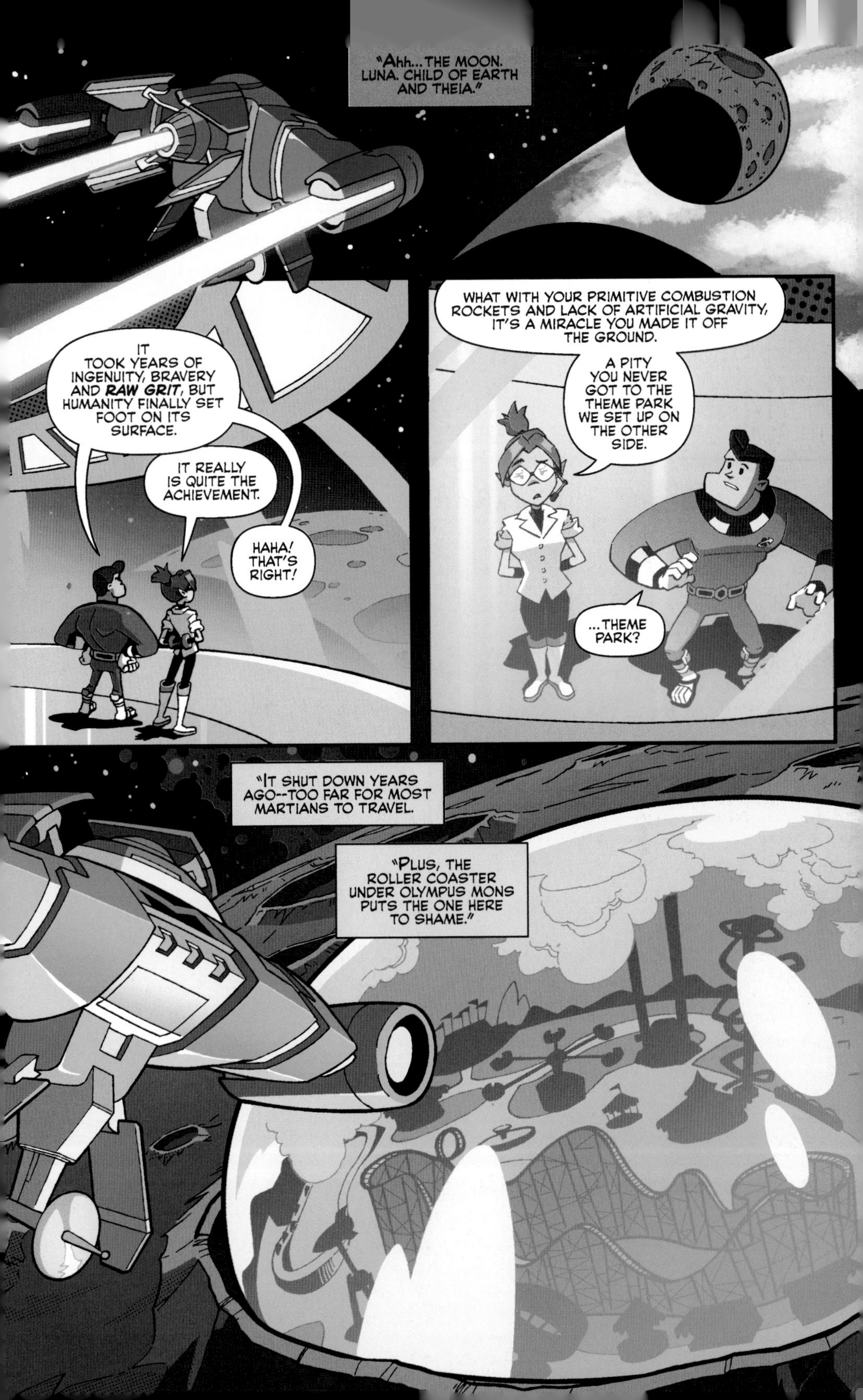
"Ahh... THE MOON. LUNA. CHILD OF EARTH AND THEIA."
IT TOOK YEARS OF INGENUITY, BRAVERY AND **RAW GRIT**, BUT HUMANITY FINALLY SET FOOT ON ITS SURFACE.
IT REALLY IS QUITE THE ACHIEVEMENT.
HAHA! THAT'S RIGHT!
WHAT WITH YOUR PRIMITIVE COMBUSTION ROCKETS AND LACK OF ARTIFICIAL GRAVITY, IT'S A MIRACLE YOU MADE IT OFF THE GROUND.
A PITY YOU NEVER GOT TO THE THEME PARK WE SET UP ON THE OTHER SIDE.
...THEME PARK?
"IT SHUT DOWN YEARS AGO--TOO FAR FOR MOST MARTIANS TO TRAVEL.
"PLUS, THE ROLLER COASTER UNDER OLYMPUS MONS PUTS THE ONE HERE TO SHAME."

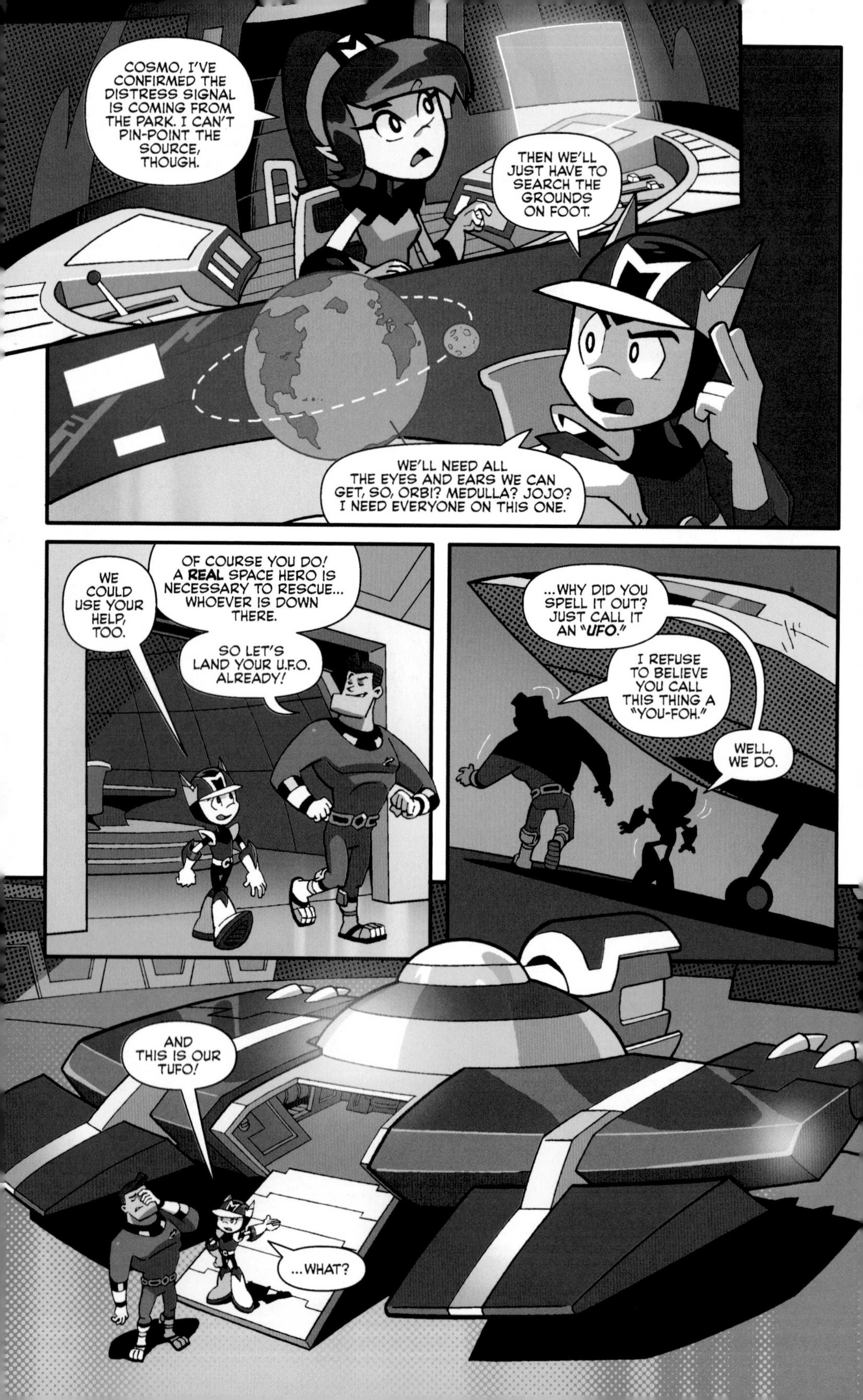

COSMO, I'VE CONFIRMED THE DISTRESS SIGNAL IS COMING FROM THE PARK. I CAN'T PIN-POINT THE SOURCE, THOUGH.
THEN WE'LL JUST HAVE TO SEARCH THE GROUNDS ON FOOT.
WE'LL NEED ALL THE EYES AND EARS WE CAN GET, SO, ORBI? MEDULLA? JOJO? I NEED EVERYONE ON THIS ONE.
WE COULD USE YOUR HELP, TOO.
OF COURSE YOU DO! A **REAL** SPACE HERO IS NECESSARY TO RESCUE... WHOEVER IS DOWN THERE.
SO LET'S LAND YOUR U.F.O. ALREADY!
...WHY DID YOU SPELL IT OUT? JUST CALL IT AN "*UFO*."
I REFUSE TO BELIEVE YOU CALL THIS THING A "YOU-FOH."
WELL, WE DO.
AND THIS IS OUR TUFO!
...WHAT?

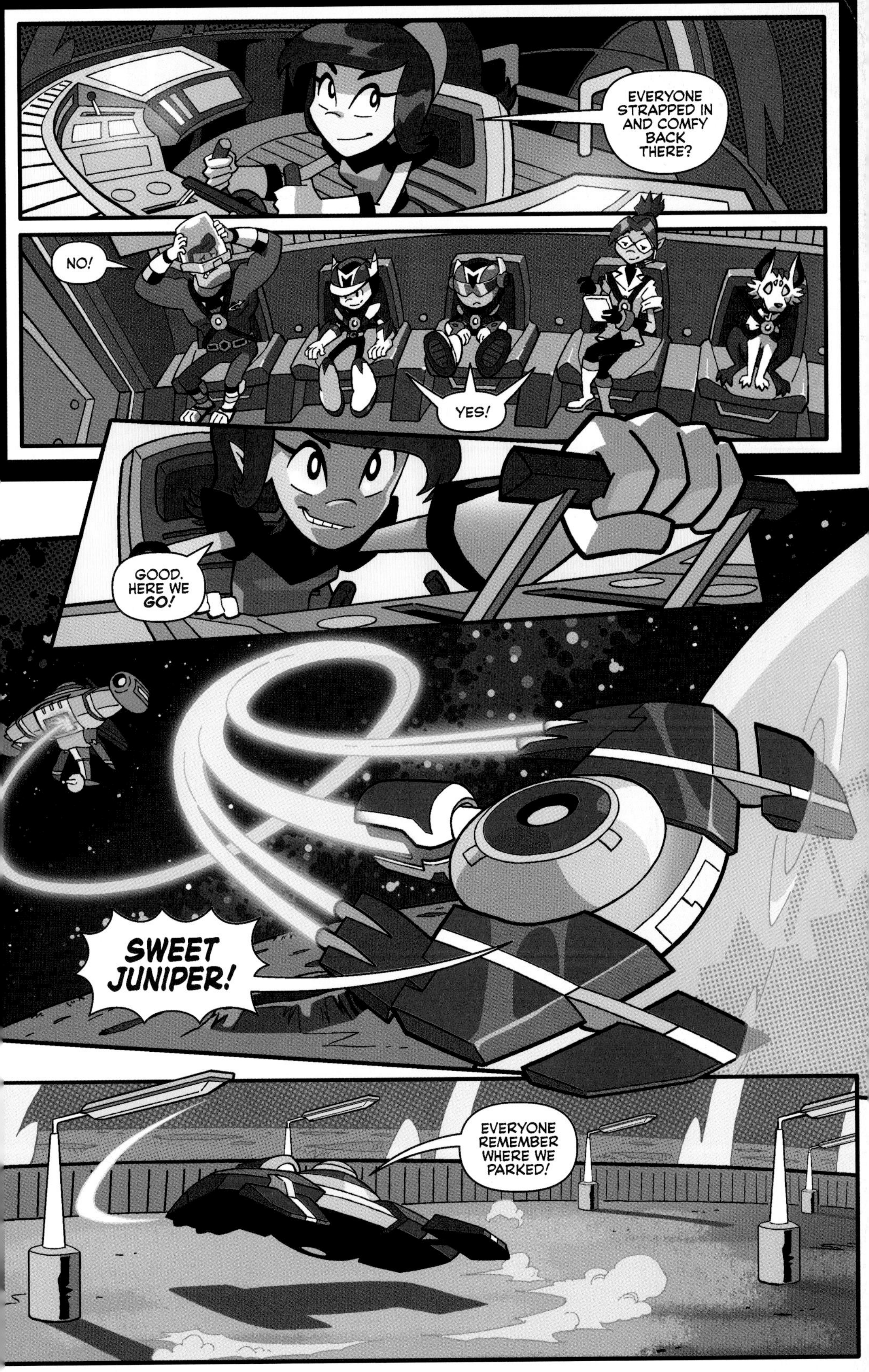
EVERYONE STRAPPED IN AND COMFY BACK THERE?
NO!
YES!
GOOD. HERE WE GO!
SWEET JUNIPER!
EVERYONE REMEMBER WHERE WE PARKED!

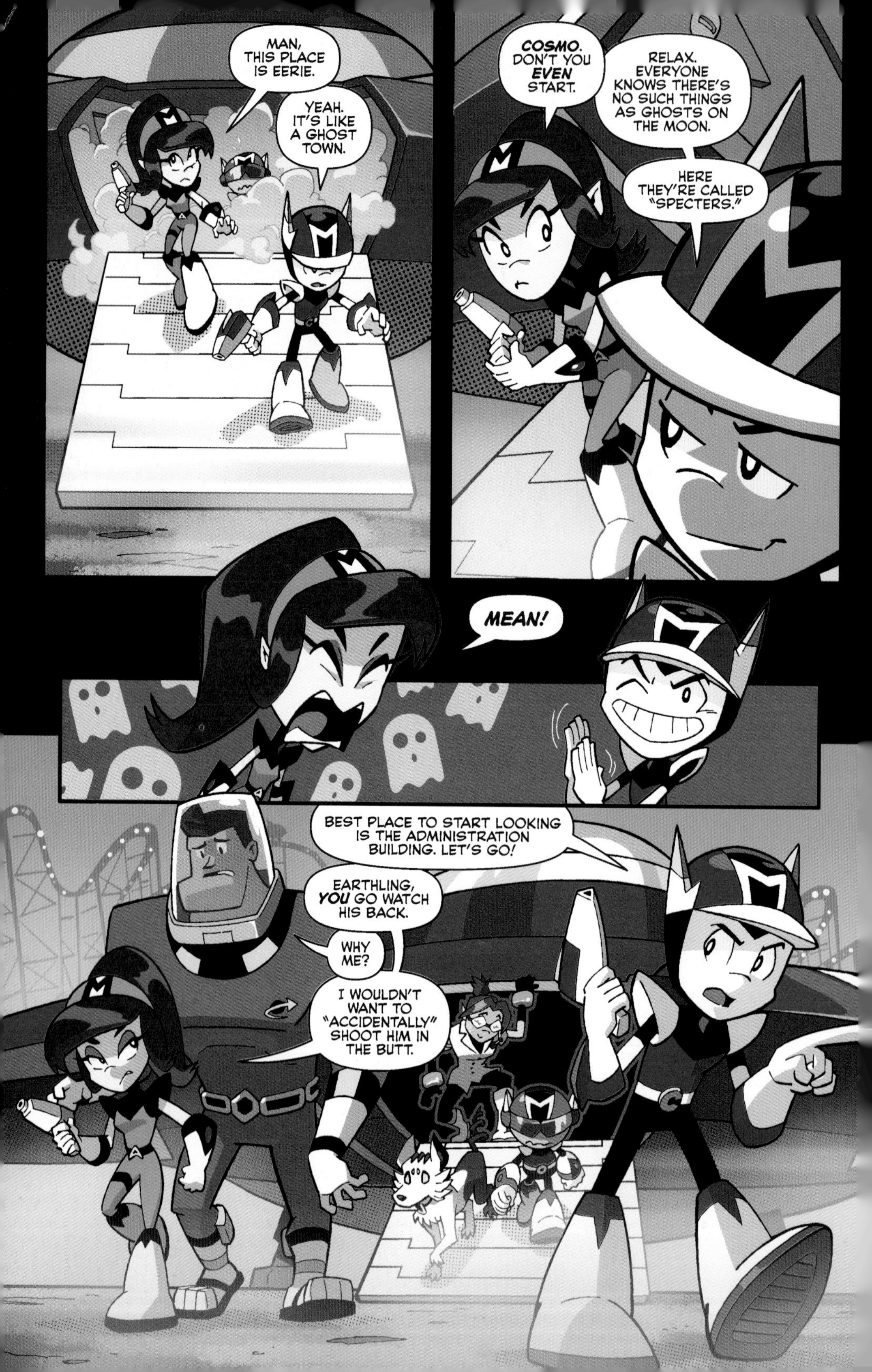
MAN, THIS PLACE IS EERIE.
YEAH. IT'S LIKE A GHOST TOWN.
COSMO. DON'T YOU EVEN START.
RELAX. EVERYONE KNOWS THERE'S NO SUCH THINGS AS GHOSTS ON THE MOON.
HERE THEY'RE CALLED "SPECTERS."
MEAN!
BEST PLACE TO START LOOKING IS THE ADMINISTRATION BUILDING. LET'S GO!
EARTHLING, YOU GO WATCH HIS BACK.
WHY ME?
I WOULDN'T WANT TO "ACCIDENTALLY" SHOOT HIM IN THE BUTT.

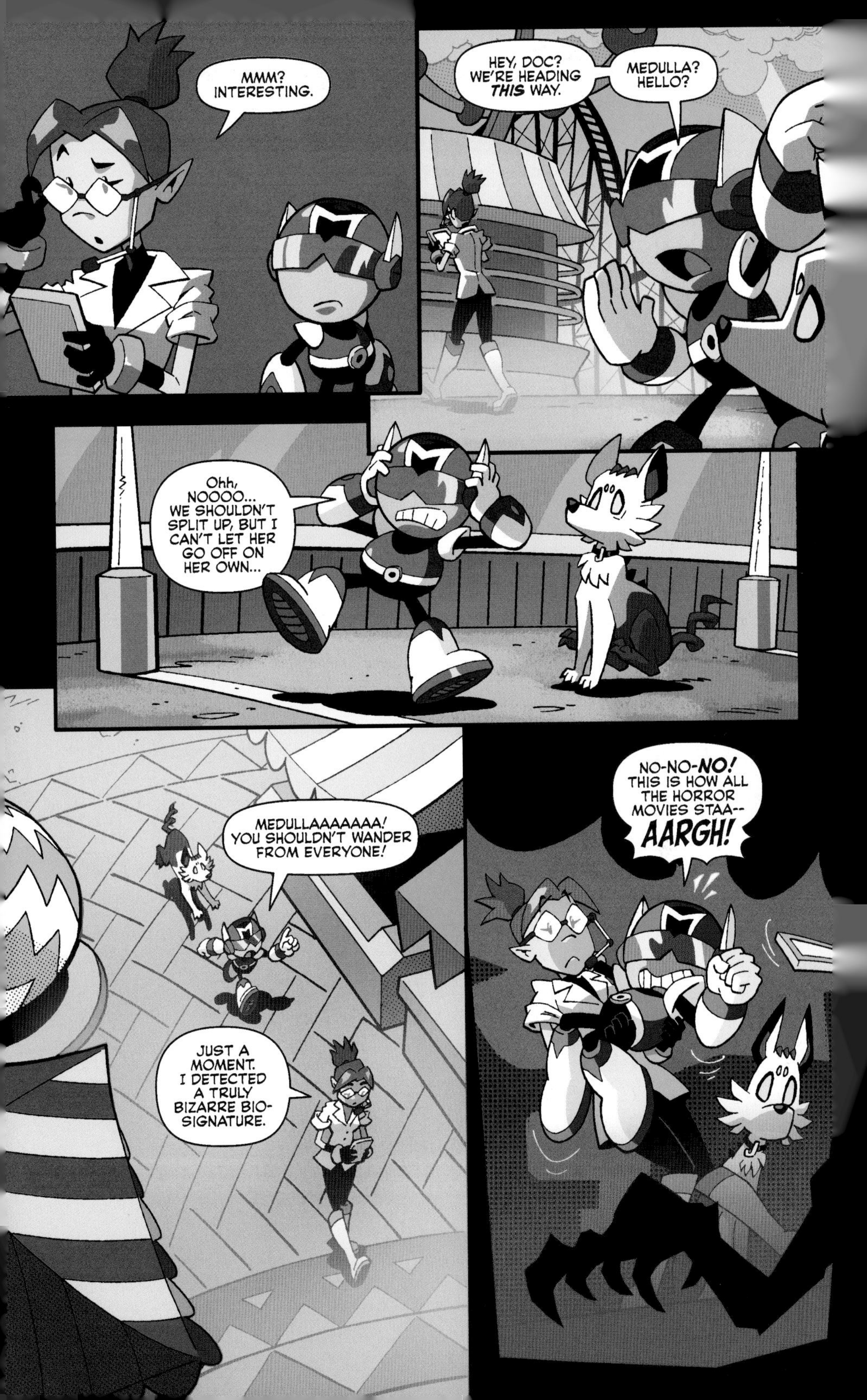
MMM? INTERESTING.
HEY, DOC? WE'RE HEADING THIS WAY.
MEDULLA? HELLO?
Ohh, NOOOO... WE SHOULDN'T SPLIT UP, BUT I CAN'T LET HER GO OFF ON HER OWN...
MEDULLAAAAAAAA! YOU SHOULDN'T WANDER FROM EVERYONE!
JUST A MOMENT. I DETECTED A TRULY BIZARRE BIO-SIGNATURE.
NO-NO-NO! THIS IS HOW ALL THE HORROR MOVIES STAA-- AARGH!

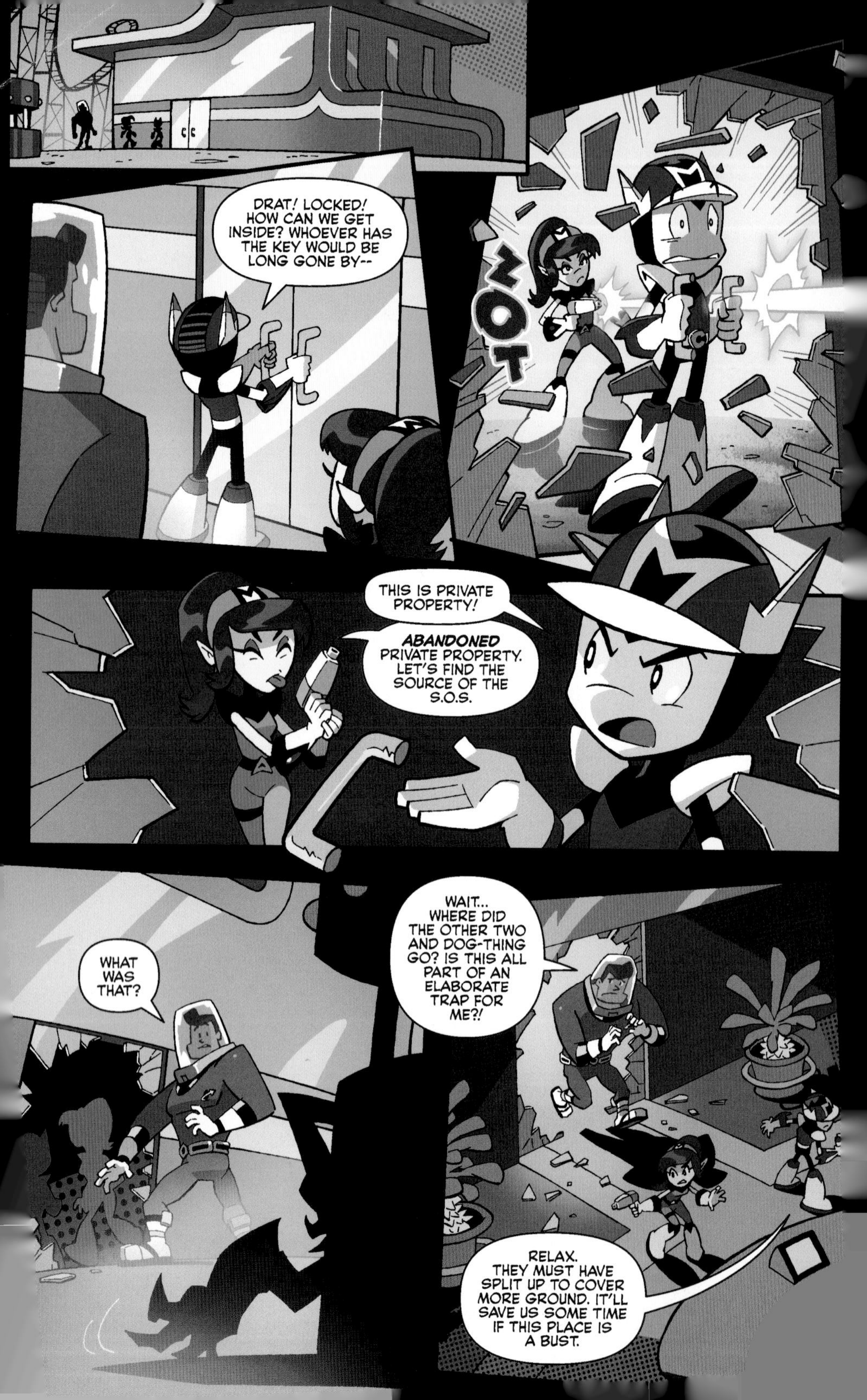
DRAT! LOCKED! HOW CAN WE GET INSIDE? WHOEVER HAS THE KEY WOULD BE LONG GONE BY--
ZOT
THIS IS PRIVATE PROPERTY!
ABANDONED PRIVATE PROPERTY. LET'S FIND THE SOURCE OF THE S.O.S.
WHAT WAS THAT?
WAIT... WHERE DID THE OTHER TWO AND DOG-THING GO? IS THIS ALL PART OF AN ELABORATE TRAP FOR ME?!
RELAX. THEY MUST HAVE SPLIT UP TO COVER MORE GROUND. IT'LL SAVE US SOME TIME IF THIS PLACE IS A BUST.

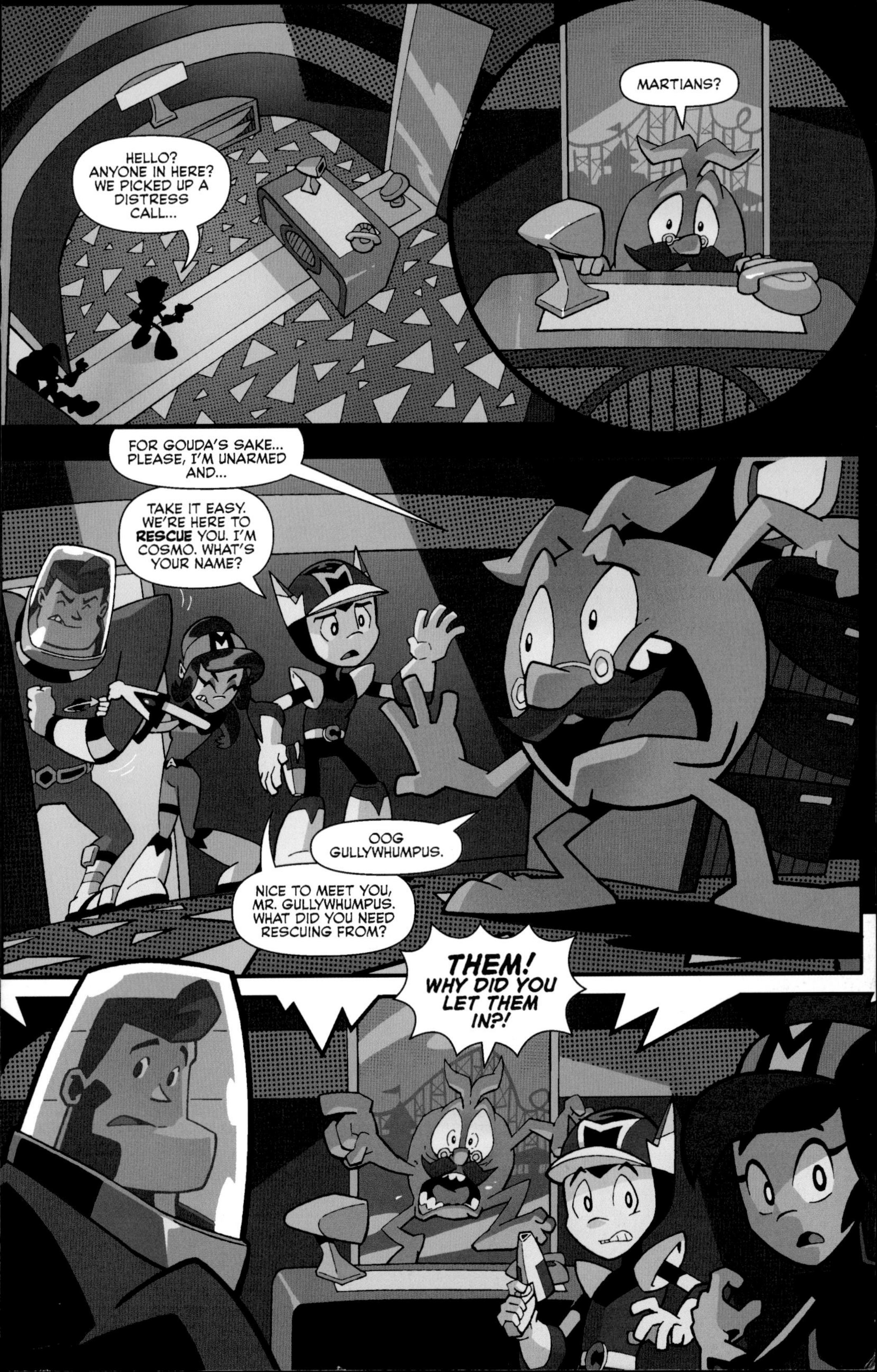
HELLO? ANYONE IN HERE? WE PICKED UP A DISTRESS CALL...
MARTIANS?
FOR GOUDA'S SAKE... PLEASE, I'M UNARMED AND...
TAKE IT EASY. WE'RE HERE TO **RESCUE** YOU. I'M COSMO. WHAT'S YOUR NAME?
OOG GULLYWHUMPUS.
NICE TO MEET YOU, MR. GULLYWHUMPUS. WHAT DID YOU NEED RESCUING FROM?
THEM! WHY DID YOU LET THEM IN?!

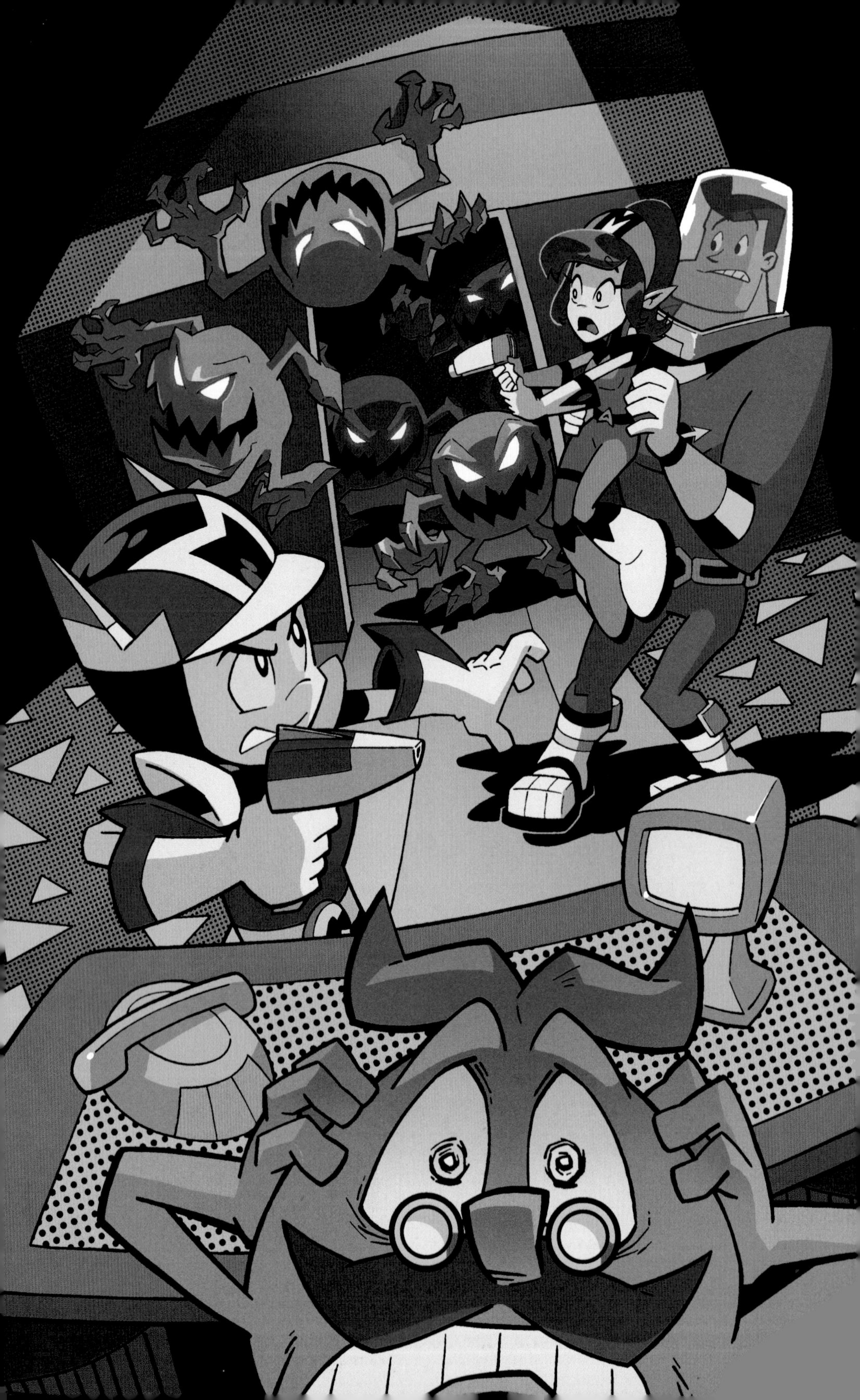

CHAPTER 2 • MOON MONSTER MAYHEM

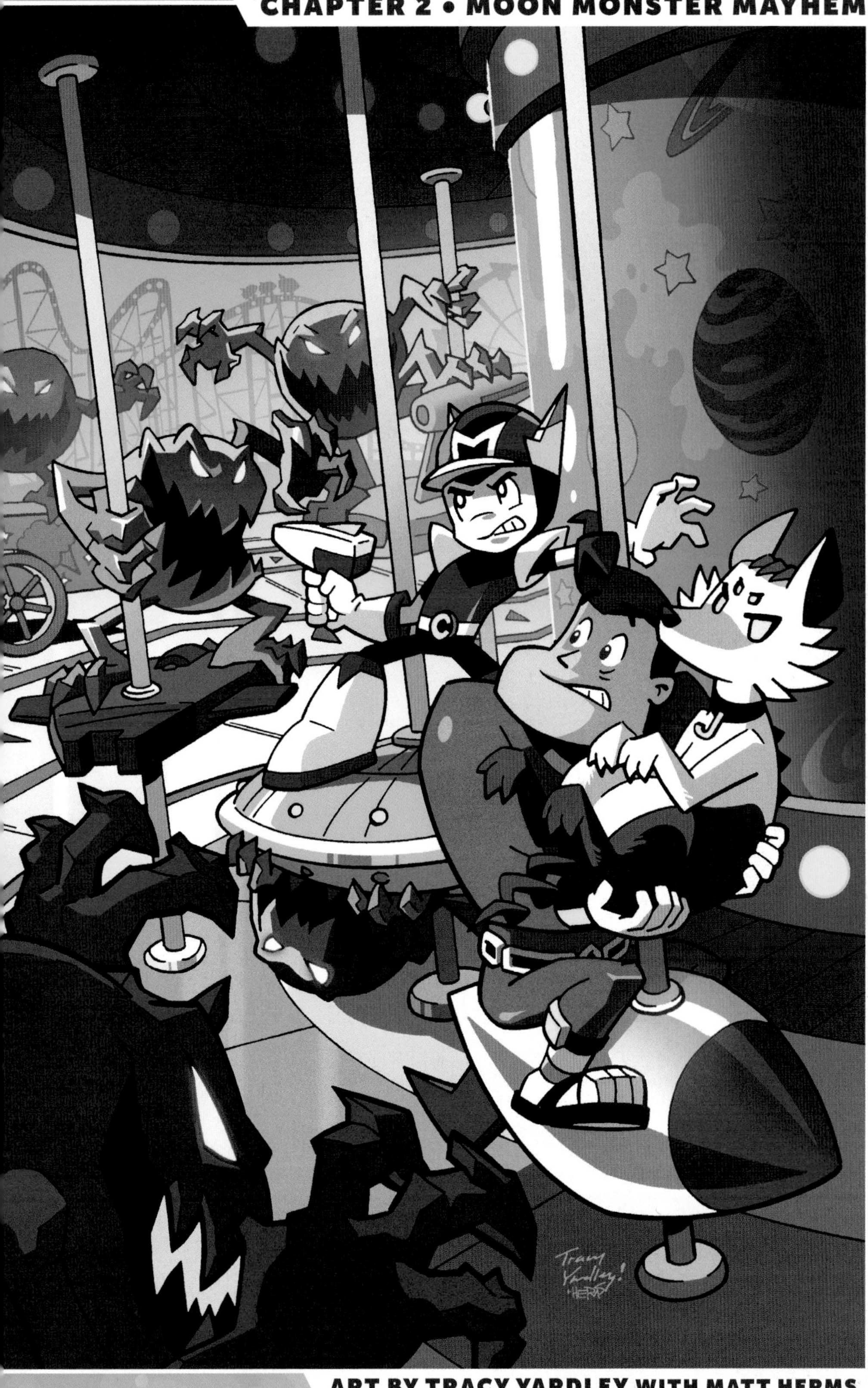
Tracy Yardley!
HERMS

ART BY TRACY YARDLEY WITH MATT HERMS

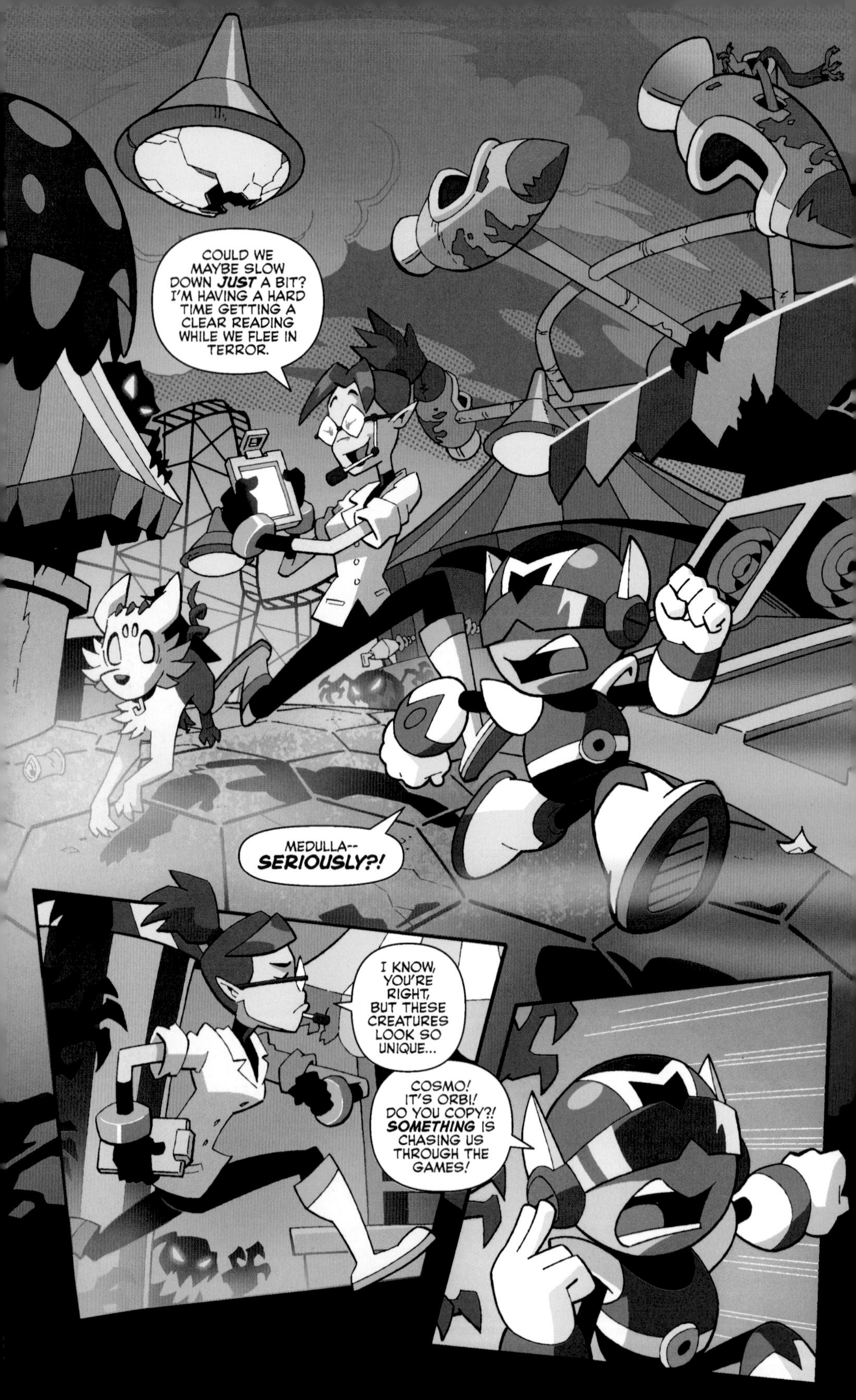
COULD WE MAYBE SLOW DOWN **JUST** A BIT? I'M HAVING A HARD TIME GETTING A CLEAR READING WHILE WE FLEE IN TERROR.
MEDULLA-- **SERIOUSLY?!**
I KNOW, YOU'RE RIGHT, BUT THESE CREATURES LOOK SO UNIQUE...
COSMO! IT'S ORBI! DO YOU COPY?! **SOMETHING** IS CHASING US THROUGH THE GAMES!

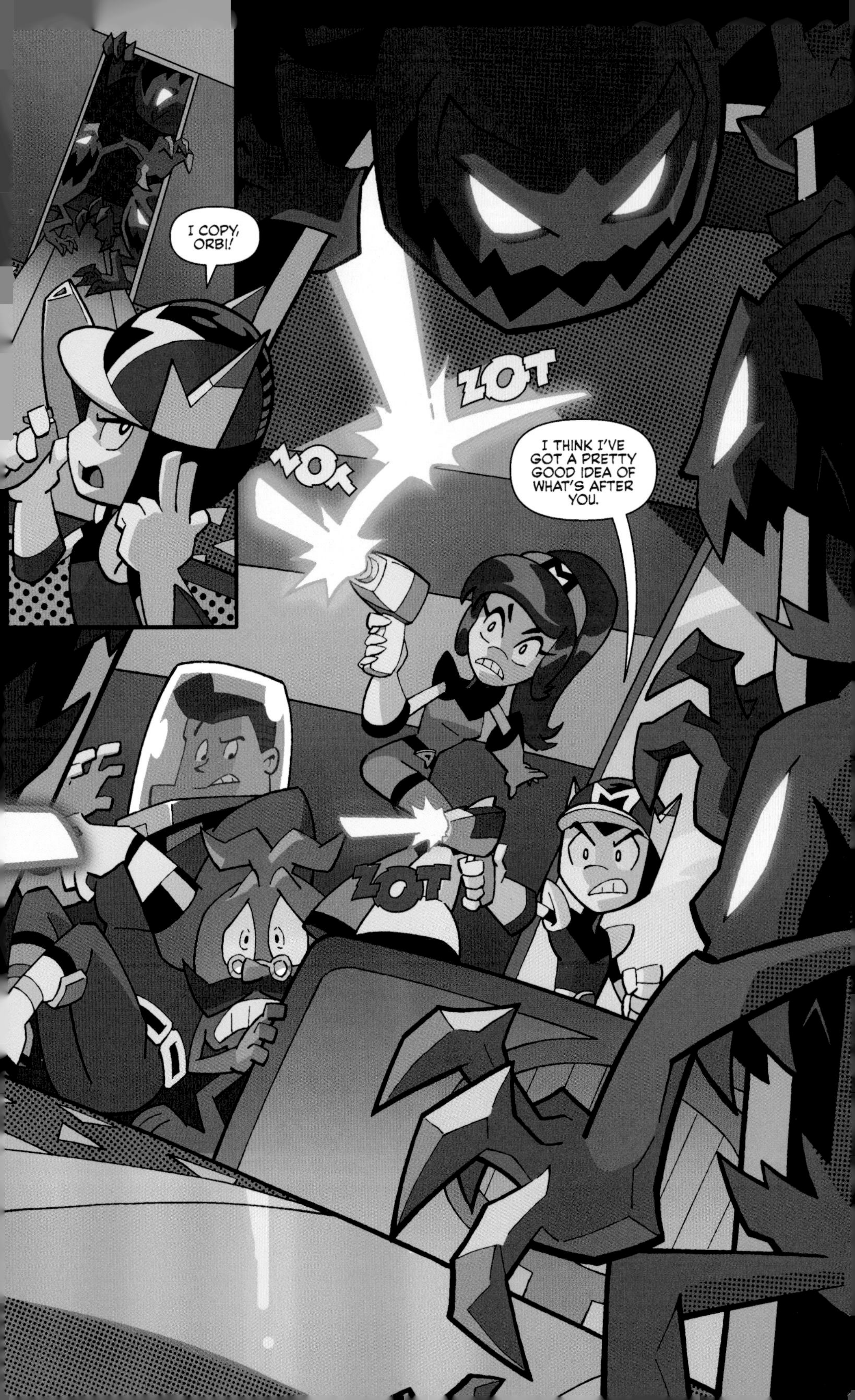
I COPY, ORBI!
ZOT
ZOT
I THINK I'VE GOT A PRETTY GOOD IDEA OF WHAT'S AFTER YOU.
ZOT

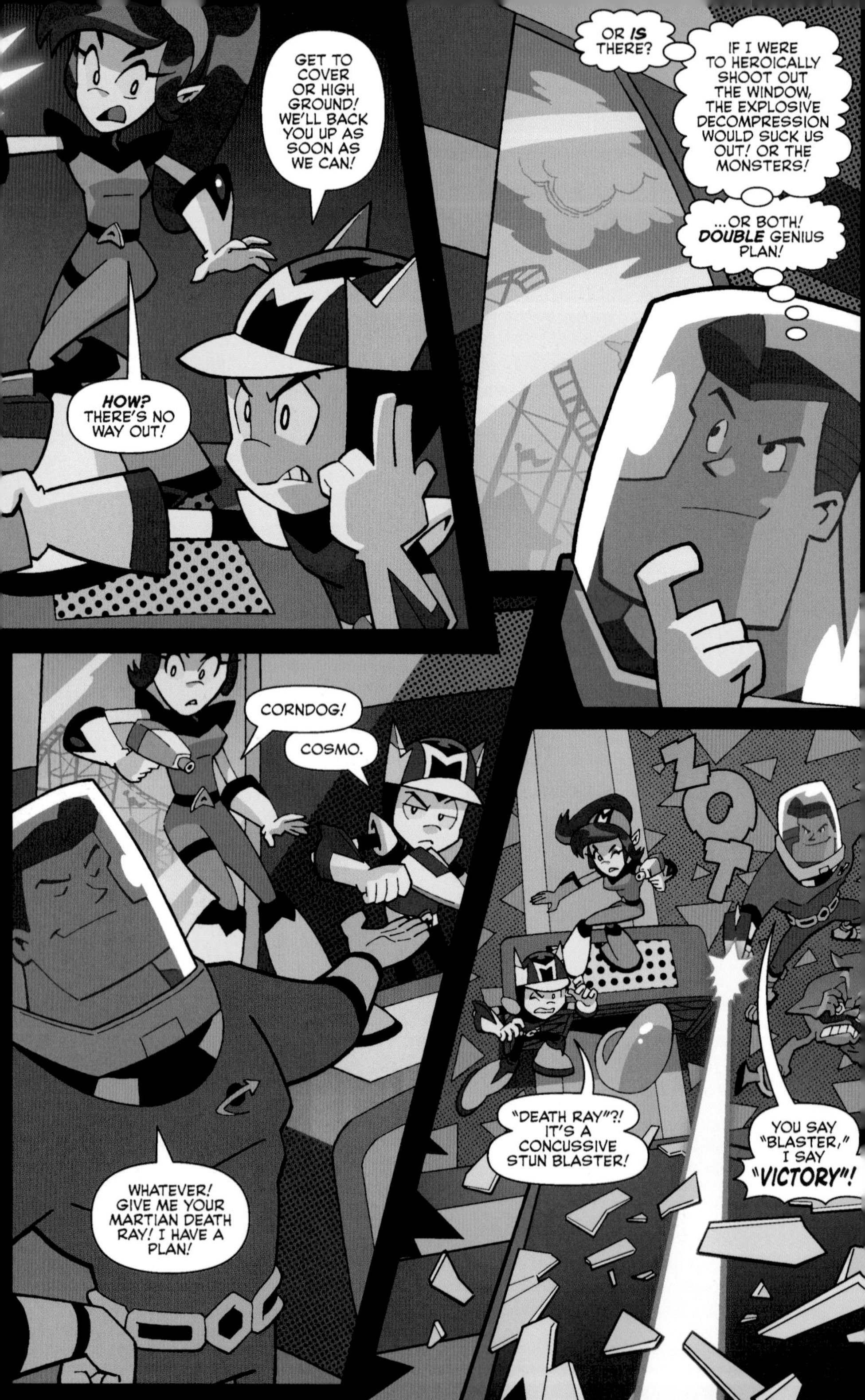
GET TO COVER OR HIGH GROUND! WE'LL BACK YOU UP AS SOON AS WE CAN!
HOW? THERE'S NO WAY OUT!
OR IS THERE?
IF I WERE TO HEROICALLY SHOOT OUT THE WINDOW, THE EXPLOSIVE DECOMPRESSION WOULD SUCK US OUT! OR THE MONSTERS!
...OR BOTH! DOUBLE GENIUS PLAN!
CORNDOG!
COSMO.
WHATEVER! GIVE ME YOUR MARTIAN DEATH RAY! I HAVE A PLAN!
ZOT
"DEATH RAY"?! IT'S A CONCUSSIVE STUN BLASTER!
YOU SAY "BLASTER," I SAY "VICTORY"!

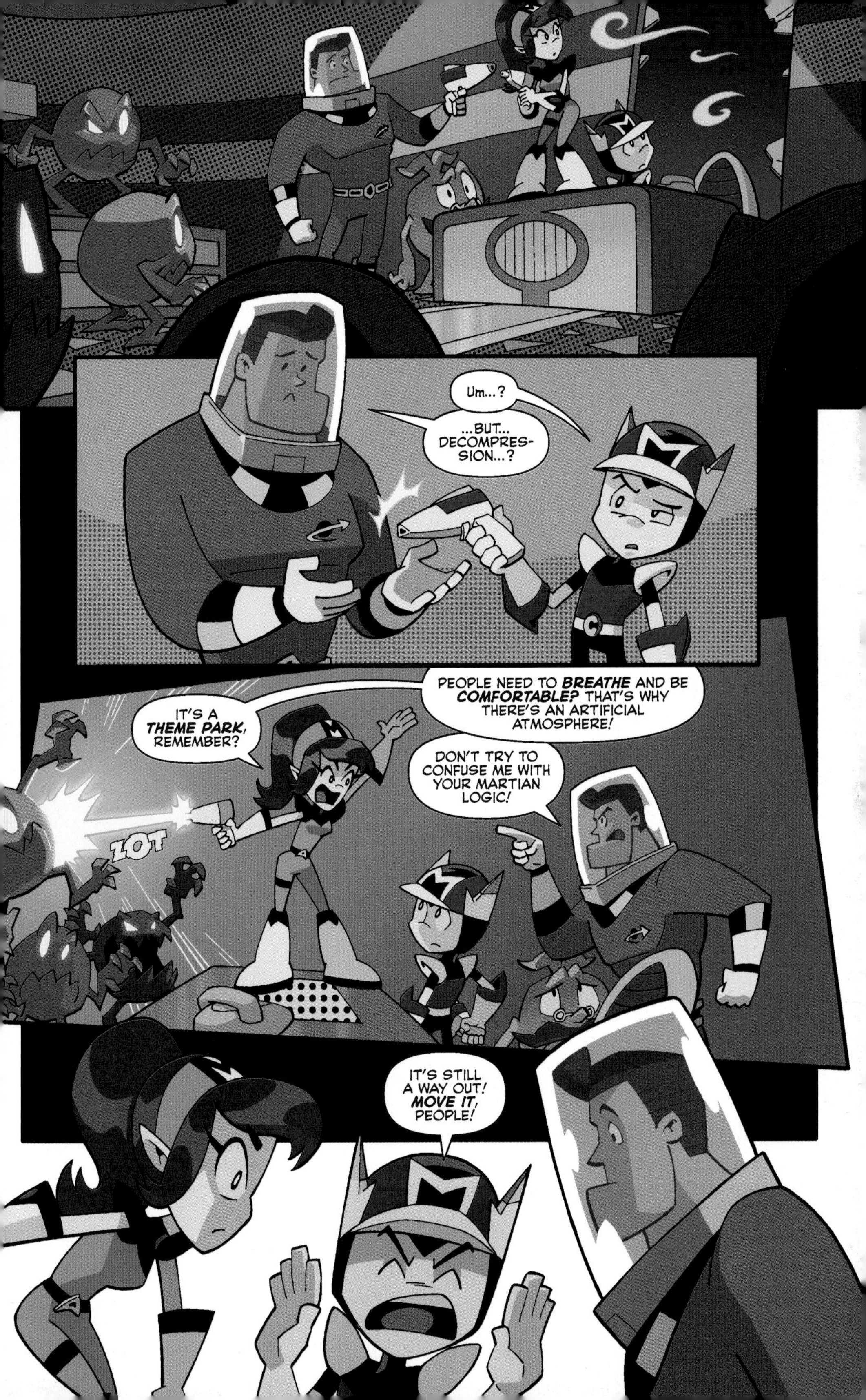
Um...?
...BUT... DECOMPRES-SION...?
IT'S A **THEME PARK**, REMEMBER?
PEOPLE NEED TO **BREATHE** AND BE **COMFORTABLE?** THAT'S WHY THERE'S AN ARTIFICIAL ATMOSPHERE!
DON'T TRY TO CONFUSE ME WITH YOUR MARTIAN LOGIC!
ZOT
IT'S STILL A WAY OUT! **MOVE IT**, PEOPLE!

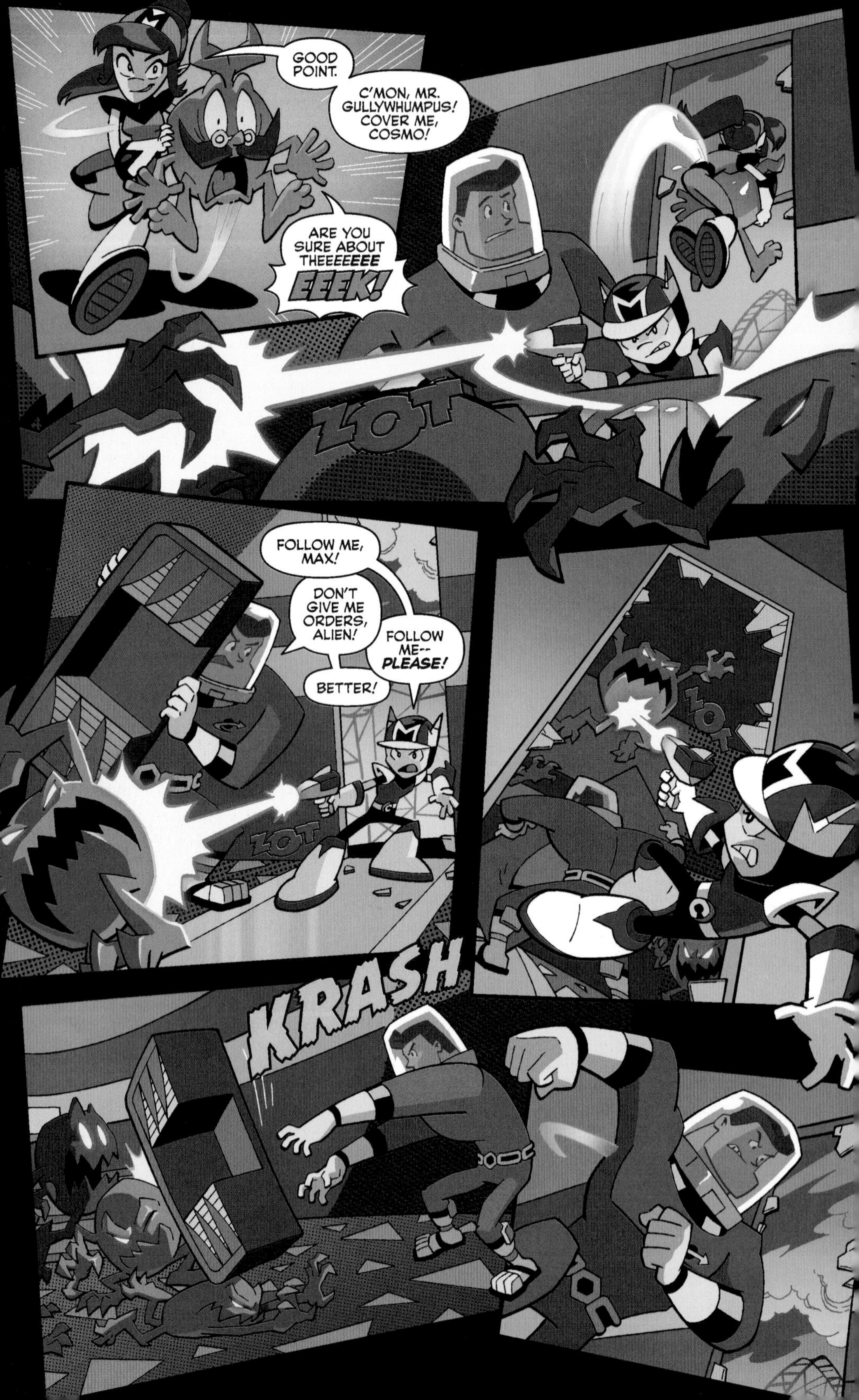
GOOD POINT.
C'MON, MR. GULLYWHUMPUS! COVER ME, COSMO!
ARE YOU SURE ABOUT THEEEEEEE EEEK!
ZOT
FOLLOW ME, MAX!
DON'T GIVE ME ORDERS, ALIEN!
FOLLOW ME-- PLEASE!
BETTER!
ZOT
ZOT
KRASH

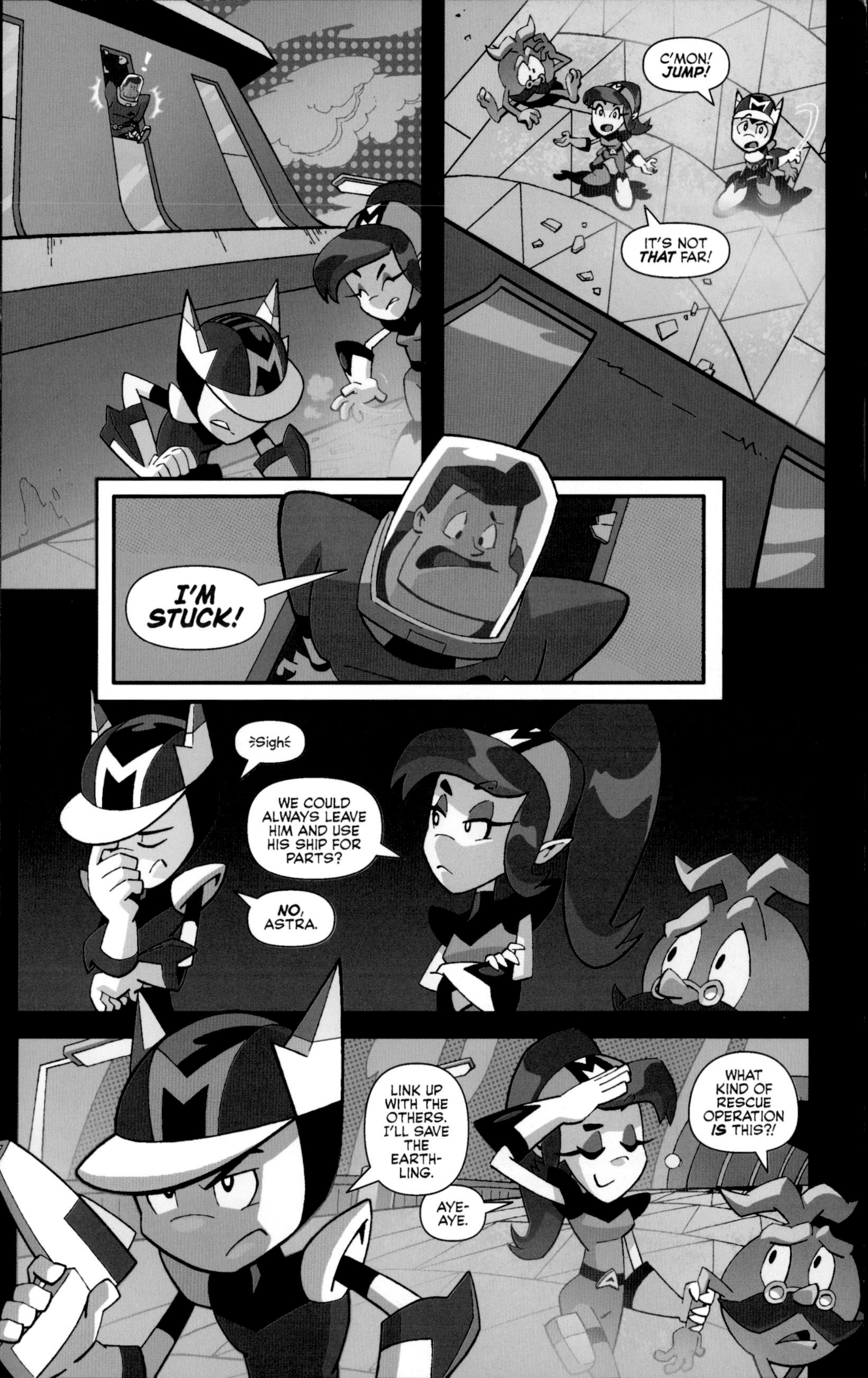
!
C'MON! JUMP!
IT'S NOT THAT FAR!
I'M STUCK!
≥Sigh≤
WE COULD ALWAYS LEAVE HIM AND USE HIS SHIP FOR PARTS?
NO, ASTRA.
LINK UP WITH THE OTHERS. I'LL SAVE THE EARTH-LING.
AYE-AYE.
WHAT KIND OF RESCUE OPERATION IS THIS?!

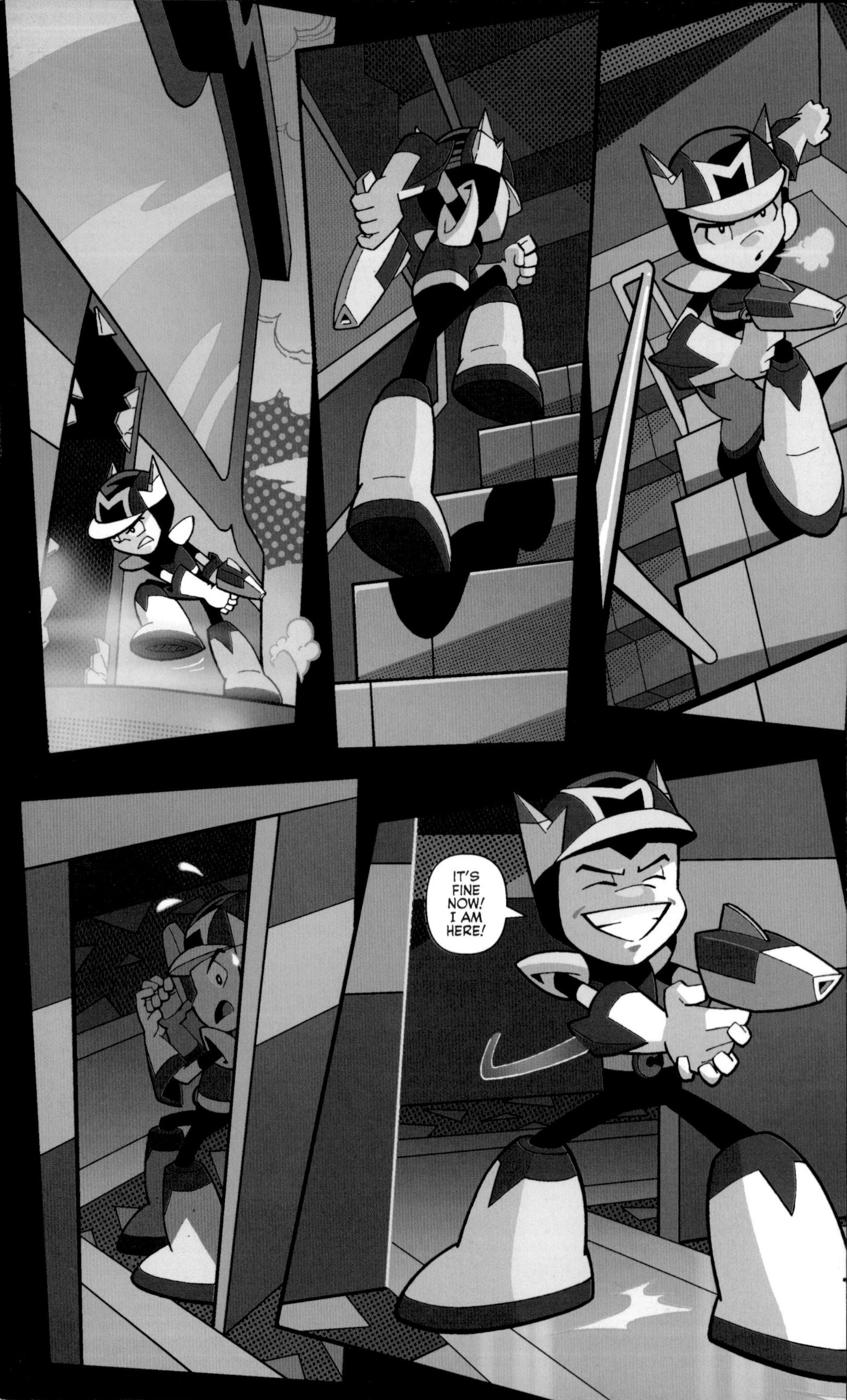
IT'S FINE NOW! I AM HERE!

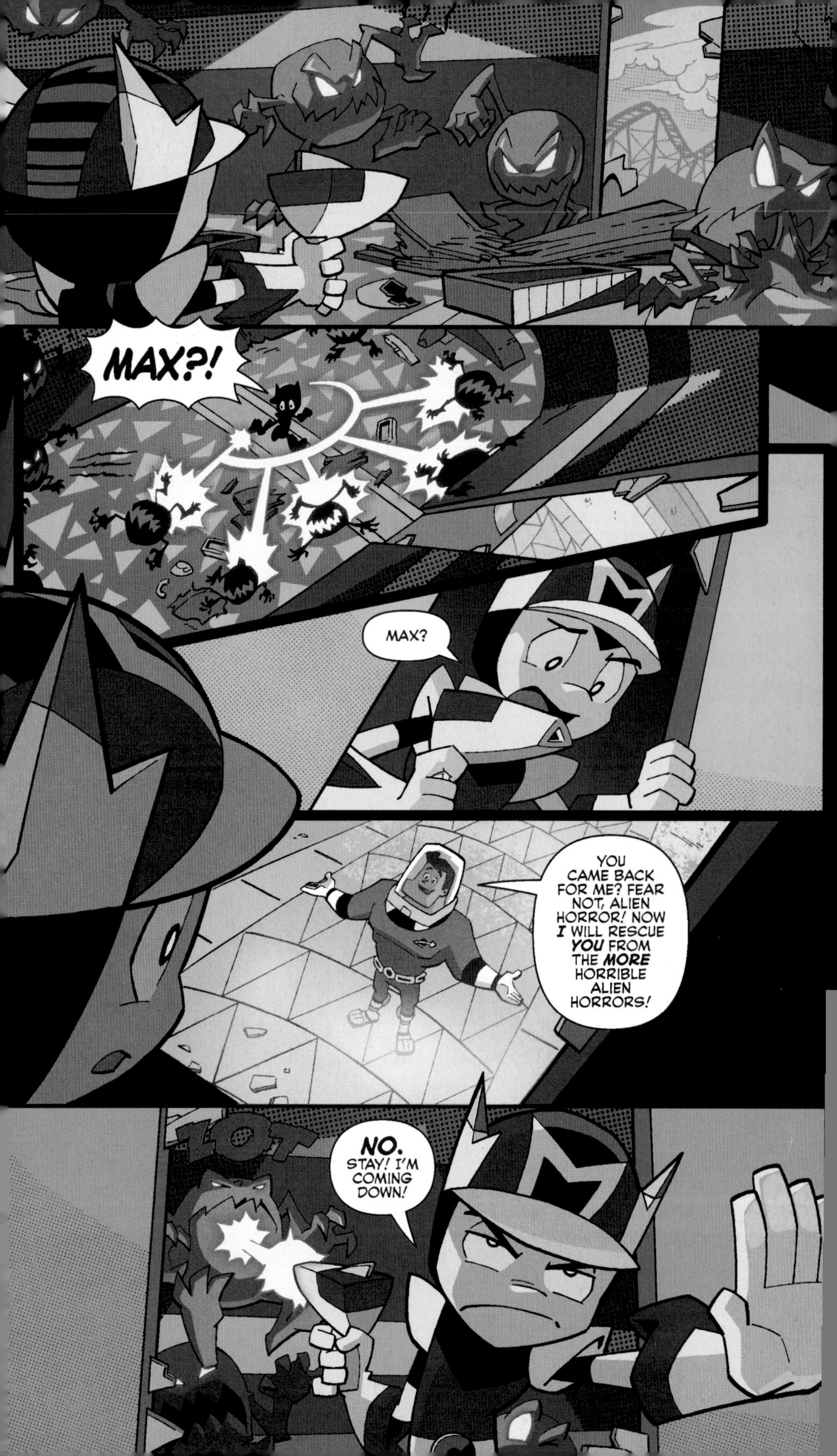
MAX?!
MAX?
YOU CAME BACK FOR ME? FEAR NOT, ALIEN HORROR! NOW I WILL RESCUE YOU FROM THE MORE HORRIBLE ALIEN HORRORS!
ZOT
NO. STAY! I'M COMING DOWN!

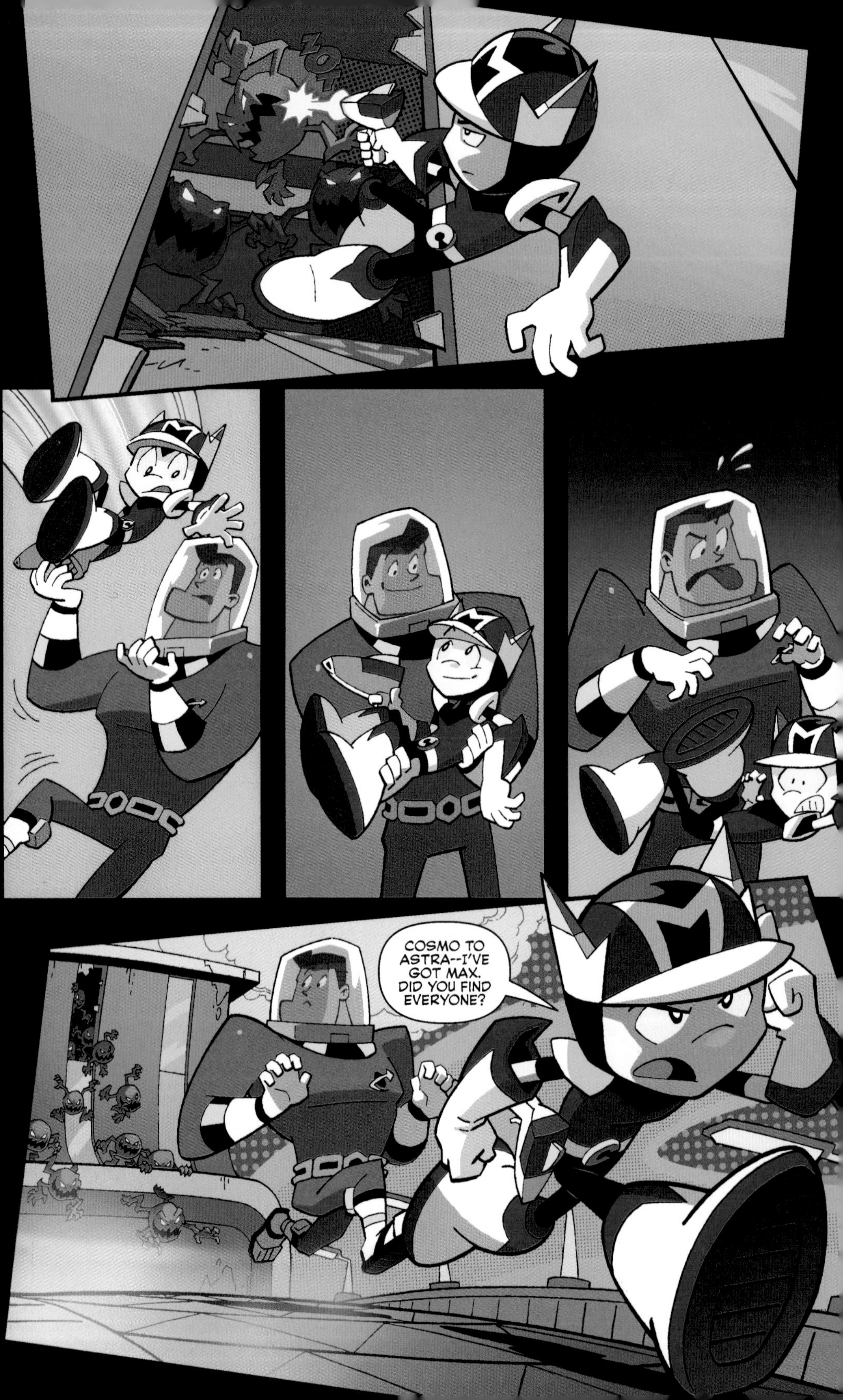
ZOT
COSMO TO ASTRA--I'VE GOT MAX. DID YOU FIND EVERYONE?

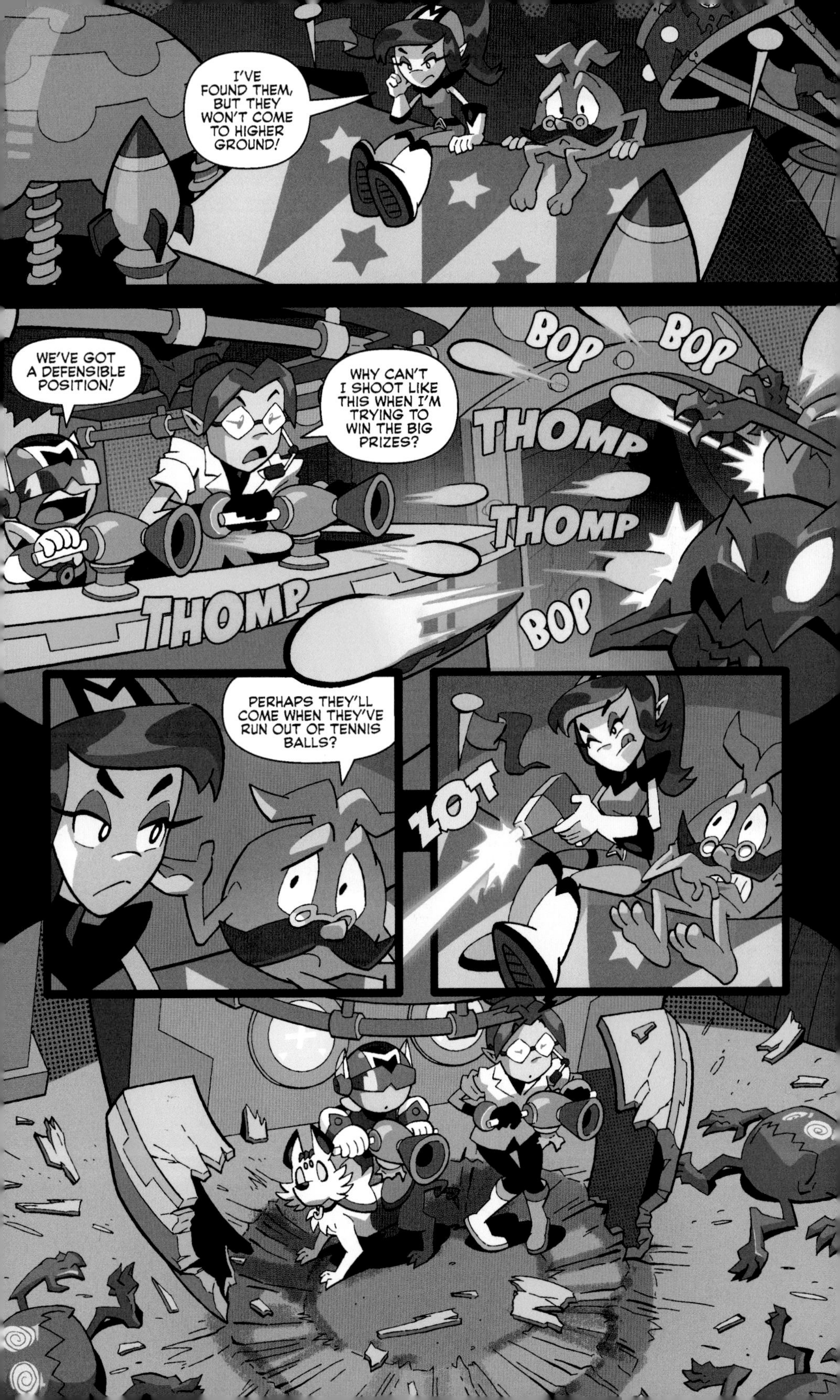
I'VE FOUND THEM, BUT THEY WON'T COME TO HIGHER GROUND!
WE'VE GOT A DEFENSIBLE POSITION!
WHY CAN'T I SHOOT LIKE THIS WHEN I'M TRYING TO WIN THE BIG PRIZES?
BOP
BOP
THOMP
THOMP
THOMP
BOP
PERHAPS THEY'LL COME WHEN THEY'VE RUN OUT OF TENNIS BALLS?
ZOT

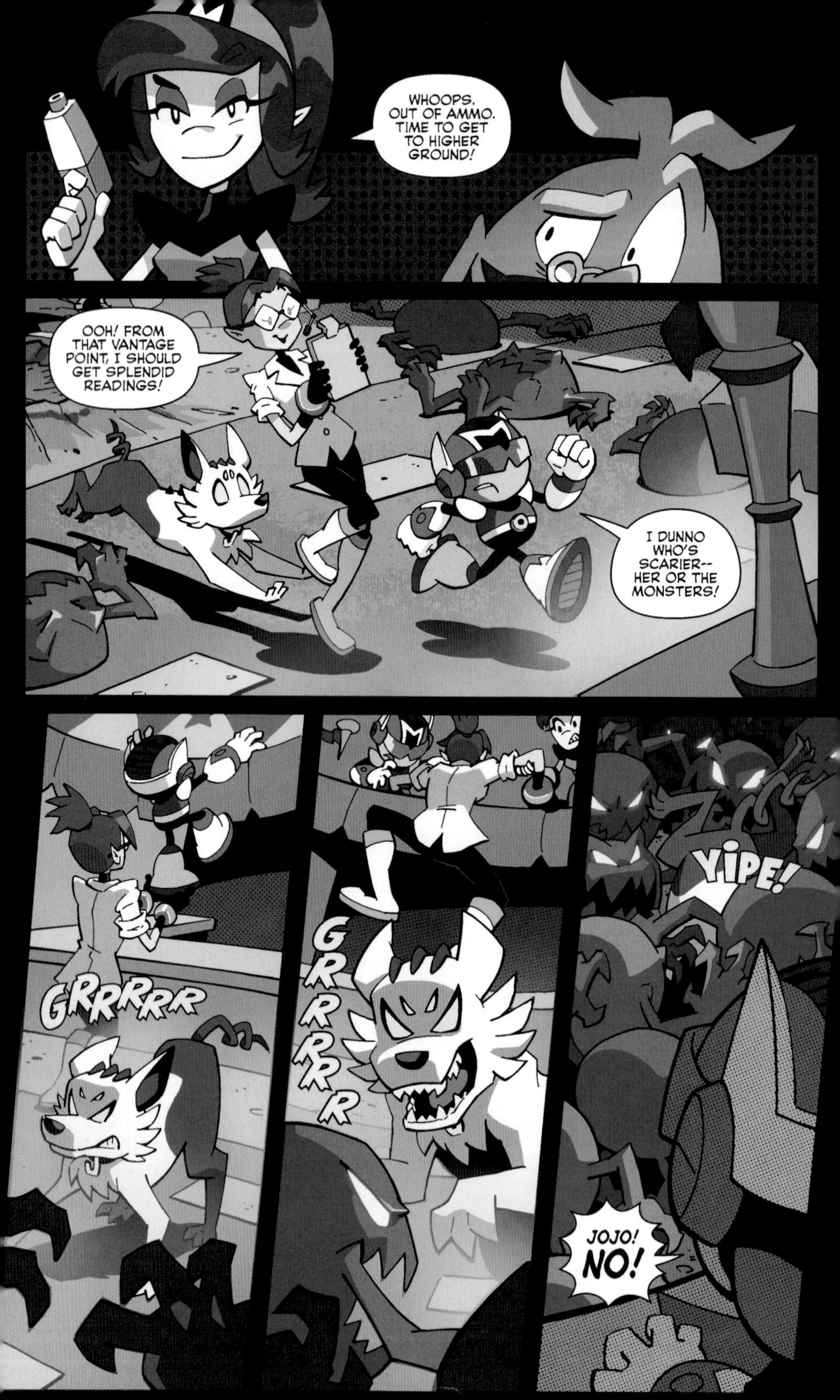

WHOOPS. OUT OF AMMO. TIME TO GET TO HIGHER GROUND!
OOH! FROM THAT VANTAGE POINT, I SHOULD GET SPLENDID READINGS!
I DUNNO WHO'S SCARIER-- HER OR THE MONSTERS!
GRRRRR
GRRRRR
YIPE!
JOJO! NO!

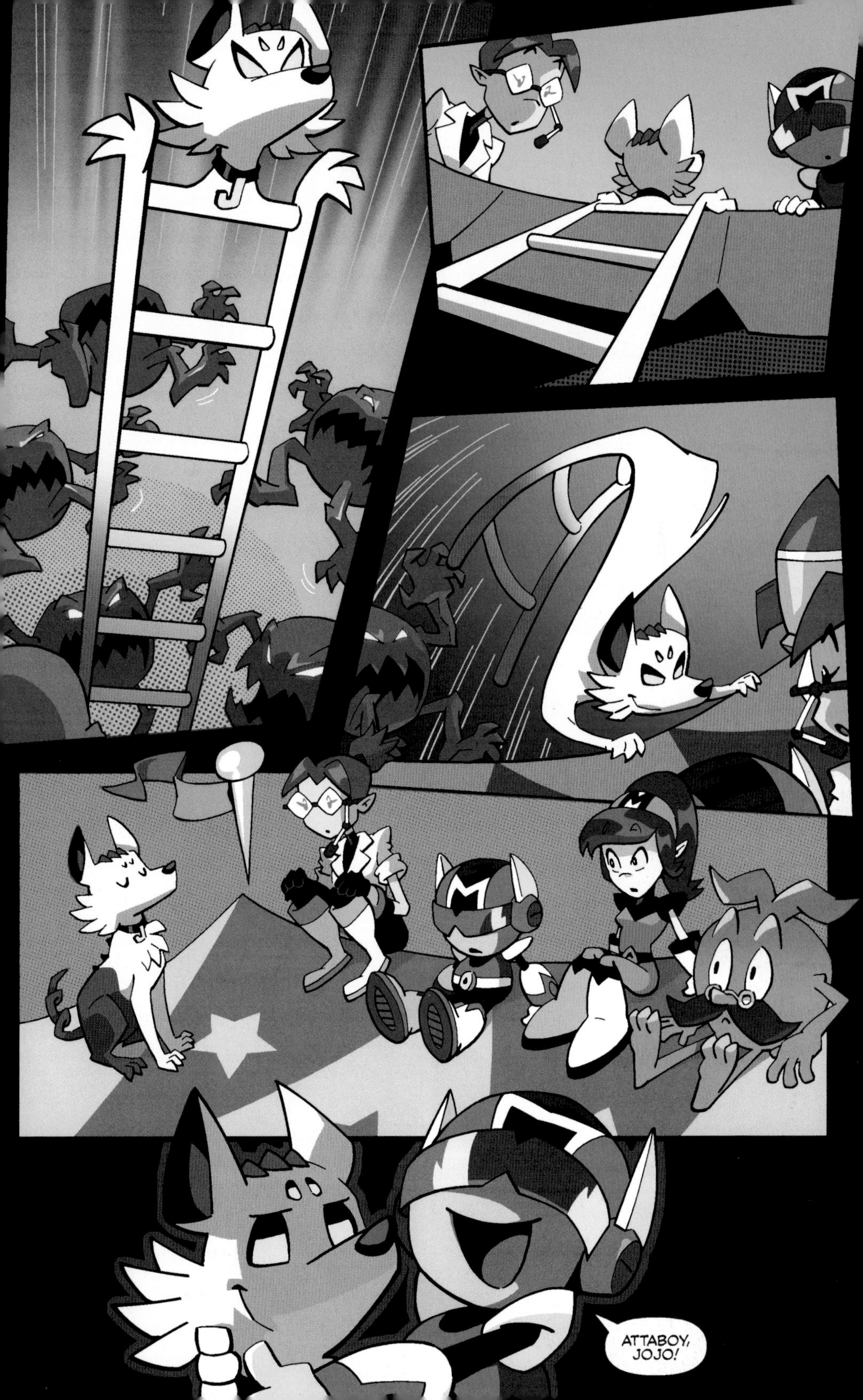
ATTABOY, JOJO!

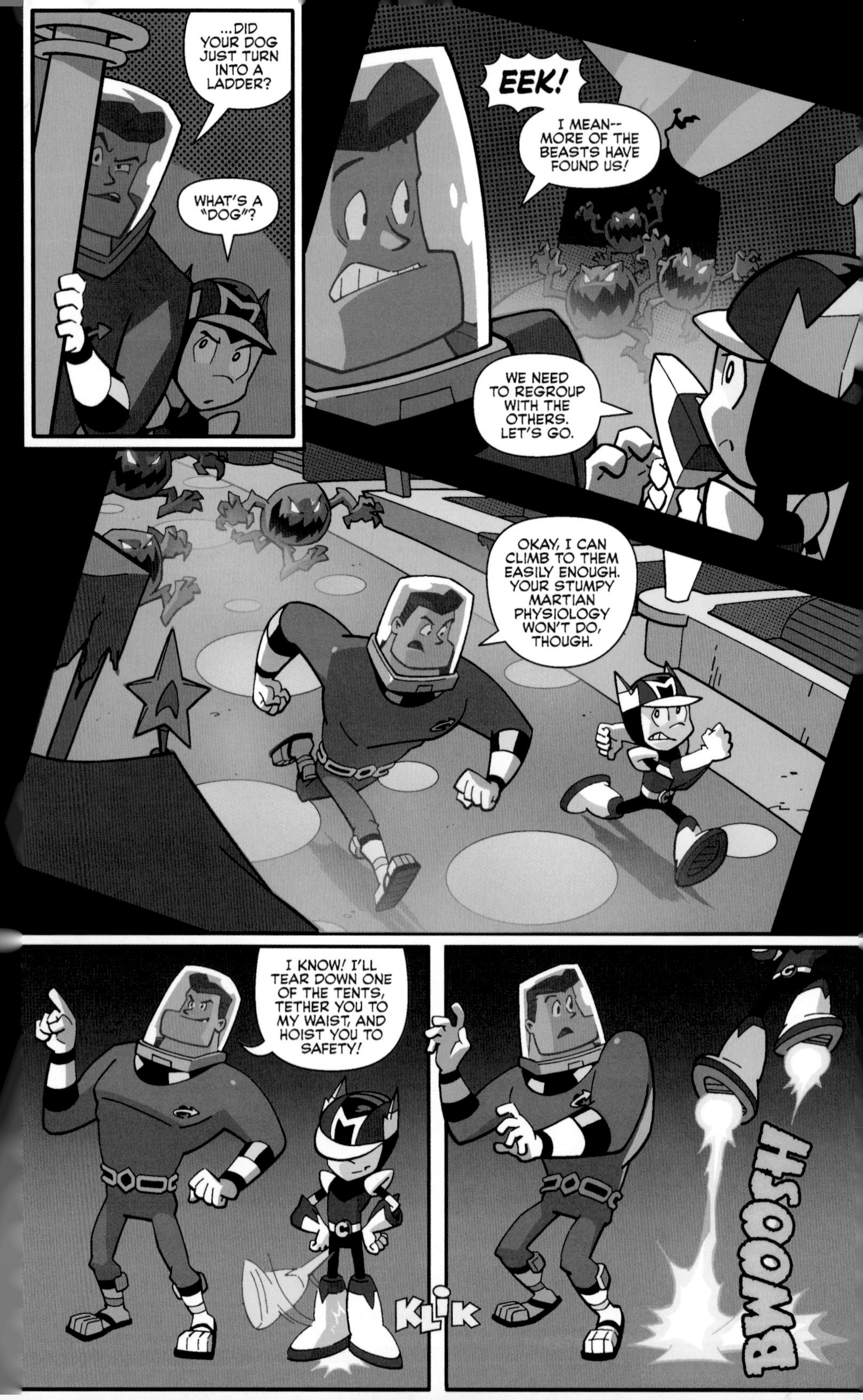
...DID YOUR DOG JUST TURN INTO A LADDER?
WHAT'S A "DOG"?
EEK!
I MEAN-- MORE OF THE BEASTS HAVE FOUND US!
WE NEED TO REGROUP WITH THE OTHERS. LET'S GO.
OKAY, I CAN CLIMB TO THEM EASILY ENOUGH. YOUR STUMPY MARTIAN PHYSIOLOGY WON'T DO, THOUGH.
I KNOW! I'LL TEAR DOWN ONE OF THE TENTS, TETHER YOU TO MY WAIST, AND HOIST YOU TO SAFETY!
KLIK
BWOOSH

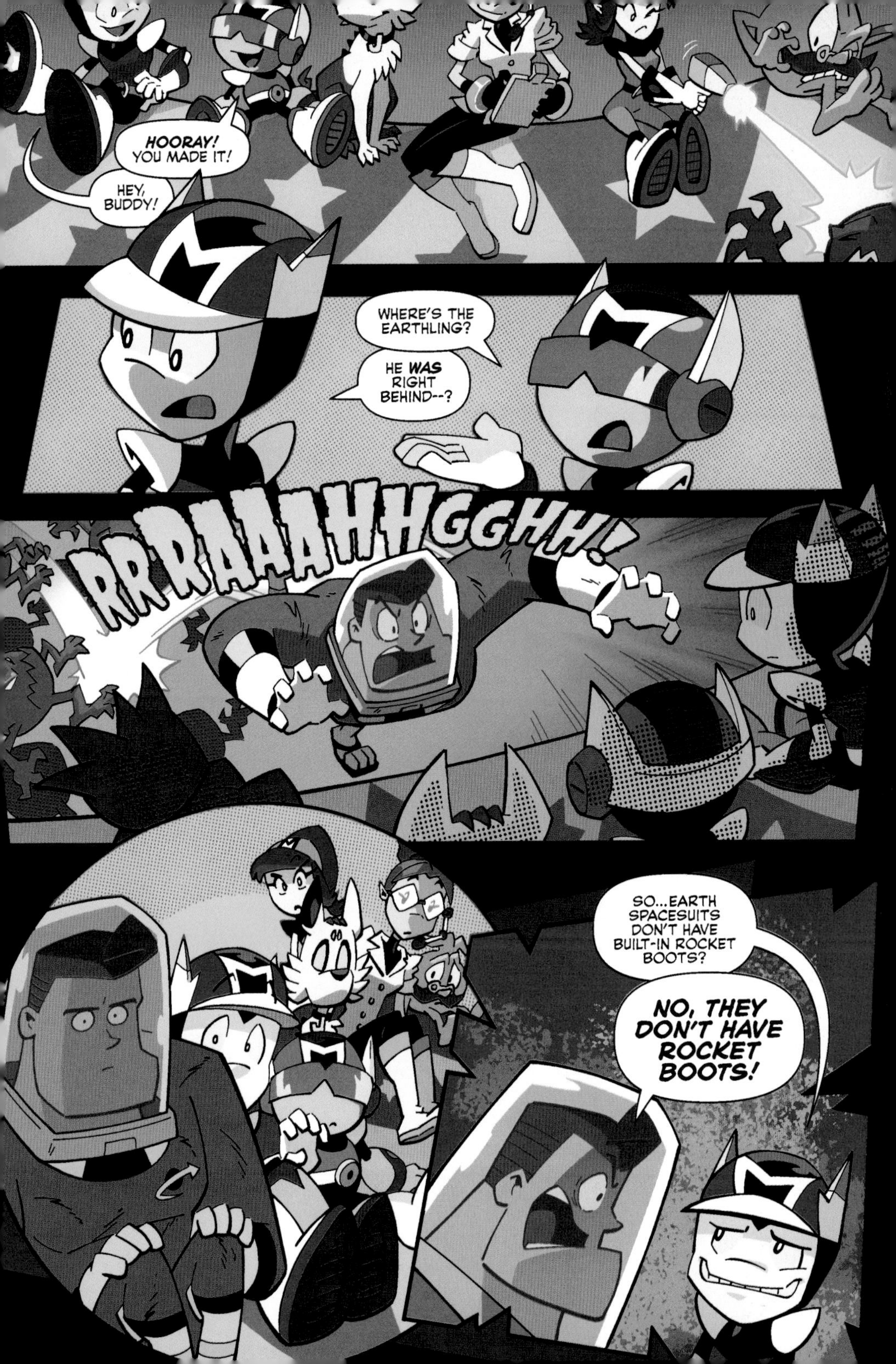
HOORAY! YOU MADE IT!
HEY, BUDDY!
WHERE'S THE EARTHLING?
HE WAS RIGHT BEHIND--?
RRRAAAHHGGHH!
SO...EARTH SPACESUITS DON'T HAVE BUILT-IN ROCKET BOOTS?
NO, THEY DON'T HAVE ROCKET BOOTS!

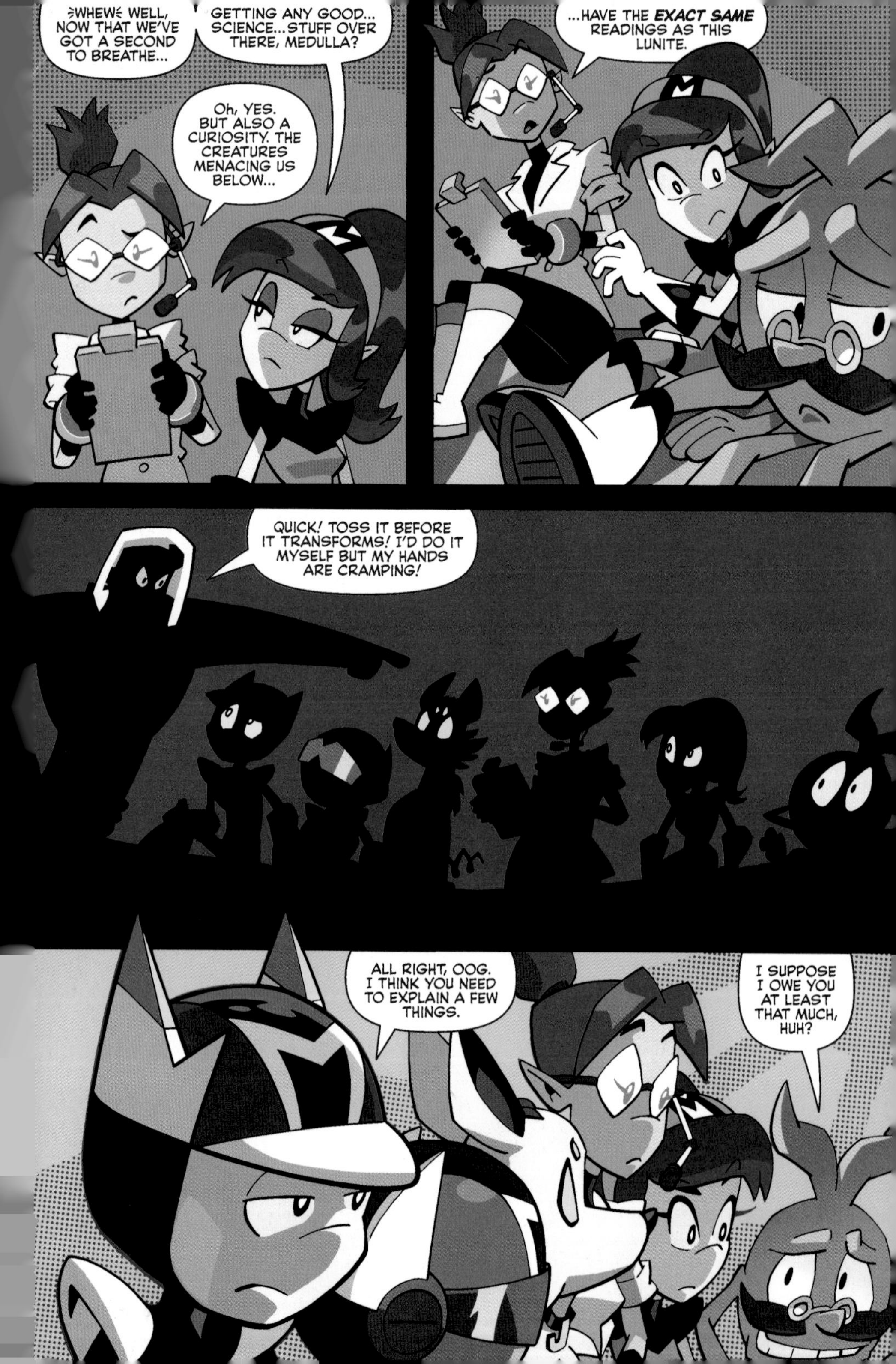

≥WHEW≤ WELL, NOW THAT WE'VE GOT A SECOND TO BREATHE...
GETTING ANY GOOD... SCIENCE...STUFF OVER THERE, MEDULLA?
Oh, YES. BUT ALSO A CURIOSITY. THE CREATURES MENACING US BELOW...
...HAVE THE EXACT SAME READINGS AS THIS LUNITE.
QUICK! TOSS IT BEFORE IT TRANSFORMS! I'D DO IT MYSELF BUT MY HANDS ARE CRAMPING!
ALL RIGHT, OOG. I THINK YOU NEED TO EXPLAIN A FEW THINGS.
I SUPPOSE I OWE YOU AT LEAST THAT MUCH, HUH?

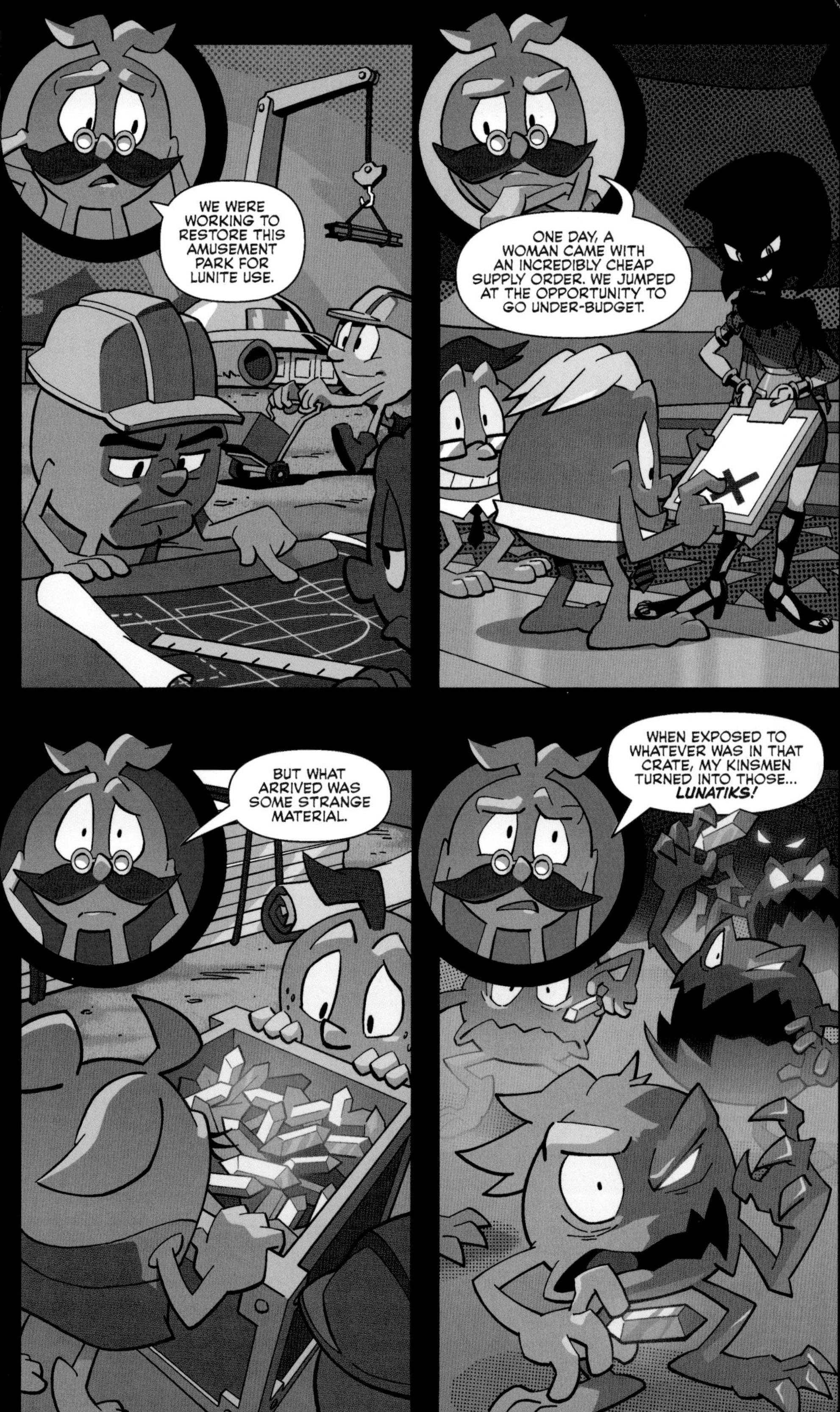
WE WERE WORKING TO RESTORE THIS AMUSEMENT PARK FOR LUNITE USE.
ONE DAY, A WOMAN CAME WITH AN INCREDIBLY CHEAP SUPPLY ORDER. WE JUMPED AT THE OPPORTUNITY TO GO UNDER-BUDGET.
BUT WHAT ARRIVED WAS SOME STRANGE MATERIAL.
WHEN EXPOSED TO WHATEVER WAS IN THAT CRATE, MY KINSMEN TURNED INTO THOSE... ***LUNATIKS!***

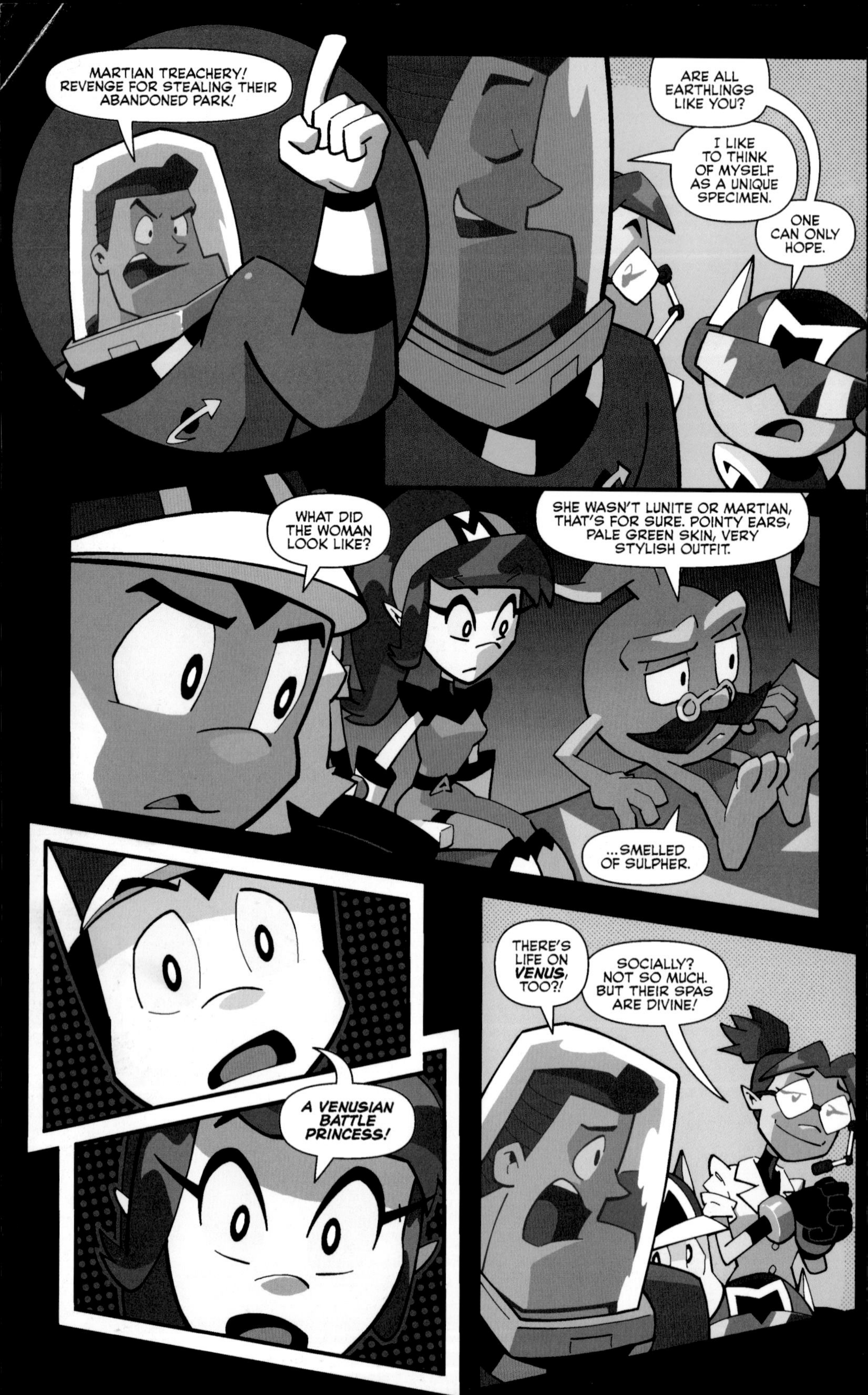
MARTIAN TREACHERY! REVENGE FOR STEALING THEIR ABANDONED PARK!
ARE ALL EARTHLINGS LIKE YOU?
I LIKE TO THINK OF MYSELF AS A UNIQUE SPECIMEN.
ONE CAN ONLY HOPE.
WHAT DID THE WOMAN LOOK LIKE?
SHE WASN'T LUNITE OR MARTIAN, THAT'S FOR SURE. POINTY EARS, PALE GREEN SKIN, VERY STYLISH OUTFIT.
...SMELLED OF SULPHER.
A VENUSIAN BATTLE PRINCESS!
THERE'S LIFE ON VENUS, TOO?!
SOCIALLY? NOT SO MUCH. BUT THEIR SPAS ARE DIVINE!

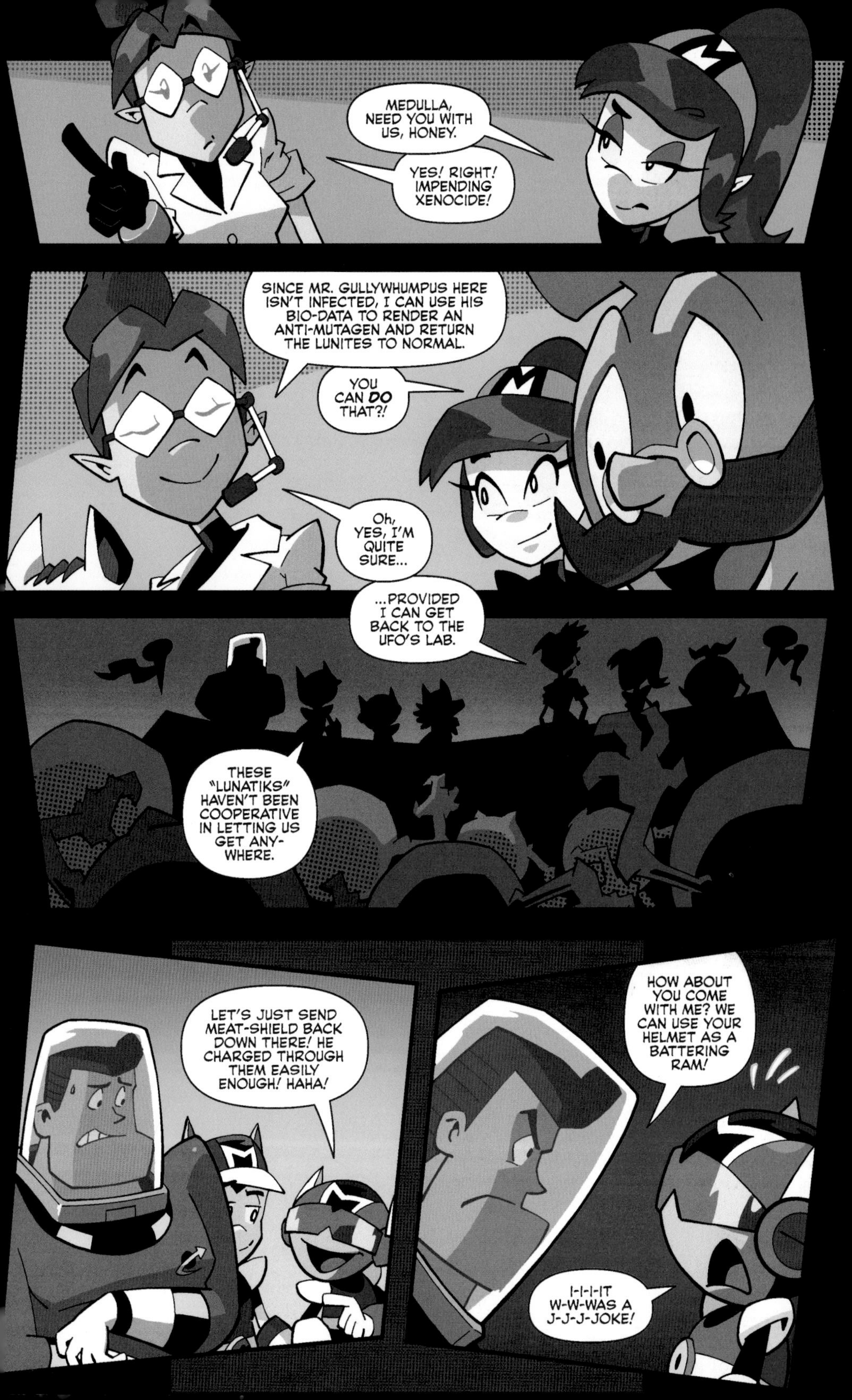
MEDULLA, NEED YOU WITH US, HONEY.
YES! RIGHT! IMPENDING XENOCIDE!
SINCE MR. GULLYWHUMPUS HERE ISN'T INFECTED, I CAN USE HIS BIO-DATA TO RENDER AN ANTI-MUTAGEN AND RETURN THE LUNITES TO NORMAL.
YOU CAN DO THAT?!
Oh, YES, I'M QUITE SURE...
...PROVIDED I CAN GET BACK TO THE UFO'S LAB.
THESE "LUNATIKS" HAVEN'T BEEN COOPERATIVE IN LETTING US GET ANY-WHERE.
LET'S JUST SEND MEAT-SHIELD BACK DOWN THERE! HE CHARGED THROUGH THEM EASILY ENOUGH! HAHA!
HOW ABOUT YOU COME WITH ME? WE CAN USE YOUR HELMET AS A BATTERING RAM!
I-I-I-IT W-W-WAS A J-J-J-JOKE!

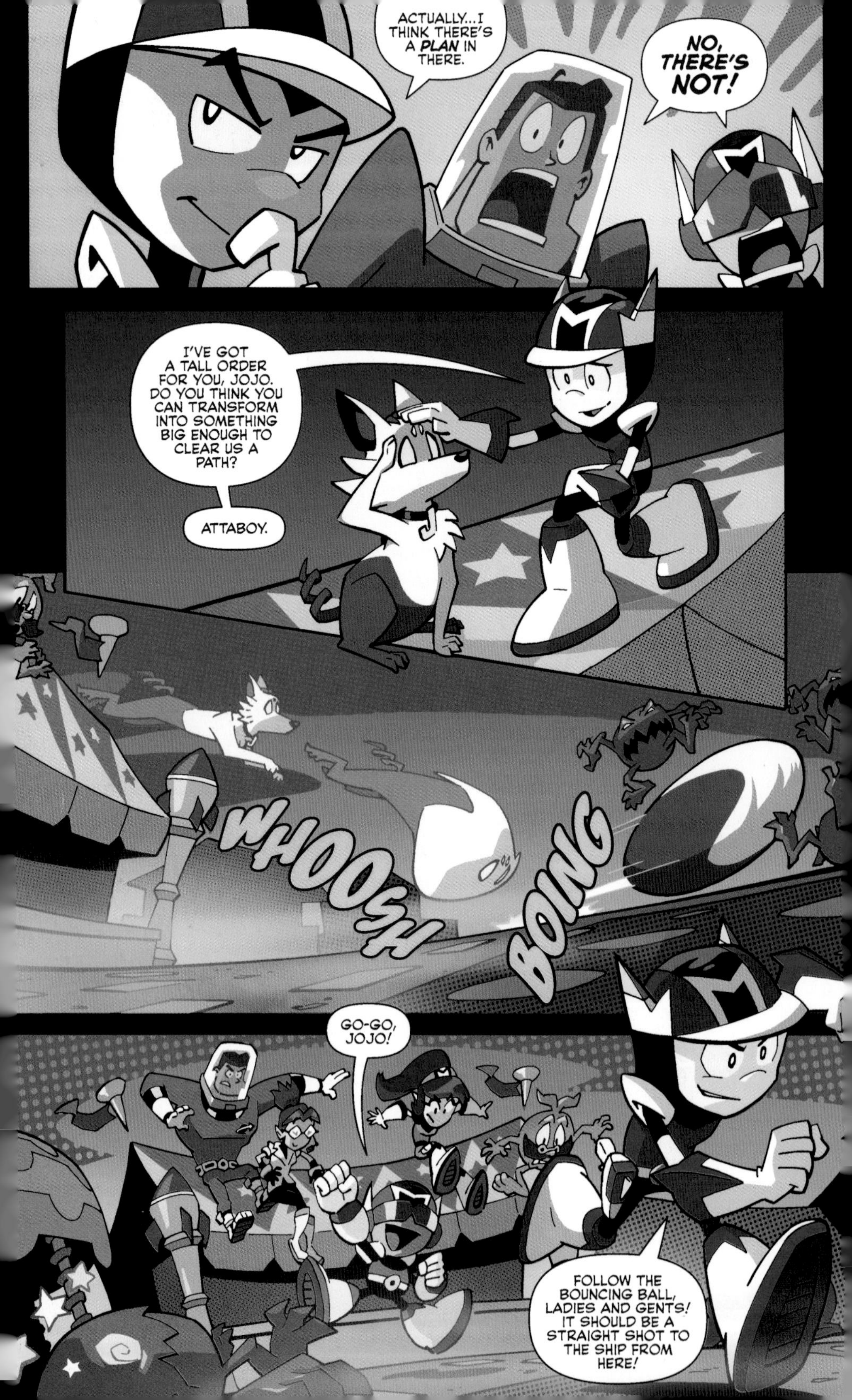
ACTUALLY...I THINK THERE'S A *PLAN* IN THERE.
NO, THERE'S NOT!
I'VE GOT A TALL ORDER FOR YOU, JOJO. DO YOU THINK YOU CAN TRANSFORM INTO SOMETHING BIG ENOUGH TO CLEAR US A PATH?
ATTABOY.
WHOOSH
BOING
GO-GO, JOJO!
FOLLOW THE BOUNCING BALL, LADIES AND GENTS! IT SHOULD BE A STRAIGHT SHOT TO THE SHIP FROM HERE!

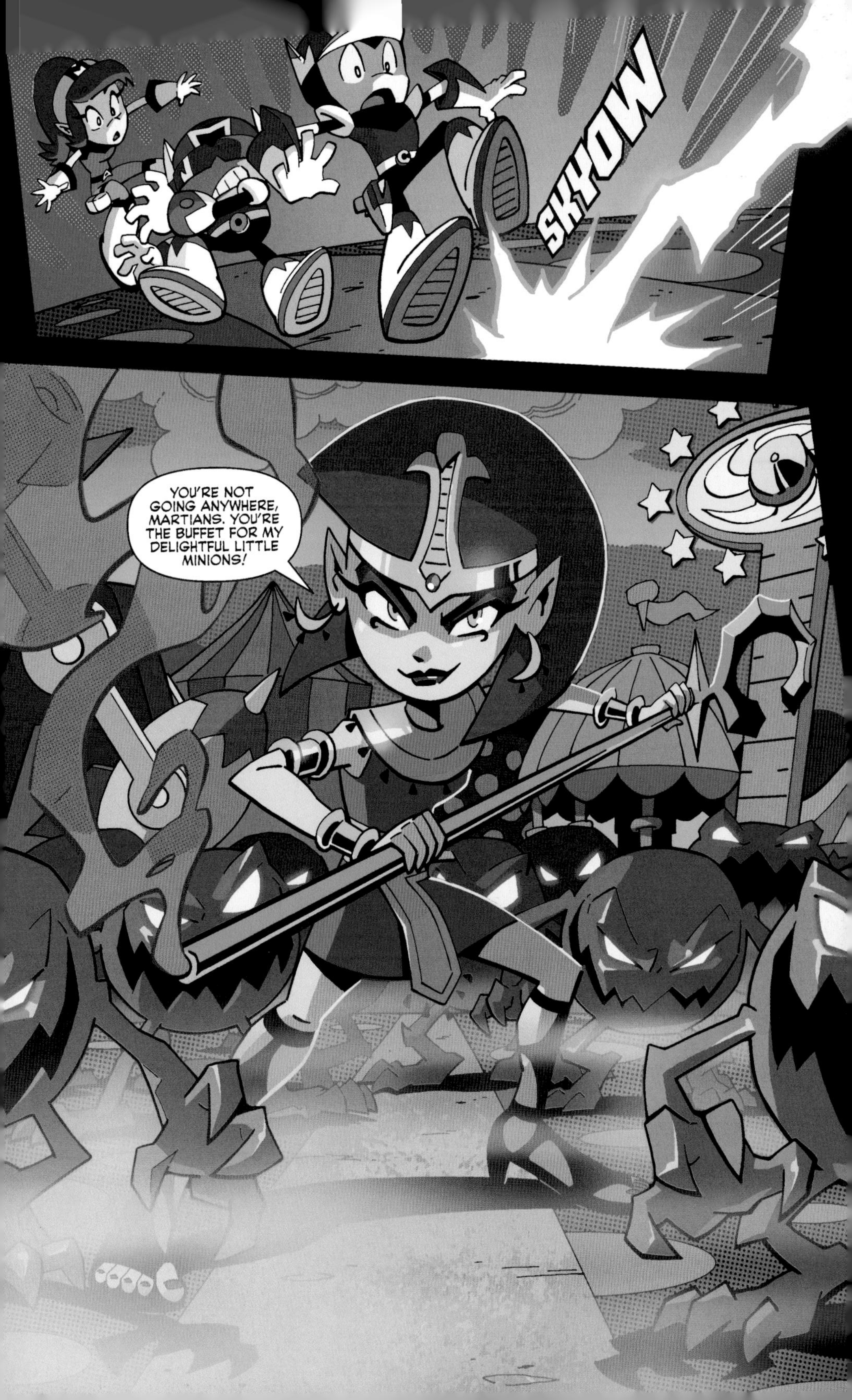

SKYOW
YOU'RE NOT GOING ANYWHERE, MARTIANS. YOU'RE THE BUFFET FOR MY DELIGHTFUL LITTLE MINIONS!

CHAPTER 3 • BATTLE PRINCESS PANIC

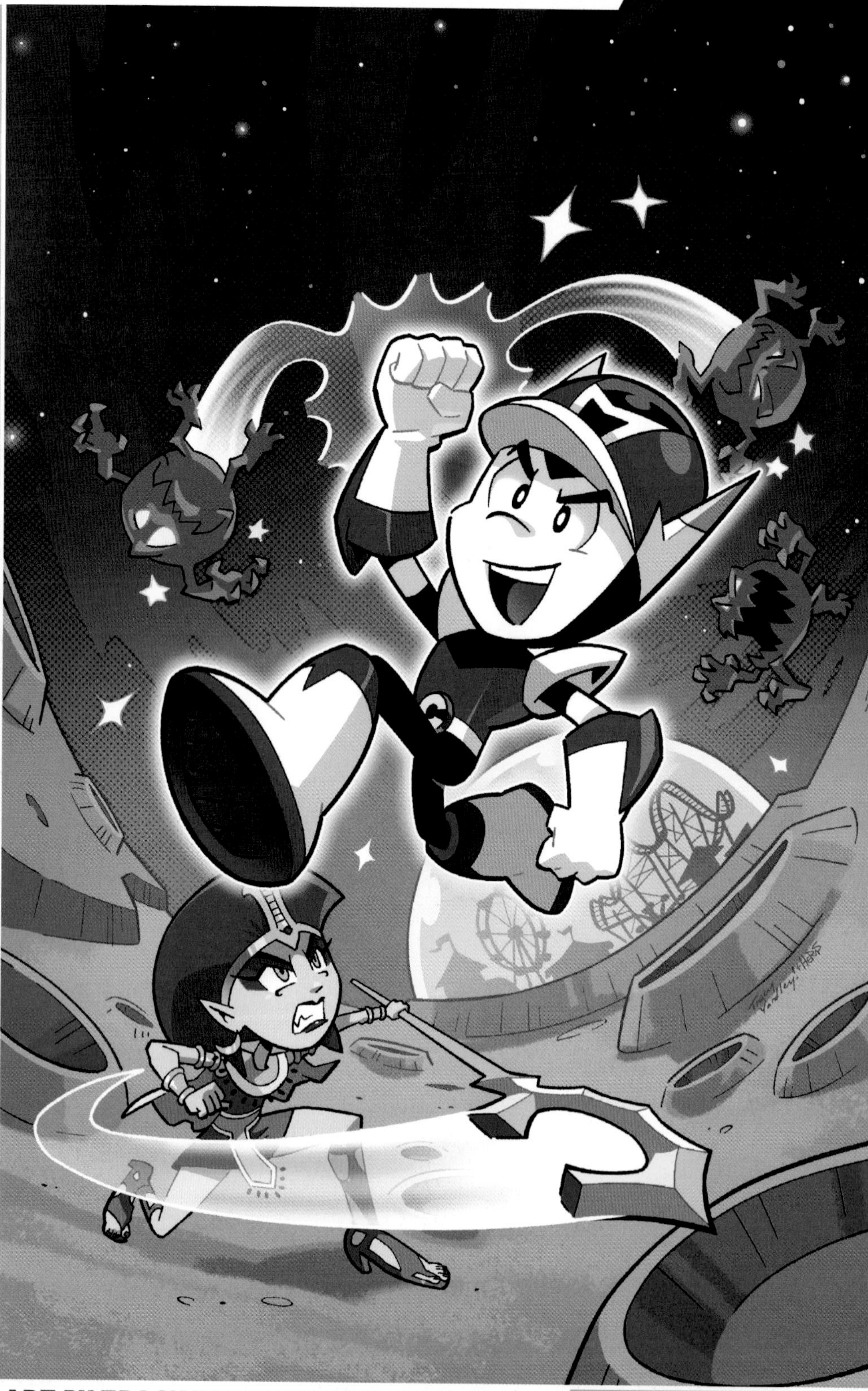

ART BY TRACY YARDLEY WITH MATT HERMS

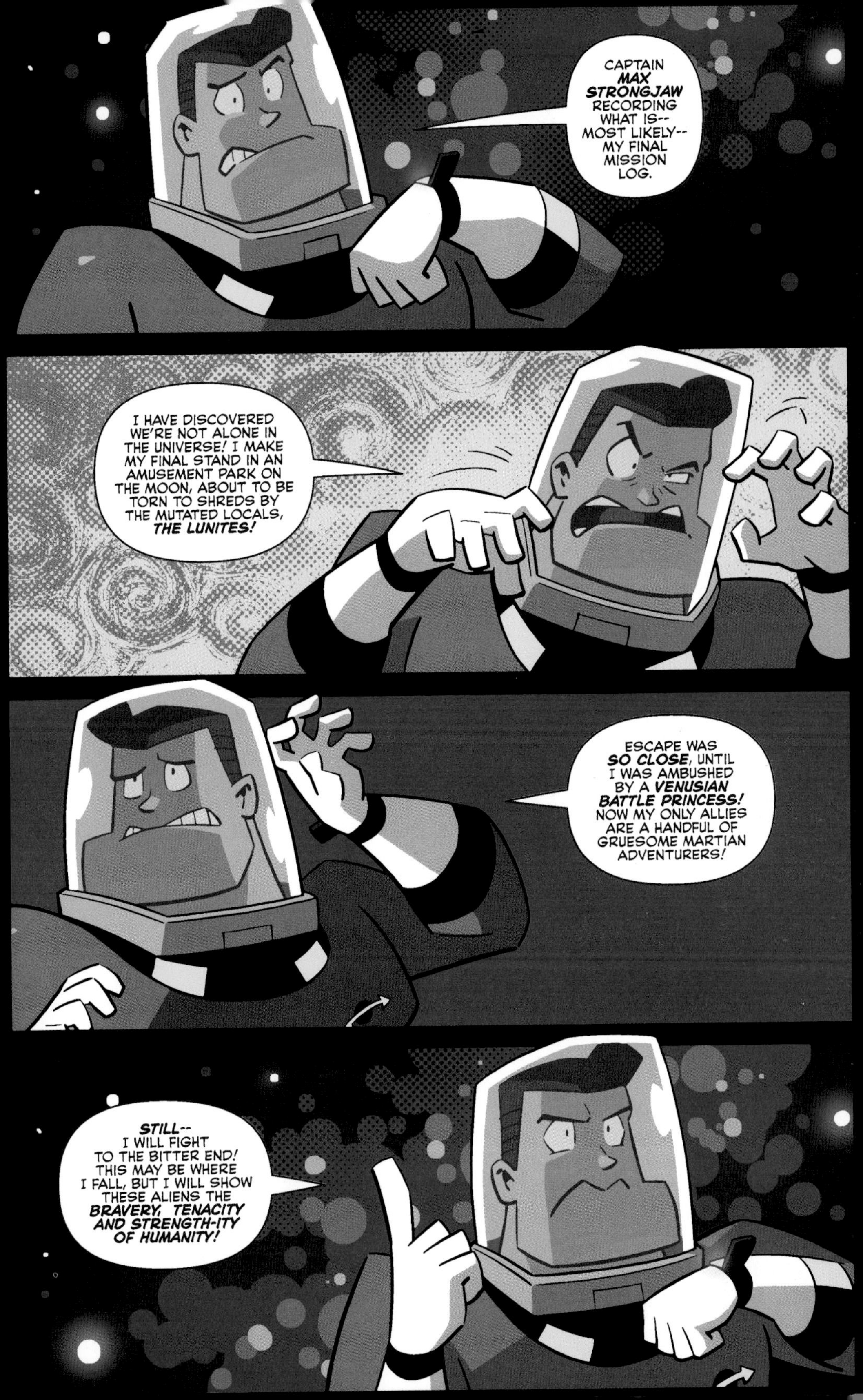
CAPTAIN *MAX STRONGJAW* RECORDING WHAT IS-- MOST LIKELY-- MY FINAL MISSION LOG.
I HAVE DISCOVERED WE'RE NOT ALONE IN THE UNIVERSE! I MAKE MY FINAL STAND IN AN AMUSEMENT PARK ON THE MOON, ABOUT TO BE TORN TO SHREDS BY THE MUTATED LOCALS, *THE LUNITES!*
ESCAPE WAS *SO CLOSE*, UNTIL I WAS AMBUSHED BY A *VENUSIAN BATTLE PRINCESS!* NOW MY ONLY ALLIES ARE A HANDFUL OF GRUESOME MARTIAN ADVENTURERS!
STILL-- I WILL FIGHT TO THE BITTER END! THIS MAY BE WHERE I FALL, BUT I WILL SHOW THESE ALIENS THE *BRAVERY, TENACITY AND STRENGTH-ITY OF HUMANITY!*

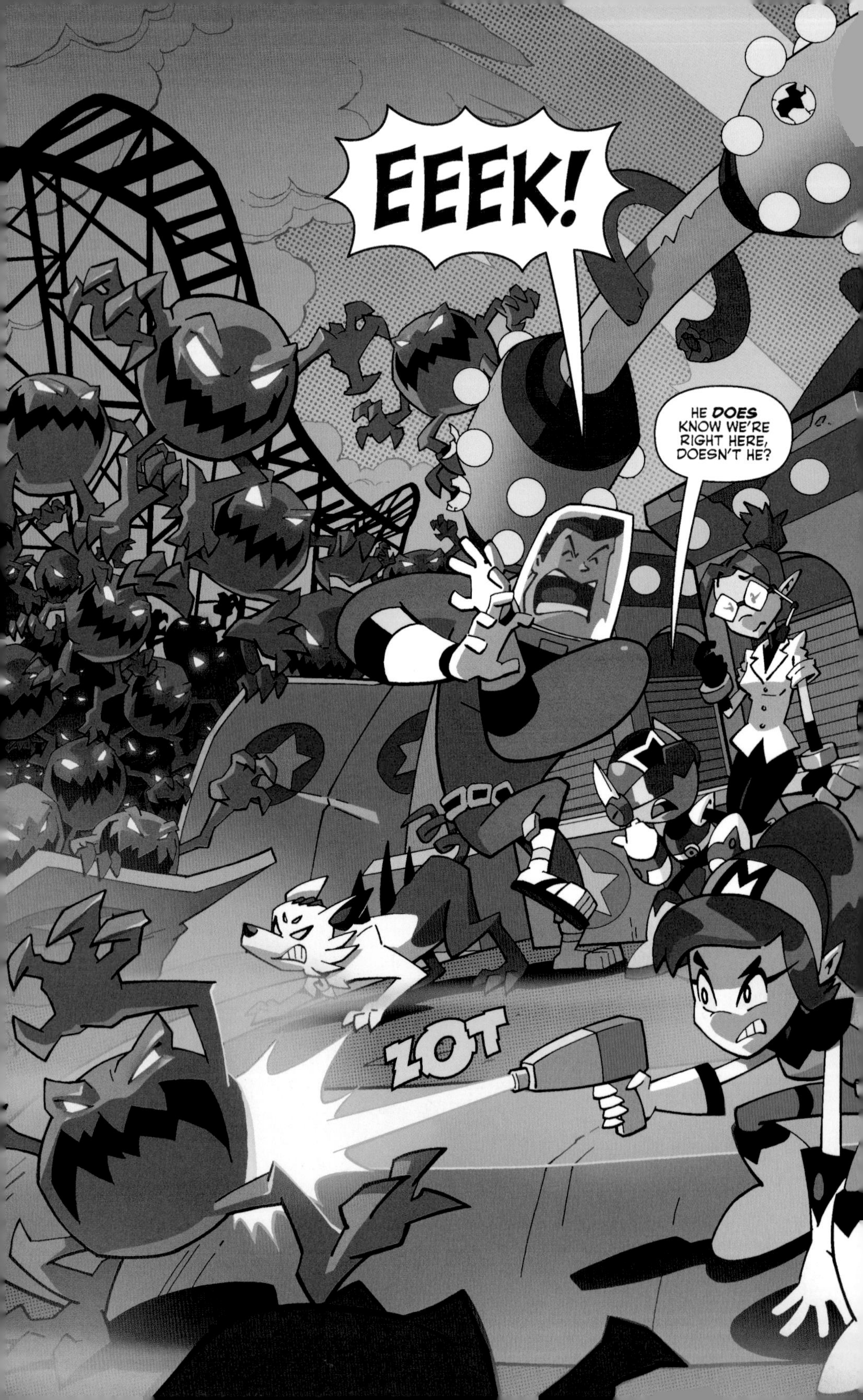
EEEK!
HE DOES KNOW WE'RE RIGHT HERE, DOESN'T HE?
ZOT

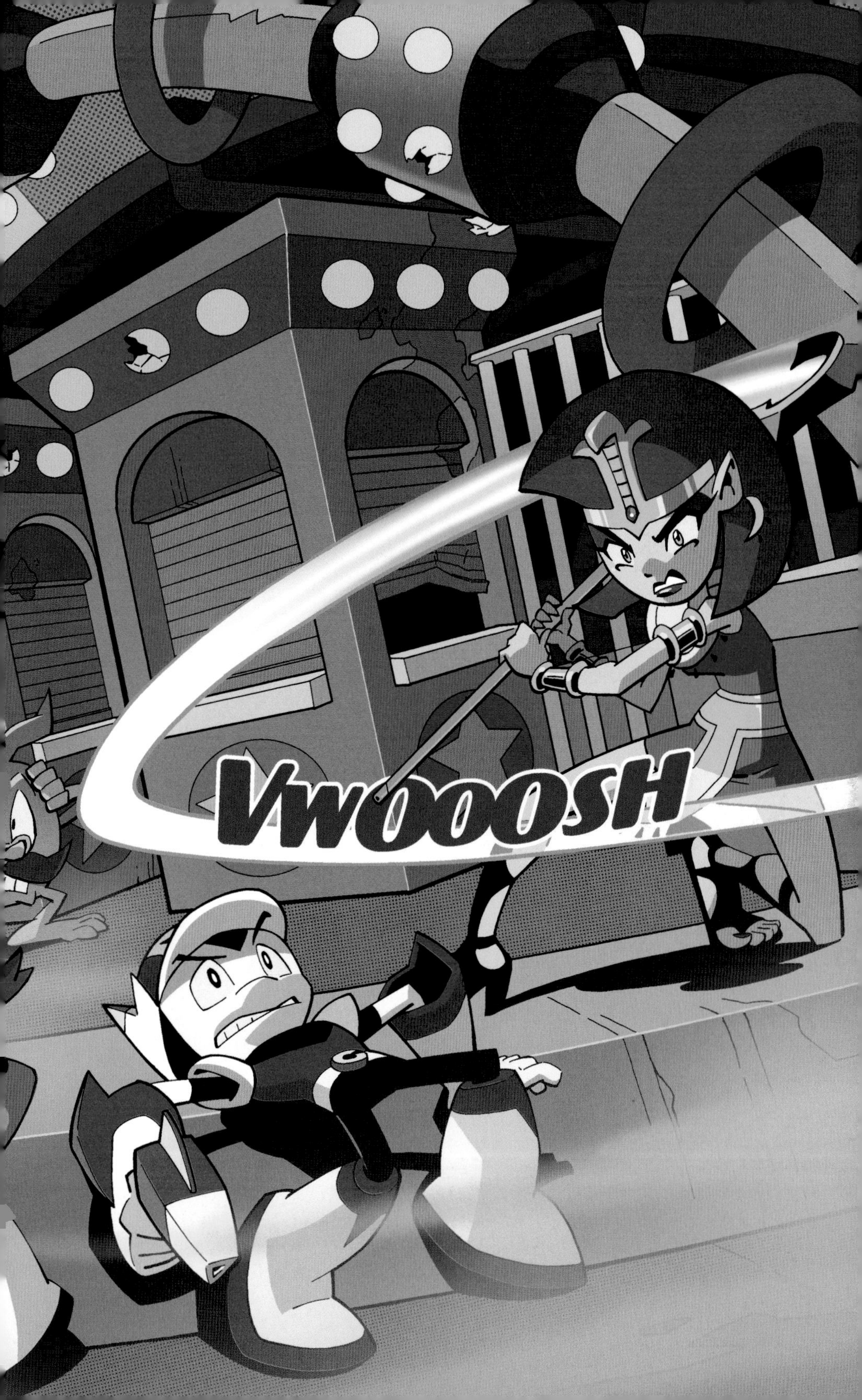
VWOOOSH

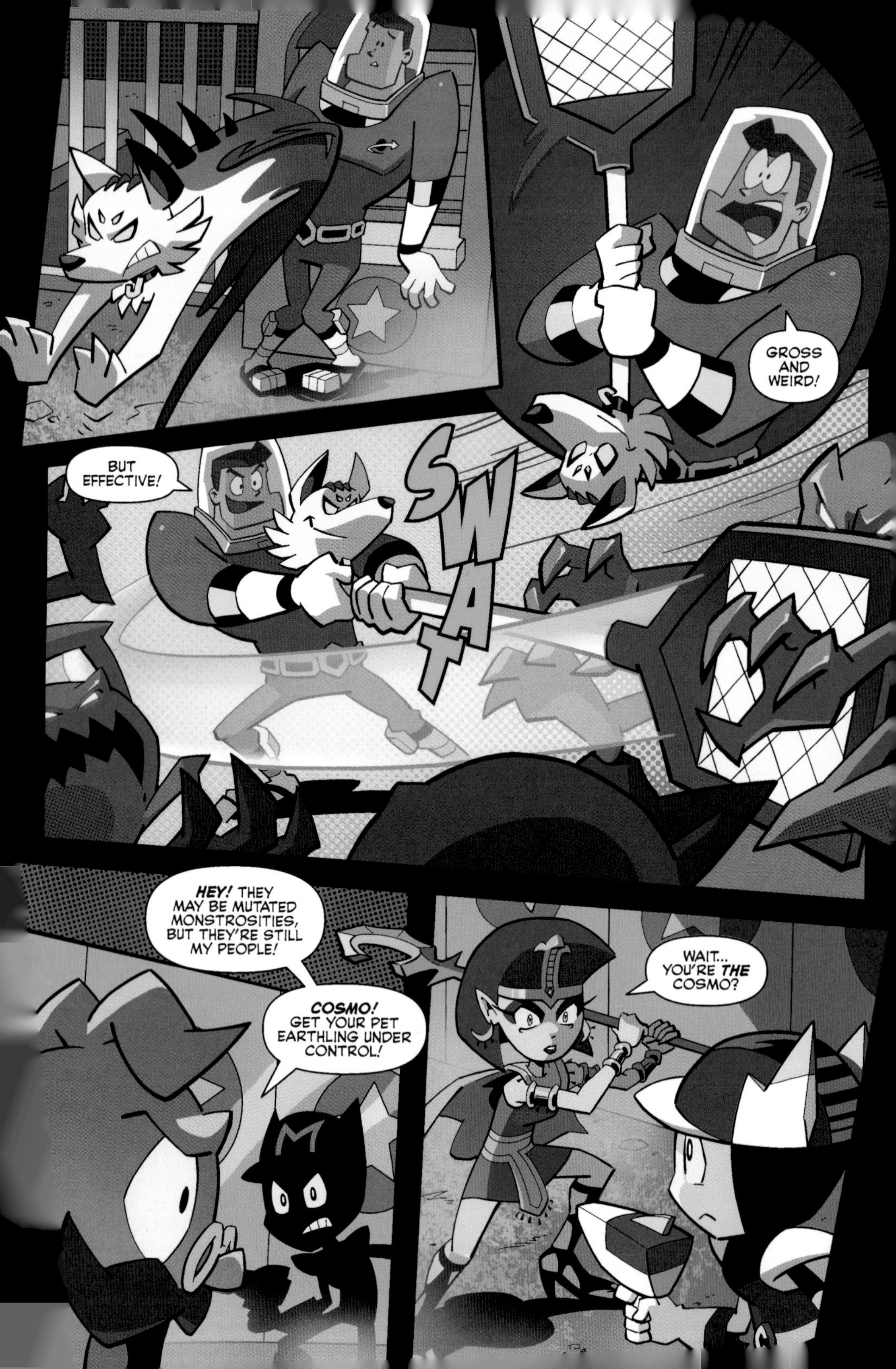
GROSS AND WEIRD!
BUT EFFECTIVE!
SWAT
HEY! THEY MAY BE MUTATED MONSTROSITIES, BUT THEY'RE STILL MY PEOPLE!
COSMO! GET YOUR PET EARTHLING UNDER CONTROL!
WAIT... YOU'RE THE COSMO?

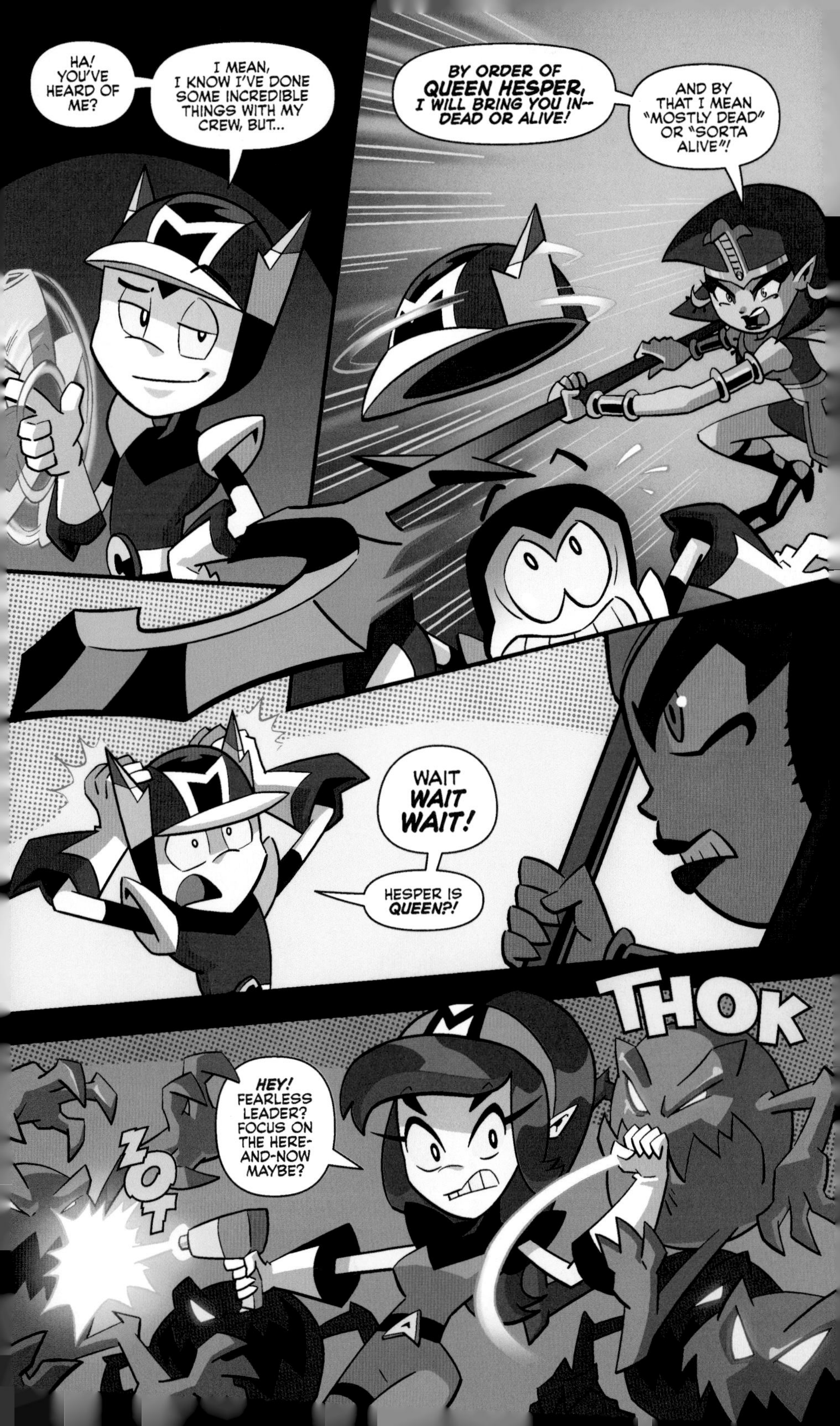
HA! YOU'VE HEARD OF ME?
I MEAN, I KNOW I'VE DONE SOME INCREDIBLE THINGS WITH MY CREW, BUT...
BY ORDER OF QUEEN HESPER, I WILL BRING YOU IN-- DEAD OR ALIVE!
AND BY THAT I MEAN "MOSTLY DEAD" OR "SORTA ALIVE"!
WAIT WAIT WAIT!
HESPER IS QUEEN?!
THOK
HEY! FEARLESS LEADER? FOCUS ON THE HERE-AND-NOW MAYBE?
ZOT

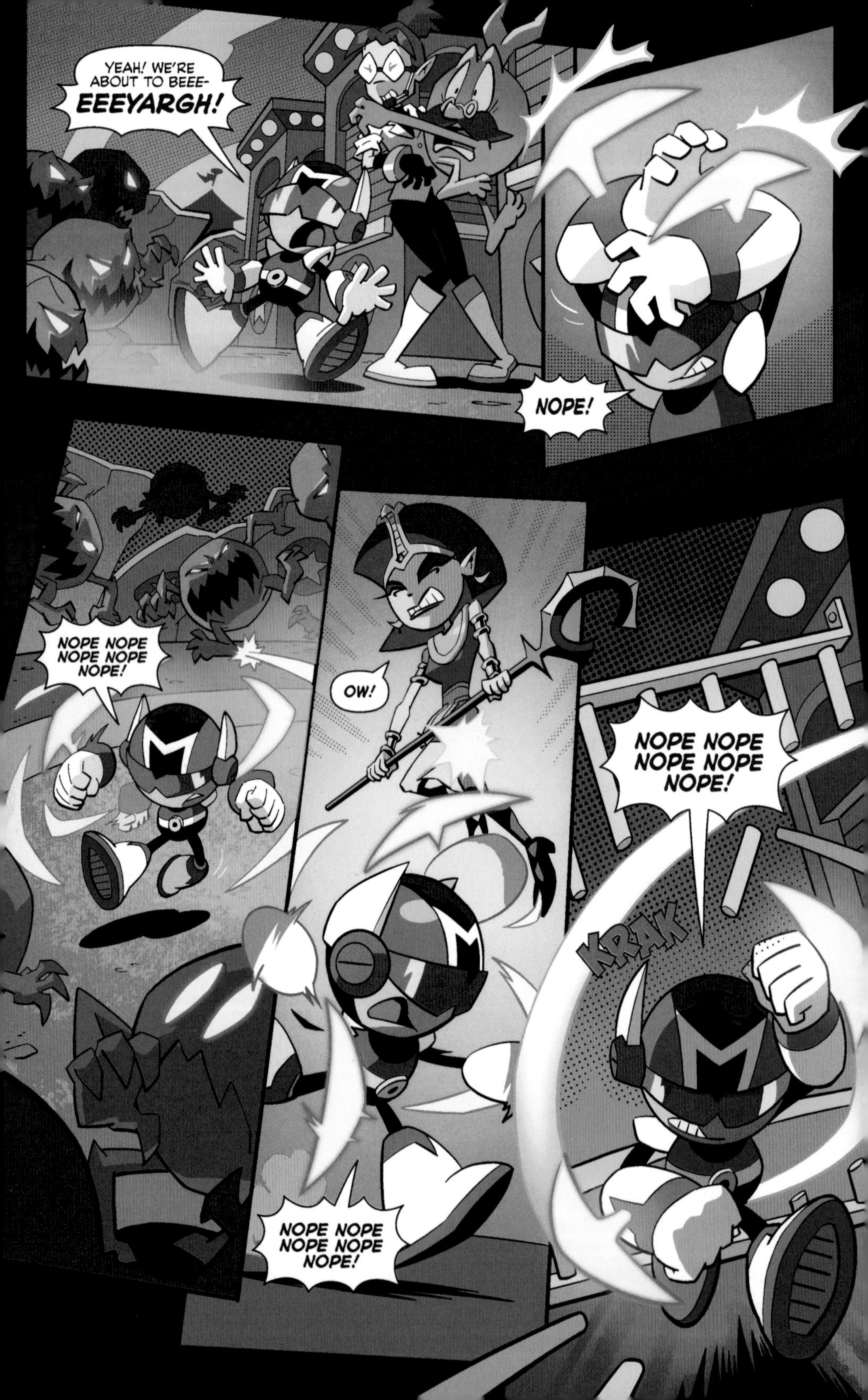
YEAH! WE'RE ABOUT TO BEEE-
EEEYARGH!
NOPE!
NOPE NOPE NOPE NOPE NOPE!
OW!
NOPE NOPE NOPE NOPE NOPE!
NOPE NOPE NOPE NOPE NOPE!
KRAK

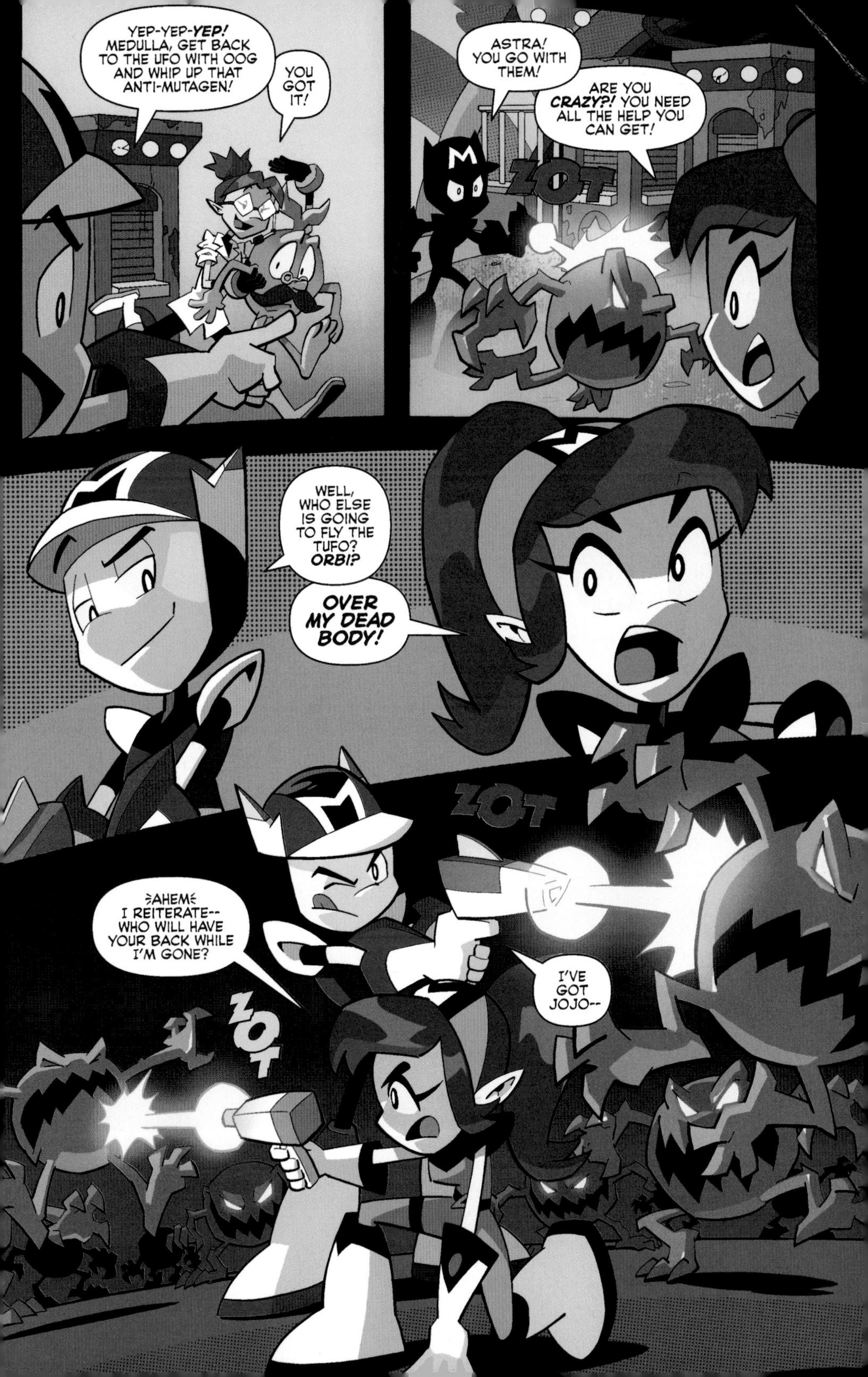
YEP-YEP-YEP! MEDULLA, GET BACK TO THE UFO WITH OOG AND WHIP UP THAT ANTI-MUTAGEN!
YOU GOT IT!
ASTRA! YOU GO WITH THEM!
ARE YOU CRAZY?! YOU NEED ALL THE HELP YOU CAN GET!
ZOT
WELL, WHO ELSE IS GOING TO FLY THE TUFO? ORBI?
OVER MY DEAD BODY!
ZOT
≥AHEM≤ I REITERATE-- WHO WILL HAVE YOUR BACK WHILE I'M GONE?
I'VE GOT JOJO--
ZOT

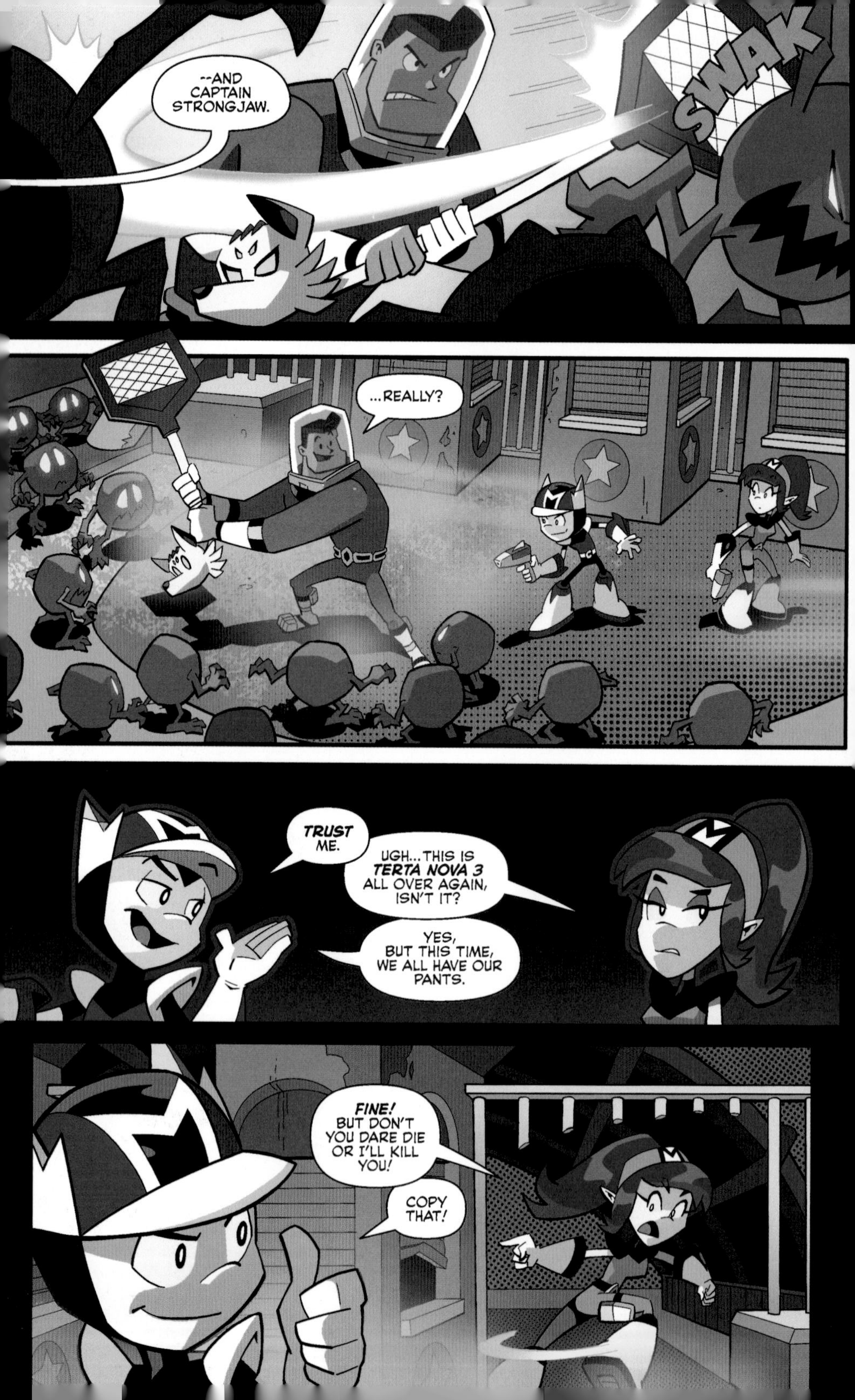
--AND CAPTAIN STRONGJAW.
SWAK
...REALLY?
TRUST ME.
UGH...THIS IS TERTA NOVA 3 ALL OVER AGAIN, ISN'T IT?
YES, BUT THIS TIME, WE ALL HAVE OUR PANTS.
FINE! BUT DON'T YOU DARE DIE OR I'LL KILL YOU!
COPY THAT!

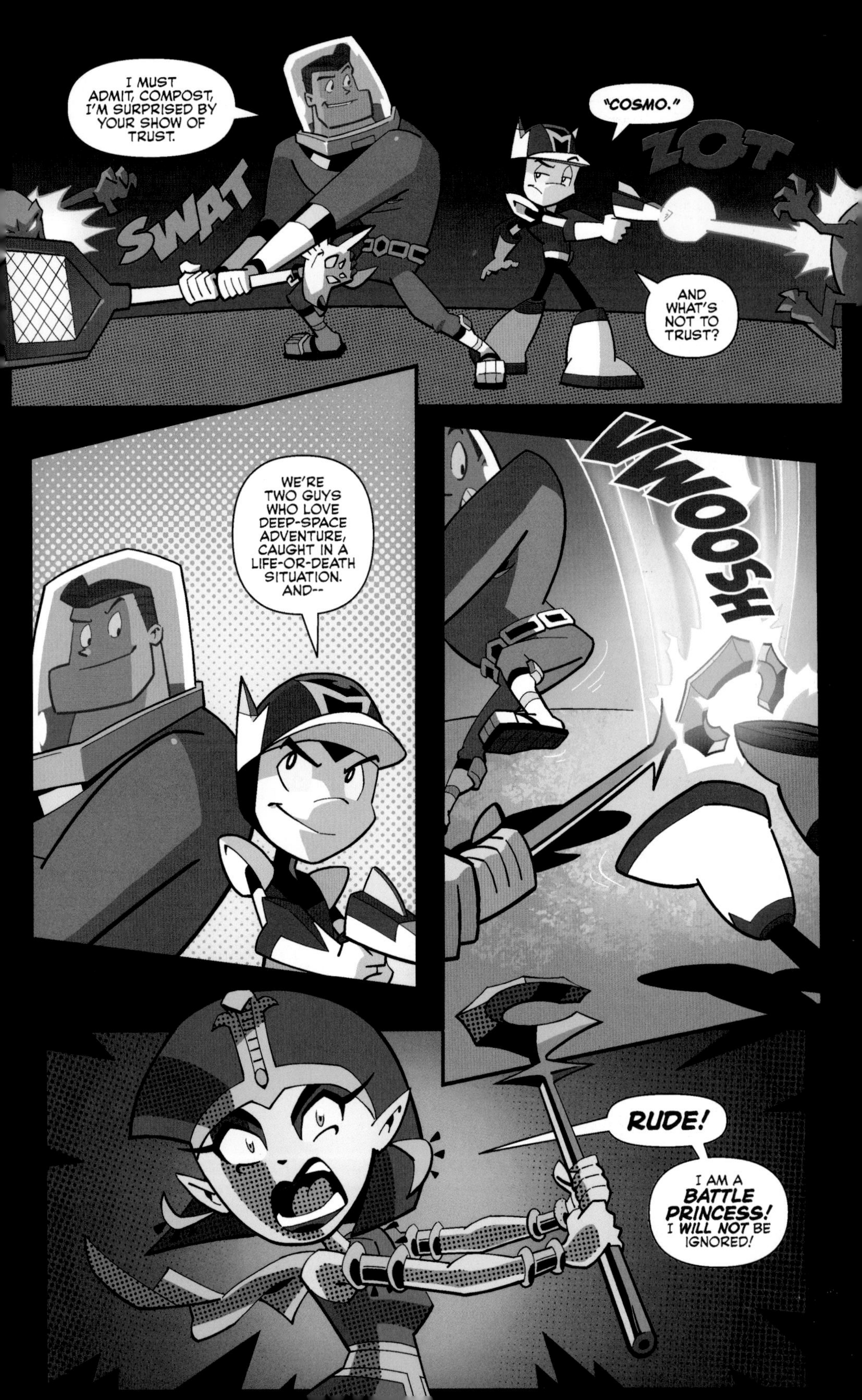
I MUST ADMIT, COMPOST, I'M SURPRISED BY YOUR SHOW OF TRUST.
SWAT
"COSMO."
ZOT
AND WHAT'S NOT TO TRUST?
WE'RE TWO GUYS WHO LOVE DEEP-SPACE ADVENTURE, CAUGHT IN A LIFE-OR-DEATH SITUATION. AND--
VWOOSH
RUDE!
I AM A BATTLE PRINCESS! I WILL NOT BE IGNORED!

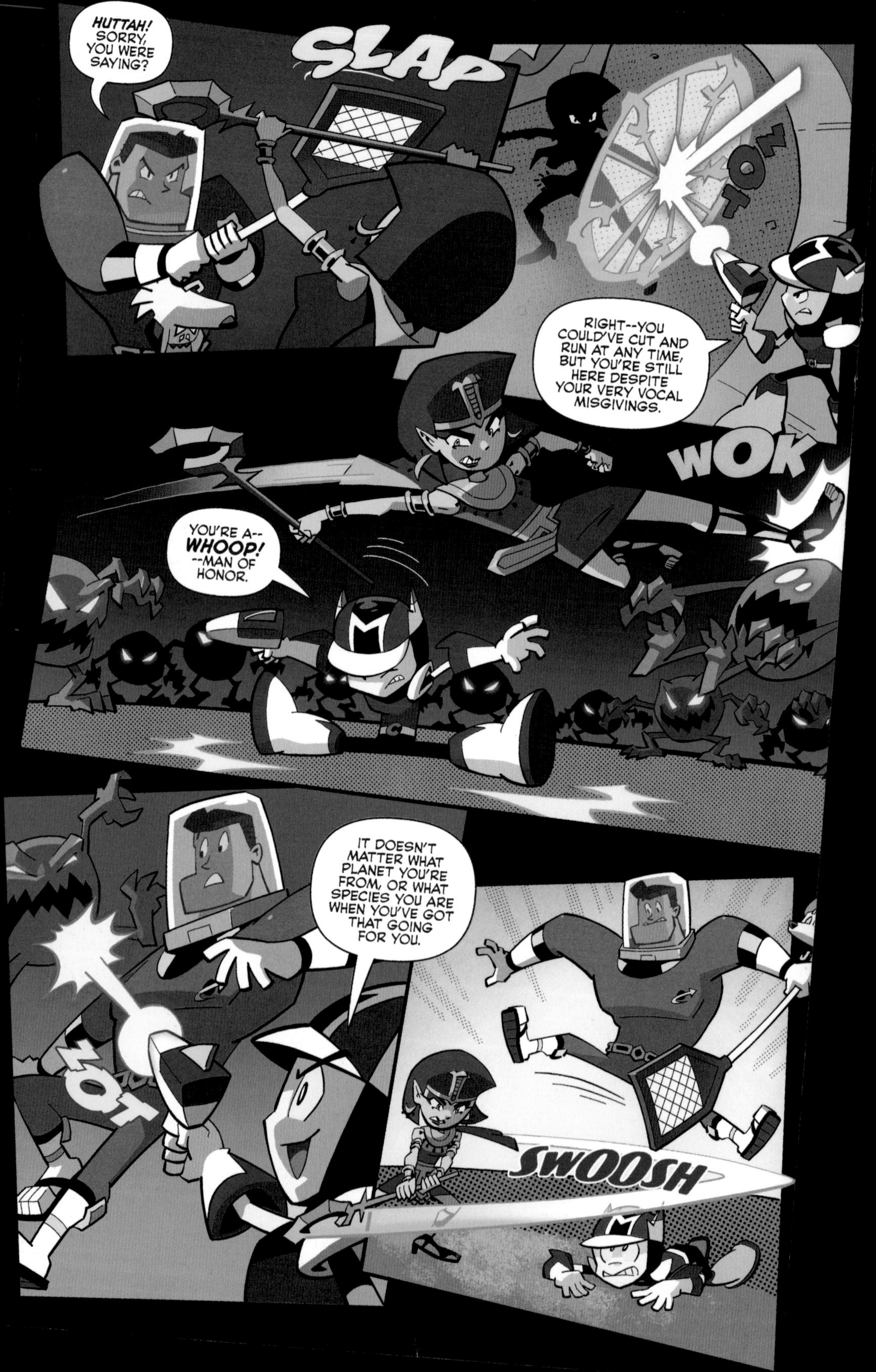
HUTTAH! SORRY, YOU WERE SAYING?
SLAP
ZOT
RIGHT--YOU COULD'VE CUT AND RUN AT ANY TIME, BUT YOU'RE STILL HERE DESPITE YOUR VERY VOCAL MISGIVINGS.
WOK
YOU'RE A-- WHOOP! --MAN OF HONOR.
IT DOESN'T MATTER WHAT PLANET YOU'RE FROM, OR WHAT SPECIES YOU ARE WHEN YOU'VE GOT THAT GOING FOR YOU.
ZOT
SWOOSH

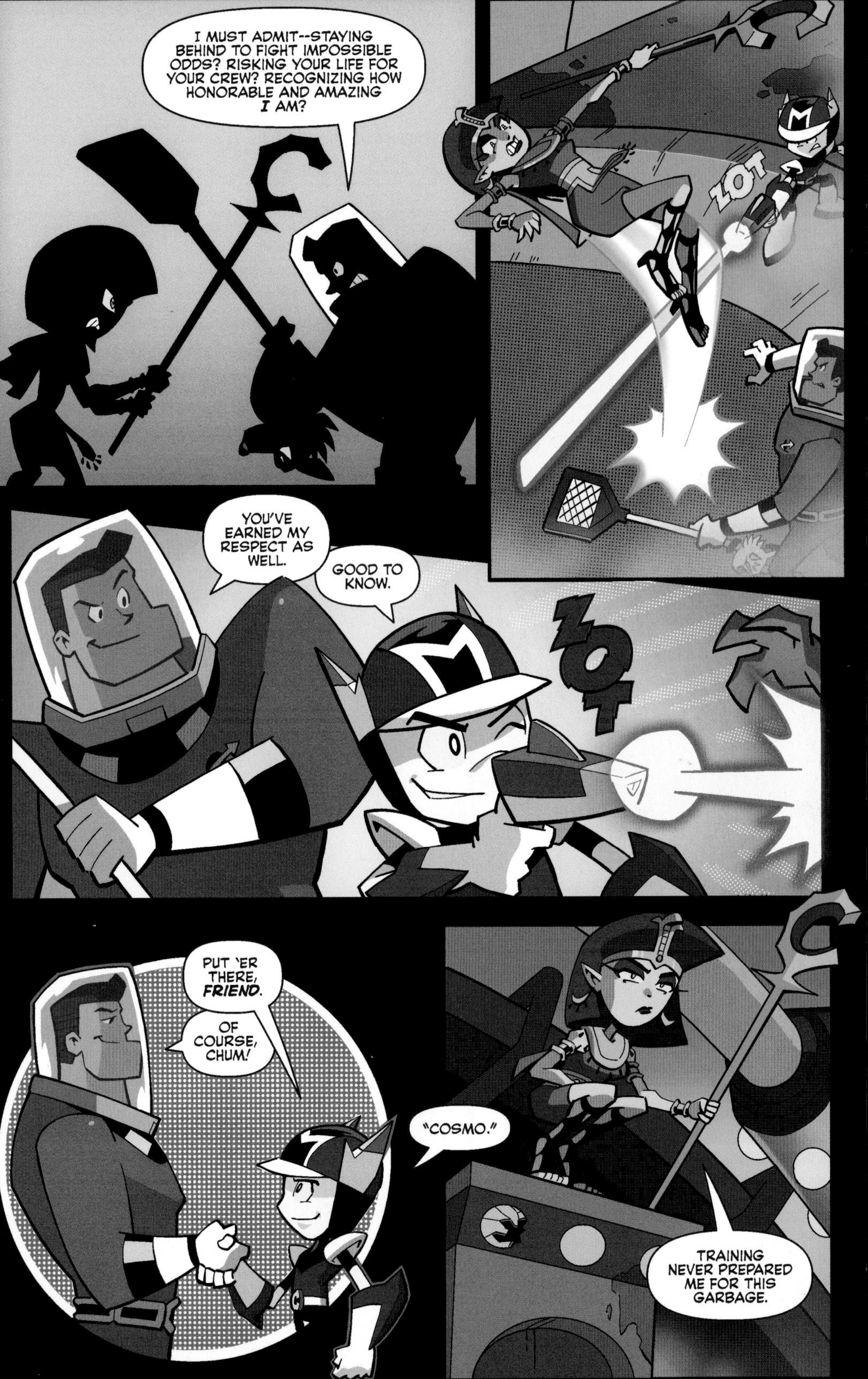

I MUST ADMIT--STAYING BEHIND TO FIGHT IMPOSSIBLE ODDS? RISKING YOUR LIFE FOR YOUR CREW? RECOGNIZING HOW HONORABLE AND AMAZING *I* AM?
ZOT
YOU'VE EARNED MY RESPECT AS WELL.
GOOD TO KNOW.
ZOT
PUT 'ER THERE, **FRIEND**.
OF COURSE, CHUM!
"COSMO."
TRAINING NEVER PREPARED ME FOR THIS GARBAGE.

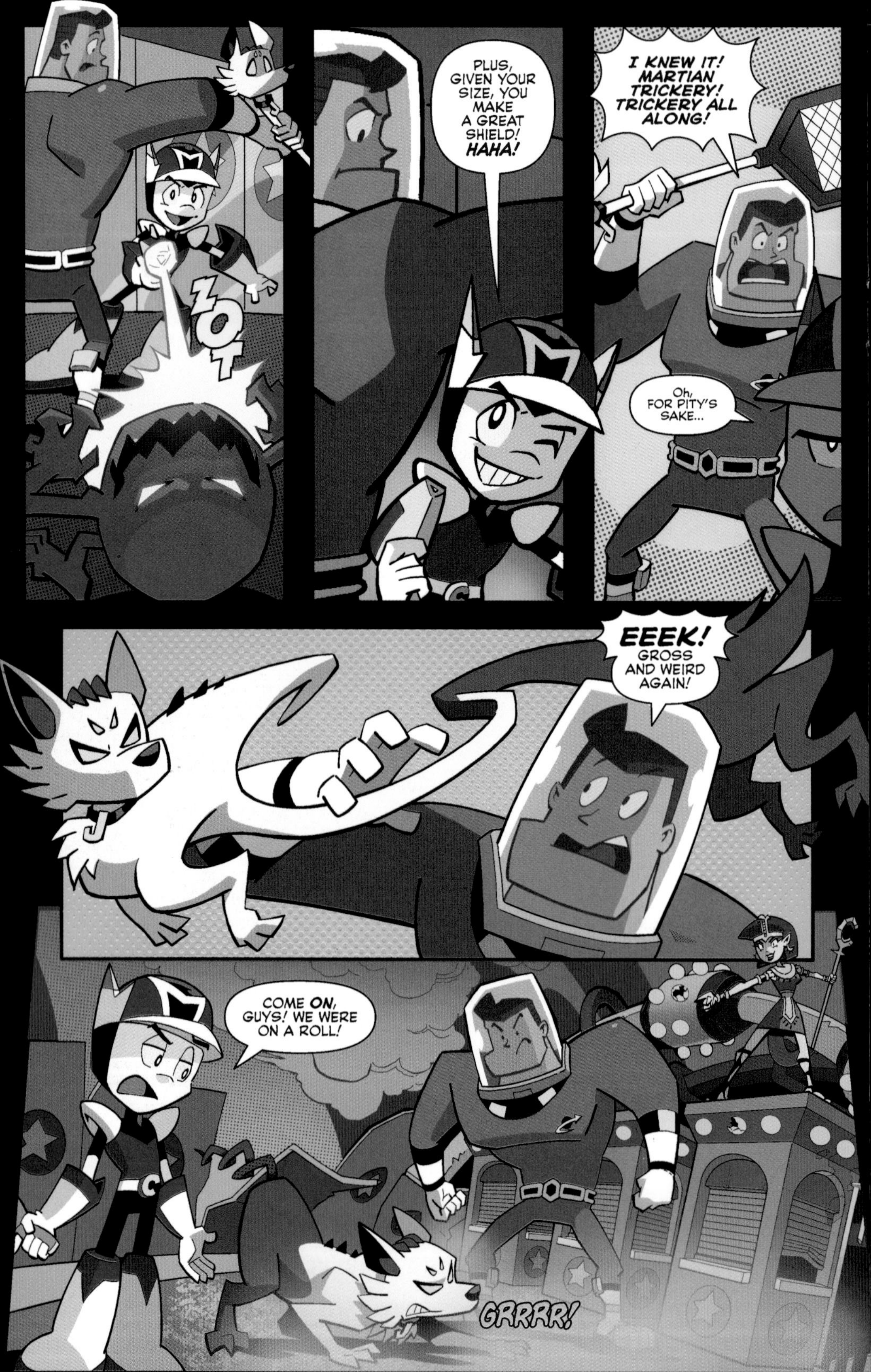
ZOT
PLUS, GIVEN YOUR SIZE, YOU MAKE A GREAT SHIELD! HAHA!
I KNEW IT! MARTIAN TRICKERY! TRICKERY ALL ALONG!
Oh, FOR PITY'S SAKE...
EEEK! GROSS AND WEIRD AGAIN!
COME ON, GUYS! WE WERE ON A ROLL!
GRRRR!

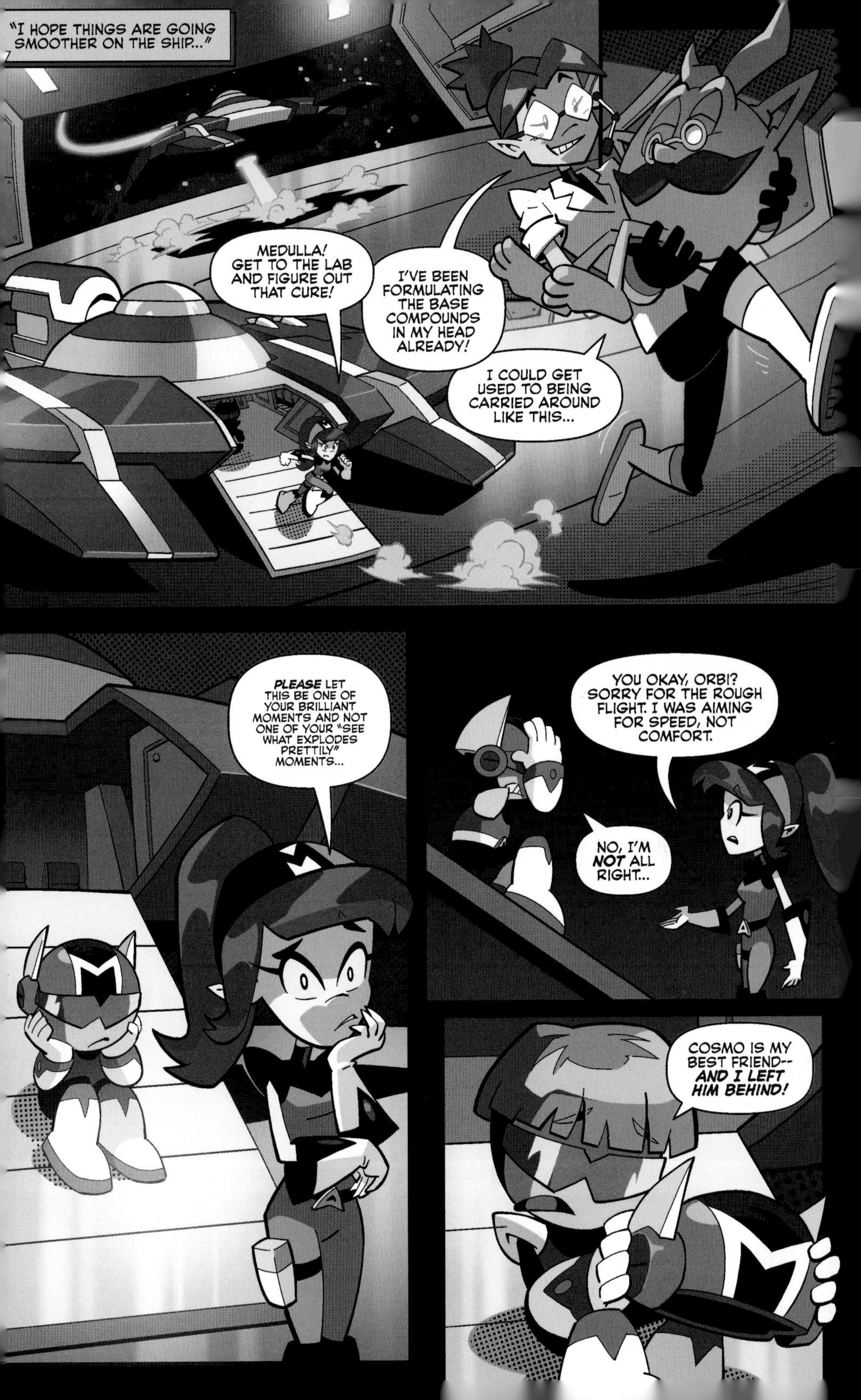
"I HOPE THINGS ARE GOING SMOOTHER ON THE SHIP..."
MEDULLA! GET TO THE LAB AND FIGURE OUT THAT CURE!
I'VE BEEN FORMULATING THE BASE COMPOUNDS IN MY HEAD ALREADY!
I COULD GET USED TO BEING CARRIED AROUND LIKE THIS...
PLEASE LET THIS BE ONE OF YOUR BRILLIANT MOMENTS AND NOT ONE OF YOUR "SEE WHAT EXPLODES PRETTILY" MOMENTS...
YOU OKAY, ORBI? SORRY FOR THE ROUGH FLIGHT. I WAS AIMING FOR SPEED, NOT COMFORT.
NO, I'M NOT ALL RIGHT...
COSMO IS MY BEST FRIEND-- AND I LEFT HIM BEHIND!

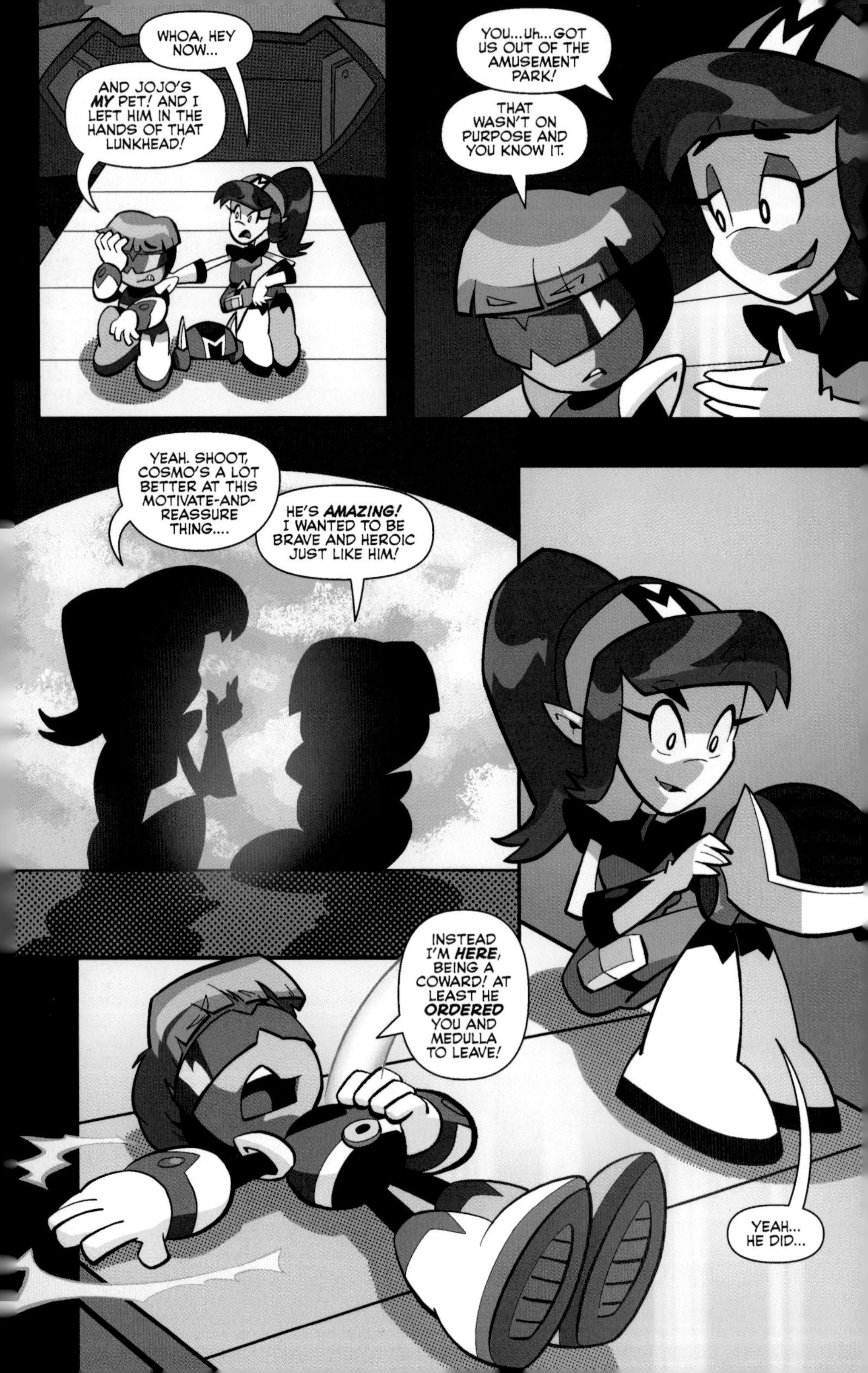
WHOA, HEY NOW...
AND JOJO'S MY PET! AND I LEFT HIM IN THE HANDS OF THAT LUNKHEAD!
YOU...Uh...GOT US OUT OF THE AMUSEMENT PARK!
THAT WASN'T ON PURPOSE AND YOU KNOW IT.
YEAH. SHOOT, COSMO'S A LOT BETTER AT THIS MOTIVATE-AND-REASSURE THING....
HE'S AMAZING! I WANTED TO BE BRAVE AND HEROIC JUST LIKE HIM!
INSTEAD I'M HERE, BEING A COWARD! AT LEAST HE ORDERED YOU AND MEDULLA TO LEAVE!
YEAH... HE DID...

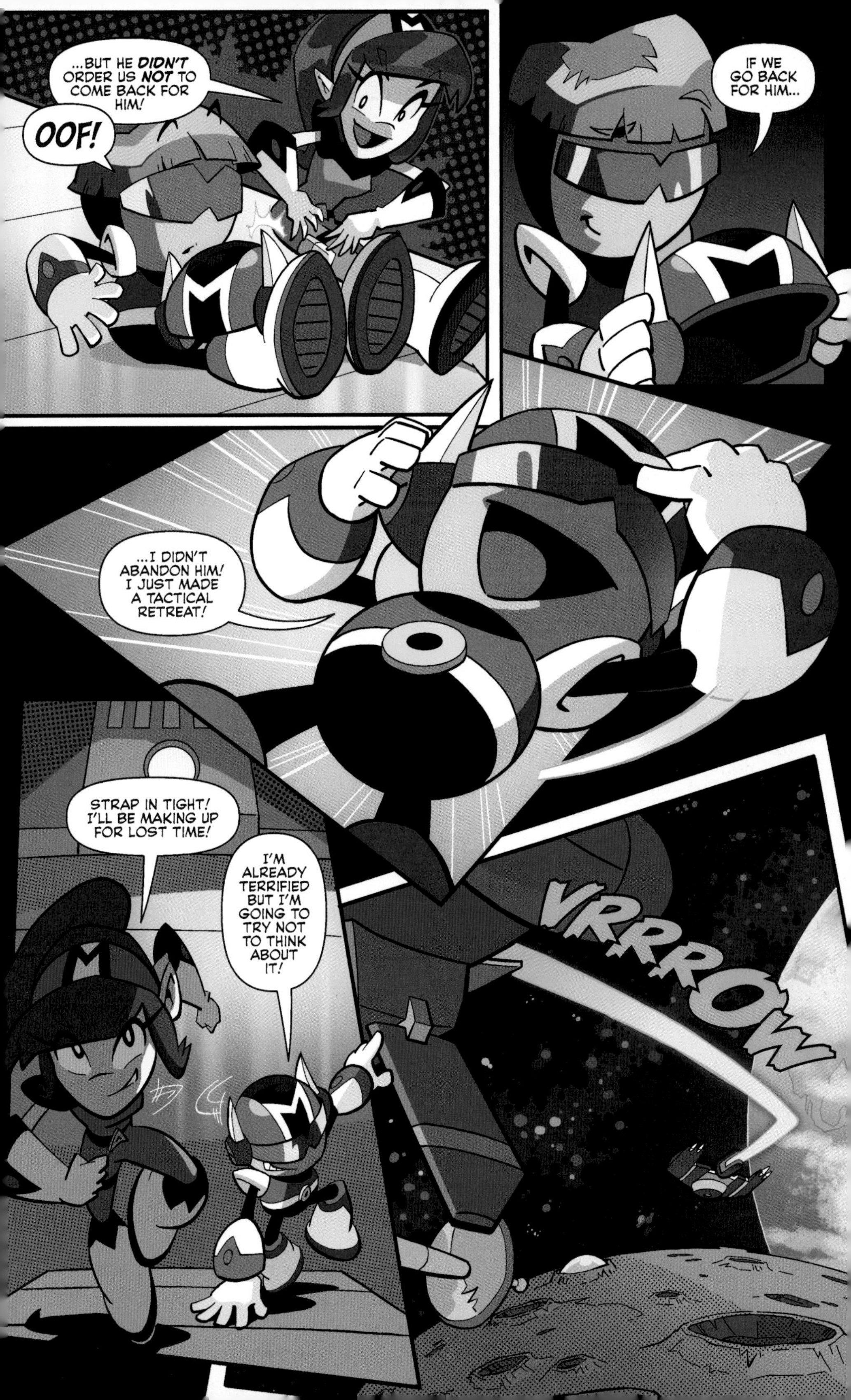
...BUT HE DIDN'T ORDER US NOT TO COME BACK FOR HIM!
OOF!
IF WE GO BACK FOR HIM...
...I DIDN'T ABANDON HIM! I JUST MADE A TACTICAL RETREAT!
STRAP IN TIGHT! I'LL BE MAKING UP FOR LOST TIME!
I'M ALREADY TERRIFIED BUT I'M GOING TO TRY NOT TO THINK ABOUT IT!
VRRROW

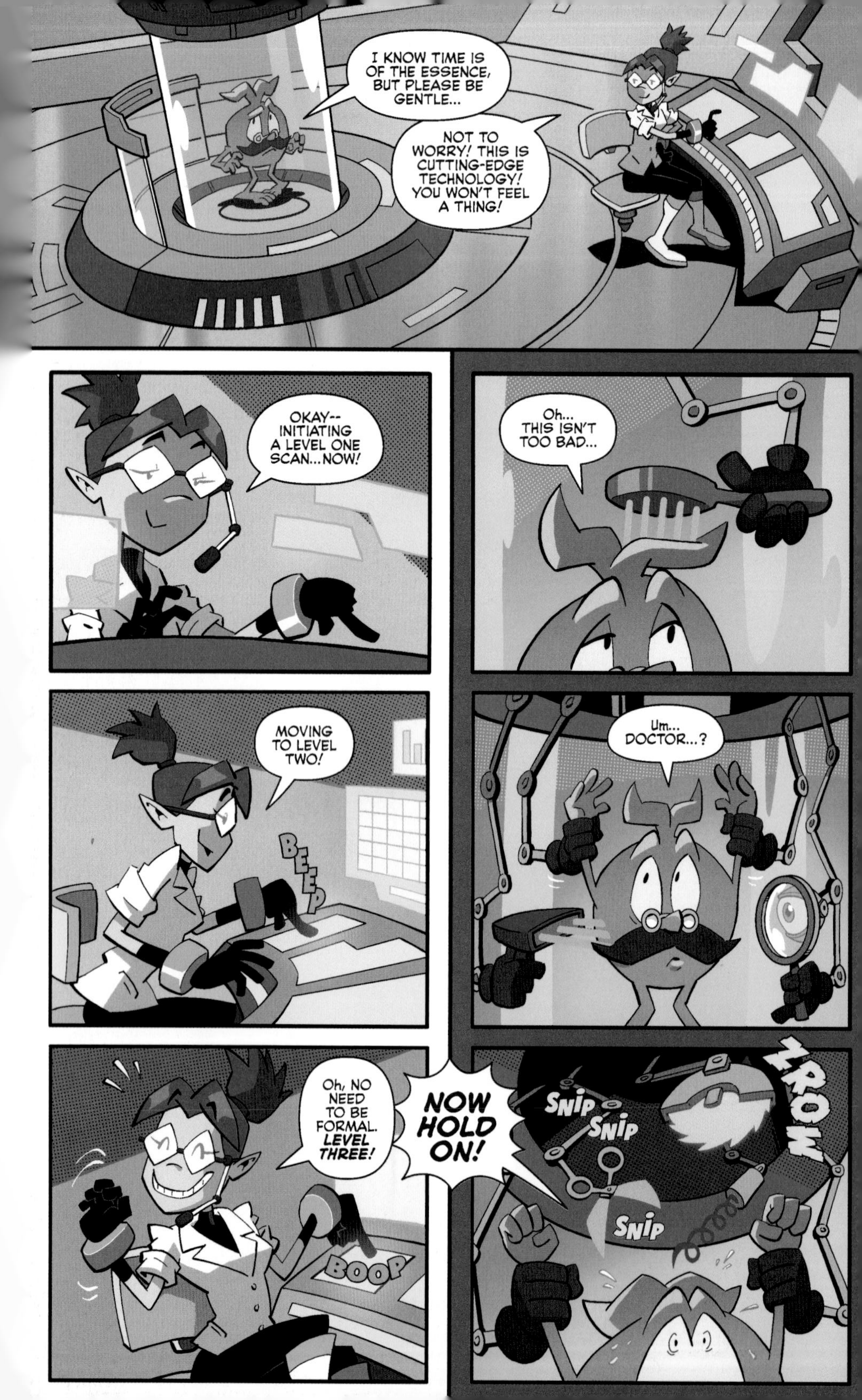
I KNOW TIME IS OF THE ESSENCE, BUT PLEASE BE GENTLE...
NOT TO WORRY! THIS IS CUTTING-EDGE TECHNOLOGY! YOU WON'T FEEL A THING!
OKAY-- INITIATING A LEVEL ONE SCAN...NOW!
Oh... THIS ISN'T TOO BAD...
MOVING TO LEVEL TWO!
BEEP
Um... DOCTOR...?
Oh, NO NEED TO BE FORMAL. LEVEL THREE!
BOOP
NOW HOLD ON!
SNIP
SNIP
SNIP
ZROW

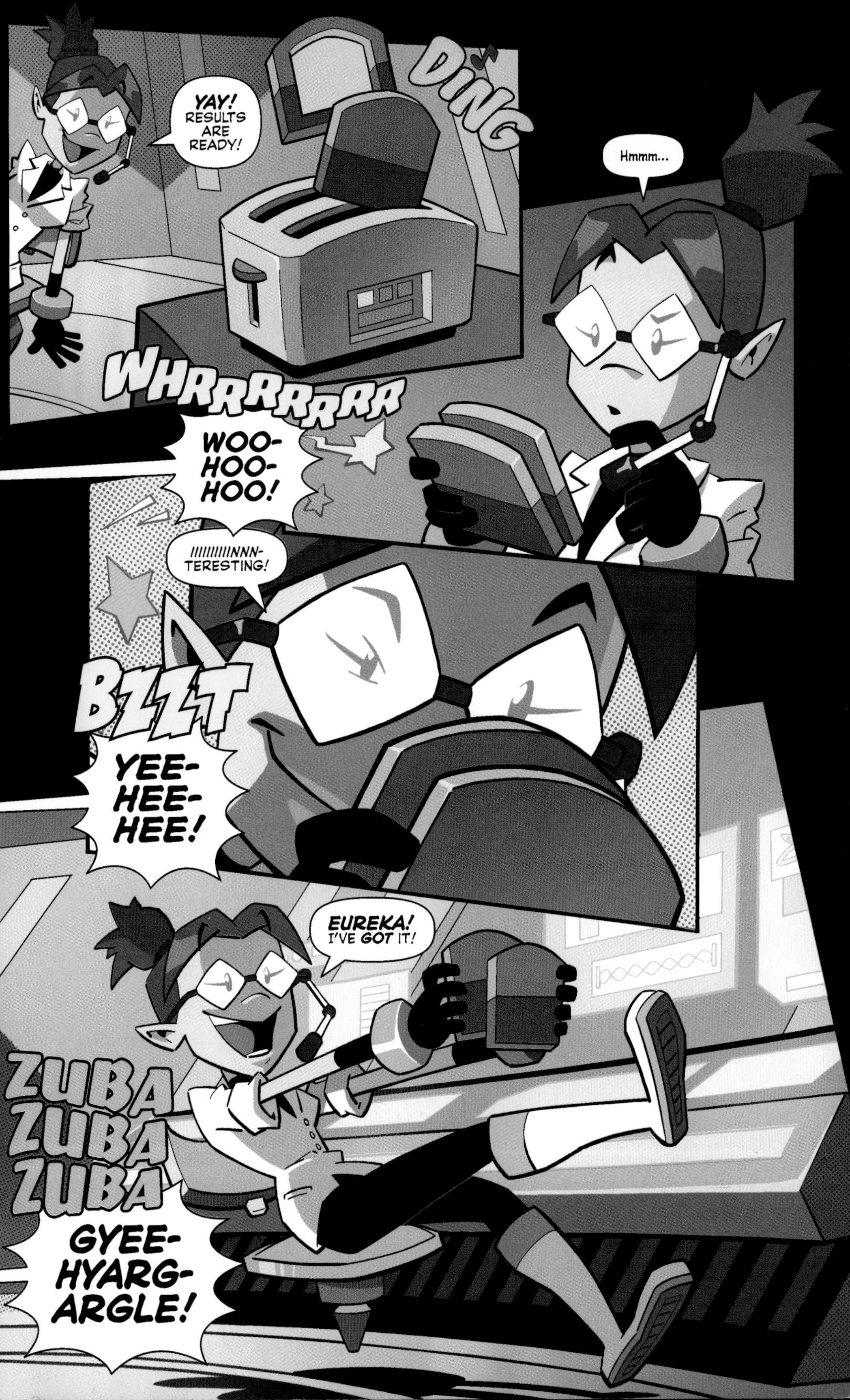
YAY! RESULTS ARE READY!
DING
WHRRRRRRRR
Hmmm...
WOO-HOO-HOO!
IIIIIIIIIINNN-TERESTING!
BZZT
YEE-HEE-HEE!
EUREKA! I'VE GOT IT!
ZUBA ZUBA ZUBA
GYEE-HYARG-ARGLE!

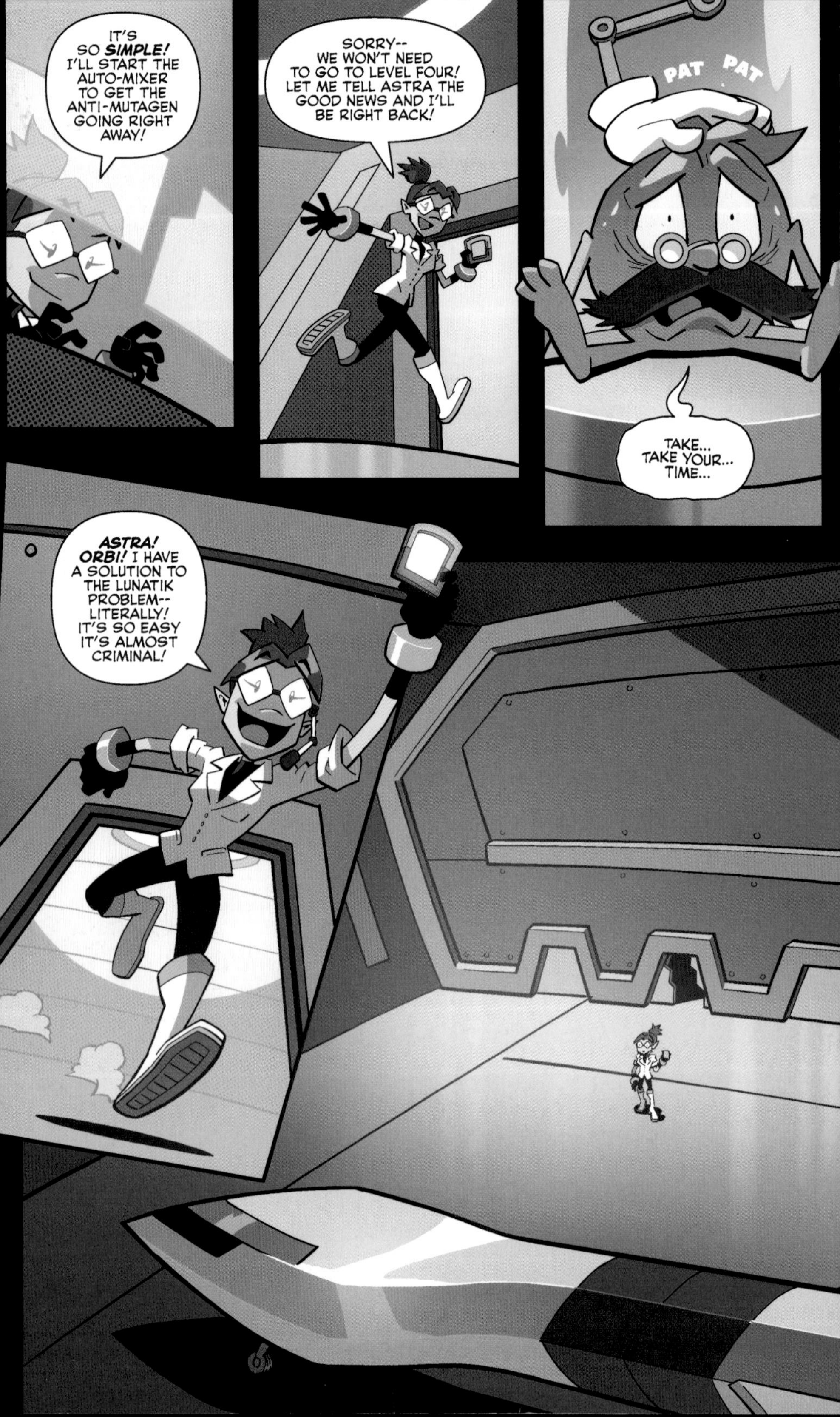
IT'S SO SIMPLE! I'LL START THE AUTO-MIXER TO GET THE ANTI-MUTAGEN GOING RIGHT AWAY!
SORRY-- WE WON'T NEED TO GO TO LEVEL FOUR! LET ME TELL ASTRA THE GOOD NEWS AND I'LL BE RIGHT BACK!
PAT PAT
TAKE... TAKE YOUR... TIME...
ASTRA! ORBI! I HAVE A SOLUTION TO THE LUNATIK PROBLEM-- LITERALLY! IT'S SO EASY IT'S ALMOST CRIMINAL!

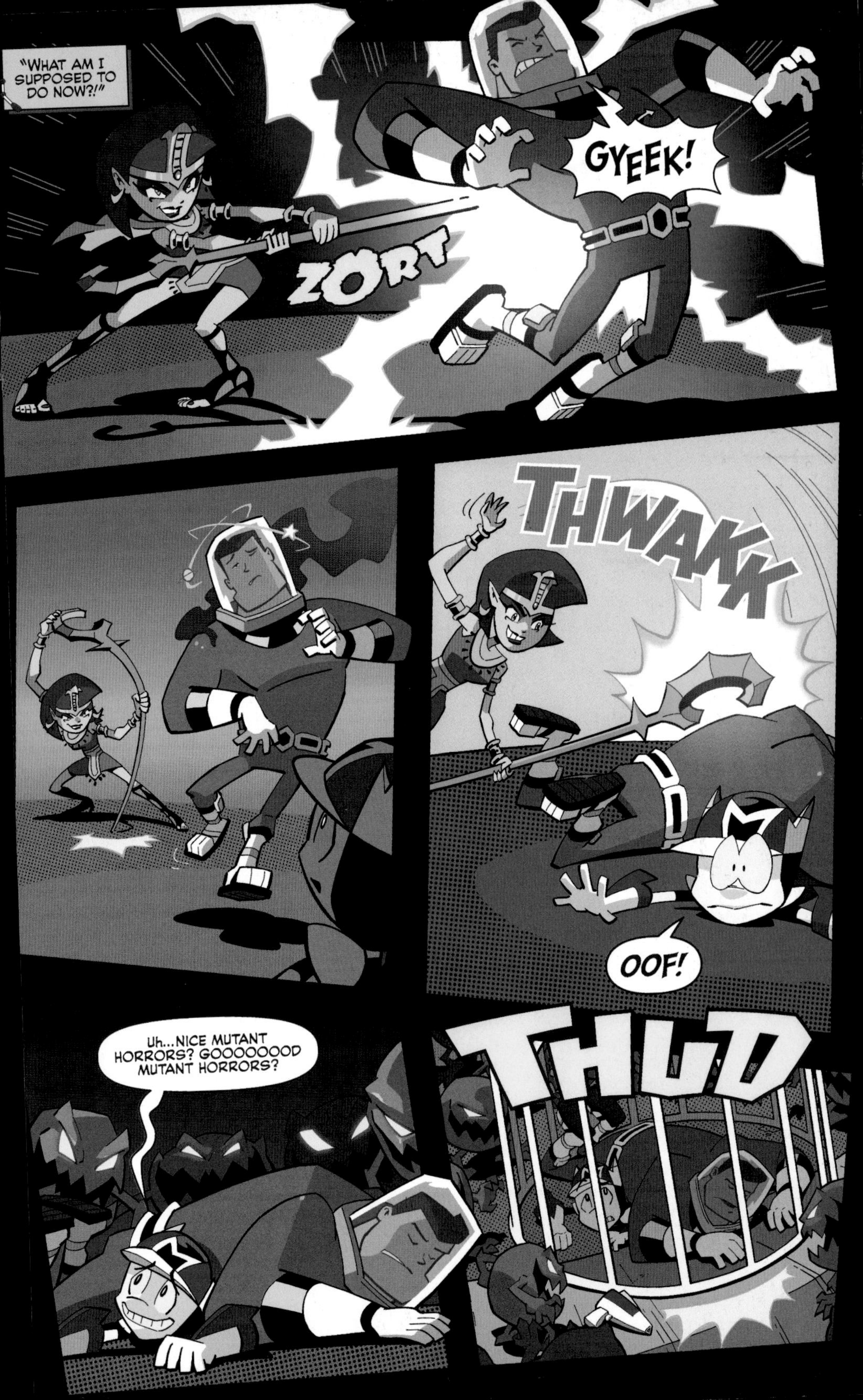
"WHAT AM I SUPPOSED TO DO NOW?!"
GYEEK!
ZORT
THWAKK
OOF!
Uh...NICE MUTANT HORRORS? GOOOOOOOD MUTANT HORRORS?
THUD

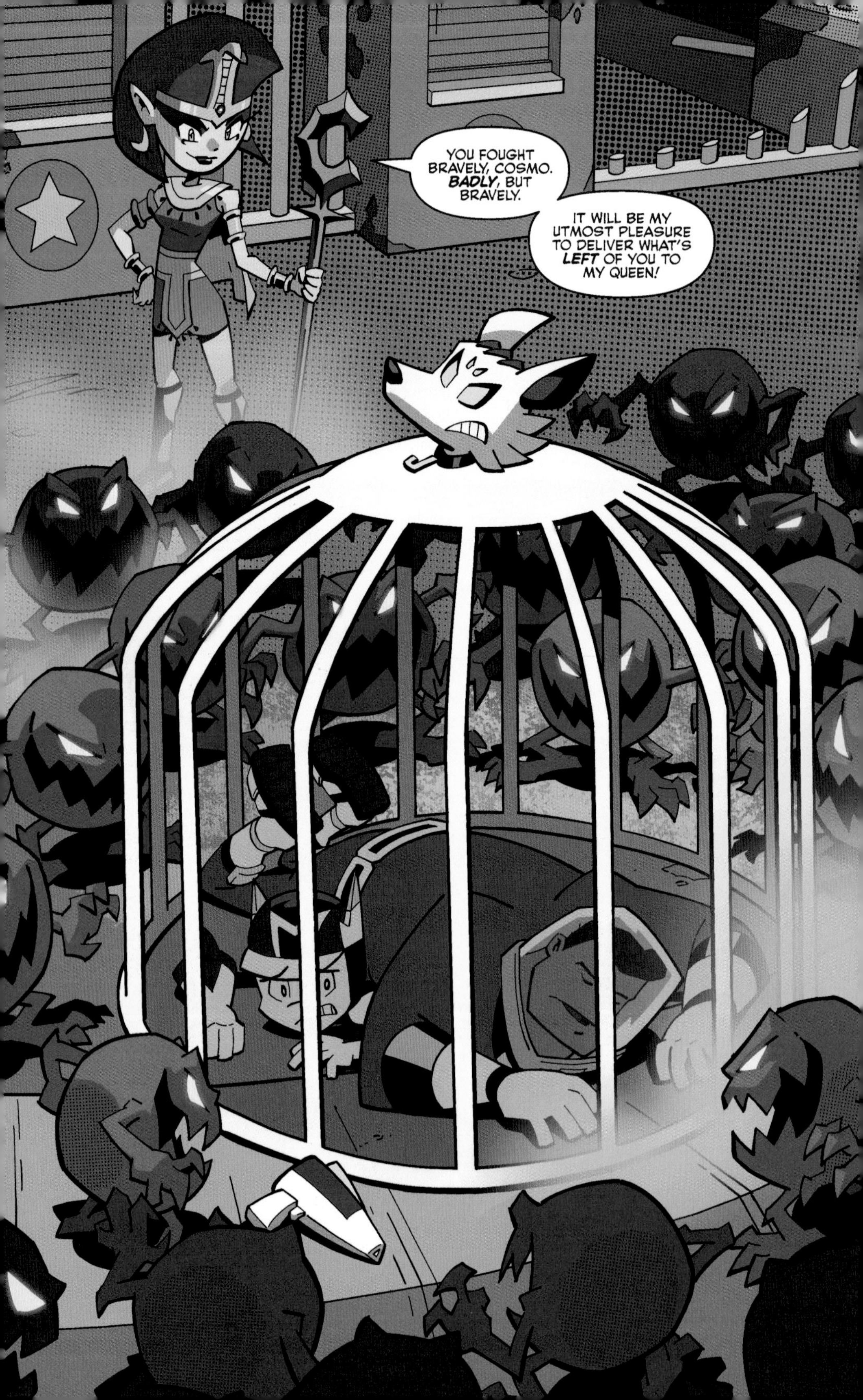
YOU FOUGHT BRAVELY, COSMO. **BADLY**, BUT BRAVELY.
IT WILL BE MY UTMOST PLEASURE TO DELIVER WHAT'S **LEFT** OF YOU TO MY QUEEN!

CHAPTER 4 • THE FINAL SHOWDOWN

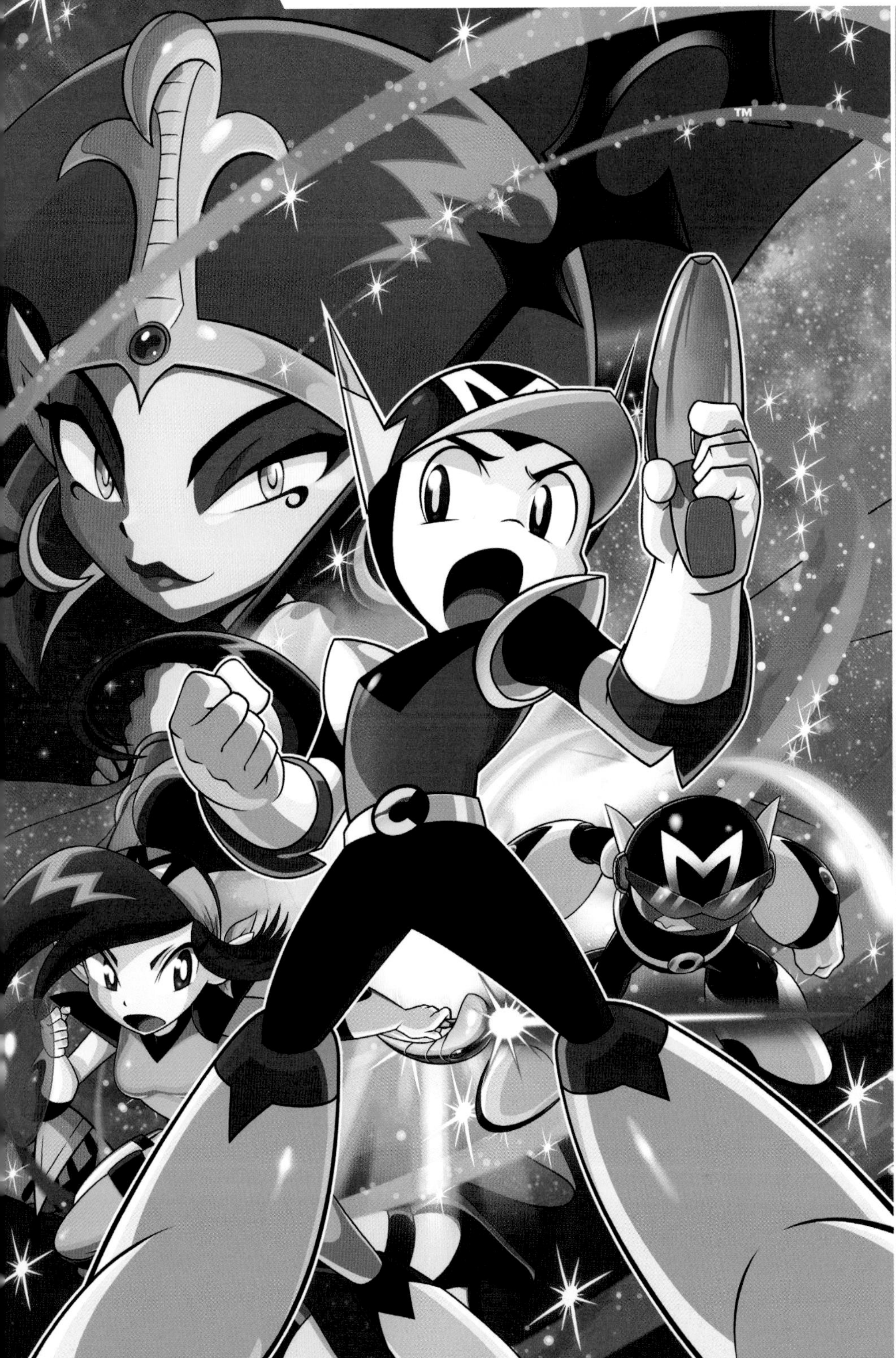

ART BY PATRICK SPAZIANTE

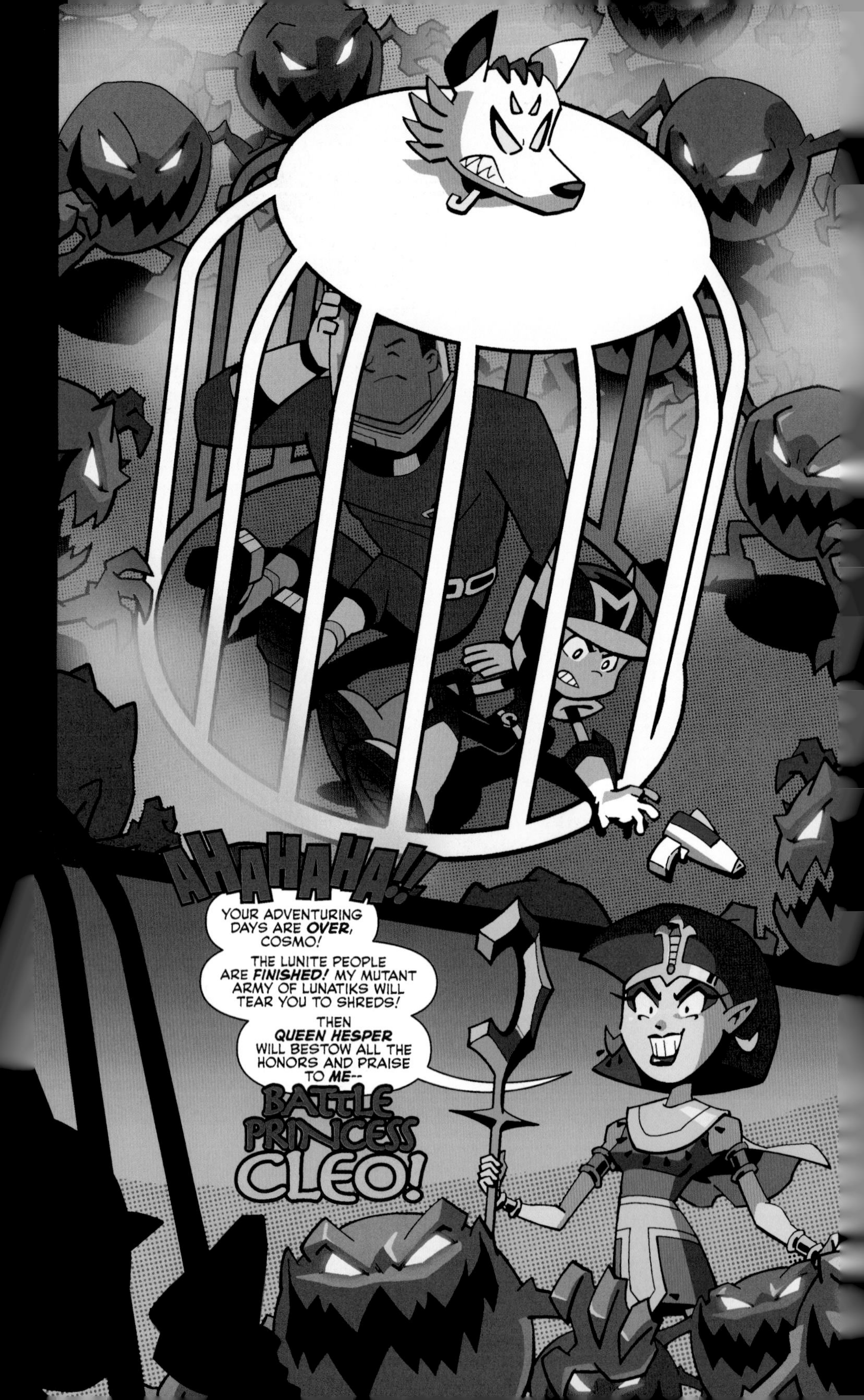
AHAHAHAHA!!
YOUR ADVENTURING DAYS ARE OVER, COSMO!
THE LUNITE PEOPLE ARE FINISHED! MY MUTANT ARMY OF LUNATIKS WILL TEAR YOU TO SHREDS!
THEN QUEEN HESPER WILL BESTOW ALL THE HONORS AND PRAISE TO ME--
BATTLE PRINCESS CLEO!

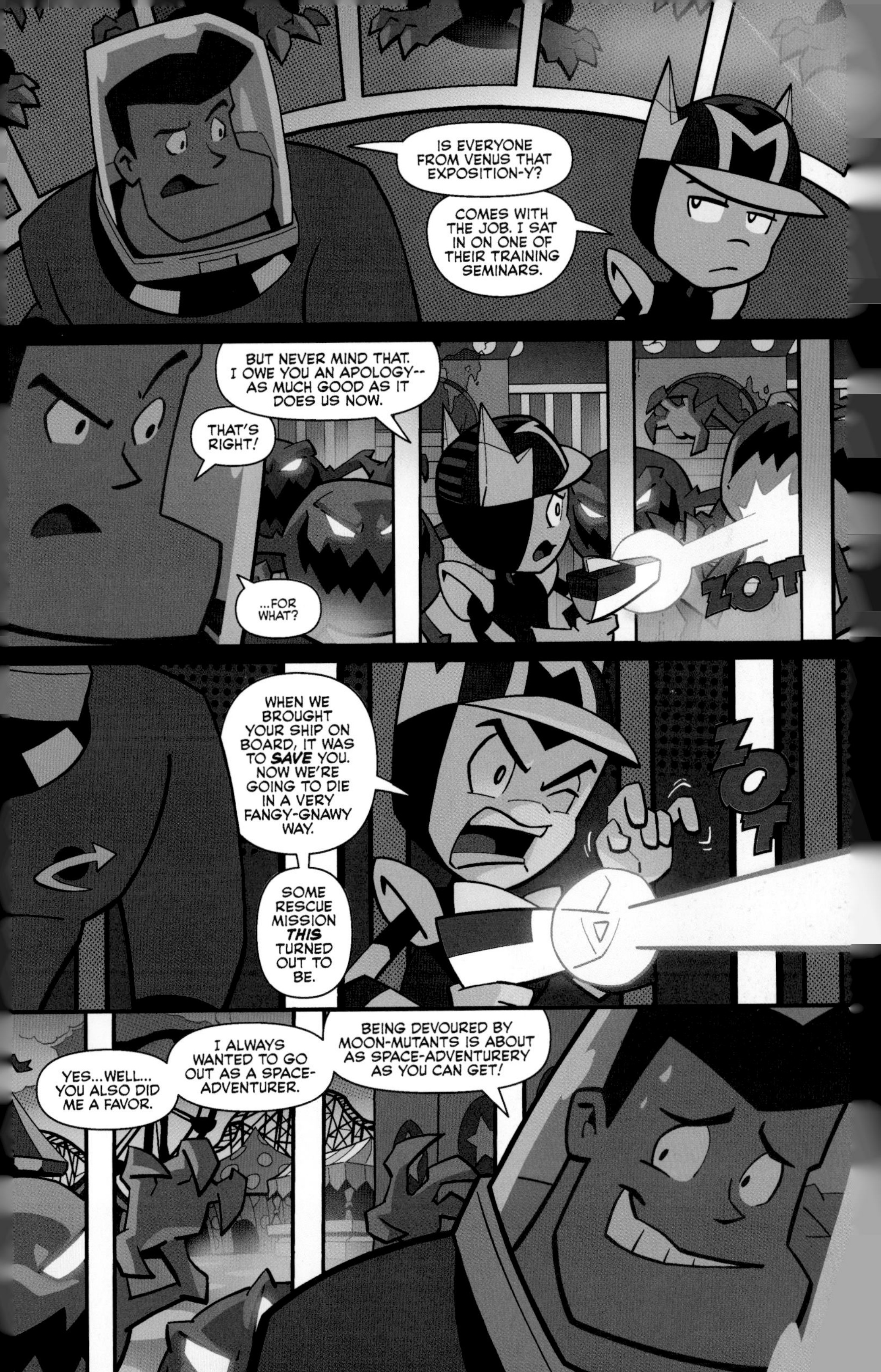

IS EVERYONE FROM VENUS THAT EXPOSITION-Y?
COMES WITH THE JOB. I SAT IN ON ONE OF THEIR TRAINING SEMINARS.
BUT NEVER MIND THAT. I OWE YOU AN APOLOGY-- AS MUCH GOOD AS IT DOES US NOW.
THAT'S RIGHT!
...FOR WHAT?
ZOT
WHEN WE BROUGHT YOUR SHIP ON BOARD, IT WAS TO *SAVE* YOU. NOW WE'RE GOING TO DIE IN A VERY FANGY-GNAWY WAY.
SOME RESCUE MISSION *THIS* TURNED OUT TO BE.
ZOT
YES...WELL... YOU ALSO DID ME A FAVOR.
I ALWAYS WANTED TO GO OUT AS A SPACE-ADVENTURER.
BEING DEVOURED BY MOON-MUTANTS IS ABOUT AS SPACE-ADVENTURERY AS YOU CAN GET!

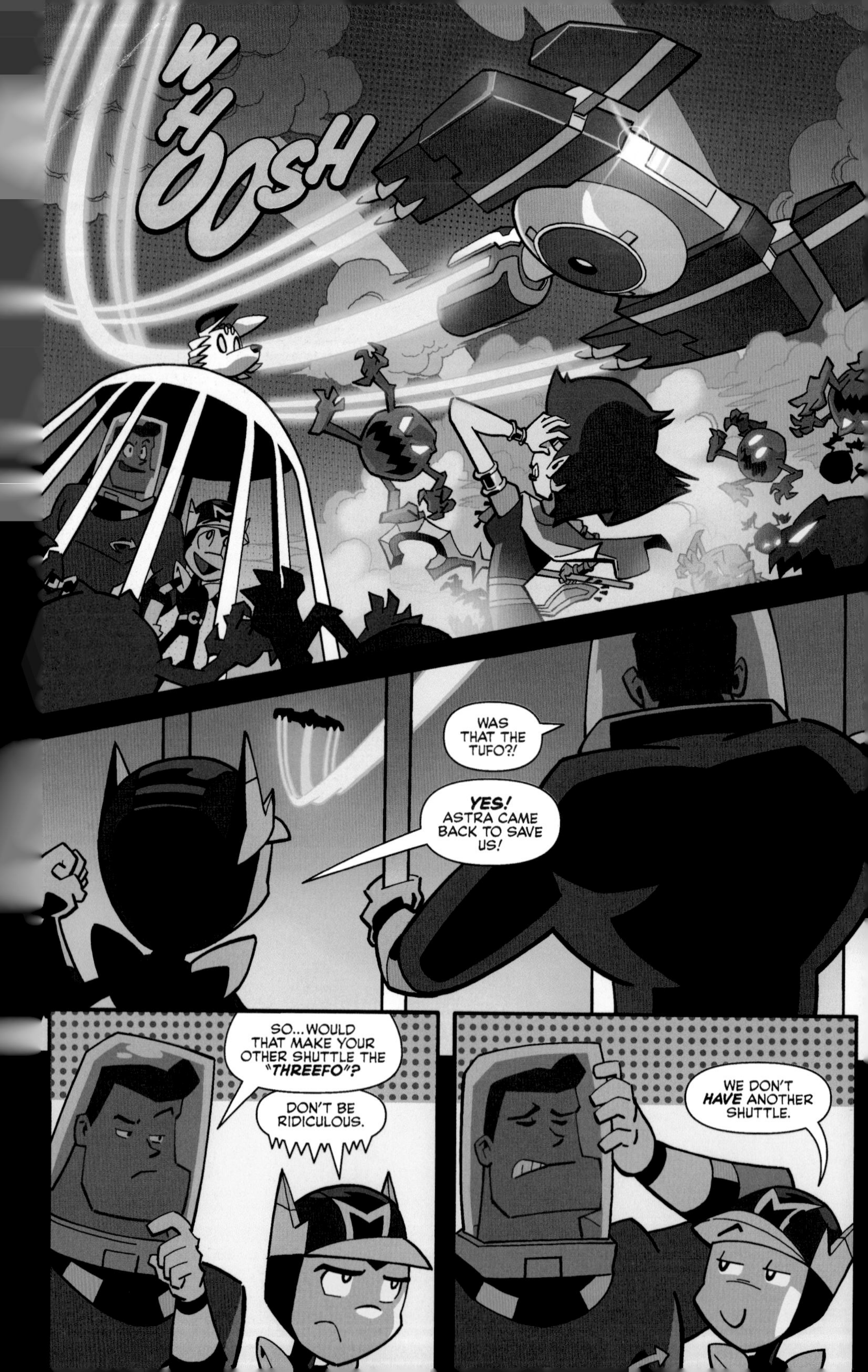
WHOOSH
WAS THAT THE TUFO?!
YES! ASTRA CAME BACK TO SAVE US!
SO...WOULD THAT MAKE YOUR OTHER SHUTTLE THE "THREEFO"?
DON'T BE RIDICULOUS.
WE DON'T HAVE ANOTHER SHUTTLE.

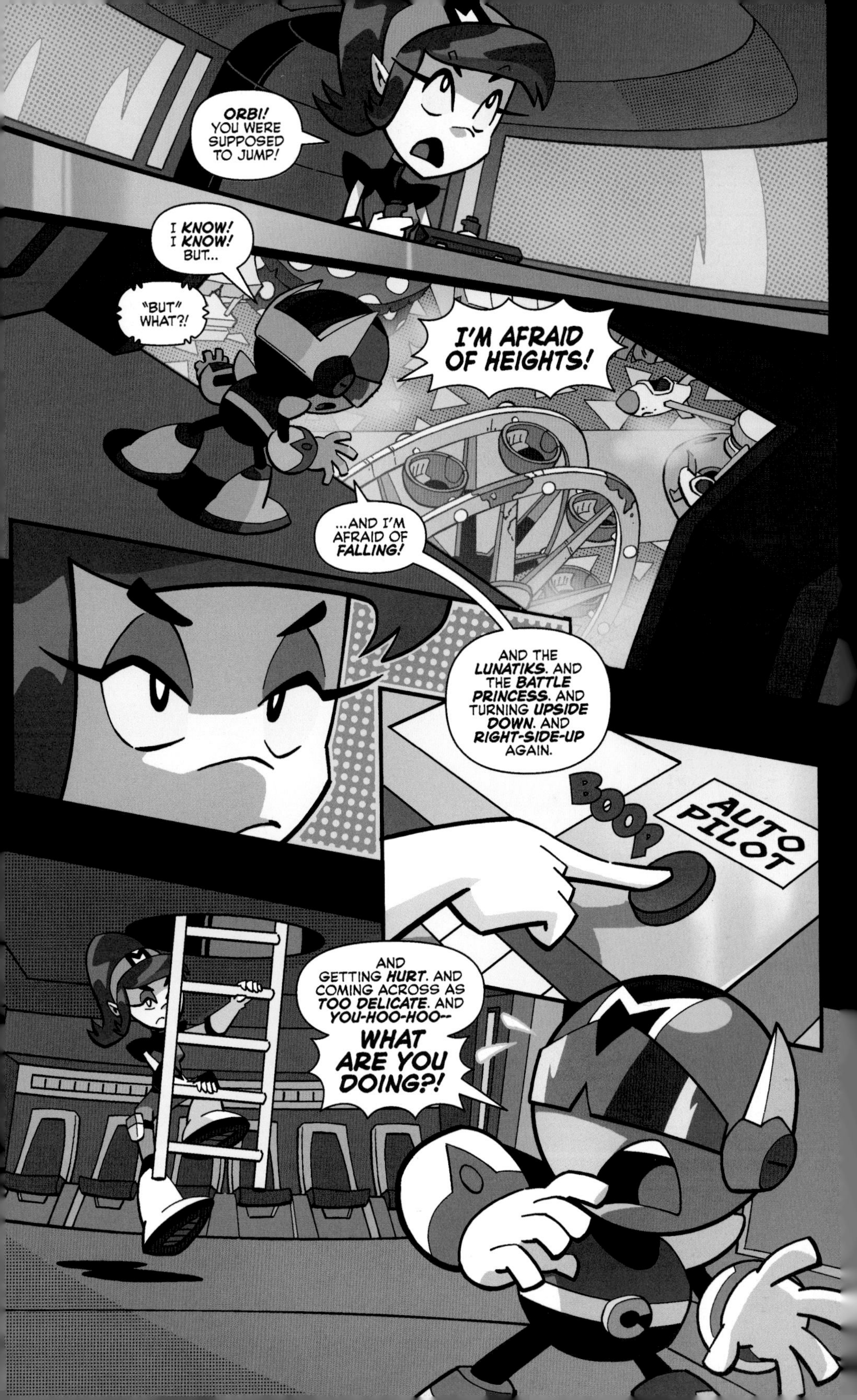

ORBI! YOU WERE SUPPOSED TO JUMP!
I KNOW! I KNOW! BUT...
"BUT" WHAT?!
I'M AFRAID OF HEIGHTS!
...AND I'M AFRAID OF FALLING!
AND THE LUNATIKS. AND THE BATTLE PRINCESS. AND TURNING UPSIDE DOWN. AND RIGHT-SIDE-UP AGAIN.
BOOP
AUTO PILOT
AND GETTING HURT. AND COMING ACROSS AS TOO DELICATE. AND YOU-HOO-HOO-- WHAT ARE YOU DOING?!

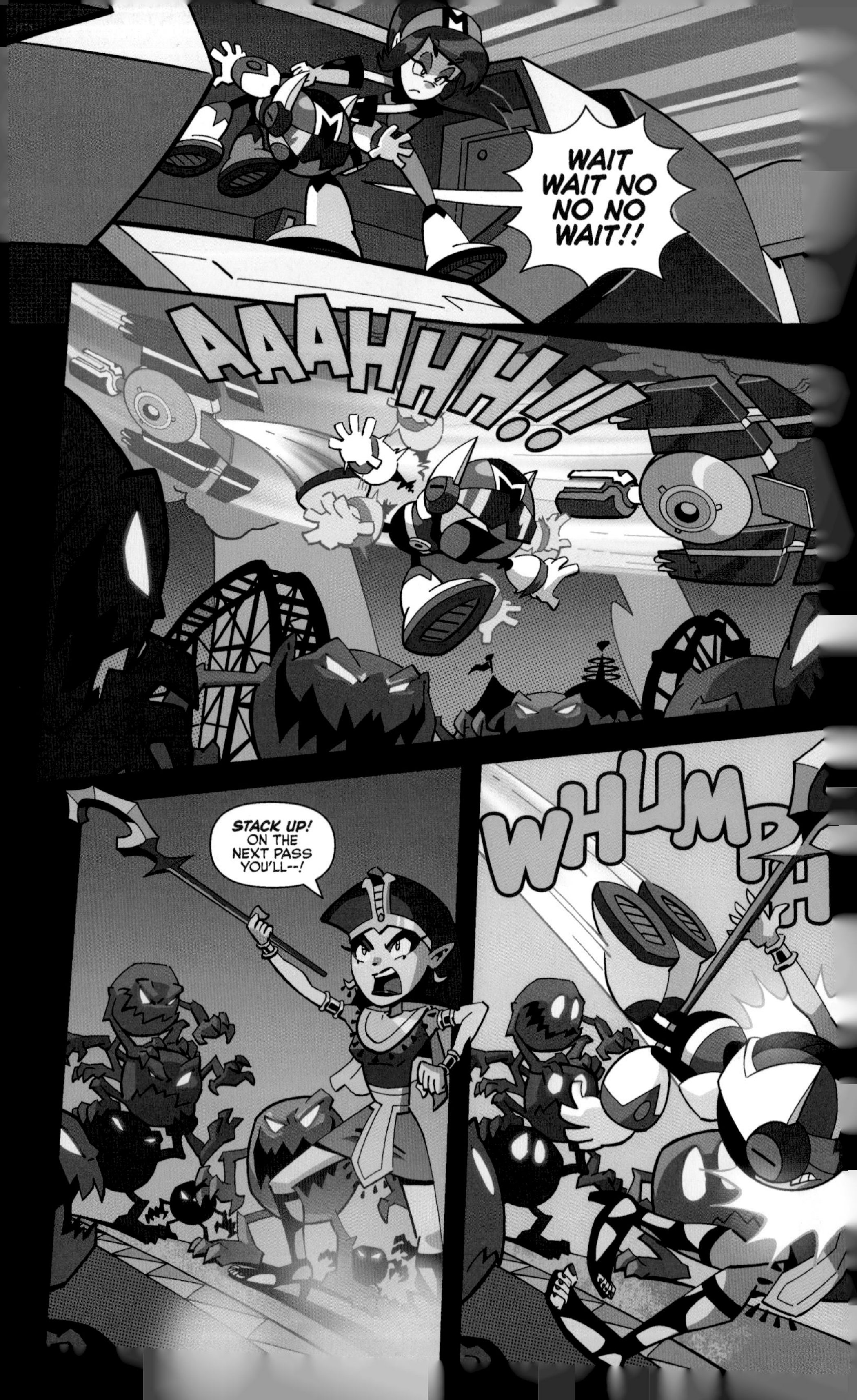
WAIT WAIT NO NO NO WAIT!!
AAAHHH!!!
STACK UP! ON THE NEXT PASS YOU'LL--!
WHUMP

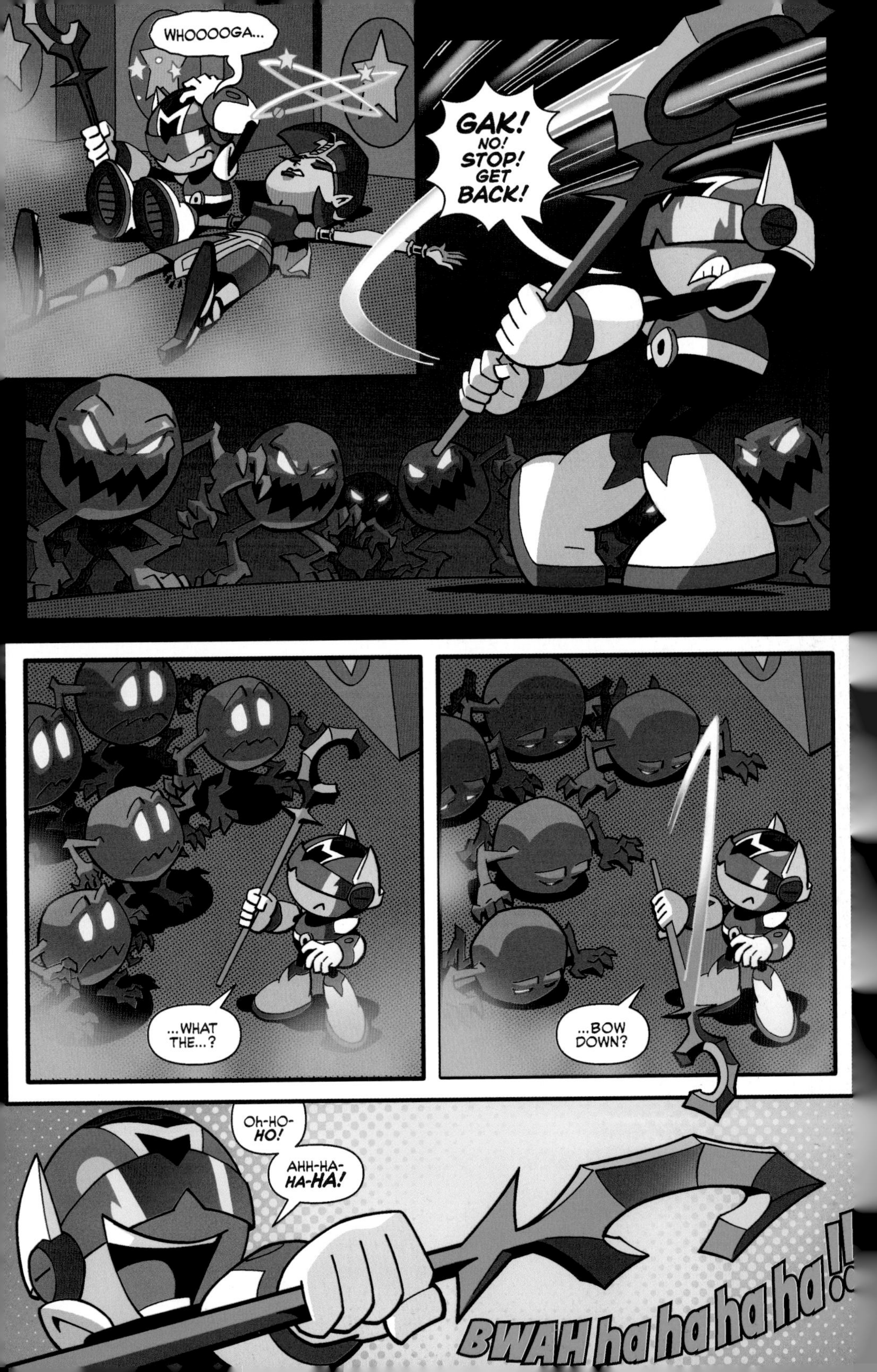
WHOOOOGA...
GAK! NO! STOP! GET BACK!
...WHAT THE...?
...BOW DOWN?
Oh-HO-HO!
AHH-HA-HA-HA!
BWAH ha ha ha ha!!

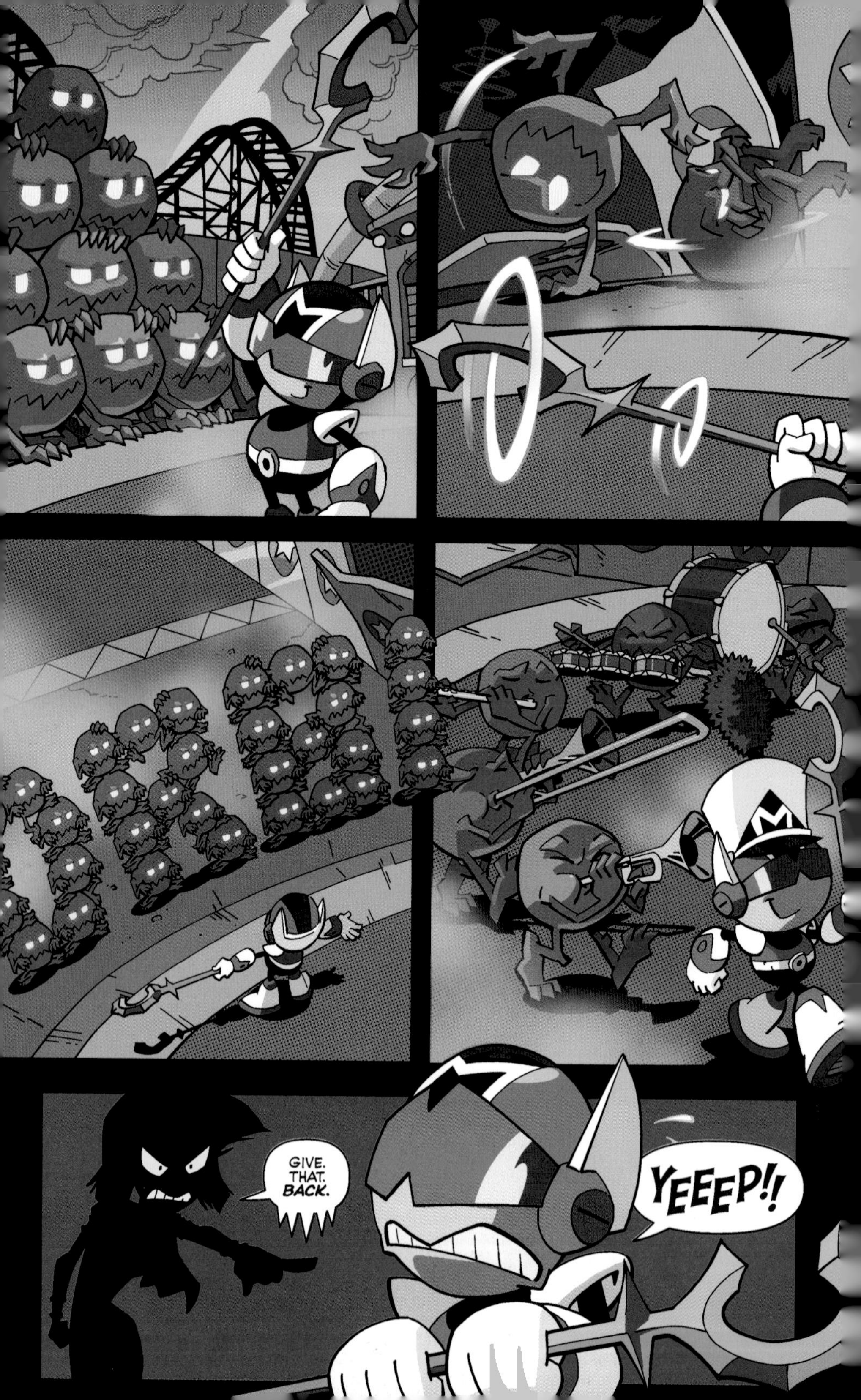
GIVE. THAT. BACK.
YEEEP!!

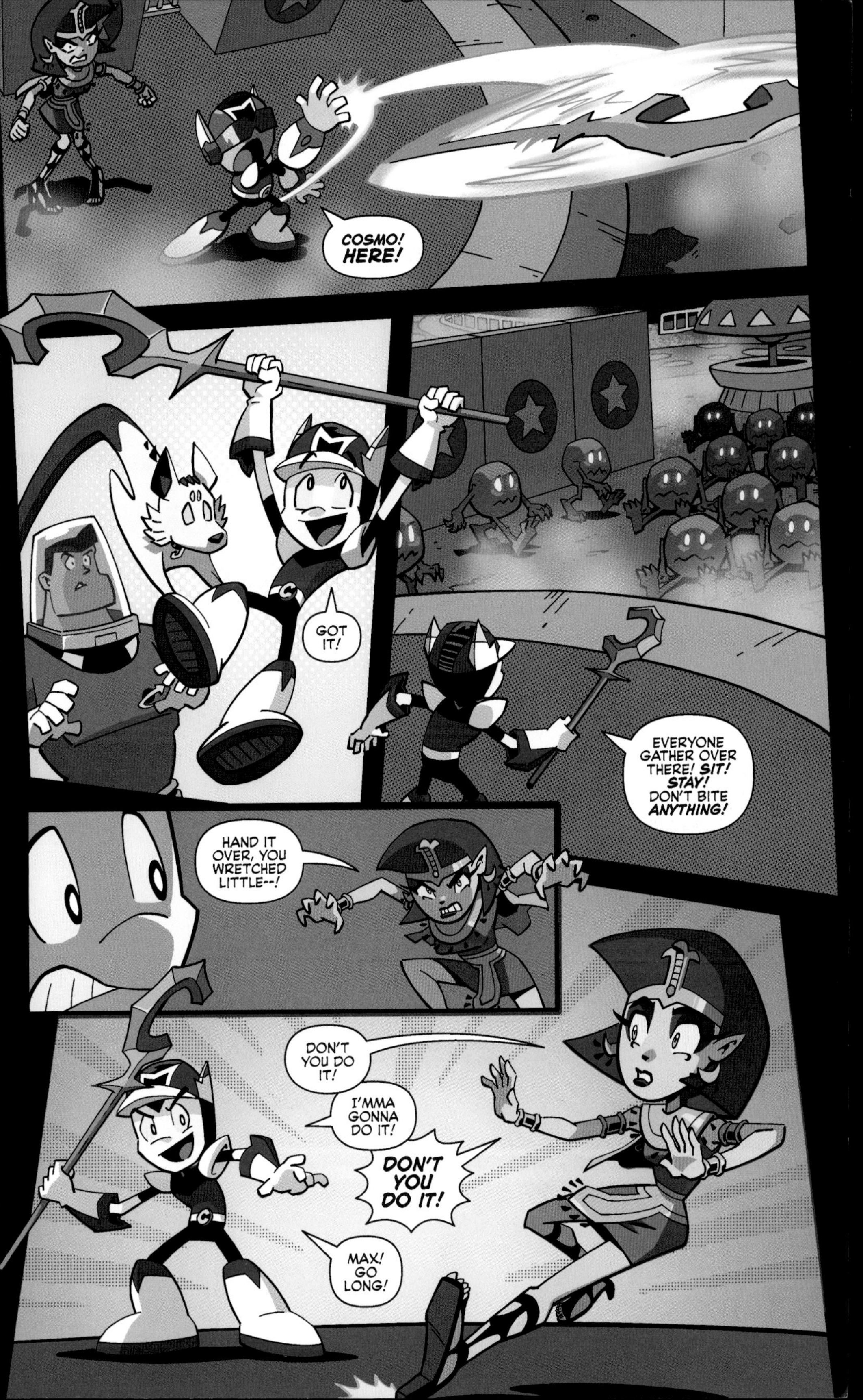
COSMO! HERE!
GOT IT!
EVERYONE GATHER OVER THERE! SIT! STAY! DON'T BITE ANYTHING!
HAND IT OVER, YOU WRETCHED LITTLE--!
DON'T YOU DO IT!
I'MMA GONNA DO IT!
DON'T YOU DO IT!
MAX! GO LONG!

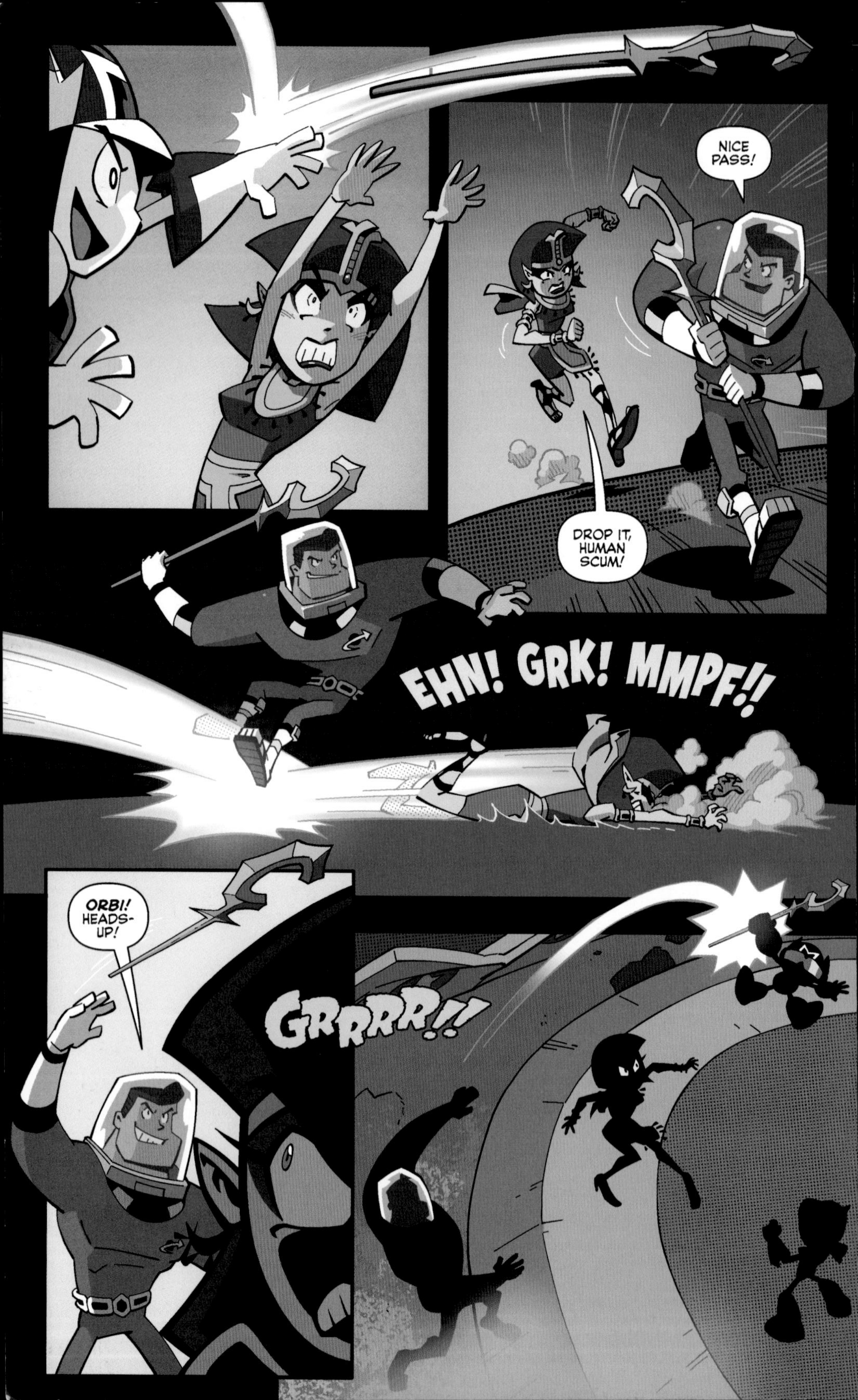
NICE PASS!
DROP IT, HUMAN SCUM!
EHN! GRK! MMPF!!
ORBI!! HEADS-UP!
GRRRRR!!

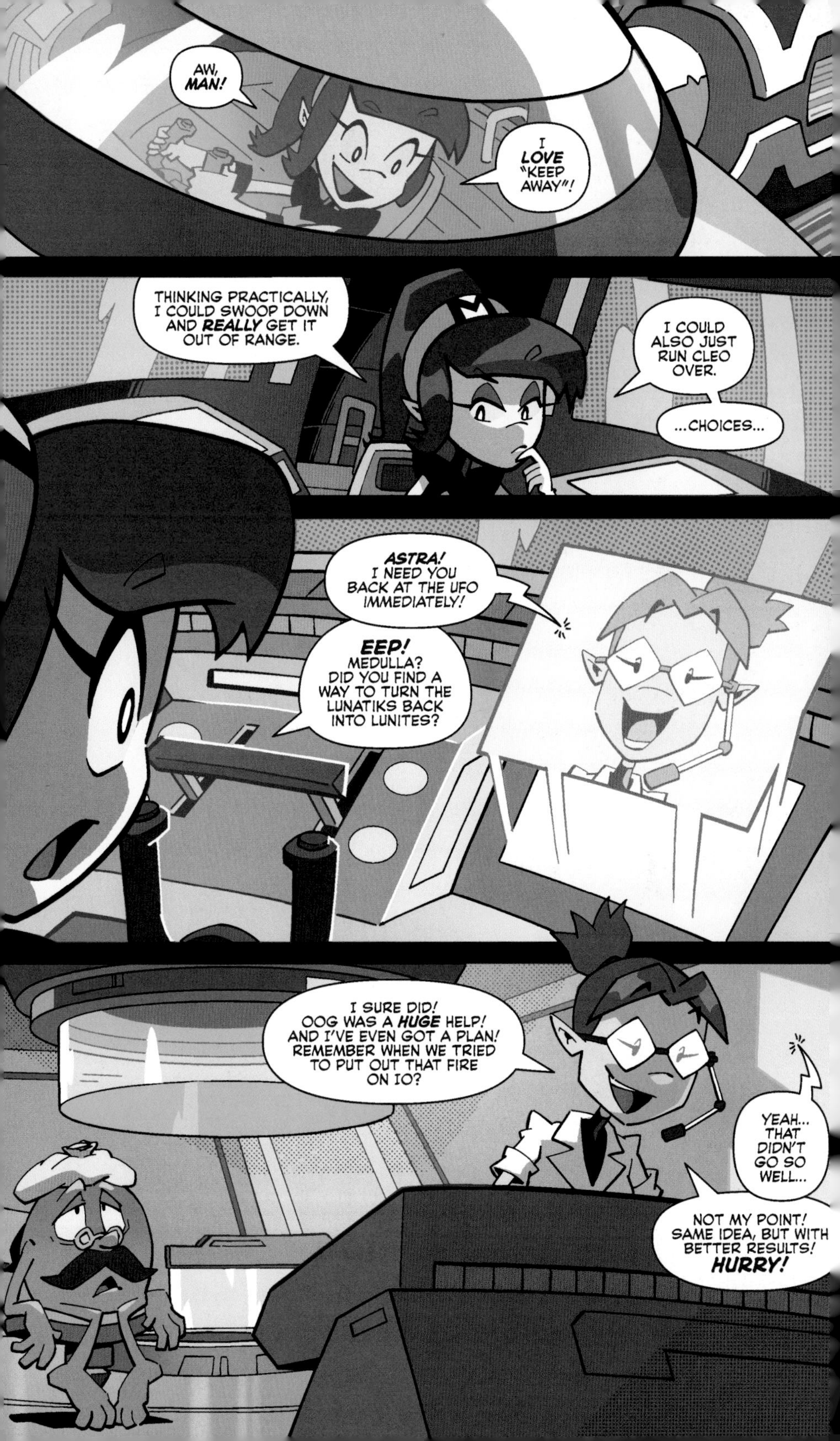
AW, MAN!
I LOVE "KEEP AWAY"!
THINKING PRACTICALLY, I COULD SWOOP DOWN AND REALLY GET IT OUT OF RANGE.
I COULD ALSO JUST RUN CLEO OVER.
...CHOICES...
ASTRA! I NEED YOU BACK AT THE UFO IMMEDIATELY!
EEP! MEDULLA? DID YOU FIND A WAY TO TURN THE LUNATIKS BACK INTO LUNITES?
I SURE DID! OOG WAS A HUGE HELP! AND I'VE EVEN GOT A PLAN! REMEMBER WHEN WE TRIED TO PUT OUT THAT FIRE ON IO?
YEAH... THAT DIDN'T GO SO WELL...
NOT MY POINT! SAME IDEA, BUT WITH BETTER RESULTS! HURRY!

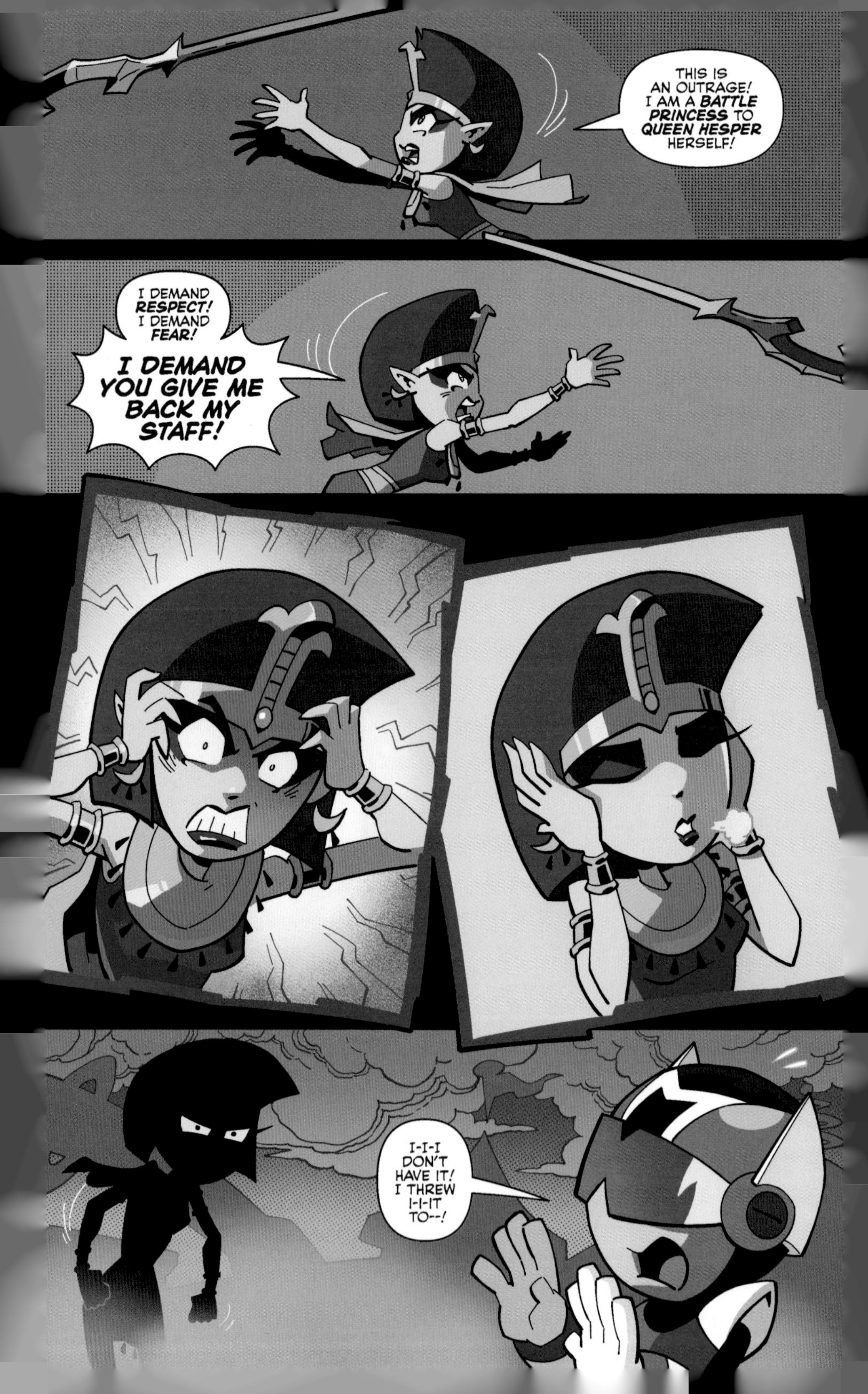
THIS IS AN OUTRAGE! I AM A BATTLE PRINCESS TO QUEEN HESPER HERSELF!
I DEMAND RESPECT! I DEMAND FEAR!
I DEMAND YOU GIVE ME BACK MY STAFF!
I-I-I DON'T HAVE IT! I THREW I-I-IT TO--!

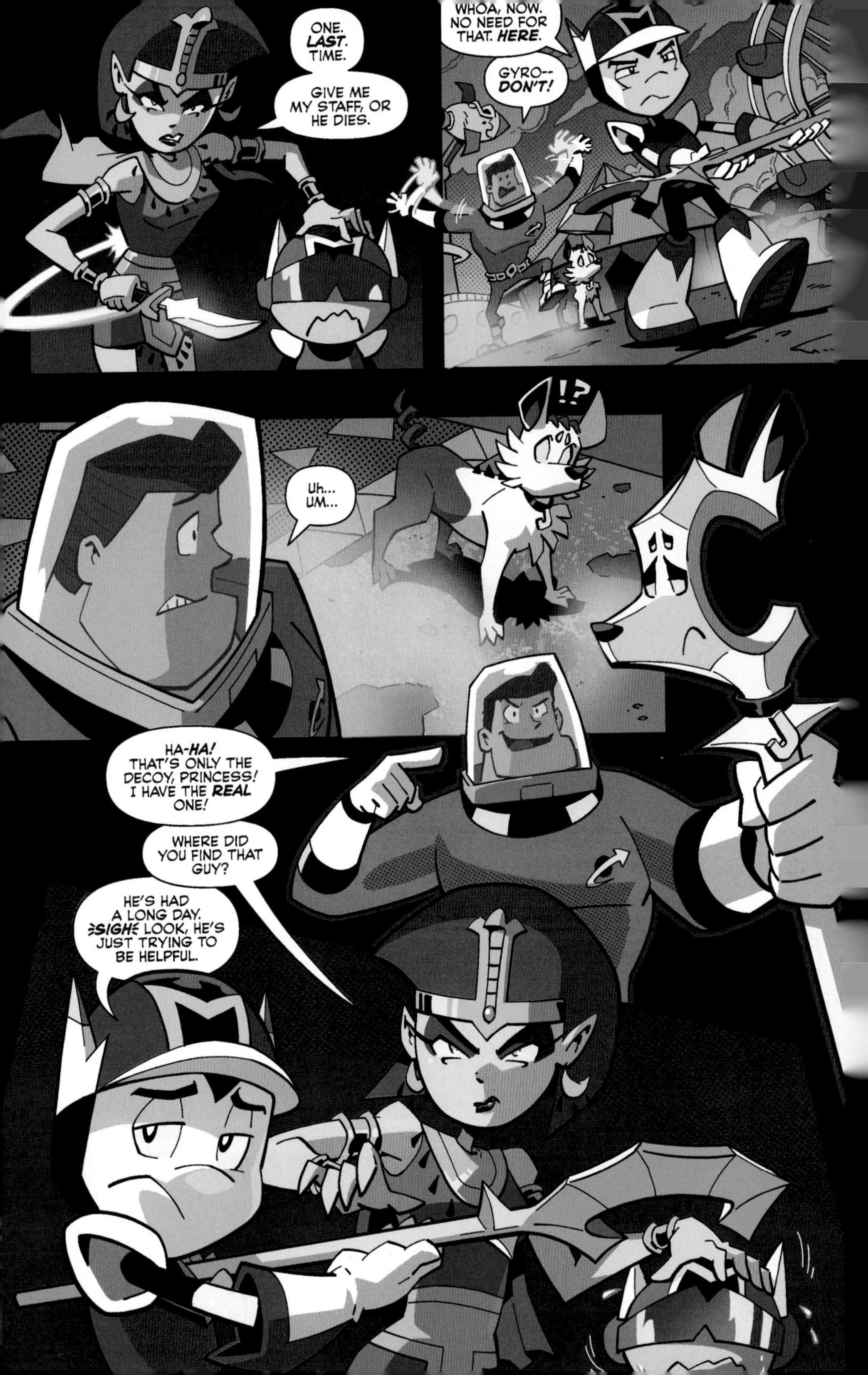

ONE. **LAST**. TIME.
GIVE ME MY STAFF, OR HE DIES.
WHOA, NOW. NO NEED FOR THAT. **HERE**.
GYRO-- **DON'T!**
!?
UH... UM...
HA-**HA!** THAT'S ONLY THE DECOY, PRINCESS! I HAVE THE **REAL** ONE!
WHERE DID YOU FIND THAT GUY?
HE'S HAD A LONG DAY. **SIGH** LOOK, HE'S JUST TRYING TO BE HELPFUL.

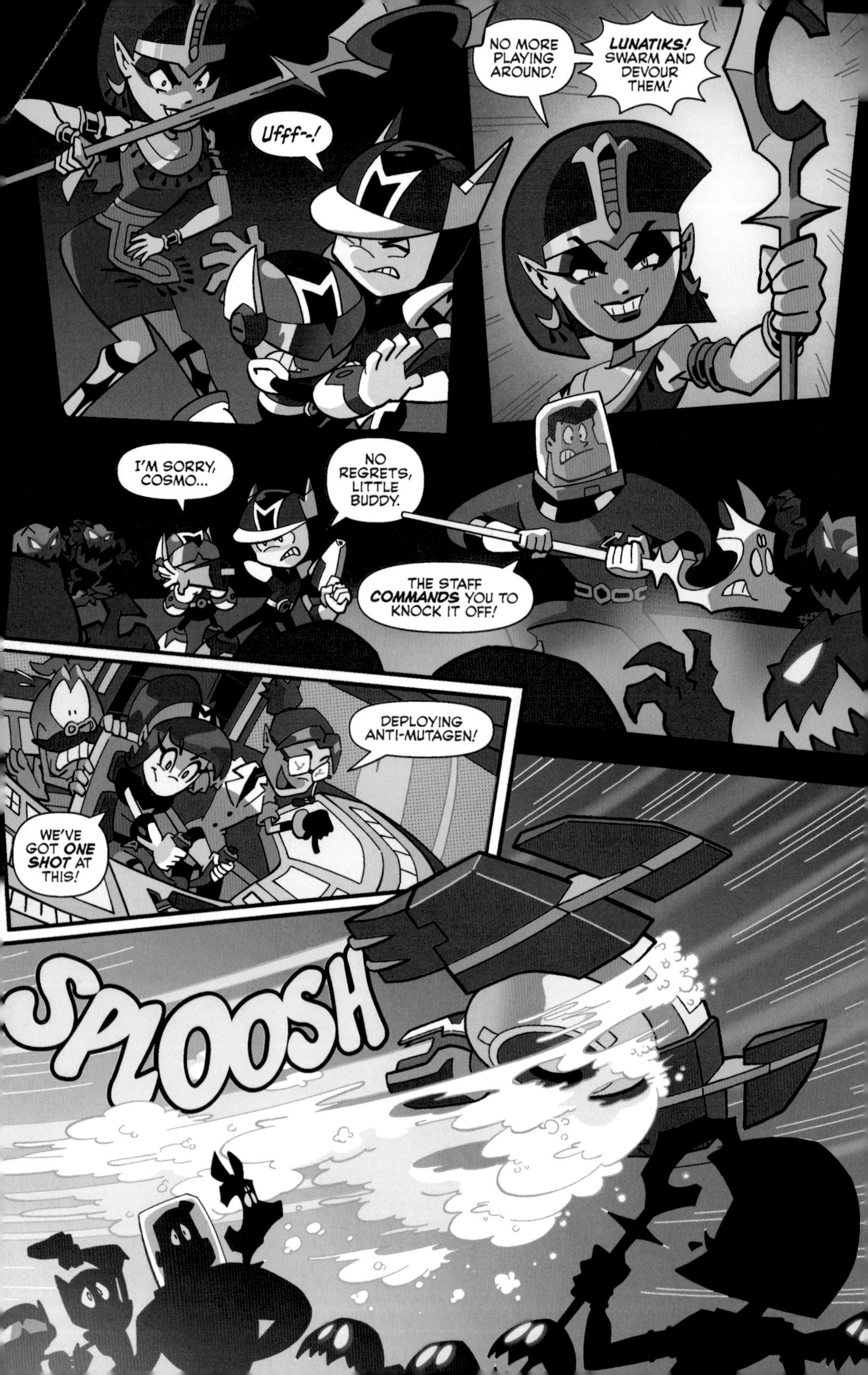
Ufff--!
NO MORE PLAYING AROUND!
LUNATIKS! SWARM AND DEVOUR THEM!
I'M SORRY, COSMO...
NO REGRETS, LITTLE BUDDY.
THE STAFF COMMANDS YOU TO KNOCK IT OFF!
DEPLOYING ANTI-MUTAGEN!
WE'VE GOT ONE SHOT AT THIS!
SPLOOSH

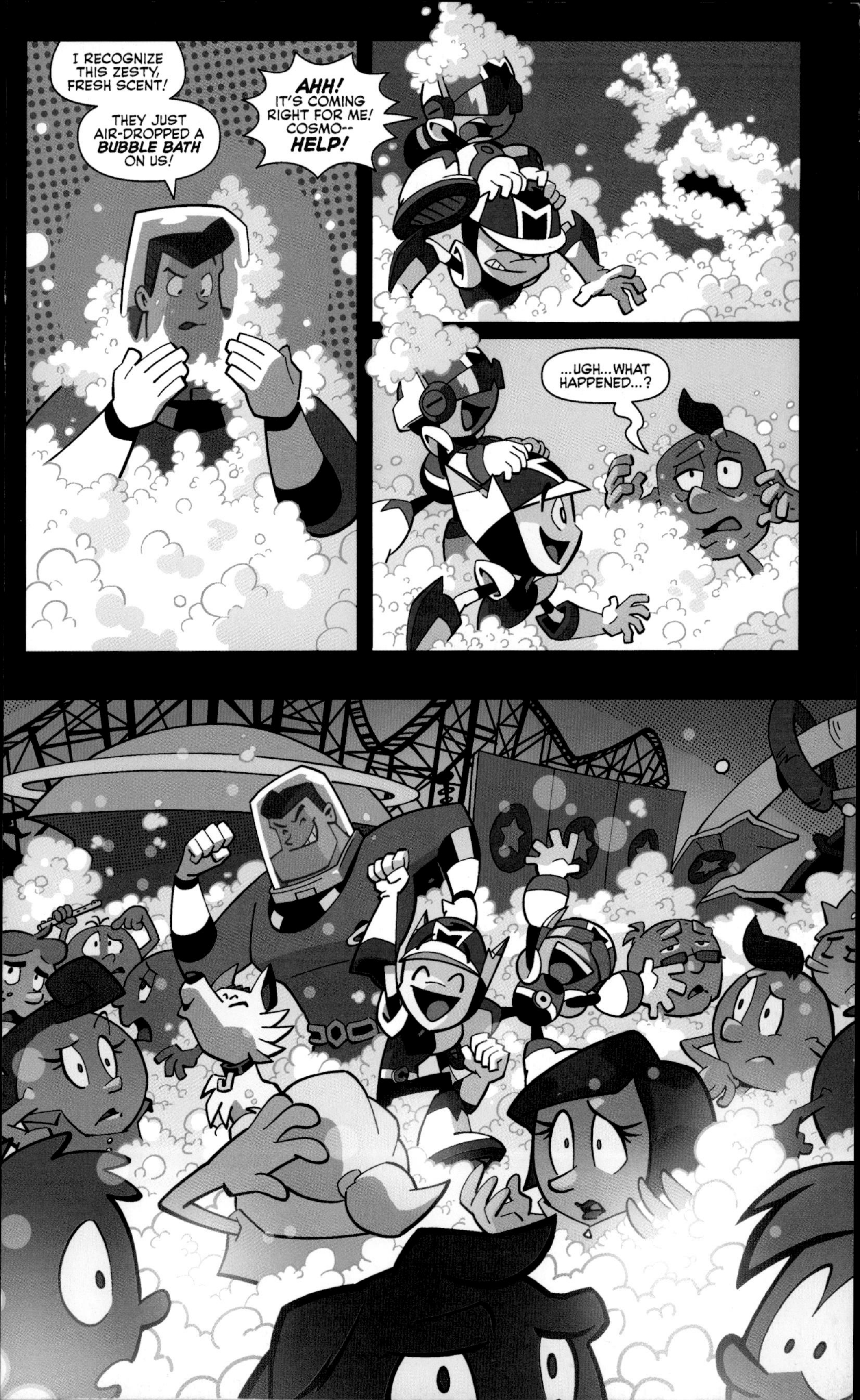
I RECOGNIZE THIS ZESTY, FRESH SCENT!
THEY JUST AIR-DROPPED A BUBBLE BATH ON US!
AHH! IT'S COMING RIGHT FOR ME! COSMO-- HELP!
...UGH...WHAT HAPPENED...?

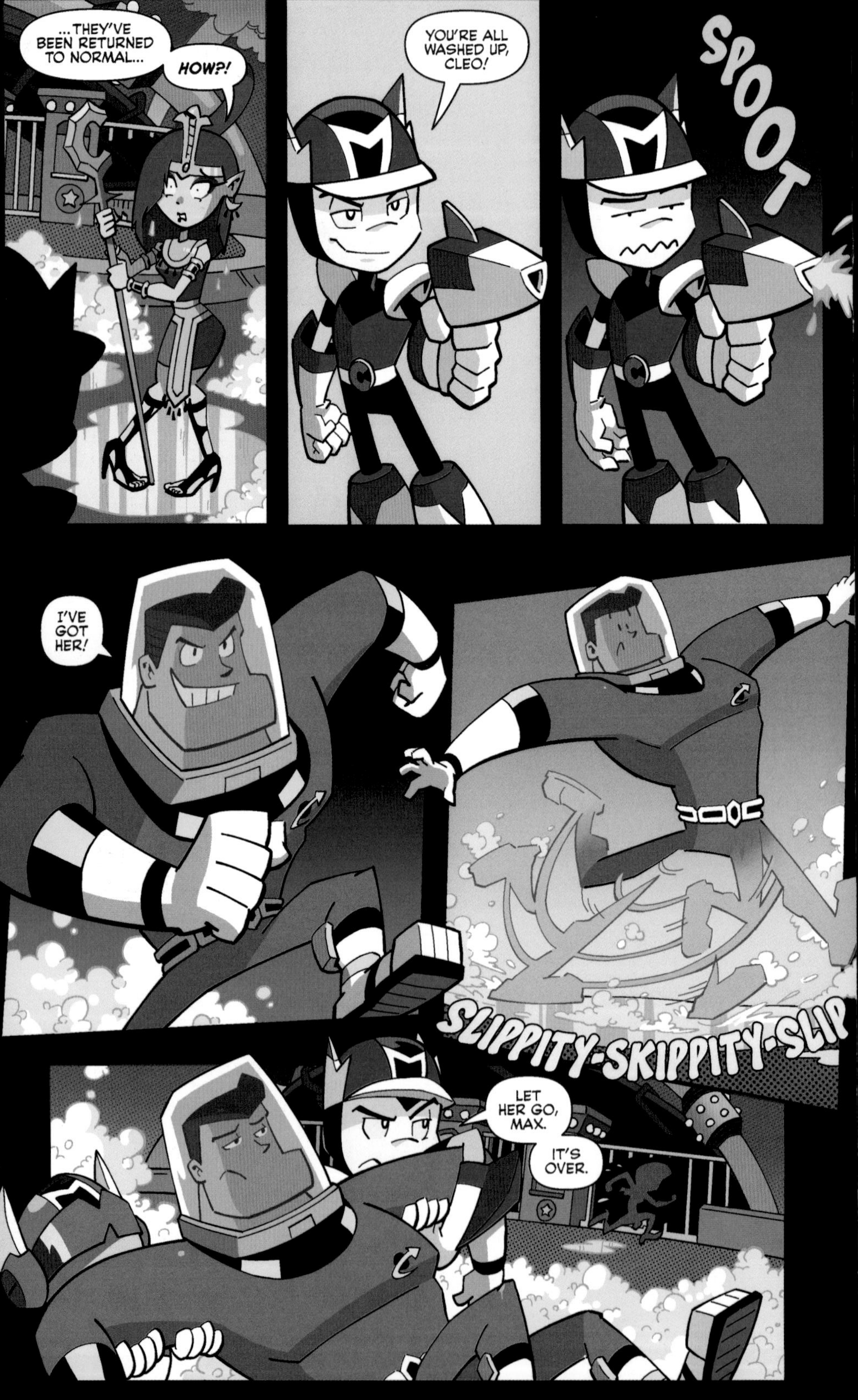
...THEY'VE BEEN RETURNED TO NORMAL...
HOW?!
YOU'RE ALL WASHED UP, CLEO!
SPOOT
I'VE GOT HER!
SLIPPITY-SKIPPITY-SLIP
LET HER GO, MAX.
IT'S OVER.

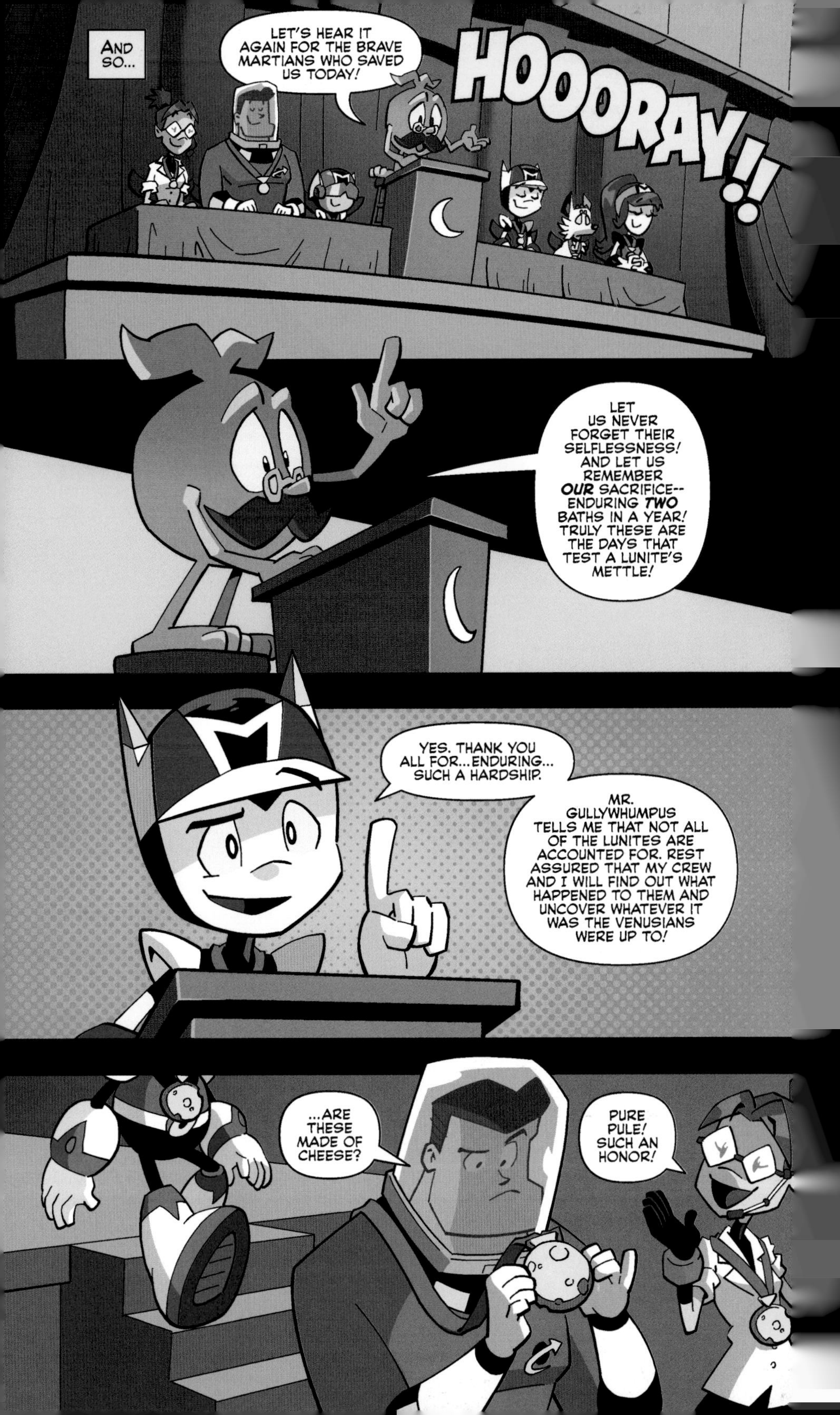
AND SO...
LET'S HEAR IT AGAIN FOR THE BRAVE MARTIANS WHO SAVED US TODAY!
HOOORAY!!
LET US NEVER FORGET THEIR SELFLESSNESS! AND LET US REMEMBER OUR SACRIFICE--ENDURING TWO BATHS IN A YEAR! TRULY THESE ARE THE DAYS THAT TEST A LUNITE'S METTLE!
YES. THANK YOU ALL FOR...ENDURING... SUCH A HARDSHIP.
MR. GULLYWHUMPUS TELLS ME THAT NOT ALL OF THE LUNITES ARE ACCOUNTED FOR. REST ASSURED THAT MY CREW AND I WILL FIND OUT WHAT HAPPENED TO THEM AND UNCOVER WHATEVER IT WAS THE VENUSIANS WERE UP TO!
...ARE THESE MADE OF CHEESE?
PURE PULE! SUCH AN HONOR!

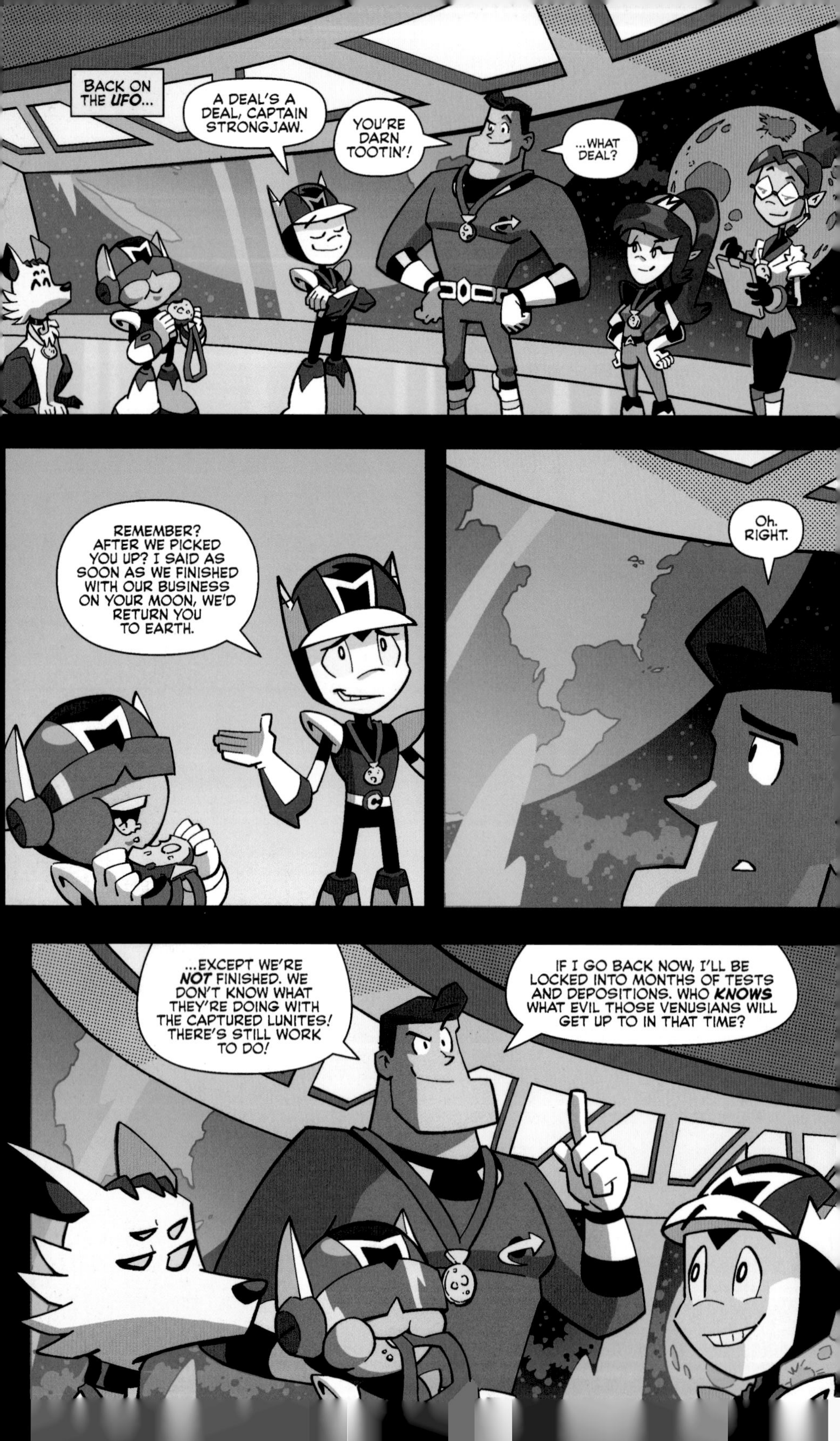
BACK ON THE *UFO*...
A DEAL'S A DEAL, CAPTAIN STRONGJAW.
YOU'RE DARN TOOTIN'!
...WHAT DEAL?
REMEMBER? AFTER WE PICKED YOU UP? I SAID AS SOON AS WE FINISHED WITH OUR BUSINESS ON YOUR MOON, WE'D RETURN YOU TO EARTH.
Oh. RIGHT.
...EXCEPT WE'RE ***NOT*** FINISHED. WE DON'T KNOW WHAT THEY'RE DOING WITH THE CAPTURED LUNITES! THERE'S STILL WORK TO DO!
IF I GO BACK NOW, I'LL BE LOCKED INTO MONTHS OF TESTS AND DEPOSITIONS. WHO ***KNOWS*** WHAT EVIL THOSE VENUSIANS WILL GET UP TO IN THAT TIME?

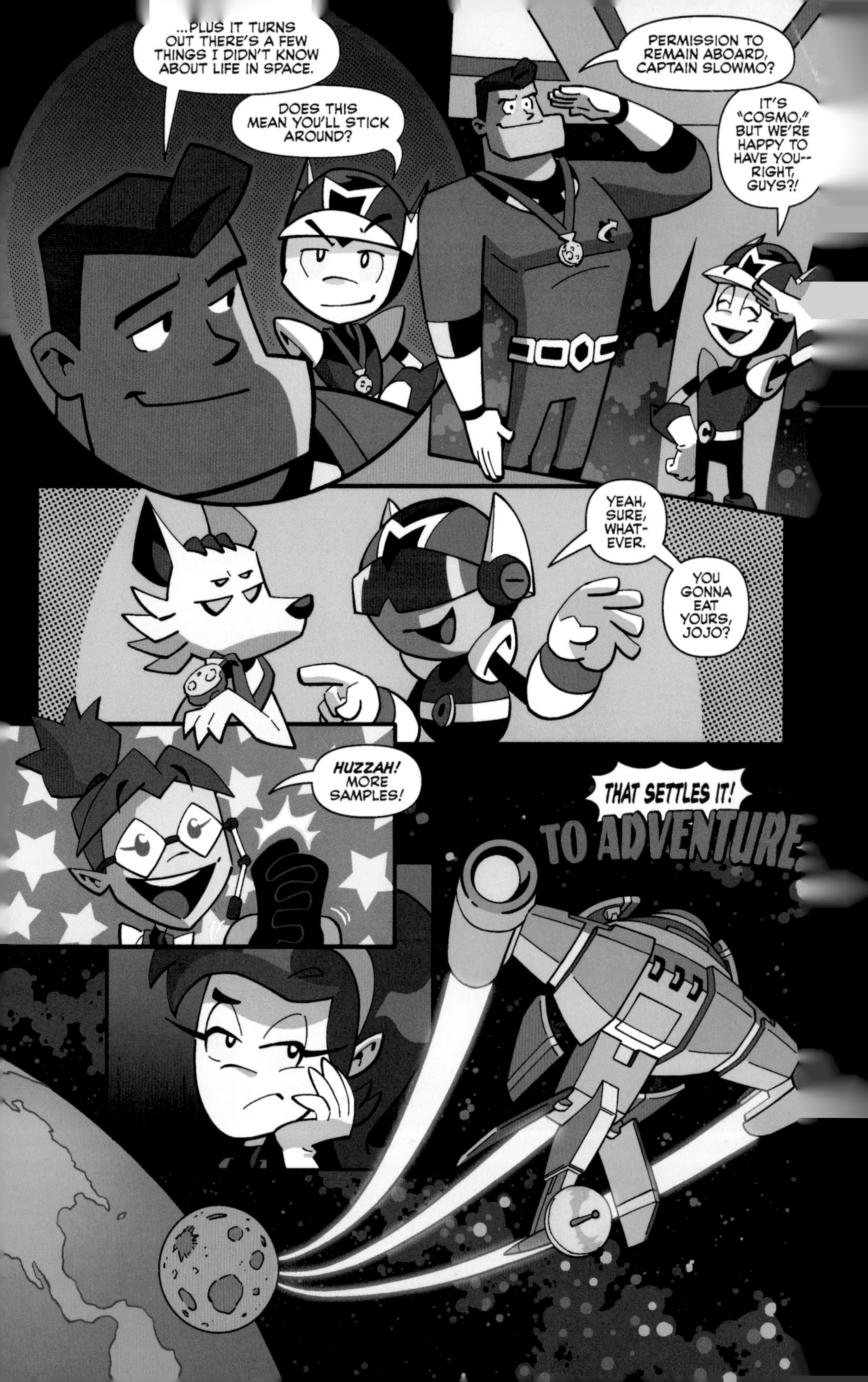
...PLUS IT TURNS OUT THERE'S A FEW THINGS I DIDN'T KNOW ABOUT LIFE IN SPACE.
DOES THIS MEAN YOU'LL STICK AROUND?
PERMISSION TO REMAIN ABOARD, CAPTAIN SLOWMO?
IT'S "COSMO," BUT WE'RE HAPPY TO HAVE YOU-- RIGHT, GUYS?!
YEAH, SURE, WHAT-EVER.
YOU GONNA EAT YOURS, JOJO?
HUZZAH! MORE SAMPLES!
THAT SETTLES IT!
TO ADVENTURE

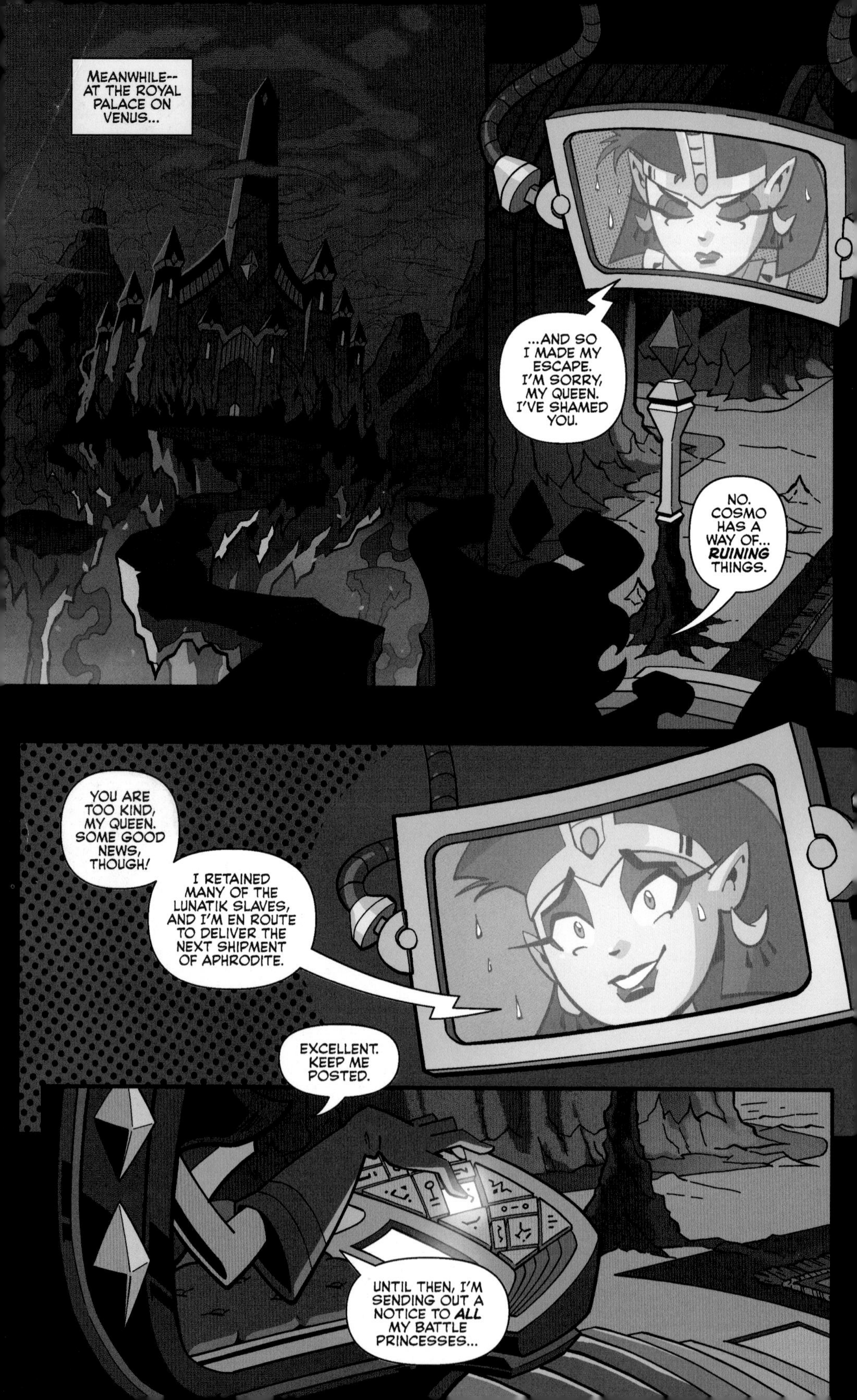
MEANWHILE--AT THE ROYAL PALACE ON VENUS...
...AND SO I MADE MY ESCAPE. I'M SORRY, MY QUEEN. I'VE SHAMED YOU.
NO. COSMO HAS A WAY OF... RUINING THINGS.
YOU ARE TOO KIND, MY QUEEN. SOME GOOD NEWS, THOUGH!
I RETAINED MANY OF THE LUNATIK SLAVES, AND I'M EN ROUTE TO DELIVER THE NEXT SHIPMENT OF APHRODITE.
EXCELLENT. KEEP ME POSTED.
UNTIL THEN, I'M SENDING OUT A NOTICE TO ALL MY BATTLE PRINCESSES...

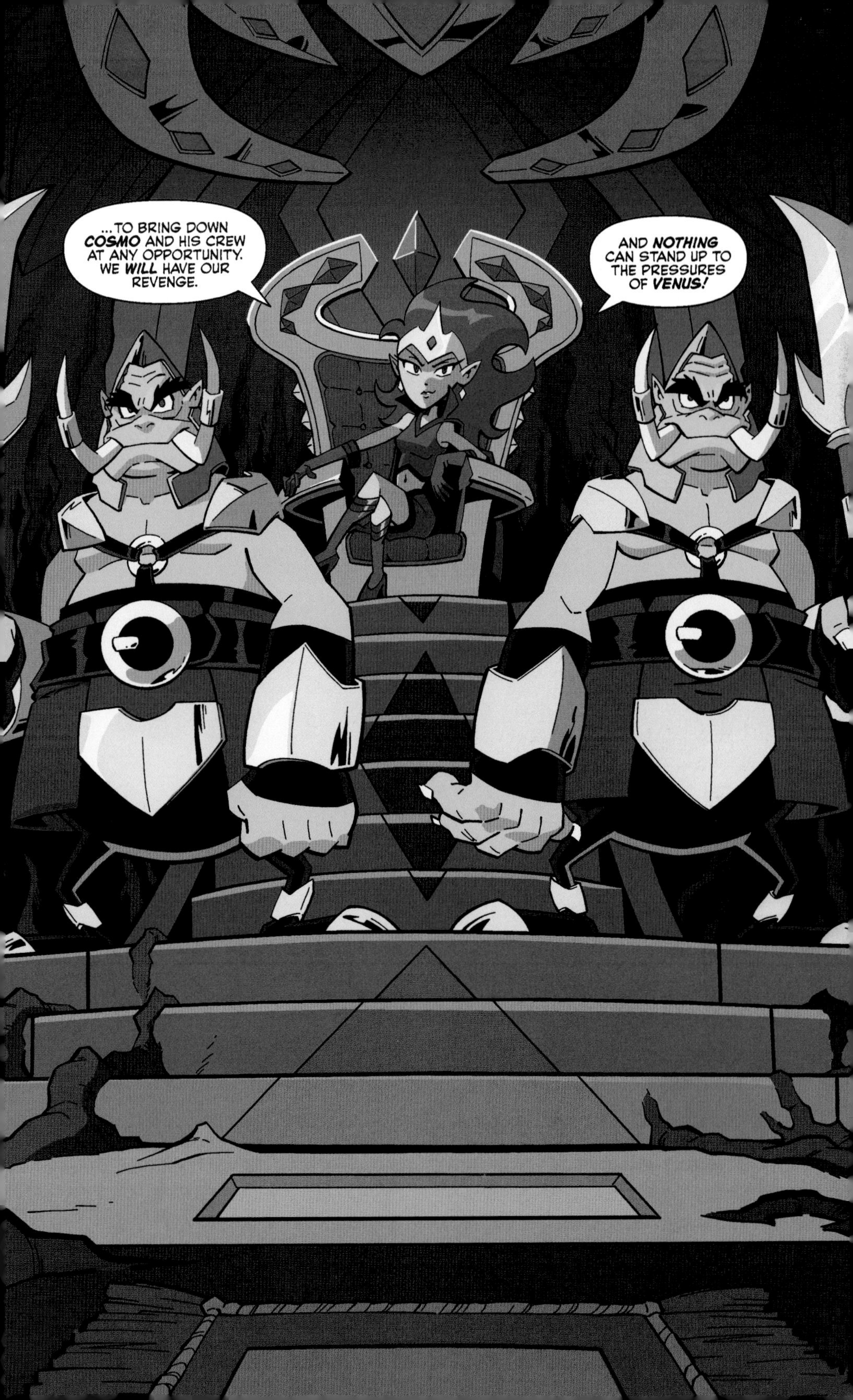
...TO BRING DOWN **COSMO** AND HIS CREW AT ANY OPPORTUNITY. WE ***WILL*** HAVE OUR REVENGE.
AND ***NOTHING*** CAN STAND UP TO THE PRESSURES OF ***VENUS!***

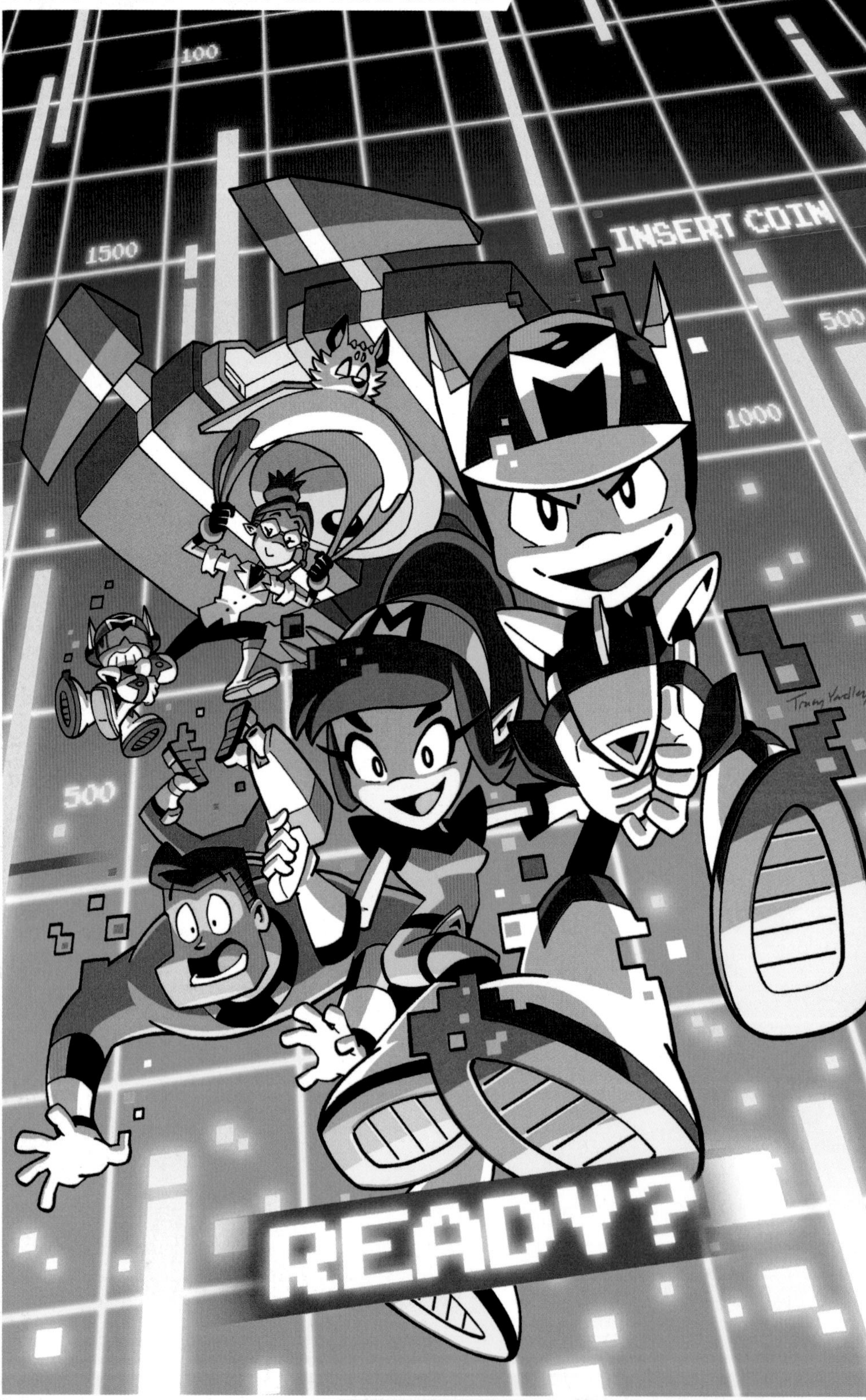
100
1500
INSERT COIN
500
1000
Tracy Yardley!
500
READY?

ART BY TRACY YARDLEY

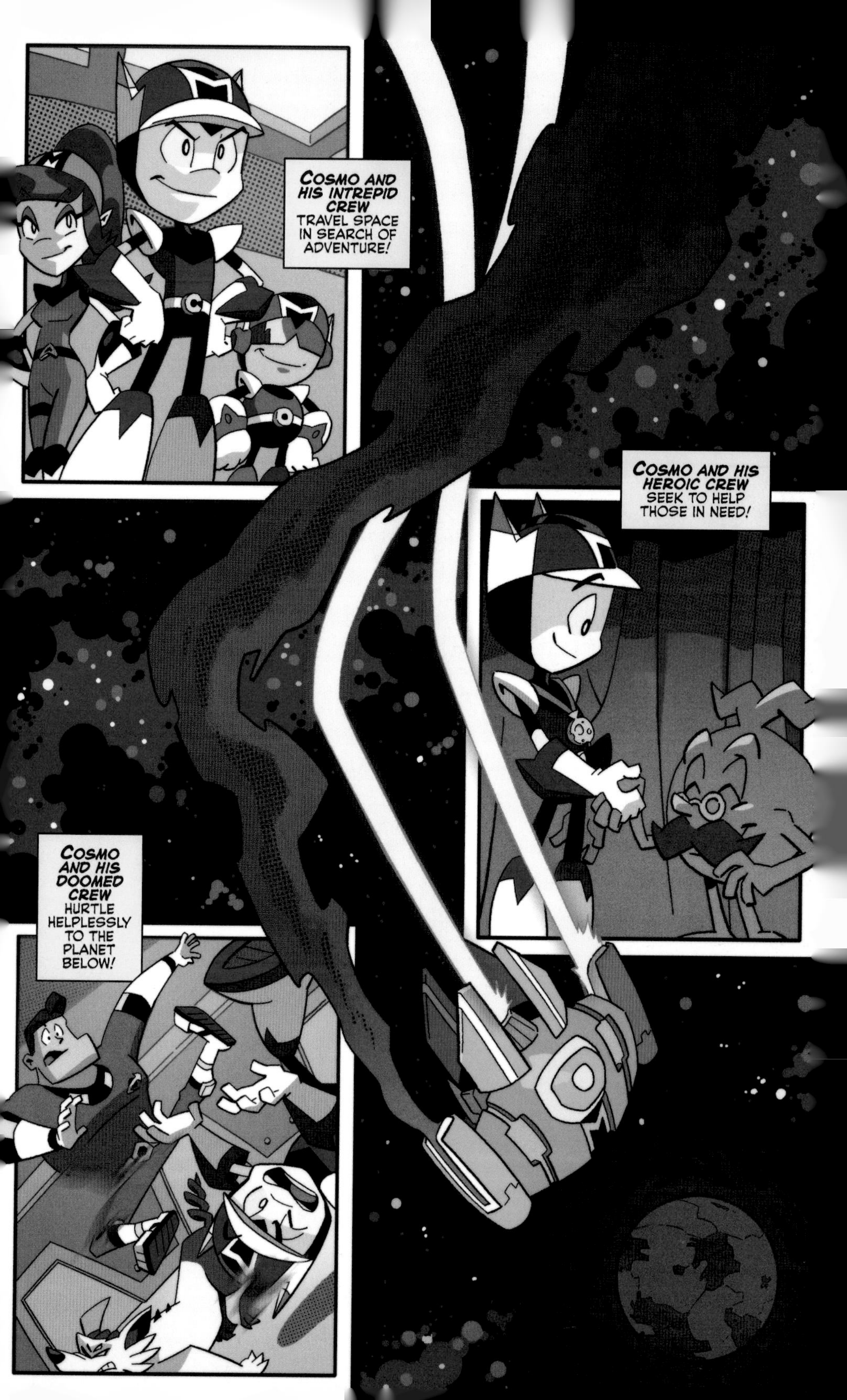
COSMO AND HIS INTREPID CREW TRAVEL SPACE IN SEARCH OF ADVENTURE!
COSMO AND HIS HEROIC CREW SEEK TO HELP THOSE IN NEED!
COSMO AND HIS DOOMED CREW HURTLE HELPLESSLY TO THE PLANET BELOW!

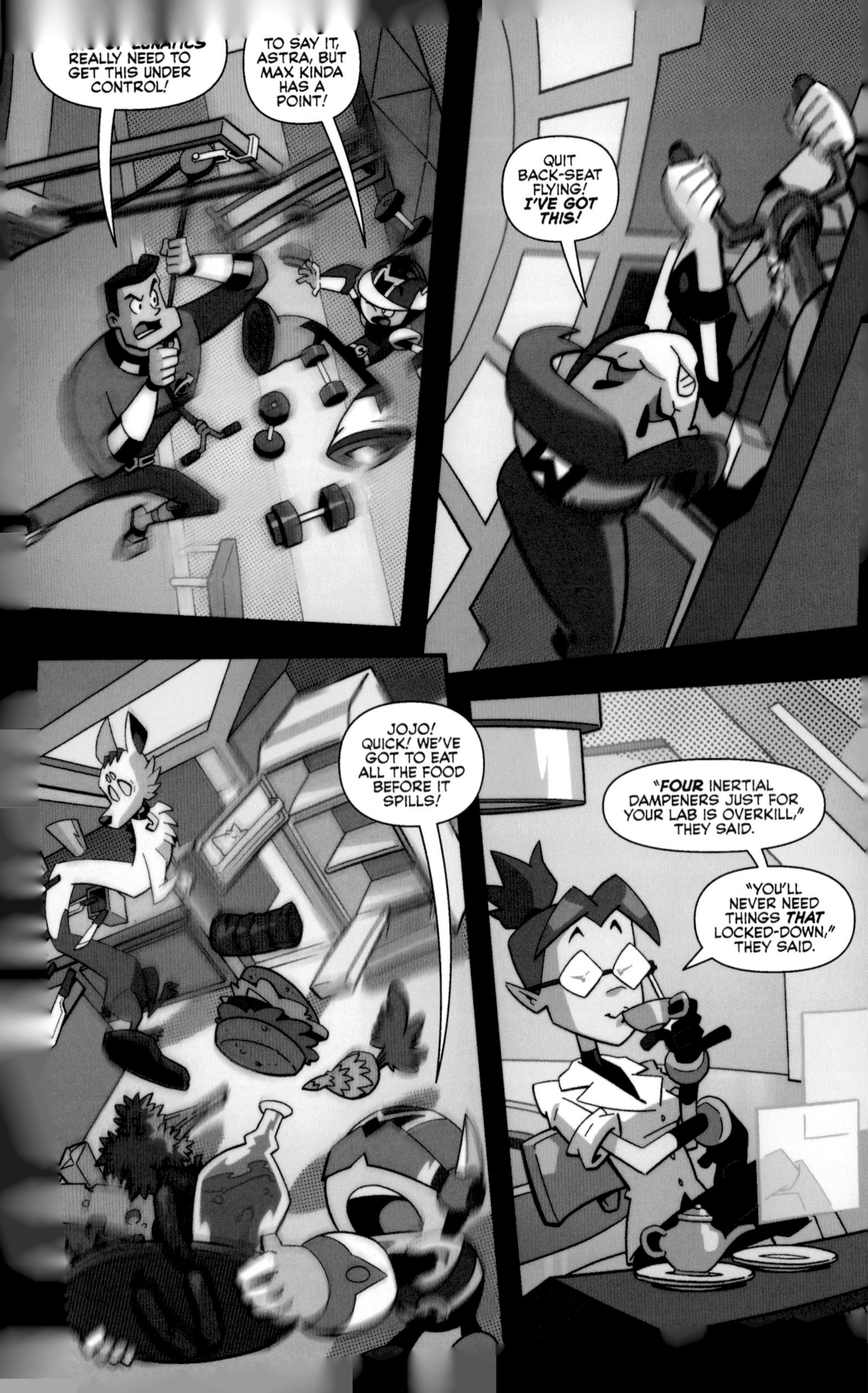
REALLY NEED TO GET THIS UNDER CONTROL!
TO SAY IT, ASTRA, BUT MAX KINDA HAS A POINT!
QUIT BACK-SEAT FLYING! I'VE GOT THIS!
JOJO! QUICK! WE'VE GOT TO EAT ALL THE FOOD BEFORE IT SPILLS!
"FOUR INERTIAL DAMPENERS JUST FOR YOUR LAB IS OVERKILL," THEY SAID.
"YOU'LL NEVER NEED THINGS THAT LOCKED-DOWN," THEY SAID.

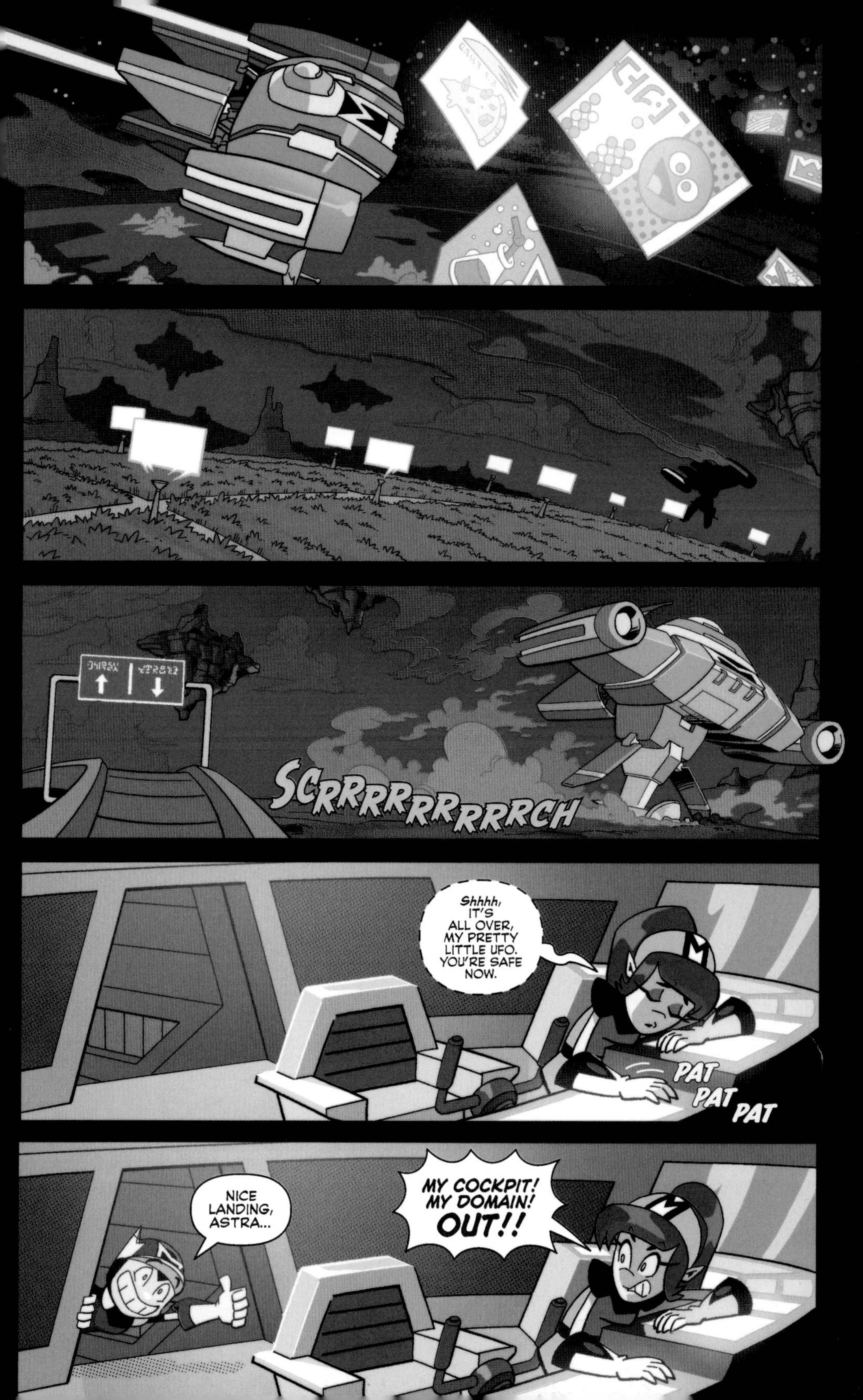
SCRRRRRRRRRRCH
Shhhh, IT'S ALL OVER, MY PRETTY LITTLE UFO. YOU'RE SAFE NOW.
PAT PAT PAT
NICE LANDING, ASTRA...
MY COCKPIT! MY DOMAIN! OUT!!

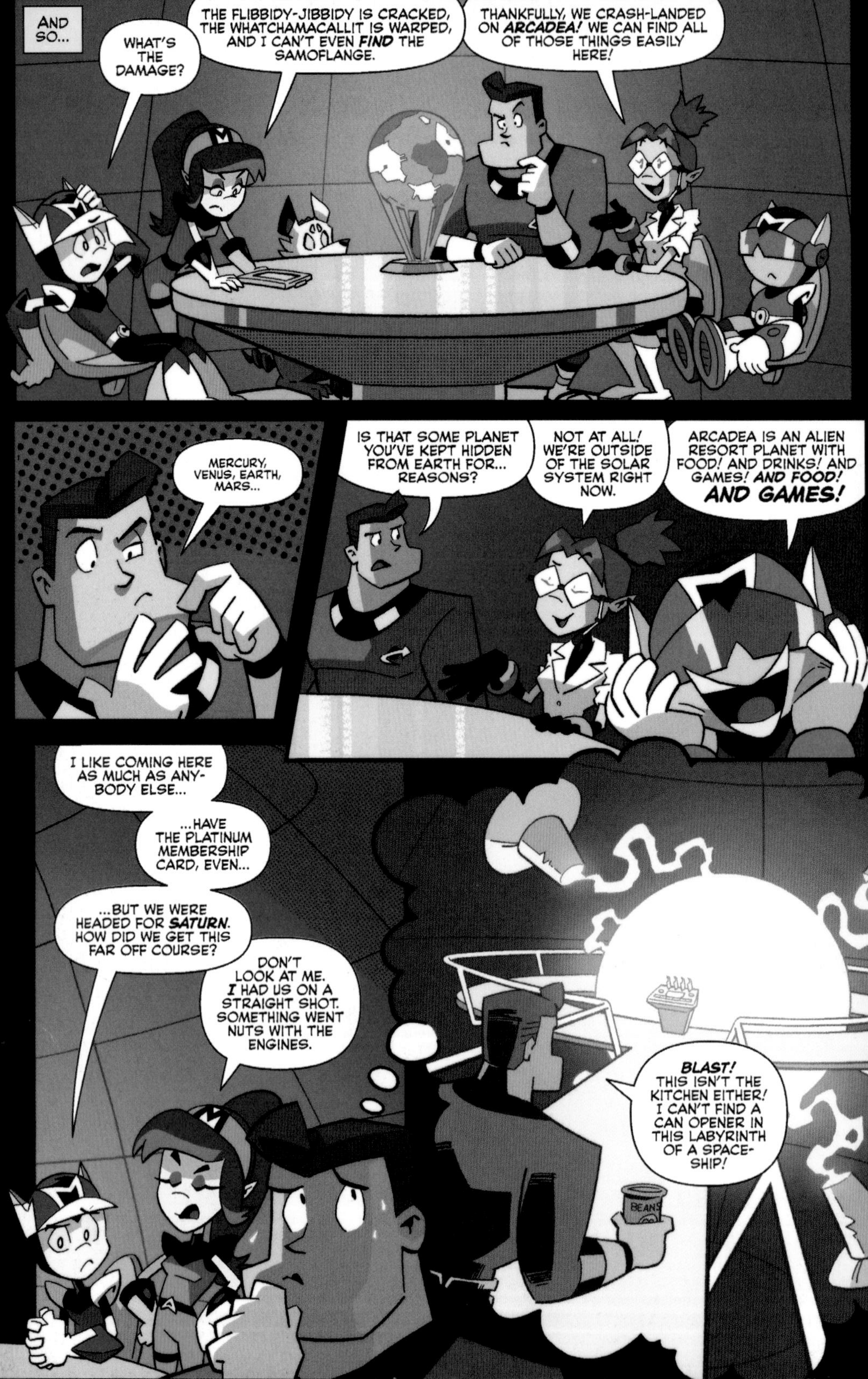
AND SO...
WHAT'S THE DAMAGE?
THE FLIBBIDY-JIBBIDY IS CRACKED, THE WHATCHAMACALLIT IS WARPED, AND I CAN'T EVEN FIND THE SAMOFLANGE.
THANKFULLY, WE CRASH-LANDED ON ARCADEA! WE CAN FIND ALL OF THOSE THINGS EASILY HERE!
MERCURY, VENUS, EARTH, MARS...
IS THAT SOME PLANET YOU'VE KEPT HIDDEN FROM EARTH FOR... REASONS?
NOT AT ALL! WE'RE OUTSIDE OF THE SOLAR SYSTEM RIGHT NOW.
ARCADEA IS AN ALIEN RESORT PLANET WITH FOOD! AND DRINKS! AND GAMES! AND FOOD! AND GAMES!
I LIKE COMING HERE AS MUCH AS ANY-BODY ELSE...
...HAVE THE PLATINUM MEMBERSHIP CARD, EVEN...
...BUT WE WERE HEADED FOR SATURN. HOW DID WE GET THIS FAR OFF COURSE?
DON'T LOOK AT ME. I HAD US ON A STRAIGHT SHOT. SOMETHING WENT NUTS WITH THE ENGINES.
BLAST! THIS ISN'T THE KITCHEN EITHER! I CAN'T FIND A CAN OPENER IN THIS LABYRINTH OF A SPACE-SHIP!
BEANS

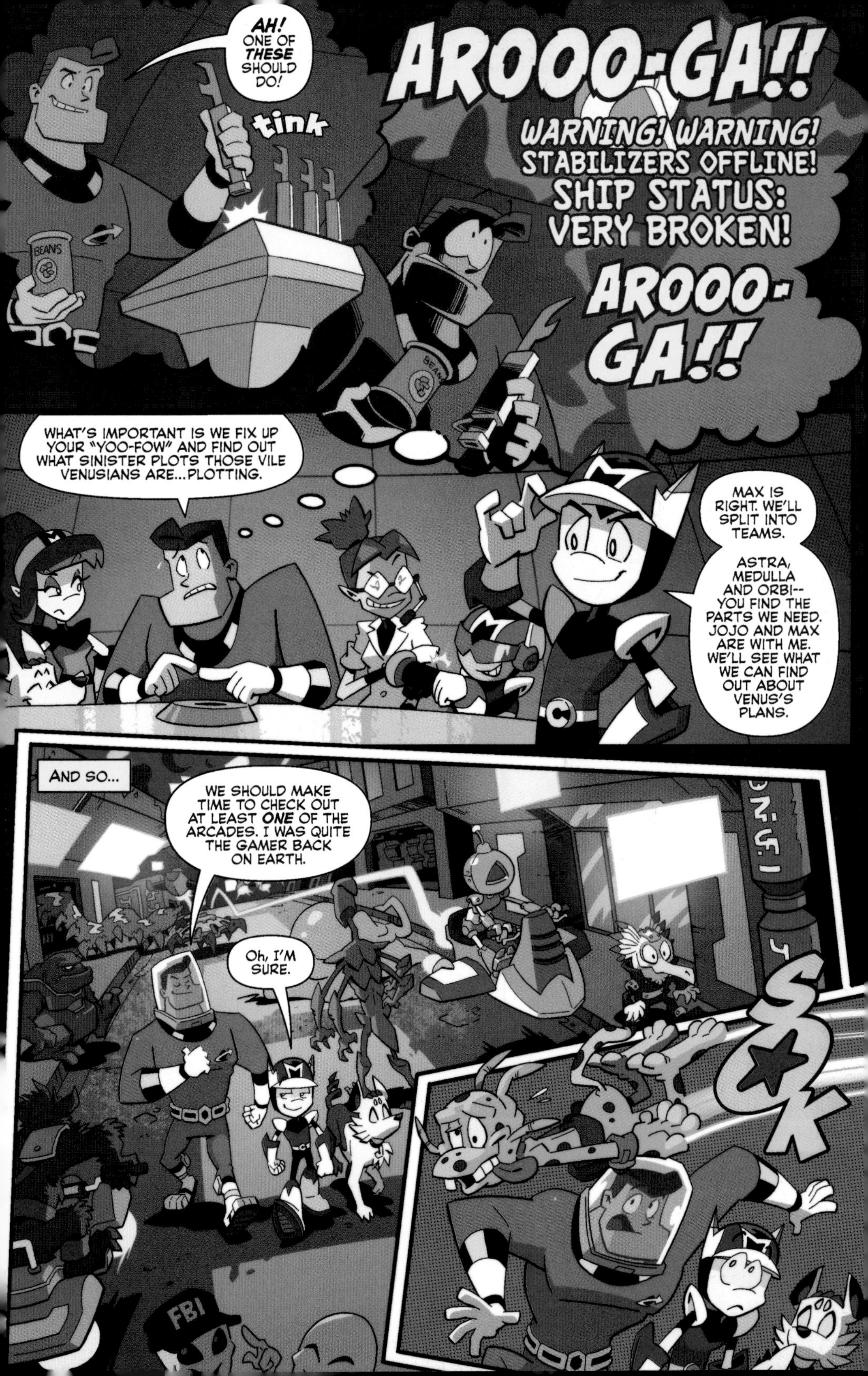
AH! ONE OF THESE SHOULD DO!
tink
AROOO-GA!!
WARNING! WARNING! STABILIZERS OFFLINE! SHIP STATUS: VERY BROKEN!
AROOO-GA!!
BEANS
WHAT'S IMPORTANT IS WE FIX UP YOUR "YOO-FOW" AND FIND OUT WHAT SINISTER PLOTS THOSE VILE VENUSIANS ARE...PLOTTING.
MAX IS RIGHT. WE'LL SPLIT INTO TEAMS.
ASTRA, MEDULLA AND ORBI-- YOU FIND THE PARTS WE NEED. JOJO AND MAX ARE WITH ME. WE'LL SEE WHAT WE CAN FIND OUT ABOUT VENUS'S PLANS.
AND SO...
WE SHOULD MAKE TIME TO CHECK OUT AT LEAST ONE OF THE ARCADES. I WAS QUITE THE GAMER BACK ON EARTH.
Oh, I'M SURE.
SMOK
FBI

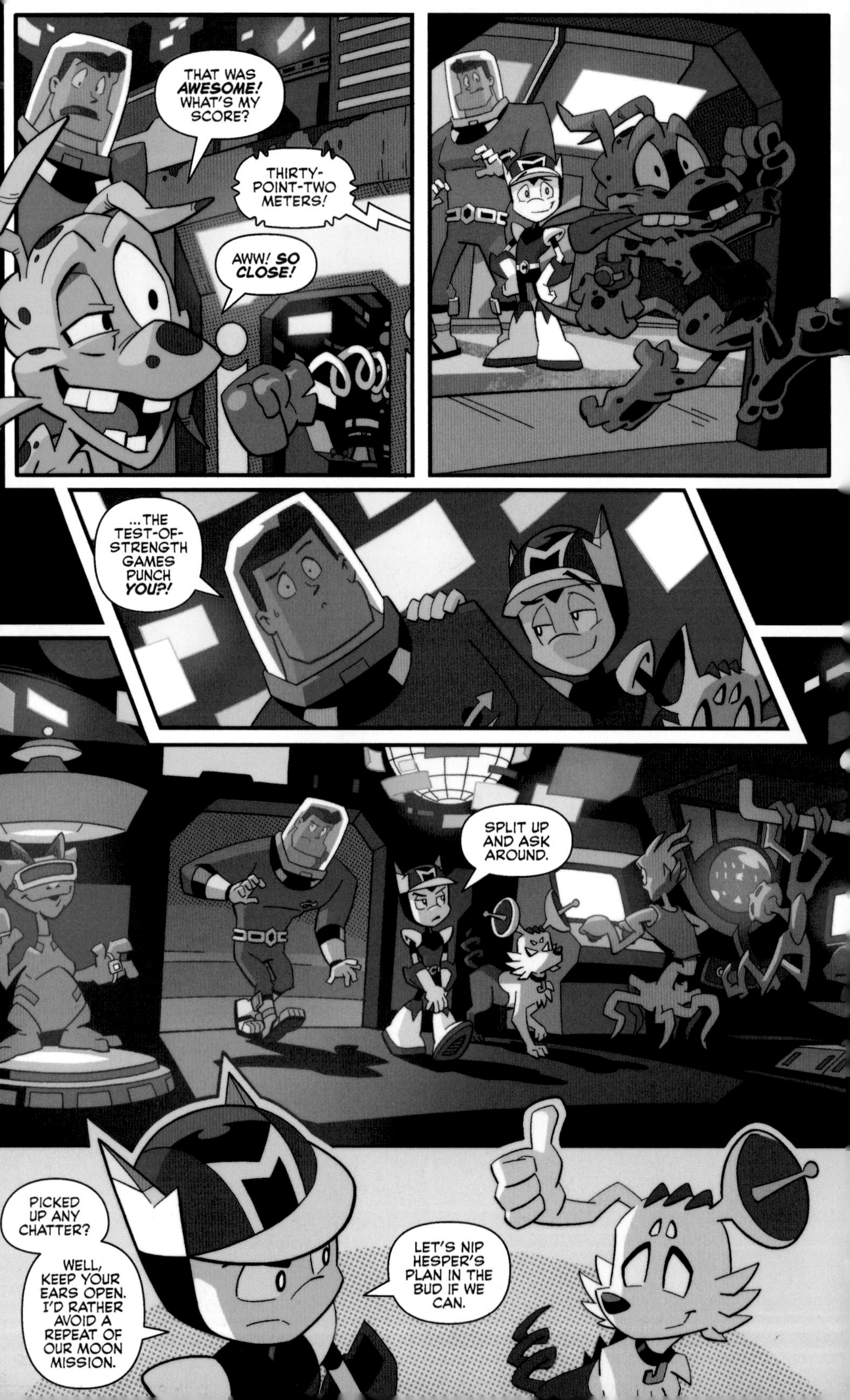
THAT WAS AWESOME! WHAT'S MY SCORE?
THIRTY-POINT-TWO METERS!
AWW! SO CLOSE!
...THE TEST-OF-STRENGTH GAMES PUNCH YOU?!
SPLIT UP AND ASK AROUND.
PICKED UP ANY CHATTER?
WELL, KEEP YOUR EARS OPEN. I'D RATHER AVOID A REPEAT OF OUR MOON MISSION.
LET'S NIP HESPER'S PLAN IN THE BUD IF WE CAN.

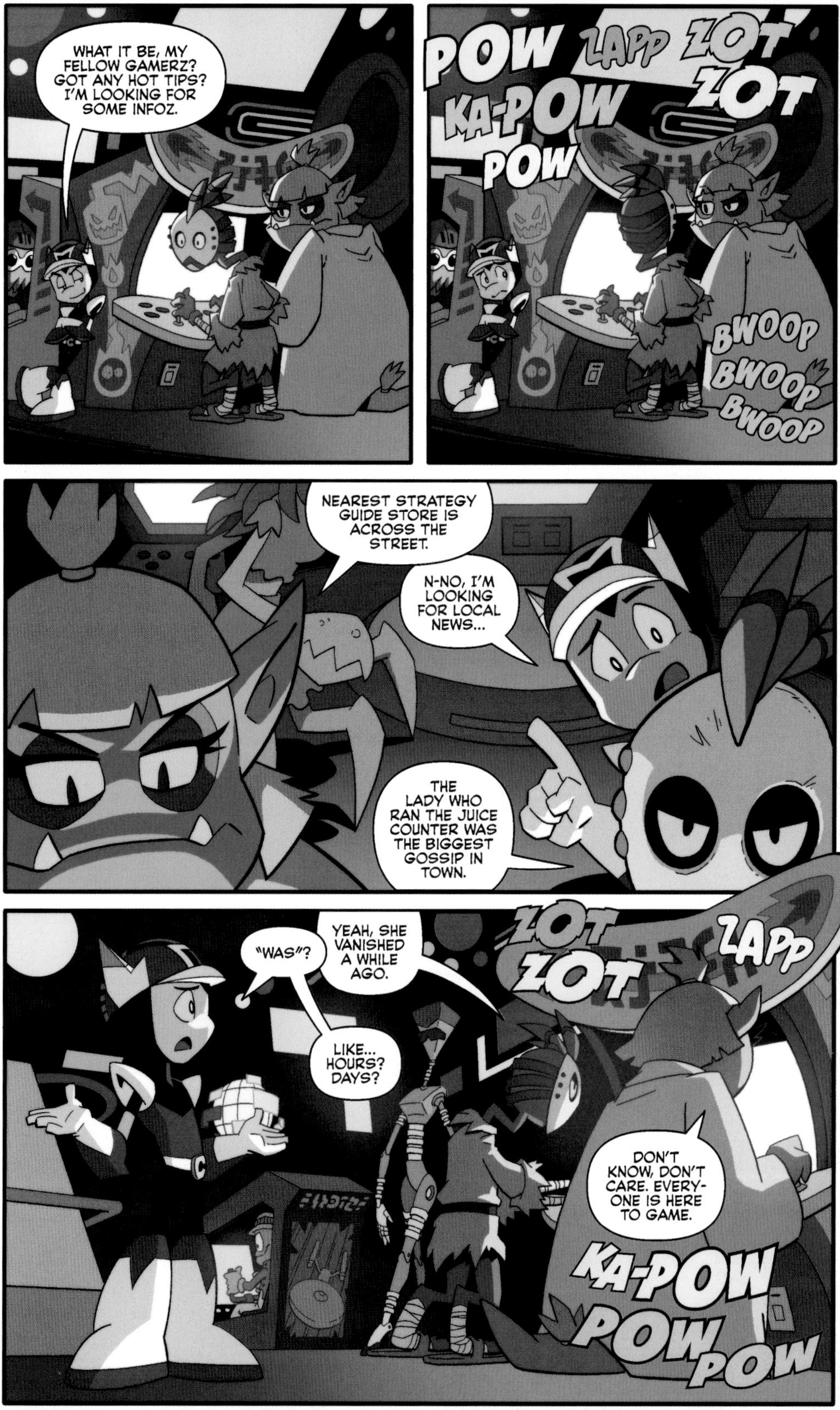

WHAT IT BE, MY FELLOW GAMERZ? GOT ANY HOT TIPS? I'M LOOKING FOR SOME INFOZ.
POW ZAPP ZOT ZOT
KA-POW
POW
BWOOP BWOOP BWOOP
NEAREST STRATEGY GUIDE STORE IS ACROSS THE STREET.
N-NO, I'M LOOKING FOR LOCAL NEWS...
THE LADY WHO RAN THE JUICE COUNTER WAS THE BIGGEST GOSSIP IN TOWN.
"WAS"?
YEAH, SHE VANISHED A WHILE AGO.
ZOT ZAPP ZOT
LIKE... HOURS? DAYS?
DON'T KNOW, DON'T CARE. EVERY-ONE IS HERE TO GAME.
KA-POW POW POW

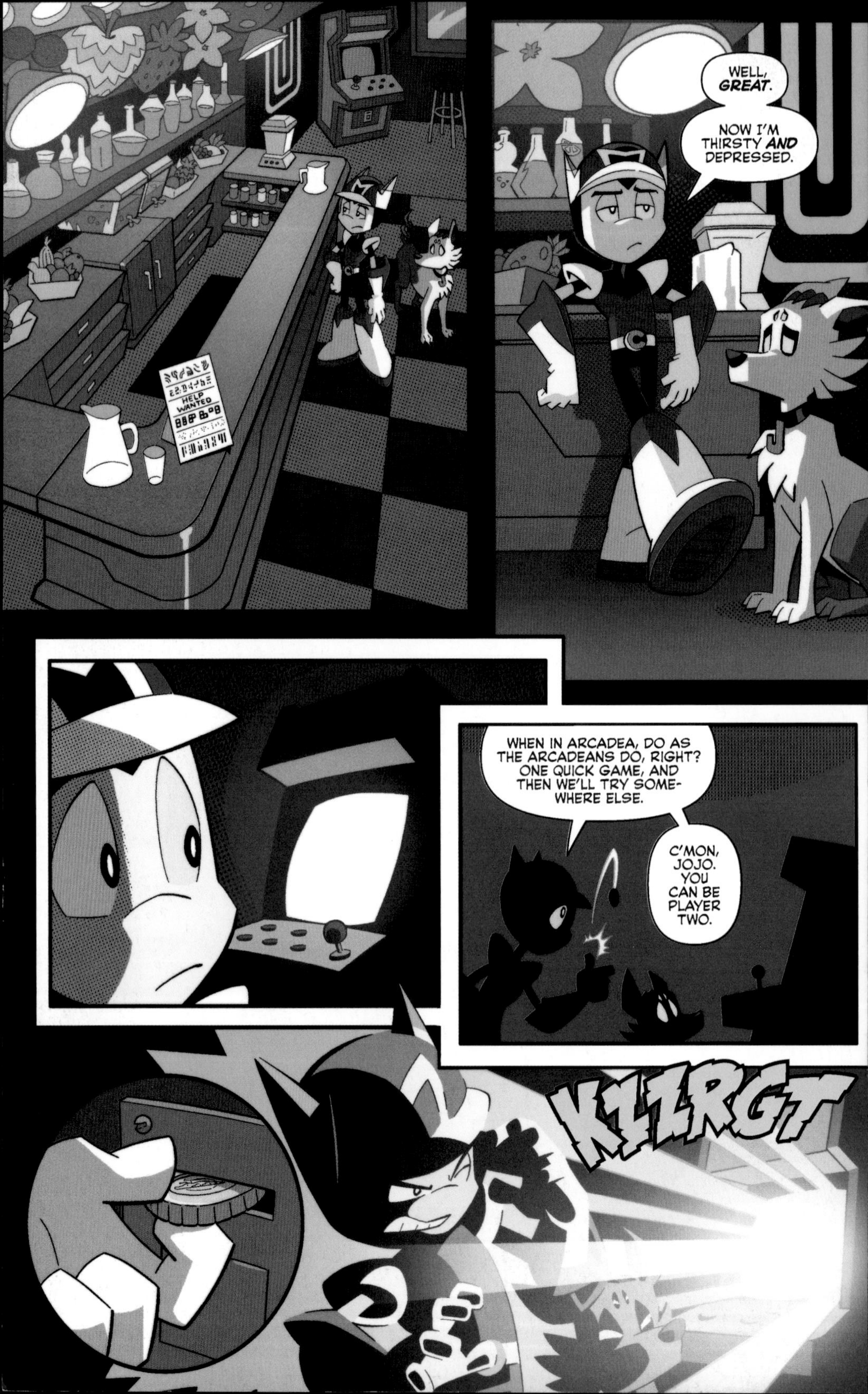
HELP WANTED
WELL, GREAT.
NOW I'M THIRSTY AND DEPRESSED.
WHEN IN ARCADEA, DO AS THE ARCADEANS DO, RIGHT? ONE QUICK GAME, AND THEN WE'LL TRY SOME-WHERE ELSE.
C'MON, JOJO. YOU CAN BE PLAYER TWO.
KZZRGT

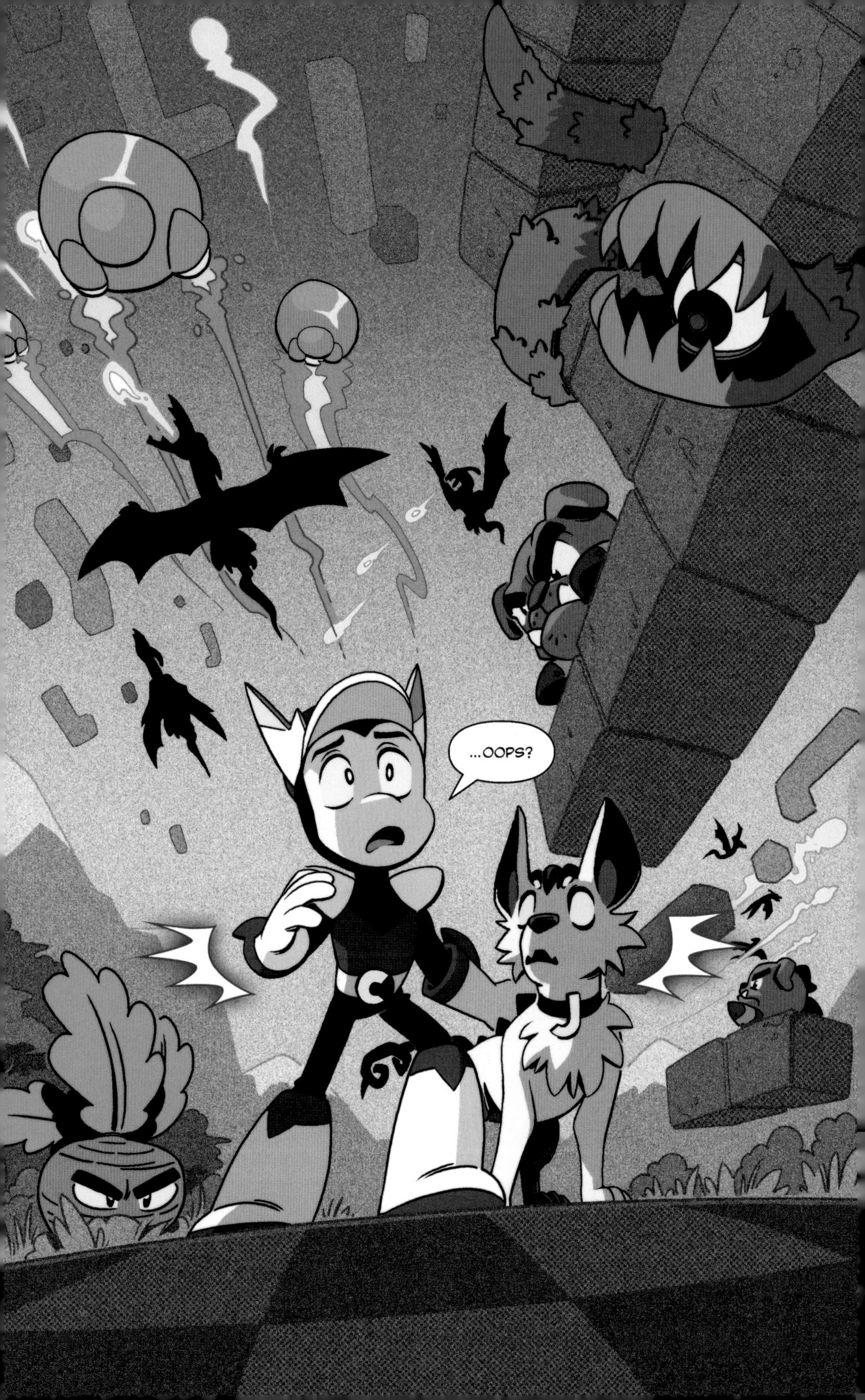
...OOPS?

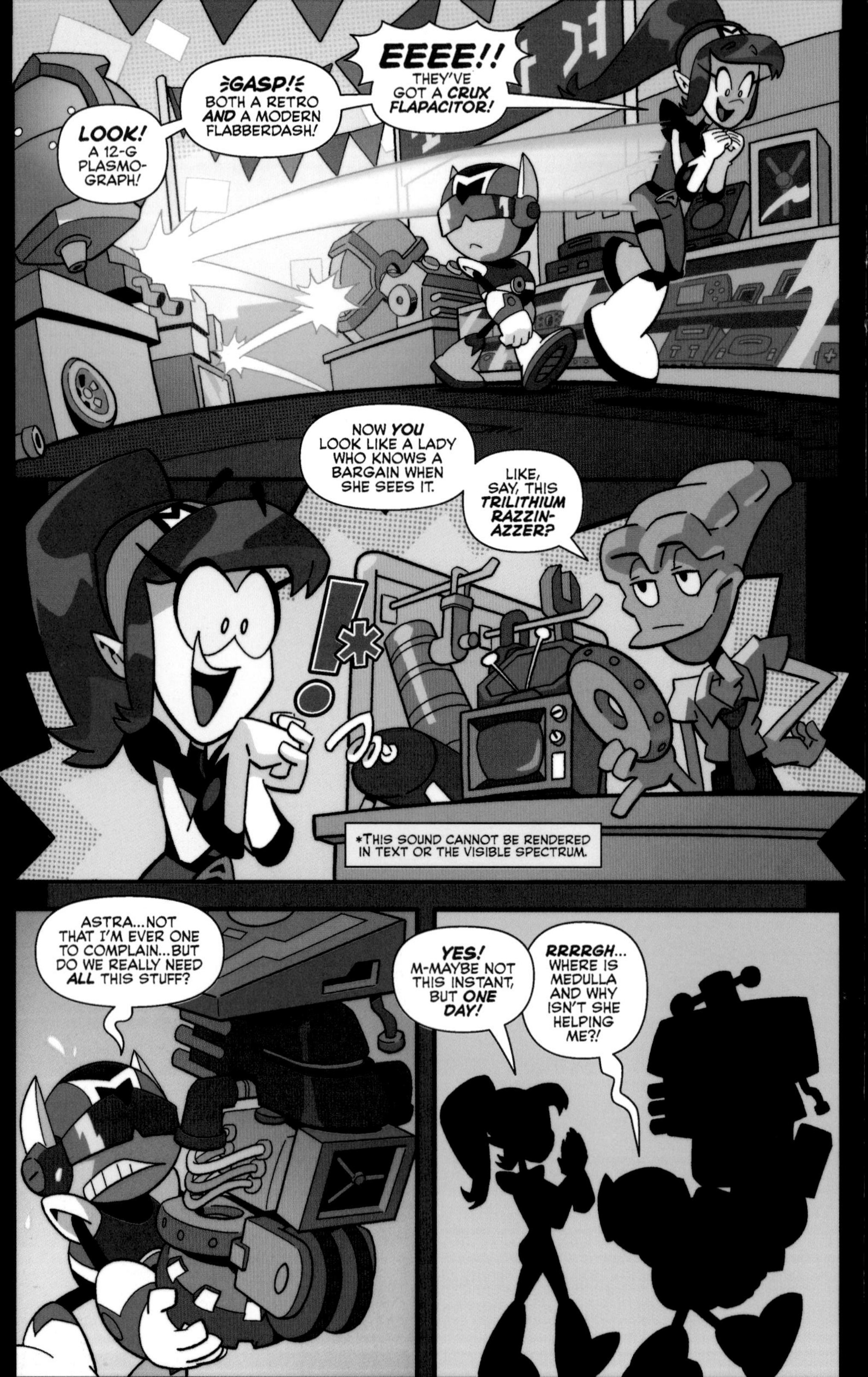
LOOK! A 12-G PLASMO-GRAPH!
GASP! BOTH A RETRO AND A MODERN FLABBERDASH!
EEEE!! THEY'VE GOT A CRUX FLAPACITOR!
NOW YOU LOOK LIKE A LADY WHO KNOWS A BARGAIN WHEN SHE SEES IT.
LIKE, SAY, THIS TRILITHIUM RAZZIN-AZZER?
!*
*THIS SOUND CANNOT BE RENDERED IN TEXT OR THE VISIBLE SPECTRUM.
ASTRA...NOT THAT I'M EVER ONE TO COMPLAIN...BUT DO WE REALLY NEED ALL THIS STUFF?
YES! M-MAYBE NOT THIS INSTANT, BUT ONE DAY!
RRRRGH... WHERE IS MEDULLA AND WHY ISN'T SHE HELPING ME?!

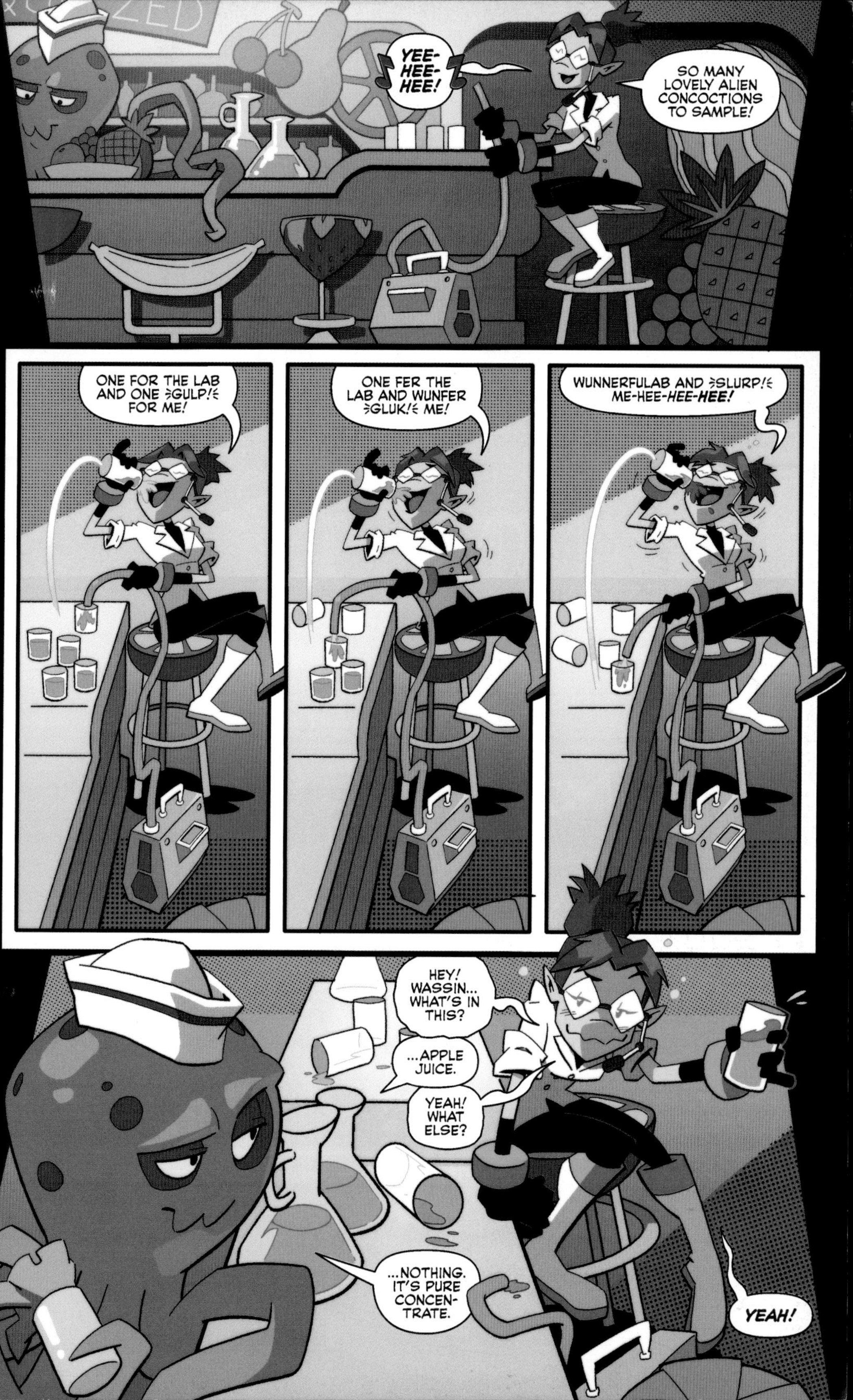
YEE-HEE-HEE!
SO MANY LOVELY ALIEN CONCOCTIONS TO SAMPLE!
ONE FOR THE LAB AND ONE ⪢GULP!⪡ FOR ME!
ONE FER THE LAB AND WUNFER ⪢GLUK!⪡ ME!
WUNNERFULAB AND ⪢SLURP!⪡ ME-HEE-*HEE*-***HEE!***
HEY! WASSIN... WHAT'S IN THIS?
...APPLE JUICE.
YEAH! WHAT ELSE?
...NOTHING. IT'S PURE CONCEN-TRATE.
YEAH!

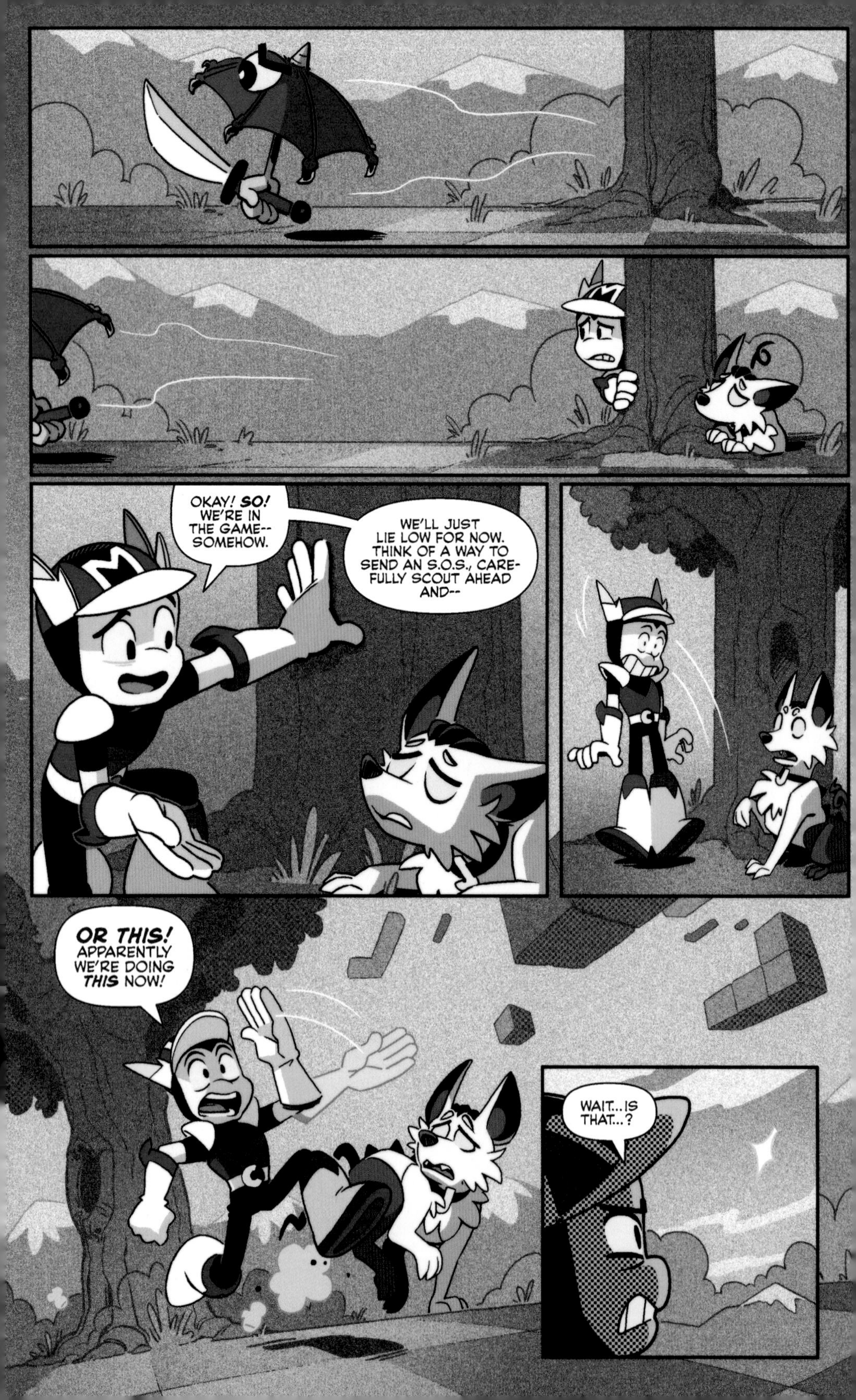
OKAY! **SO!** WE'RE IN THE GAME--SOMEHOW.
WE'LL JUST LIE LOW FOR NOW. THINK OF A WAY TO SEND AN S.O.S., CAREFULLY SCOUT AHEAD AND--
OR THIS! APPARENTLY WE'RE DOING ***THIS*** NOW!
WAIT...IS THAT...?

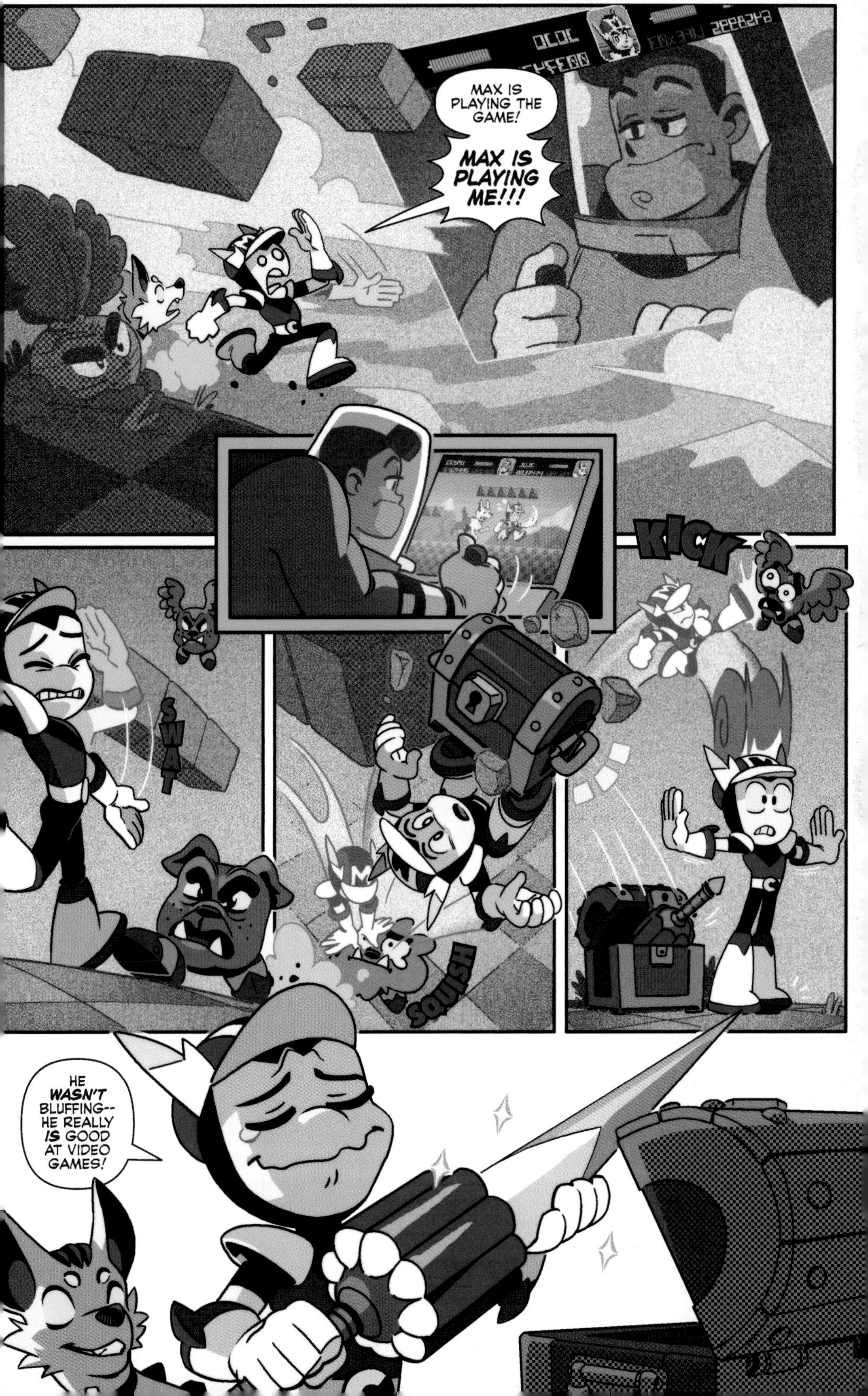
MAX IS PLAYING THE GAME!
MAX IS PLAYING ME!!!
SWAT
KICK
SQUISH
HE WASN'T BLUFFING-- HE REALLY IS GOOD AT VIDEO GAMES!

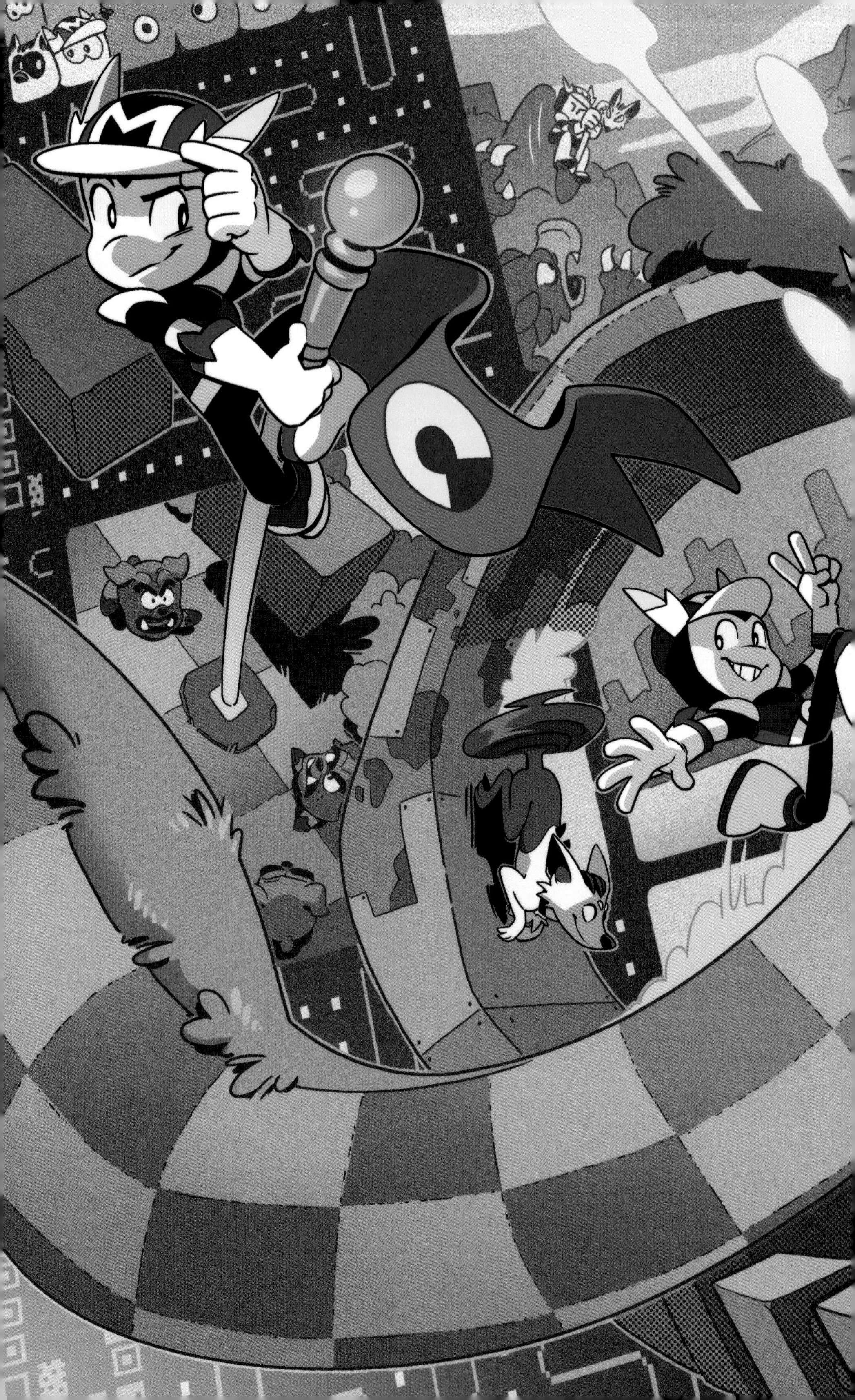

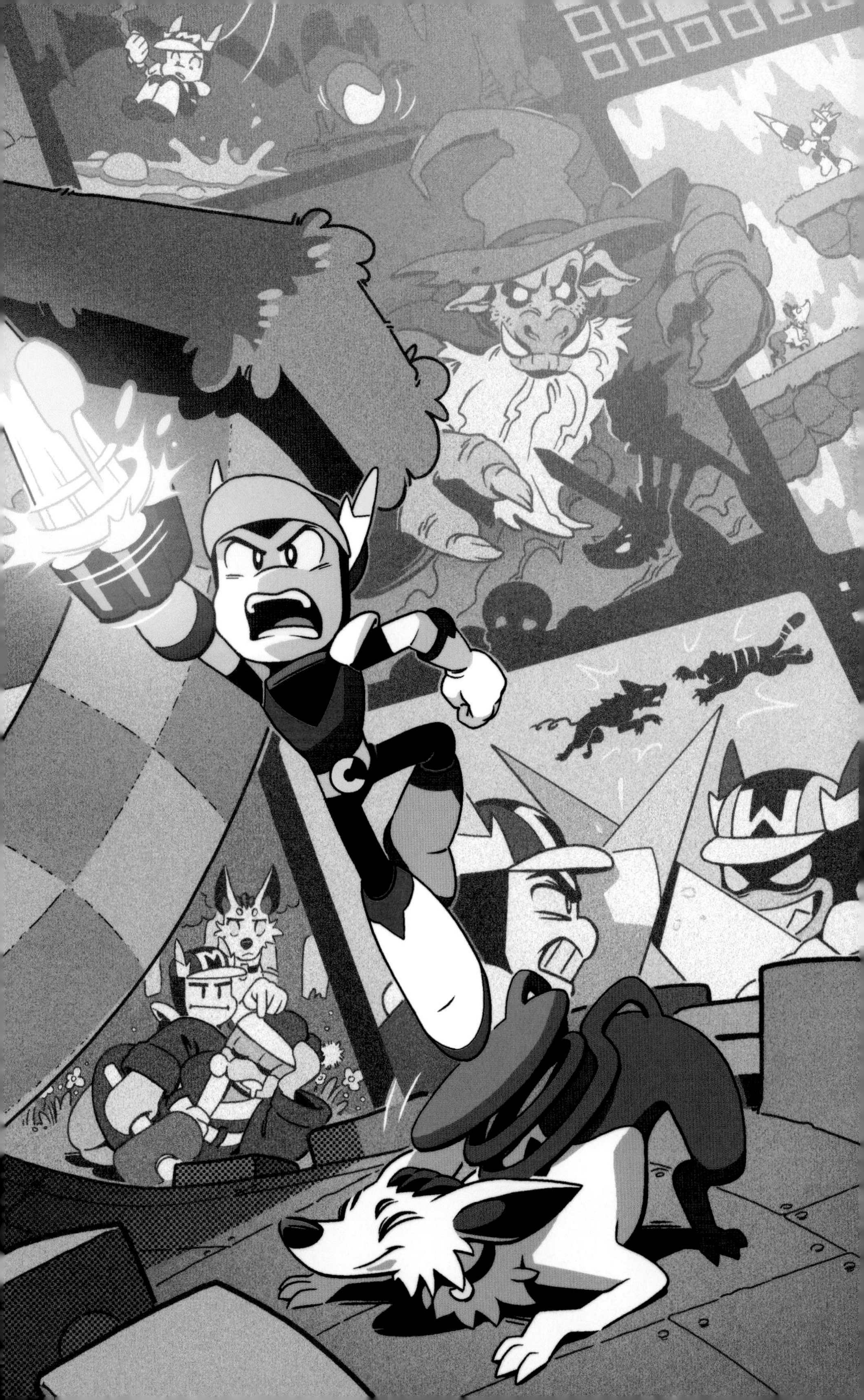

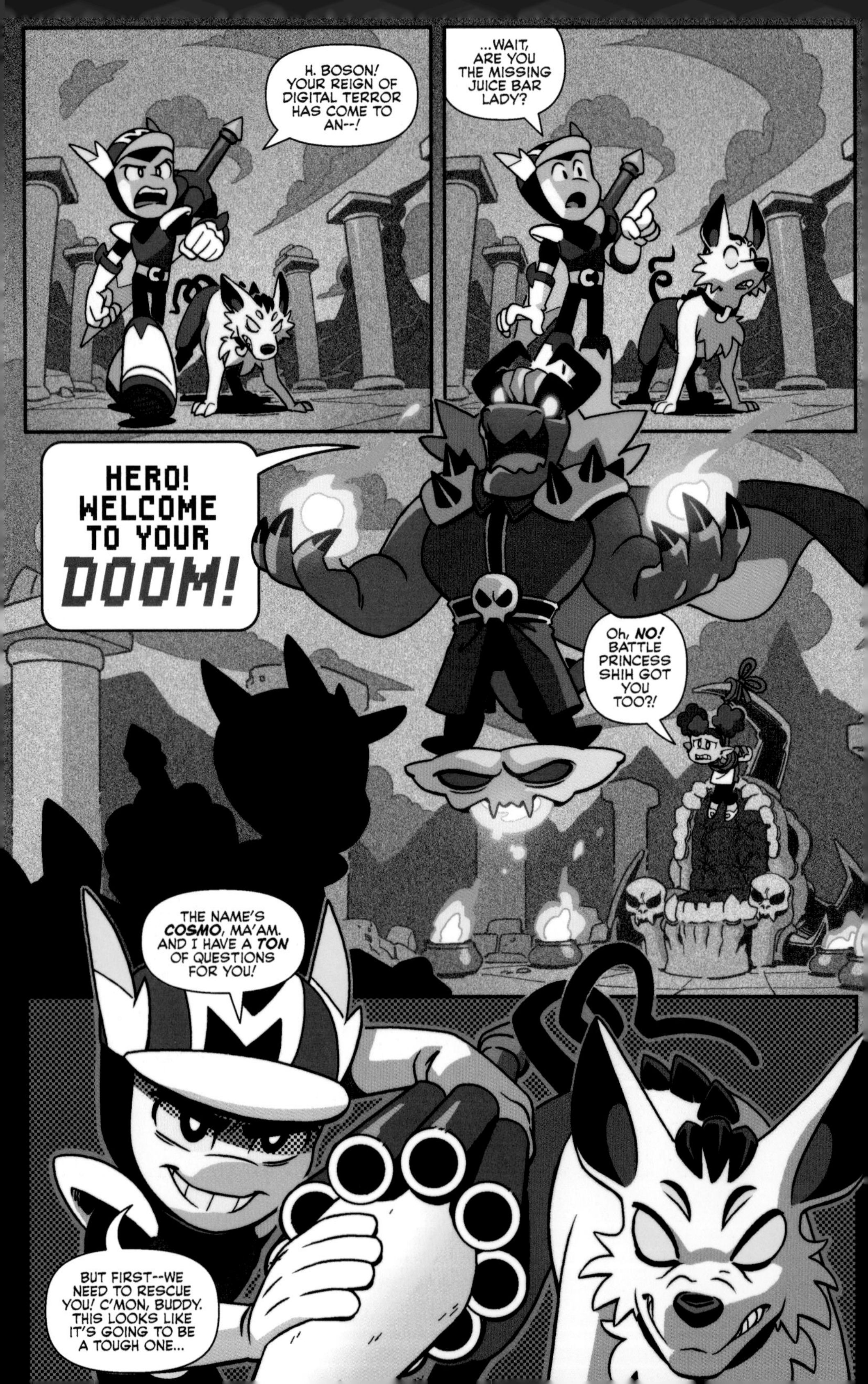
H. BOSON! YOUR REIGN OF DIGITAL TERROR HAS COME TO AN--!
...WAIT, ARE YOU THE MISSING JUICE BAR LADY?
HERO! WELCOME TO YOUR DOOM!
Oh, NO! BATTLE PRINCESS SHIH GOT YOU TOO?!
THE NAME'S COSMO, MA'AM. AND I HAVE A TON OF QUESTIONS FOR YOU!
BUT FIRST--WE NEED TO RESCUE YOU! C'MON, BUDDY. THIS LOOKS LIKE IT'S GOING TO BE A TOUGH ONE...

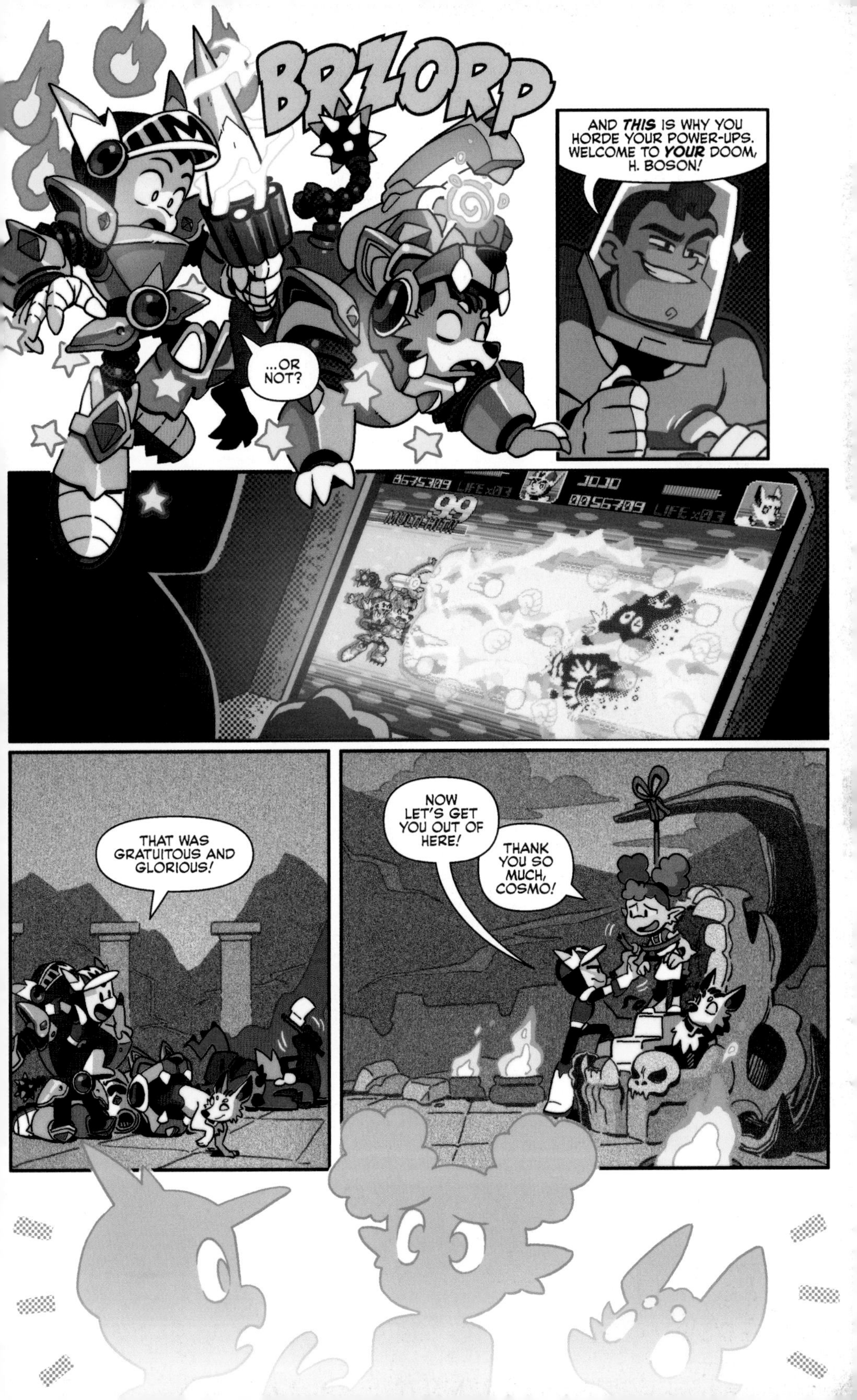
BRZORP
AND THIS IS WHY YOU HORDE YOUR POWER-UPS. WELCOME TO YOUR DOOM, H. BOSON!
...OR NOT?
8675309 LIFE x03
JOJO
0056709 LIFE x03
99
THAT WAS GRATUITOUS AND GLORIOUS!
NOW LET'S GET YOU OUT OF HERE!
THANK YOU SO MUCH, COSMO!

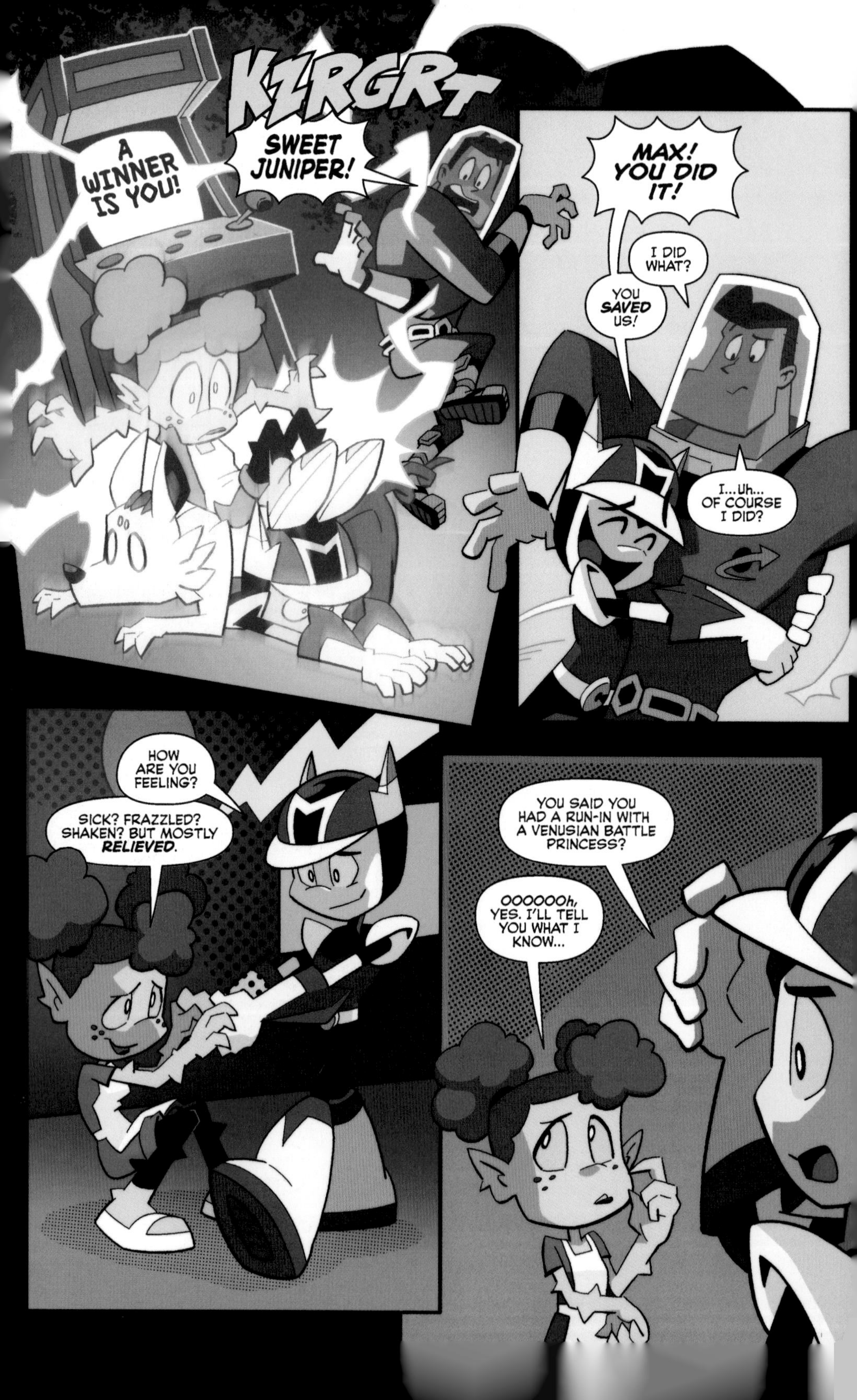
KZRGRT
A WINNER IS YOU!
SWEET JUNIPER!
MAX! YOU DID IT!
I DID WHAT?
YOU *SAVED* US!
I...Uh... OF COURSE I DID?
HOW ARE YOU FEELING?
SICK? FRAZZLED? SHAKEN? BUT MOSTLY ***RELIEVED***.
YOU SAID YOU HAD A RUN-IN WITH A VENUSIAN BATTLE PRINCESS?
OOOOOOh, YES. I'LL TELL YOU WHAT I KNOW...

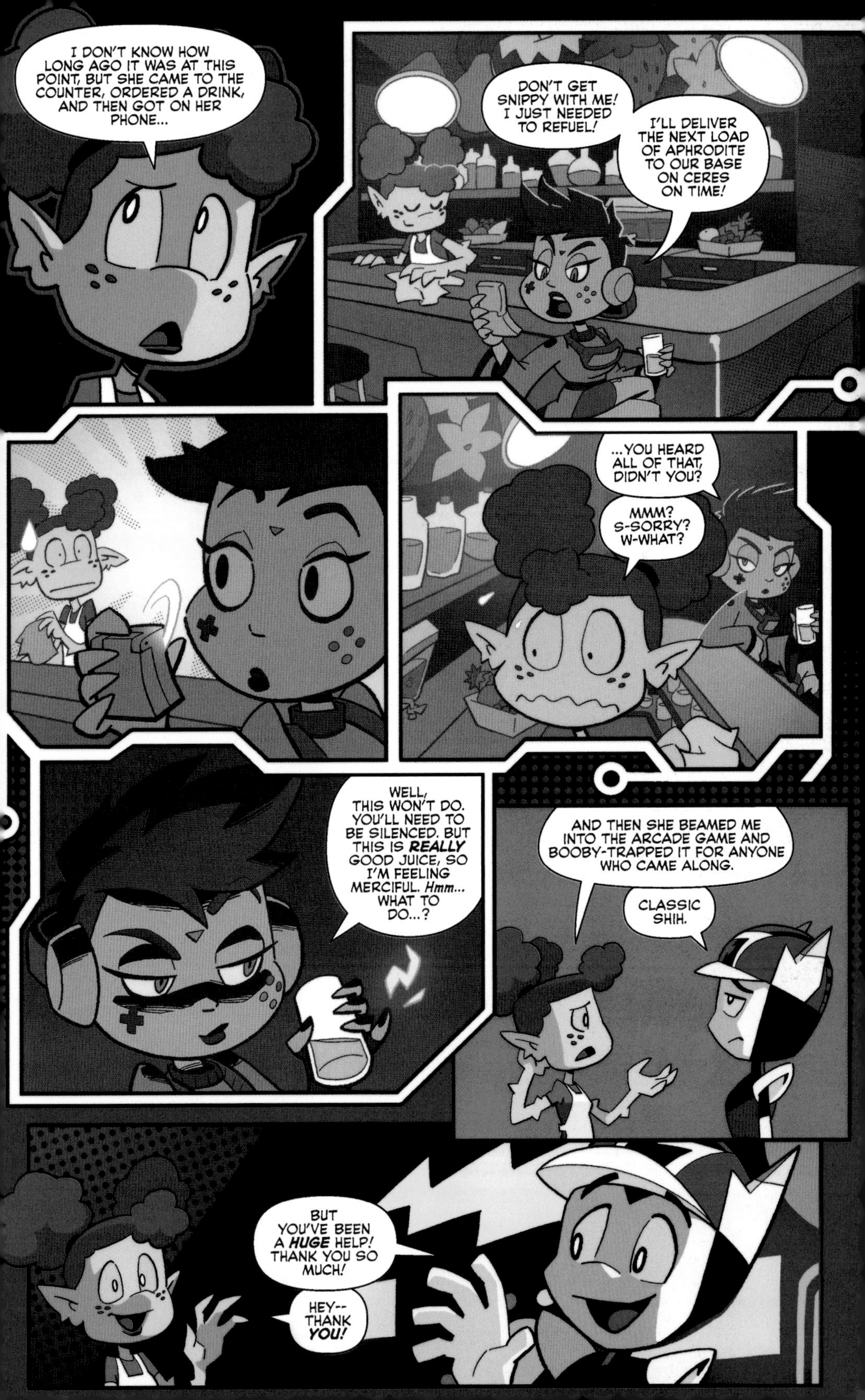
I DON'T KNOW HOW LONG AGO IT WAS AT THIS POINT, BUT SHE CAME TO THE COUNTER, ORDERED A DRINK, AND THEN GOT ON HER PHONE...
DON'T GET SNIPPY WITH ME! I JUST NEEDED TO REFUEL!
I'LL DELIVER THE NEXT LOAD OF APHRODITE TO OUR BASE ON CERES ON TIME!
...YOU HEARD ALL OF THAT, DIDN'T YOU?
MMM? S-SORRY? W-WHAT?
WELL, THIS WON'T DO. YOU'LL NEED TO BE SILENCED. BUT THIS IS REALLY GOOD JUICE, SO I'M FEELING MERCIFUL. Hmm... WHAT TO DO...?
AND THEN SHE BEAMED ME INTO THE ARCADE GAME AND BOOBY-TRAPPED IT FOR ANYONE WHO CAME ALONG.
CLASSIC SHIH.
BUT YOU'VE BEEN A HUGE HELP! THANK YOU SO MUCH!
HEY-- THANK YOU!

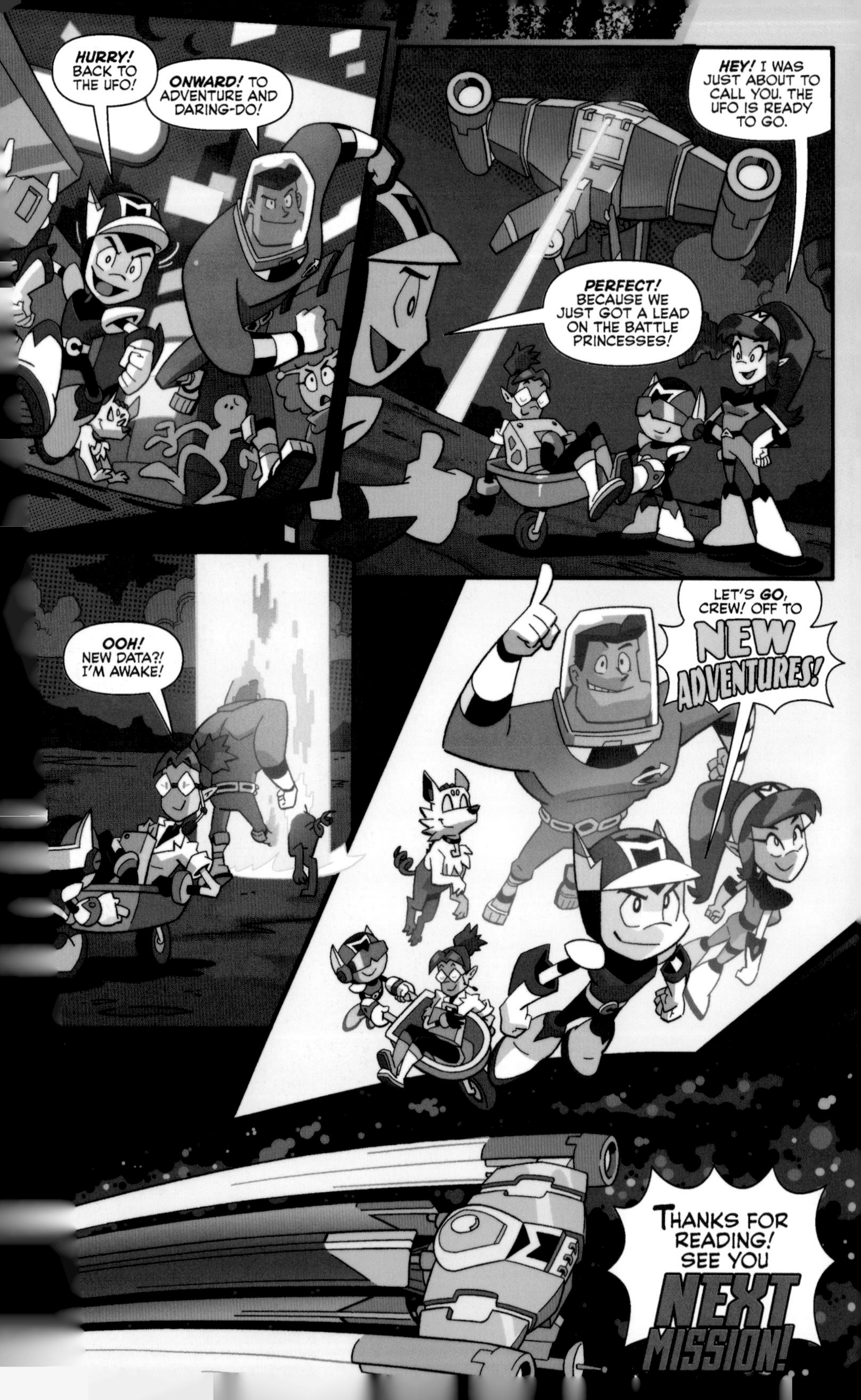

HURRY! BACK TO THE UFO!
ONWARD! TO ADVENTURE AND DARING-DO!
HEY! I WAS JUST ABOUT TO CALL YOU. THE UFO IS READY TO GO.
PERFECT! BECAUSE WE JUST GOT A LEAD ON THE BATTLE PRINCESSES!
OOH! NEW DATA?! I'M AWAKE!
LET'S GO, CREW! OFF TO NEW ADVENTURES!
THANKS FOR READING! SEE YOU NEXT MISSION!

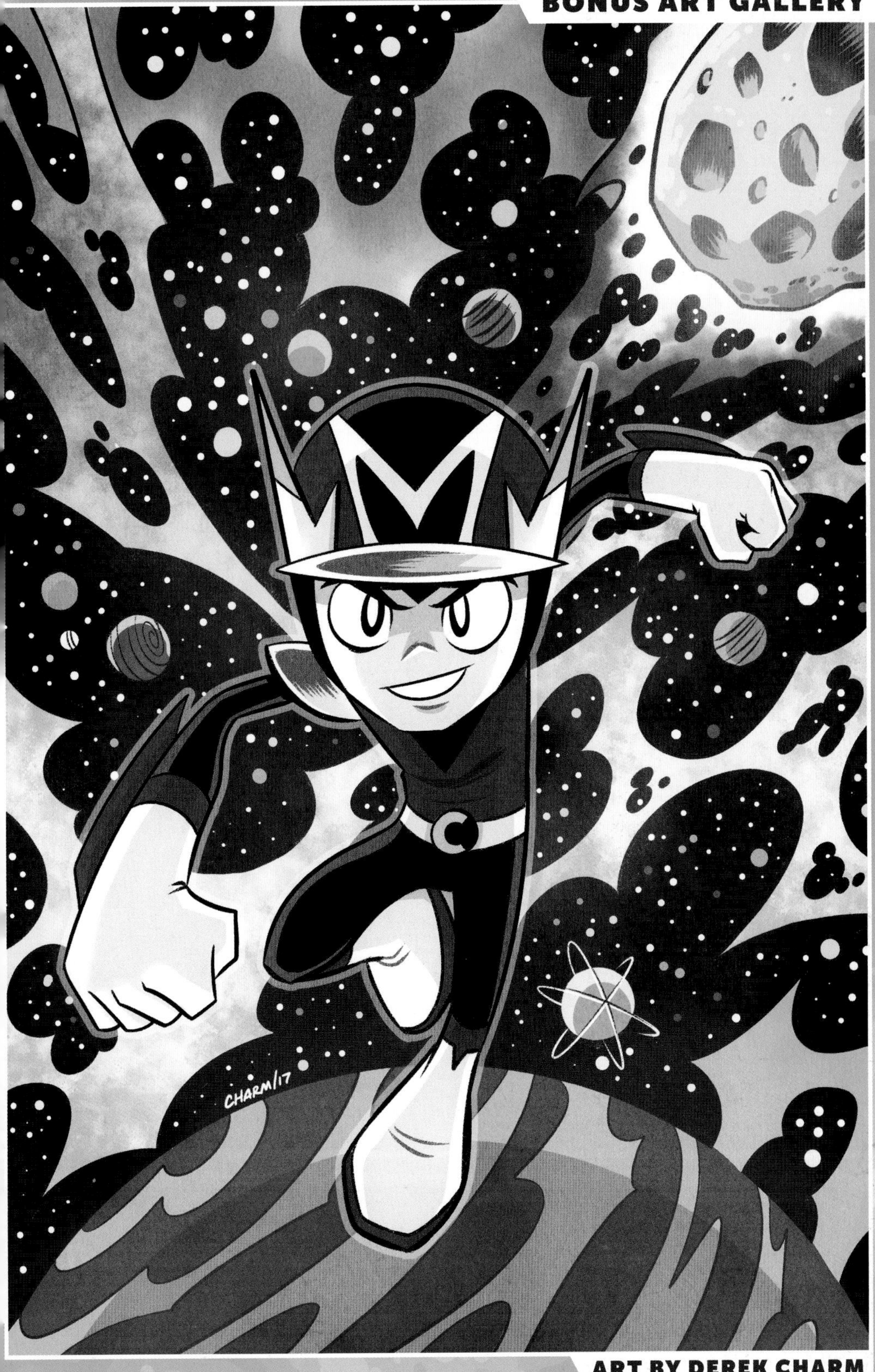
CHARM/17

ART BY DEREK CHARM

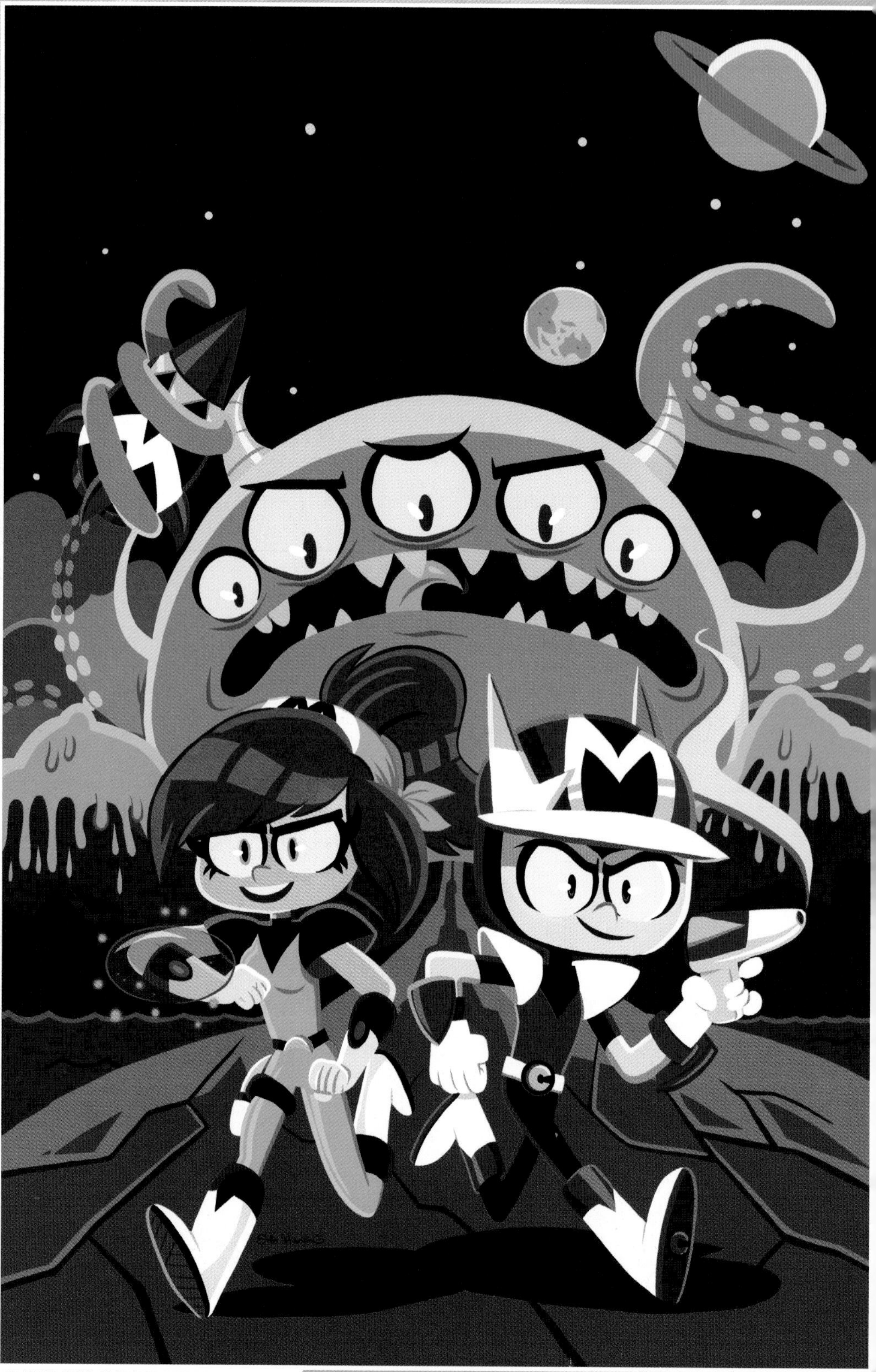

ART BY ERIN HUNTING

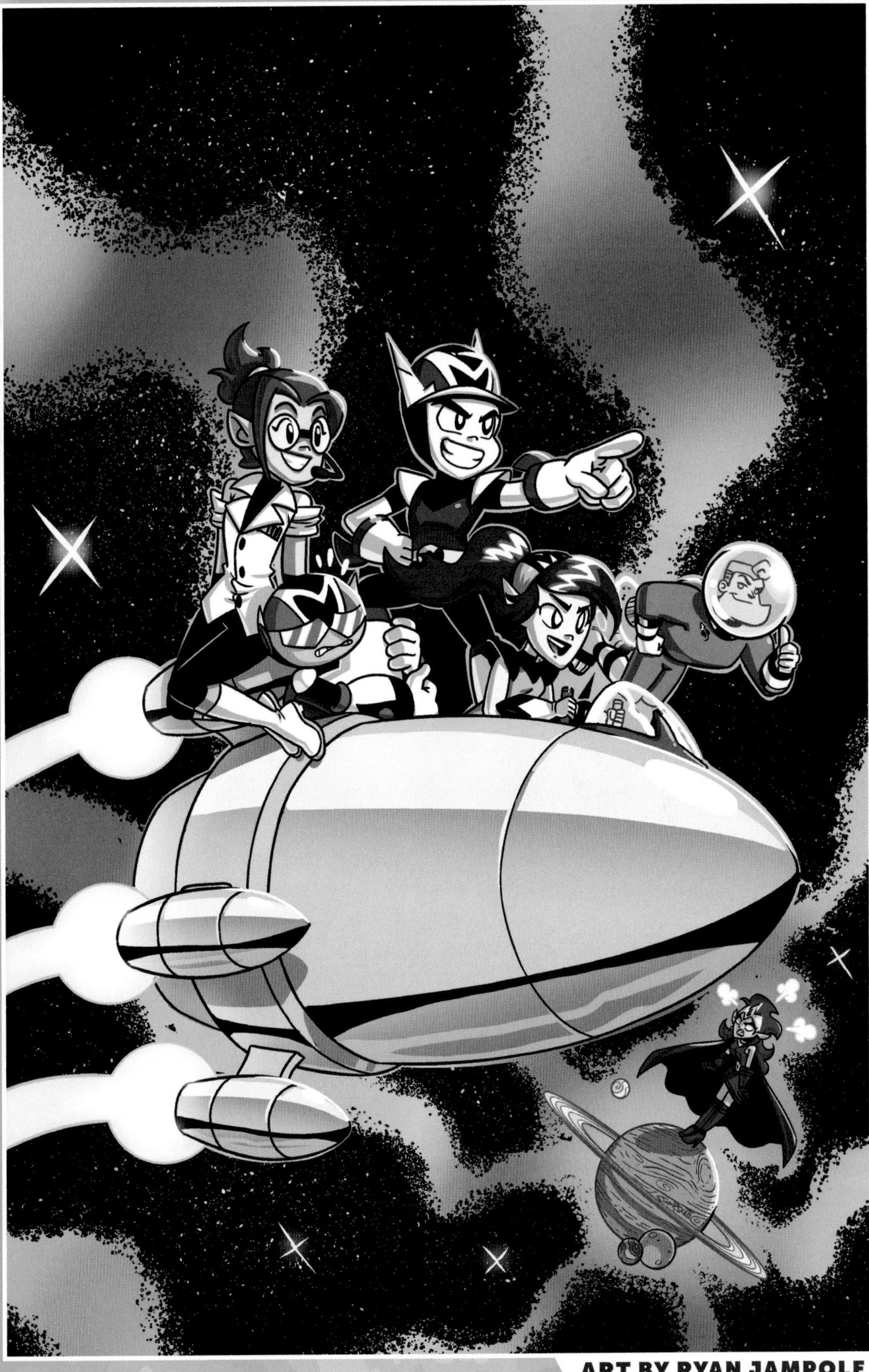

ART BY RYAN JAMPOLE

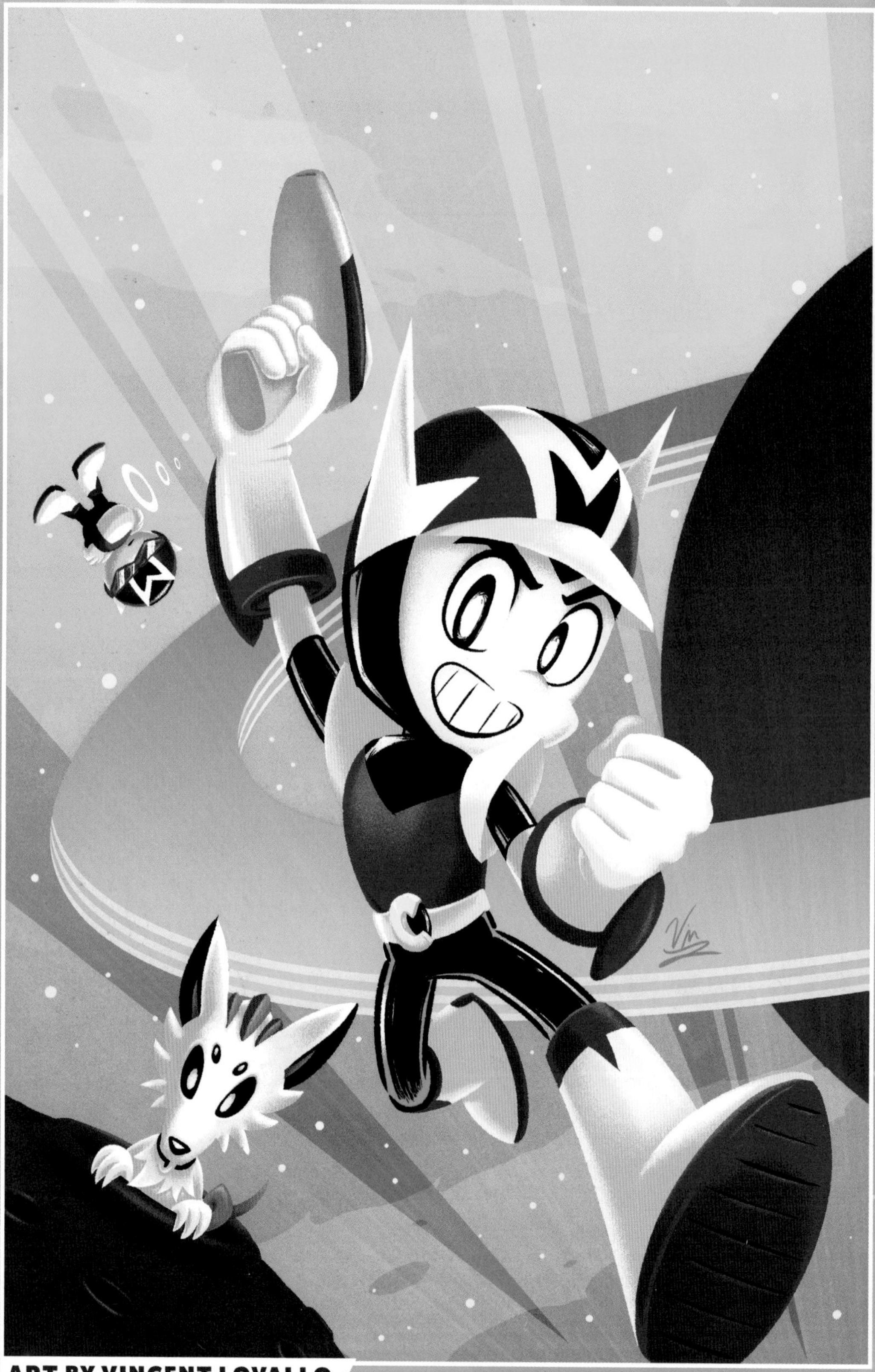

ART BY VINCENT LOVALLO

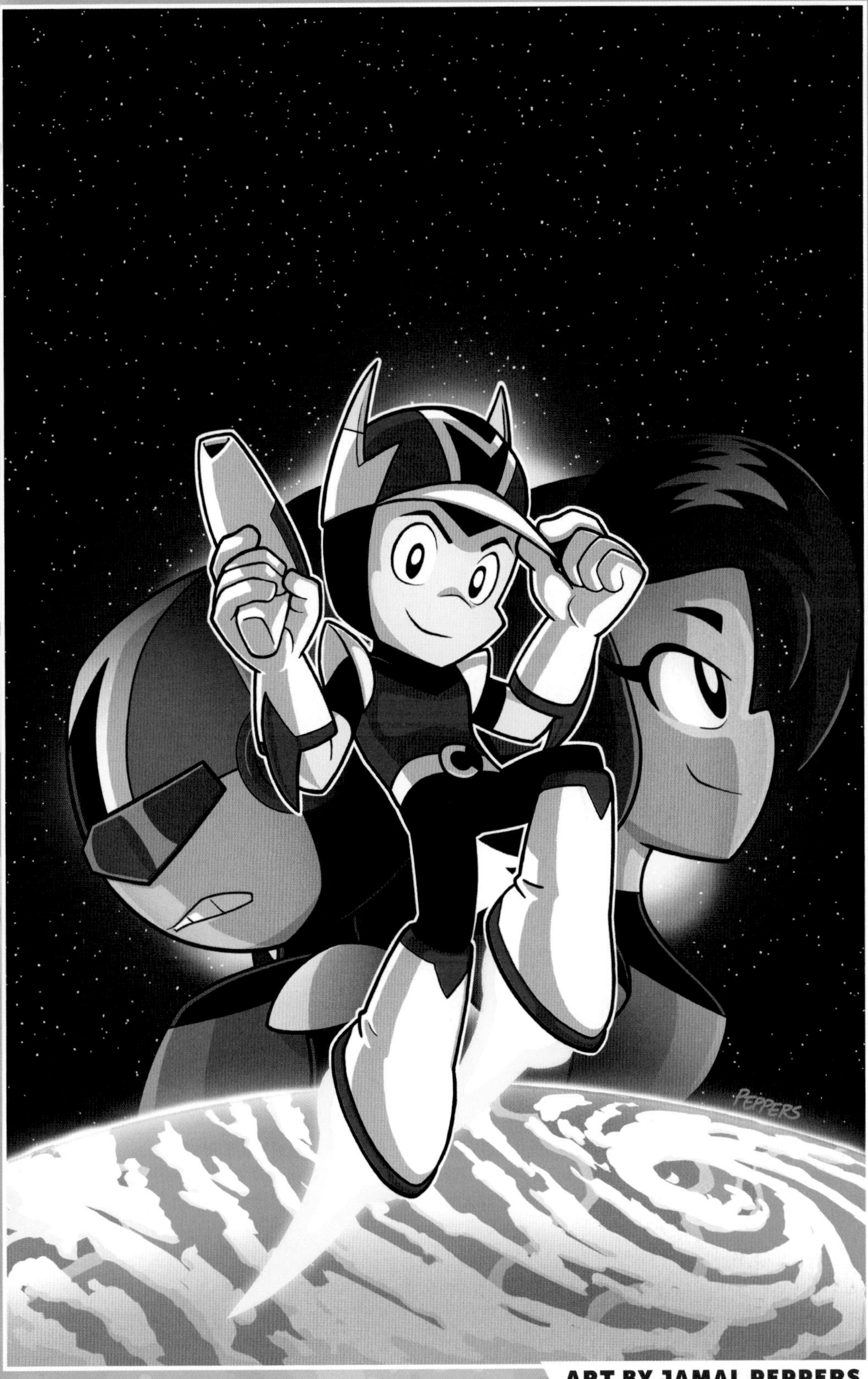
PEPPERS

ART BY JAMAL PEPPERS

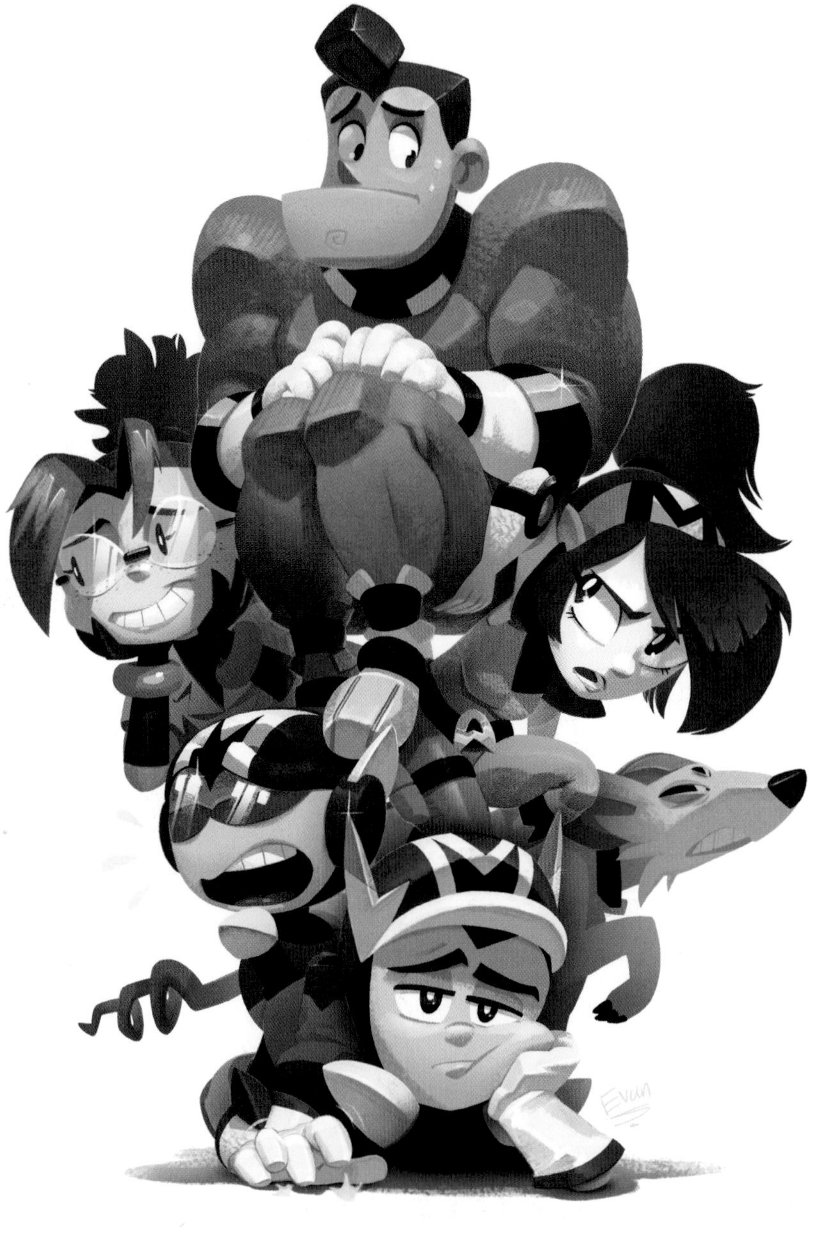

ART BY EVAN STANLEY

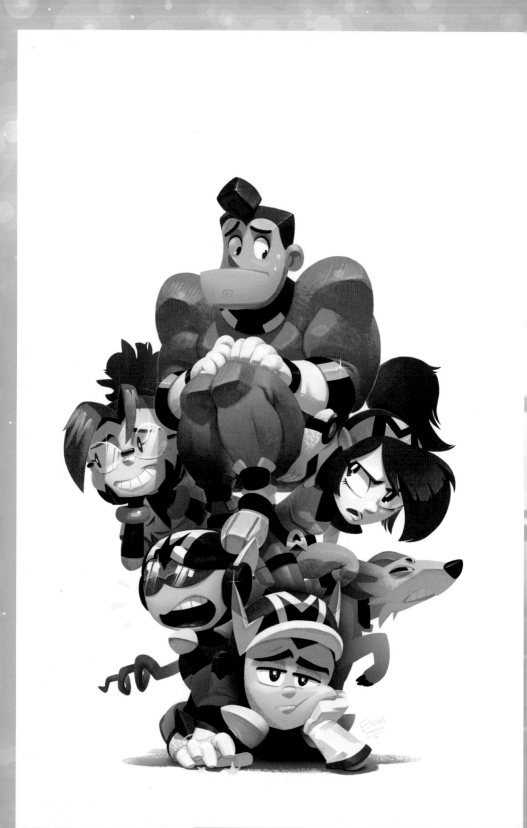

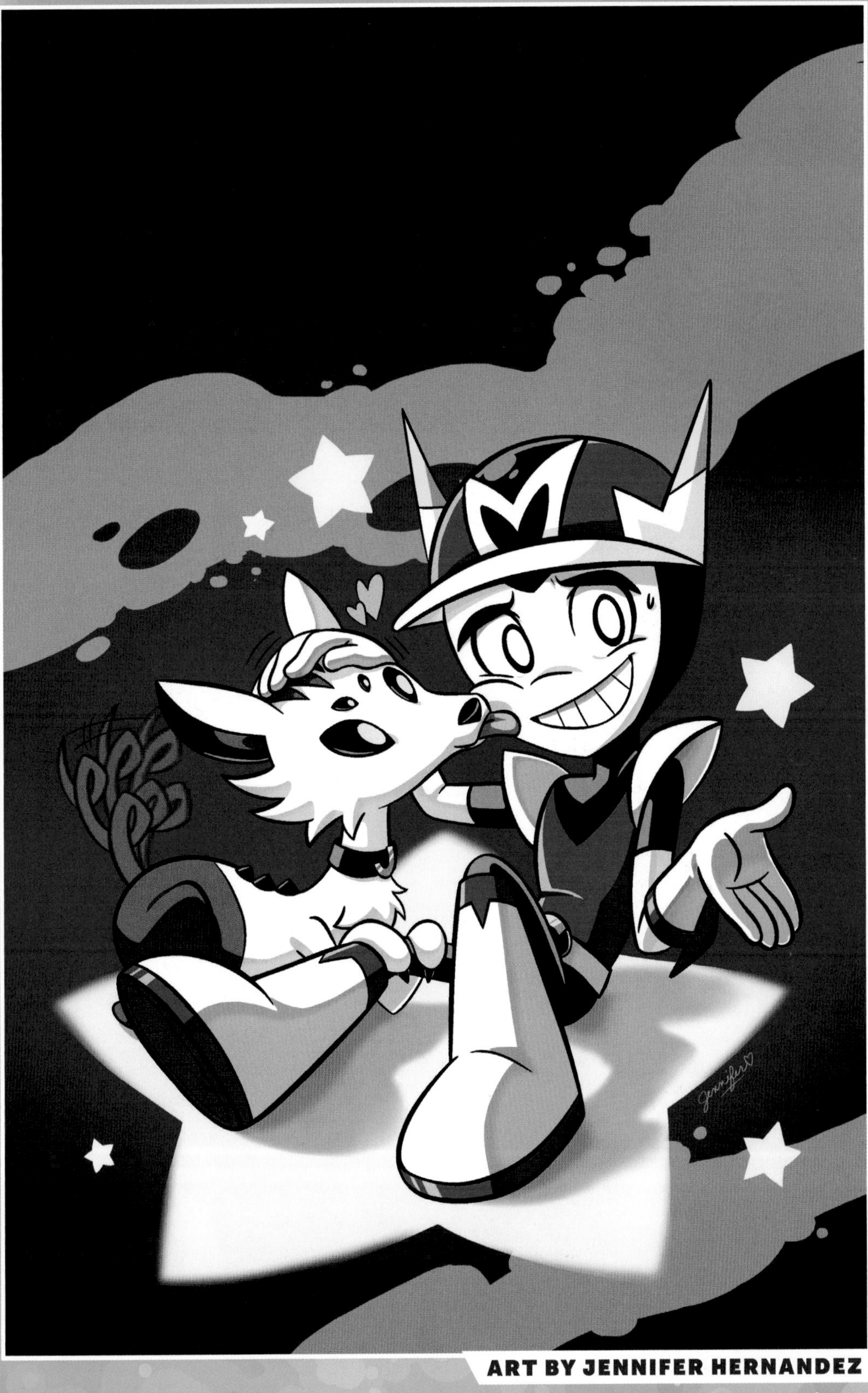

ART BY JENNIFER HERNANDEZ

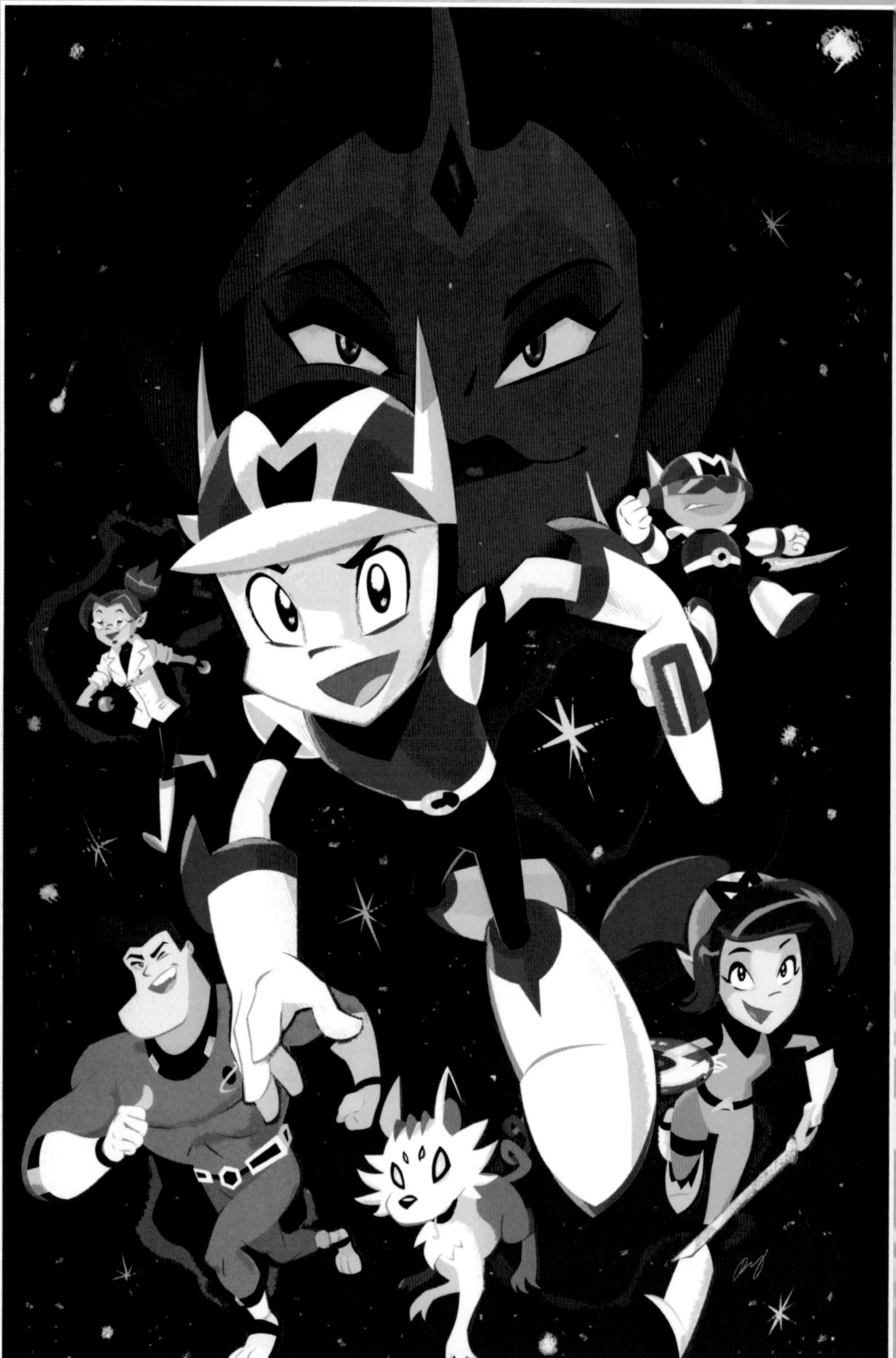

ART BY DAN SCHOENING

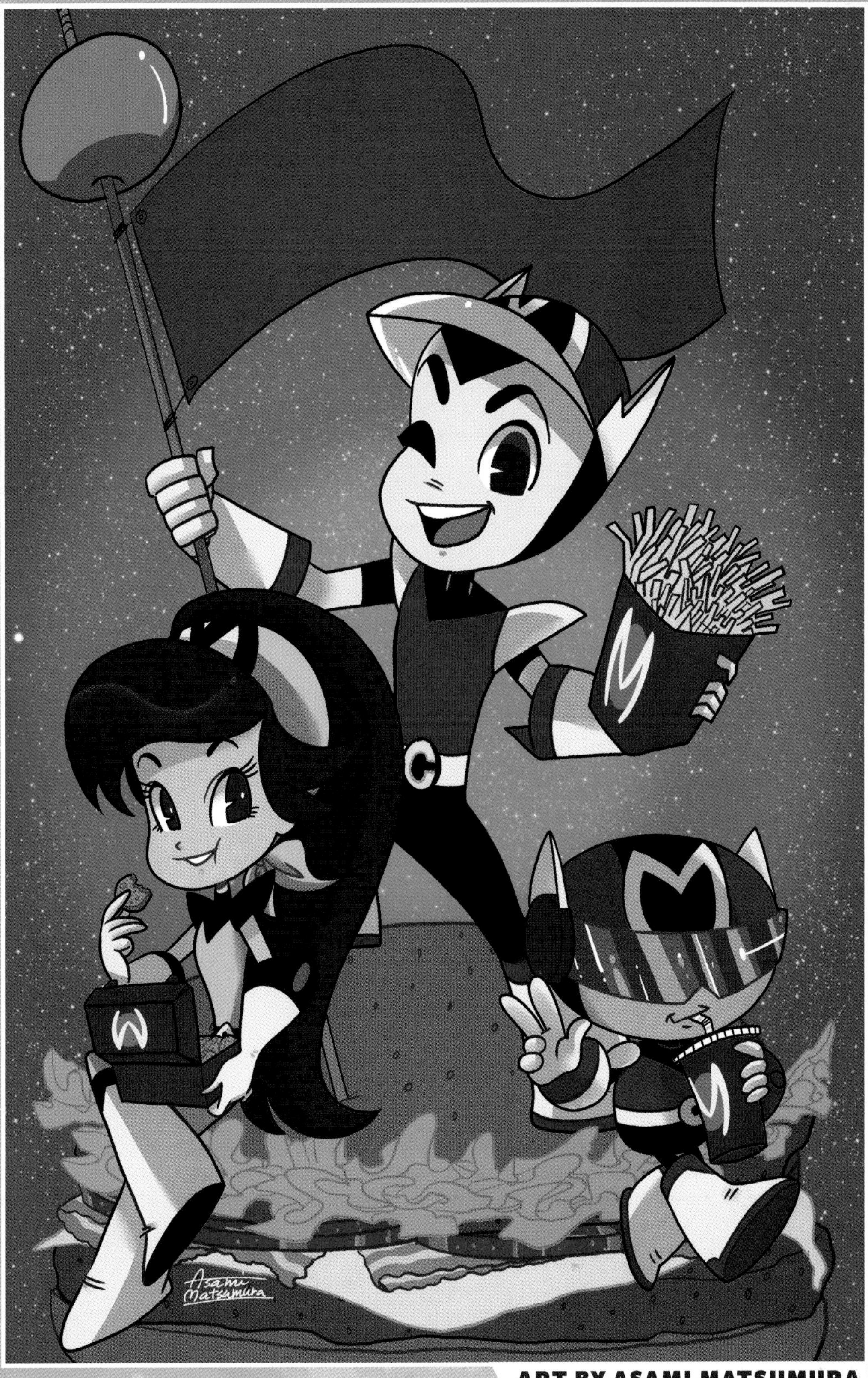
Asami Matsumura

ART BY ASAMI MATSUMURA

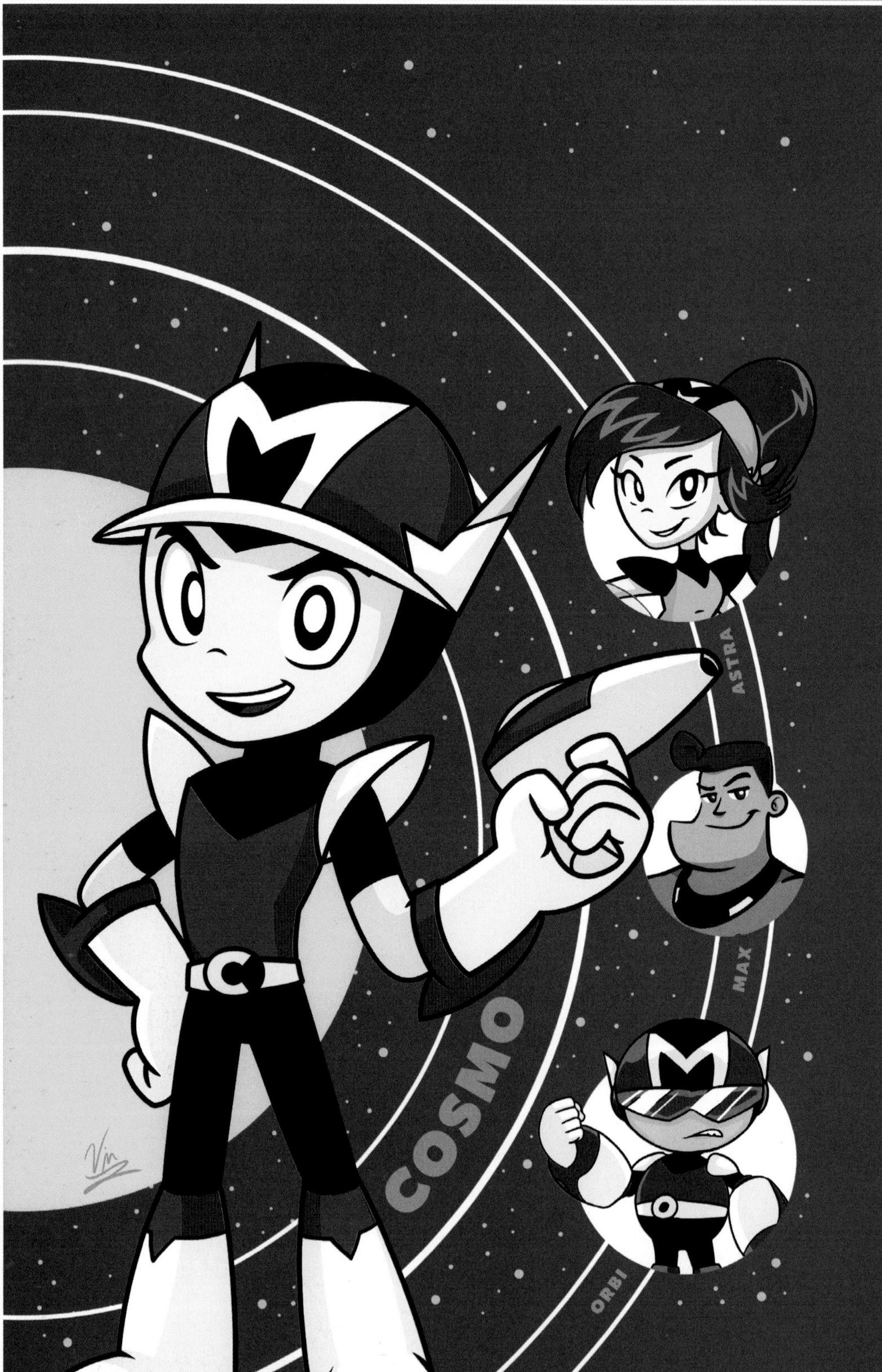
COSMO
ASTRA
MAX
ORBI

ART BY VINCENT LOVALLO

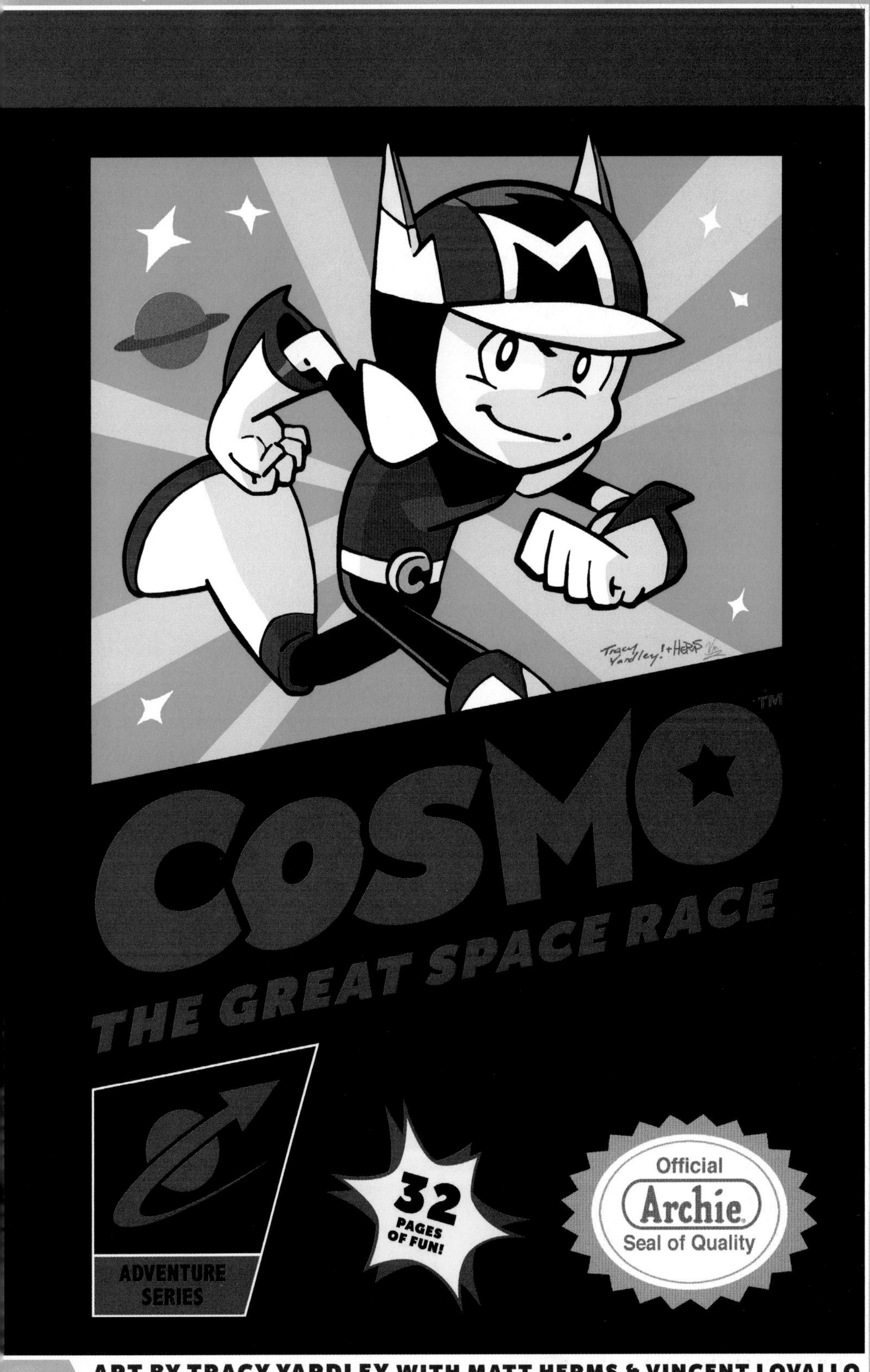
COSMO™
THE GREAT SPACE RACE
32 PAGES OF FUN!
Official Archie® Seal of Quality
ADVENTURE SERIES

ART BY TRACY YARDLEY WITH MATT HERMS & VINCENT LOVALLO

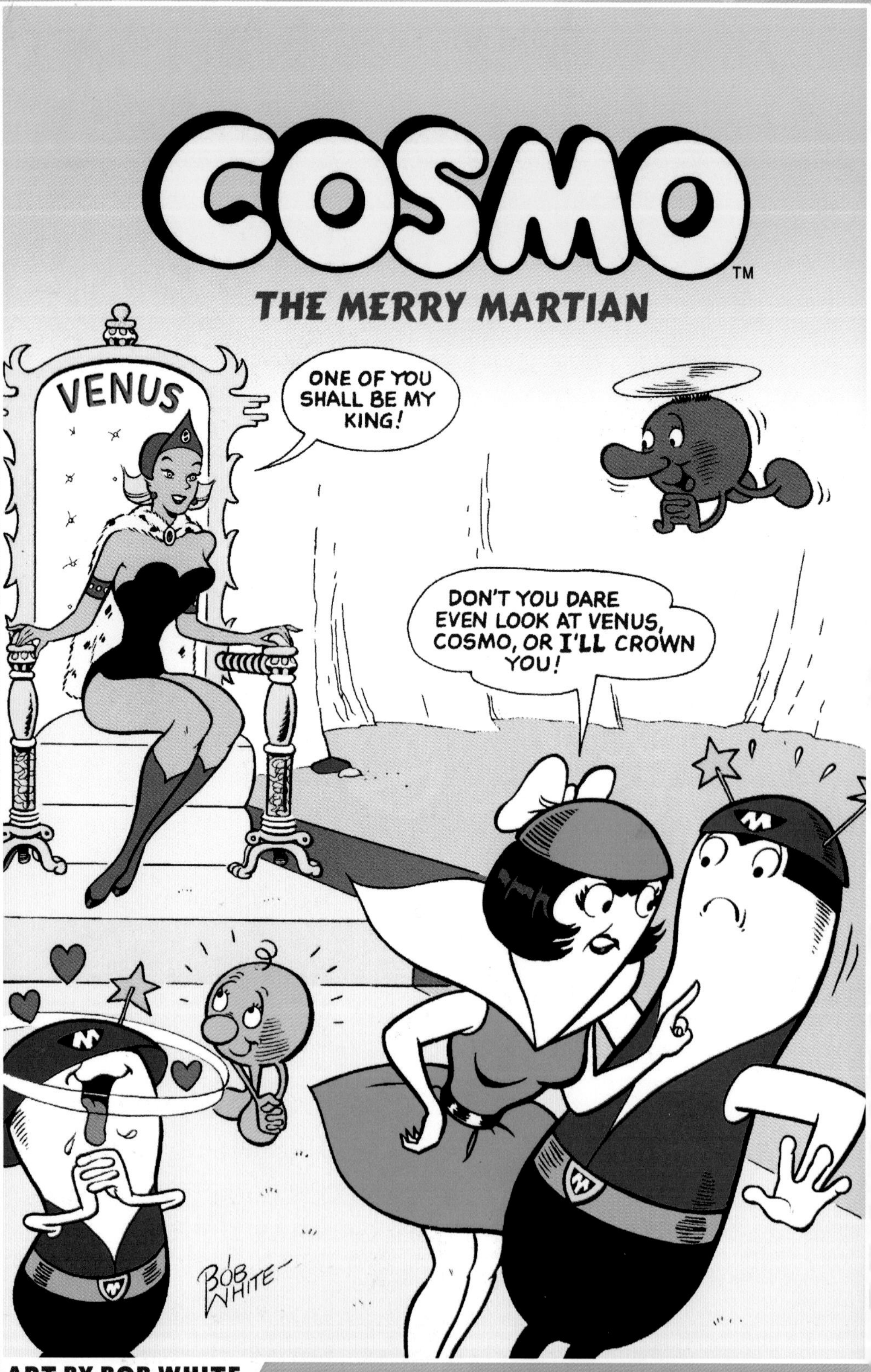
COSMO
THE MERRY MARTIAN
VENUS
ONE OF YOU SHALL BE MY KING!
DON'T YOU DARE EVEN LOOK AT VENUS, COSMO, OR I'LL CROWN YOU!
BOB WHITE

ART BY BOB WHITE

DATA FILE: COSMO

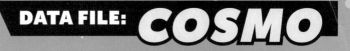

The adventure-hungry captain. Swashbuckling and confident, he can find a way out of any jam. Given he leads a crew of eccentric shipmates, Cosmo is bailing them out of danger more often than not!

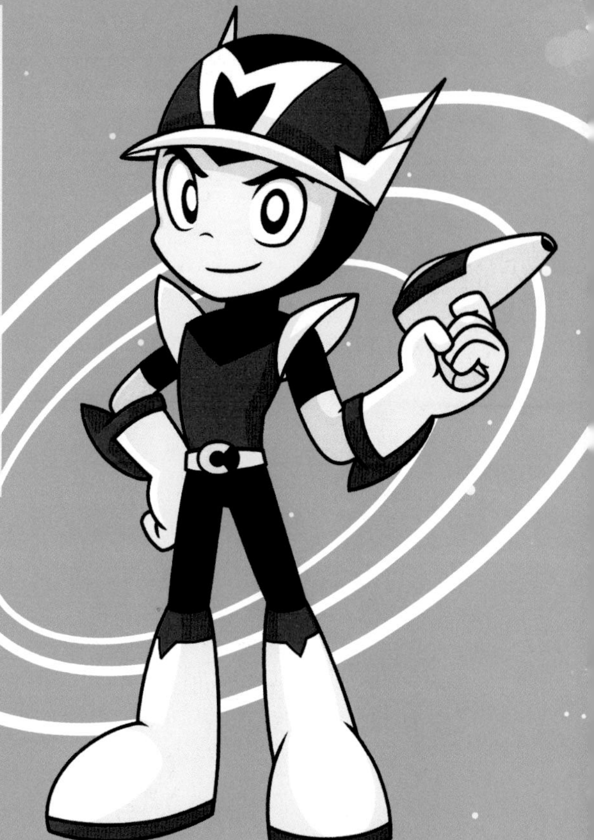

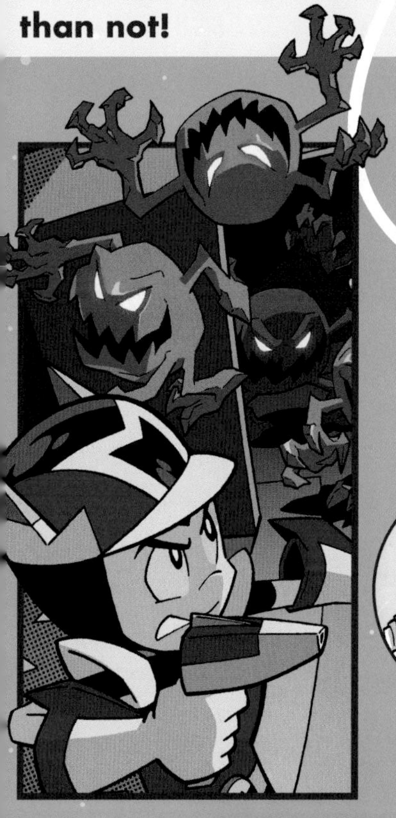

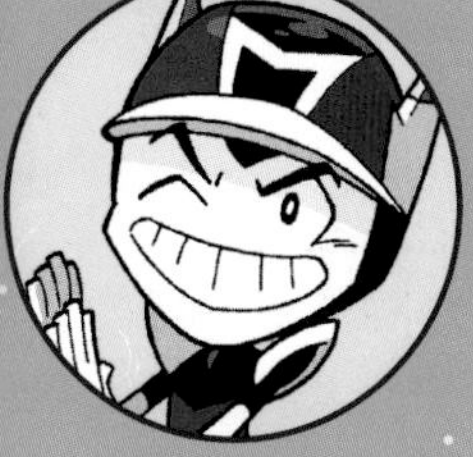

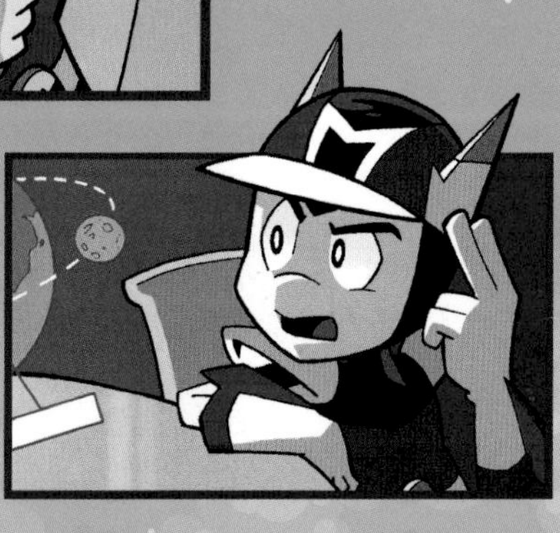

Name: Cosmo

Home planet: Mars

Age: 20

Likes: Adventuring with friends, jokes, indie rock, BBQ sauce

Dislikes: Evildoers, wrinkled apparel, honey mustard

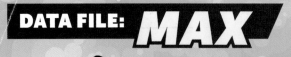

DATA FILE: MAX

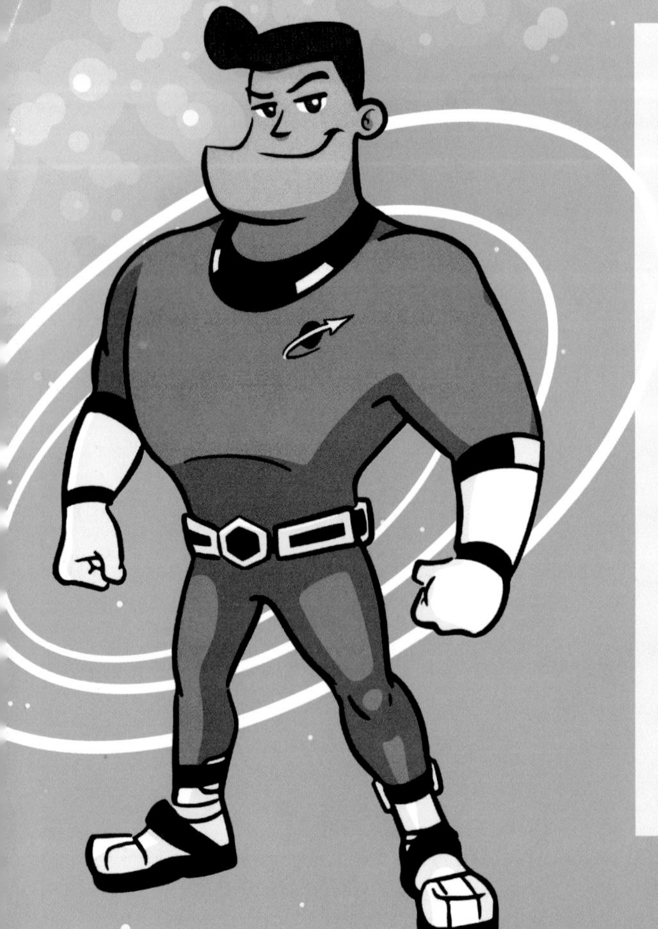

A human astronaut from the near-future. He was sent out to explore Mars in search for signs of life. Instead, Cosmo found (and rescued) him. Arrogant and out of his depth, Max tries to take command at all the wrong times. When push comes to shove, Max is a team player when it matters most.

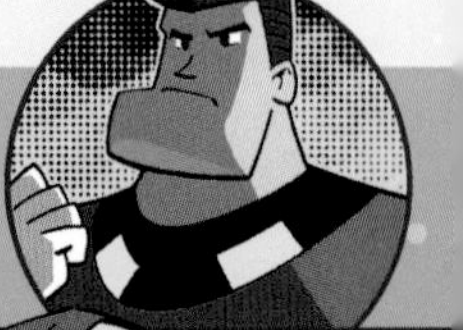

Name: Max Strongjaw

Home planet: Earth

Age: 28

Likes: Exploration, weight training, arcade games, pulled pork

Dislikes: Romantic comedies, bossy people, potato salad

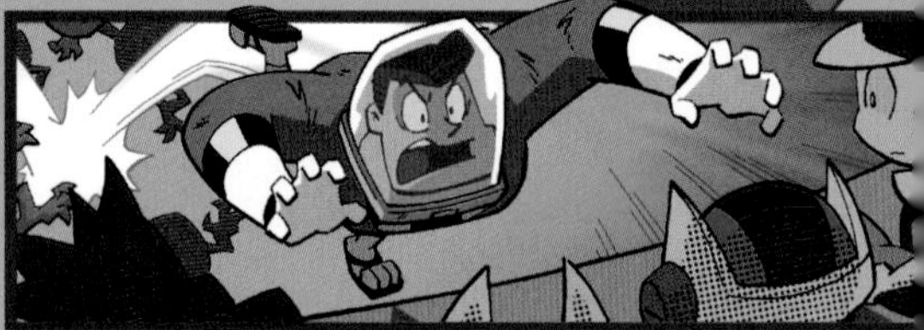

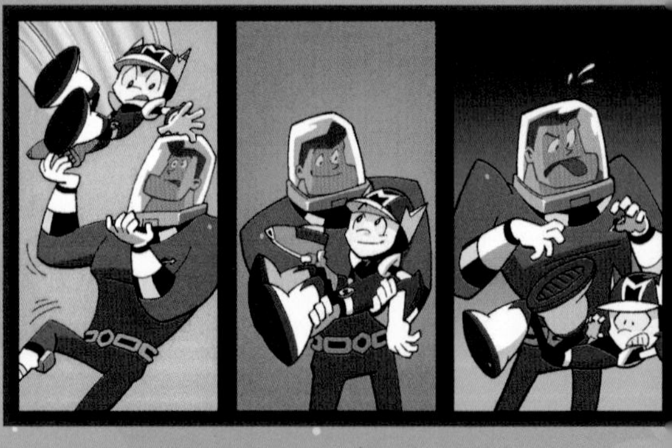

DATA FILE: MEDULLA

A bright yet eccentric Martian scientist who is also considered to be the "gadget gal" of the group. A touch older than the others, but no less adventurous, Medulla exploits Cosmo and the crew's various adventures as a means of testing out her new inventions.

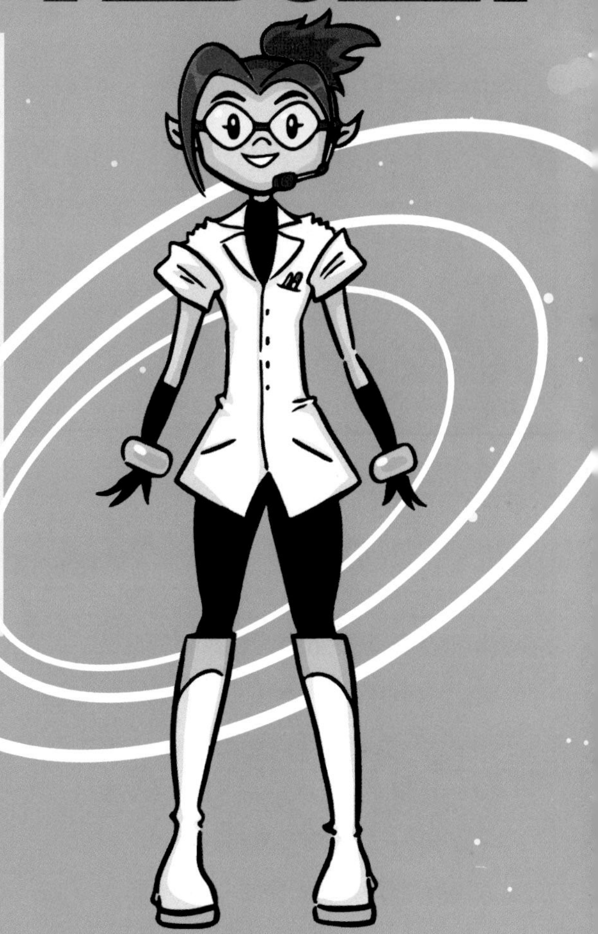

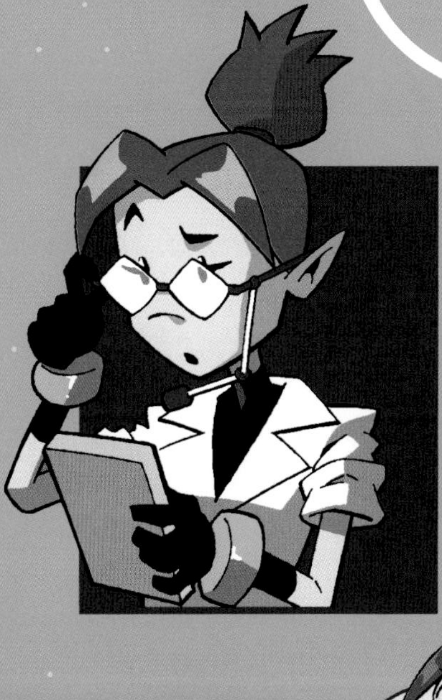

Name: Medulla

Home planet: Mars

Age: 29

Likes: Experimentation, reading, sudoku, spas, 1000% fruit juice

Dislikes: contact lenses, bar soap, teen romance, pushy people, cilantro

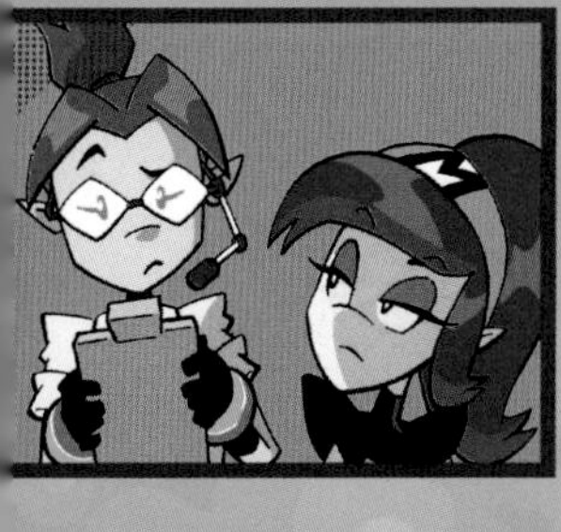

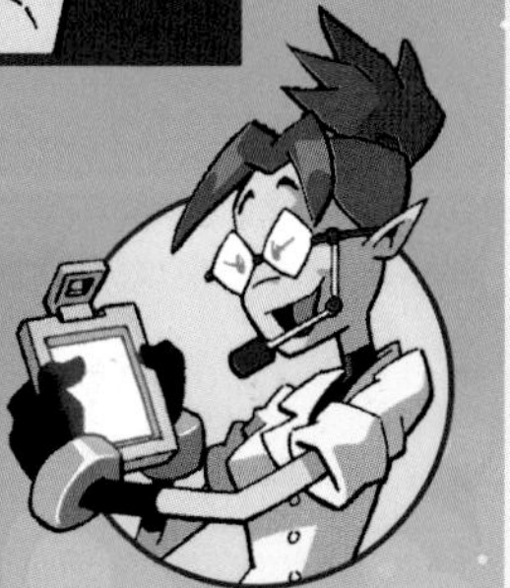

DATA FILE: ORBI & JOJO

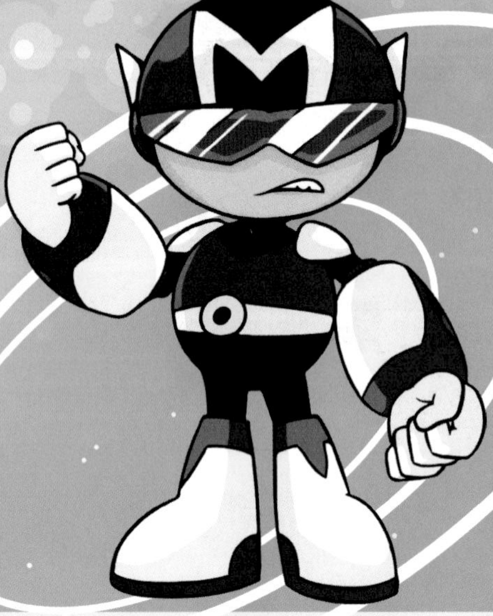

Orbi is Cosmo's best friend. While he wants to be a hero like Cosmo and talks a big talk, he doesn't have the nerves to back it up. To his credit, he's always willing to lend a hand and can usually bail himself out of danger with enough frantic flailing.

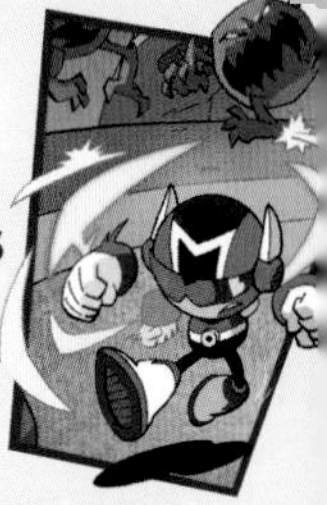

Name: Orbi

Home planet: Mars

Age: 13

Likes: Snacking, animals, video games, tranquility

Dislikes: monsters, chaos, peas, bright lights

Jojo is Orbi's pet "dog" with metamorphic abilities. Often coming across as gruff and disinterested, he's obviously intelligent enough to interact with the crew. In secret, he is an ancient and nomadic hero–a legend among his people.

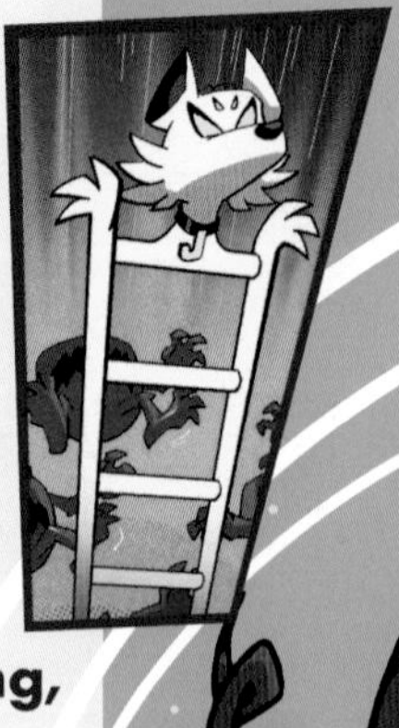

Name: Jojo

Home planet: Unknown

Age: Unknown

Likes: Adventuring, sleeping, hunting, treats

Dislikes: dishonesty, overly affectionate people, crowds

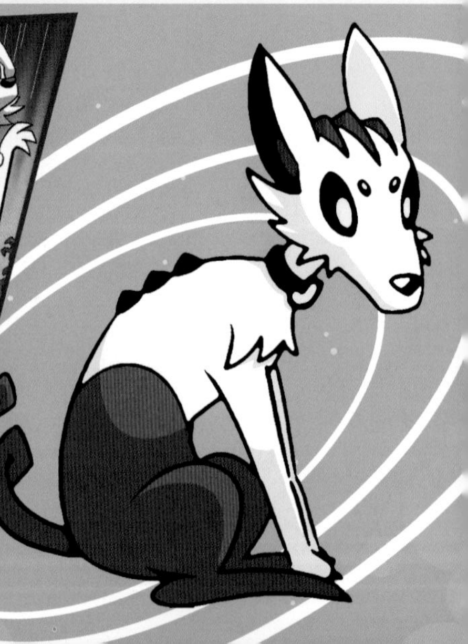

DATA FILE: ASTRA

Astra is the crew's pilot and wild card. She's eager to take on challenges—even unreasonable ones—but never purposefully at the expense of the crew.

She has a running romantic rivalry with Cosmo; they're both somewhat interested, but it's more fun to one-up each other.

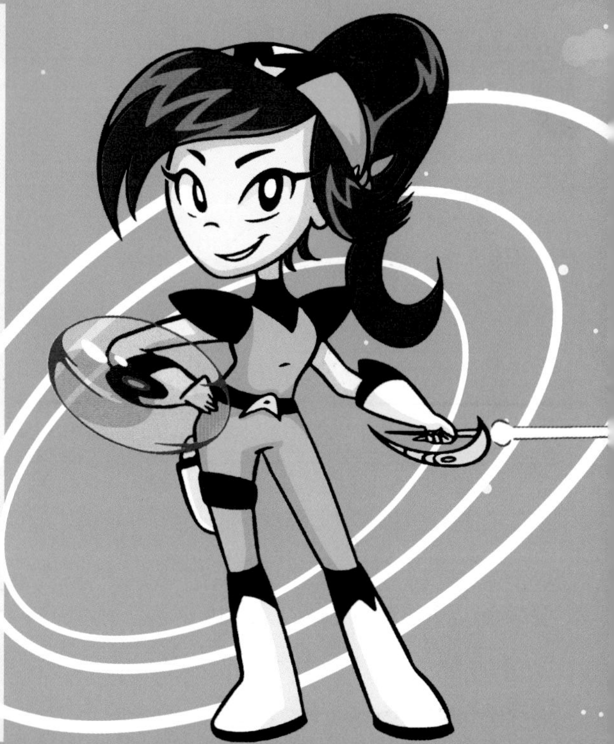

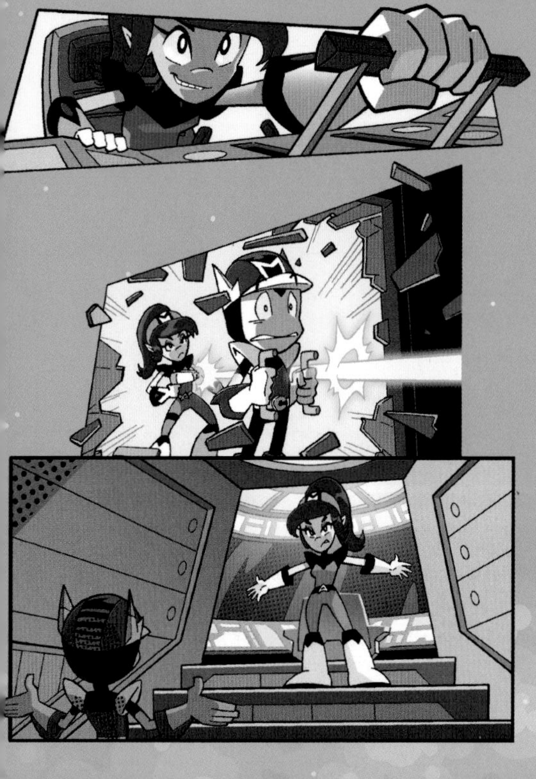

Name: Astra

Home planet: Mars

Age: 19

Likes: Flying vehicles, fencing, acrobatics, cinnamon rolls

Dislikes: Ghosts, waiting, invasion of privacy, bean sprouts

SERIES CONCEPT ART

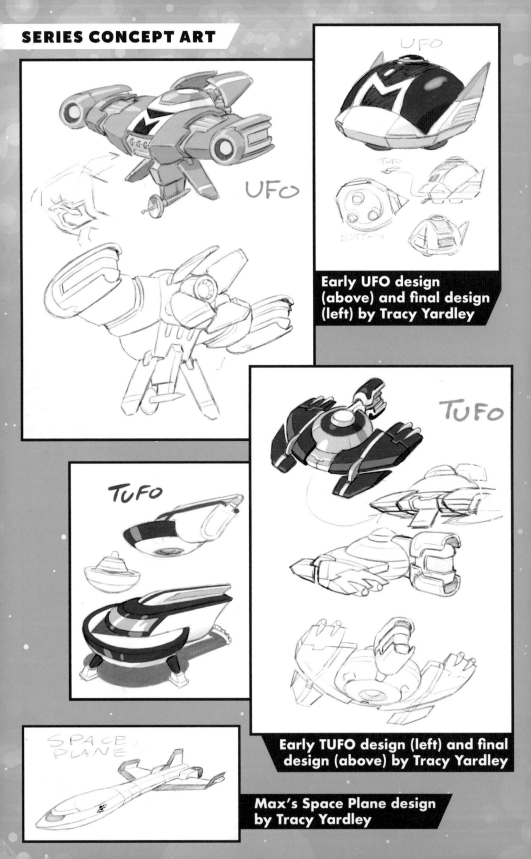

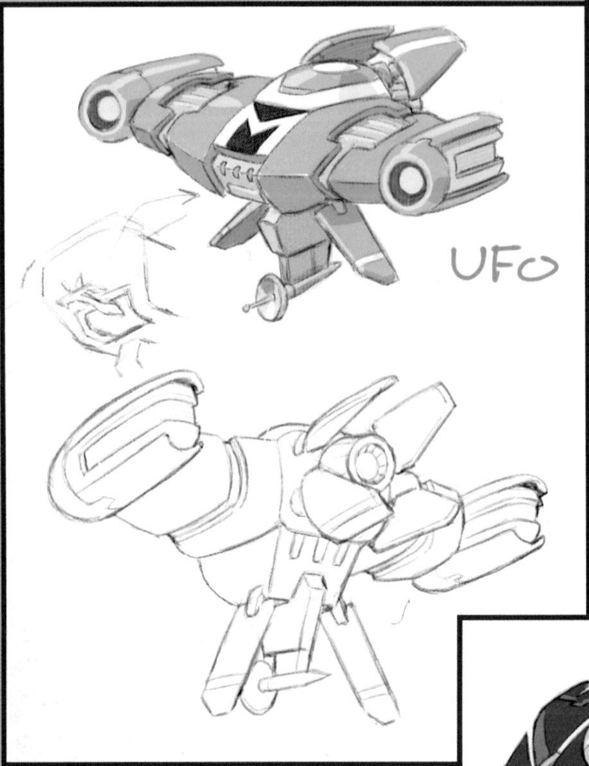
UFO

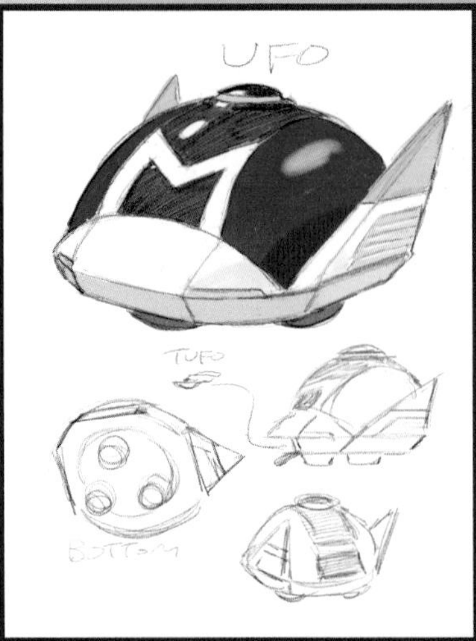
UFO
TUFO
BOTTOM

Early UFO design (above) and final design (left) by Tracy Yardley

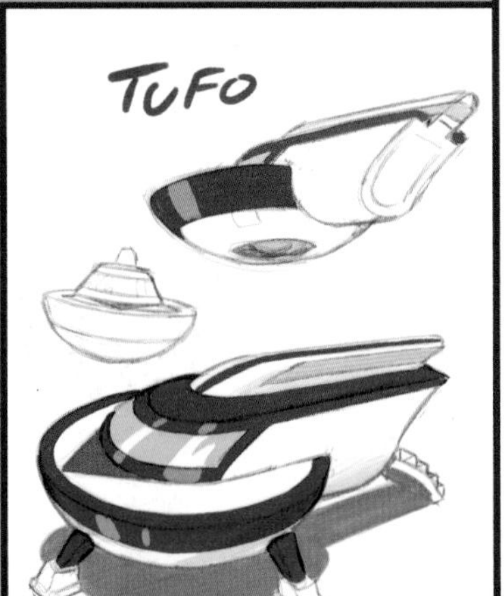
TUFO

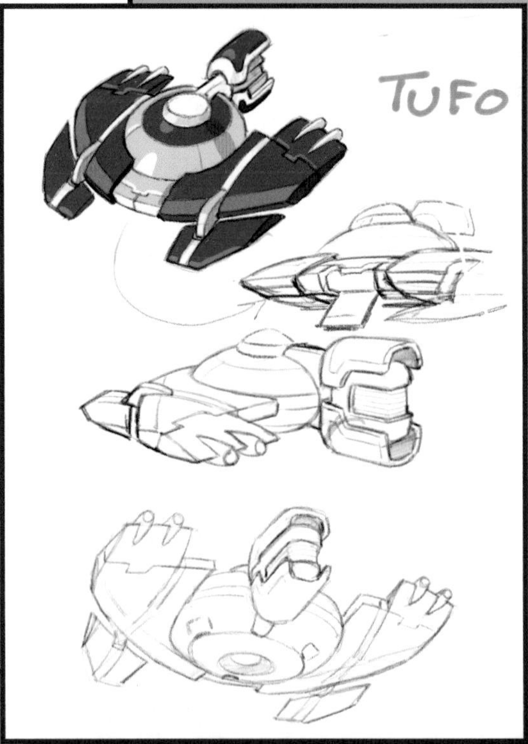
TUFO

Early TUFO design (left) and final design (above) by Tracy Yardley

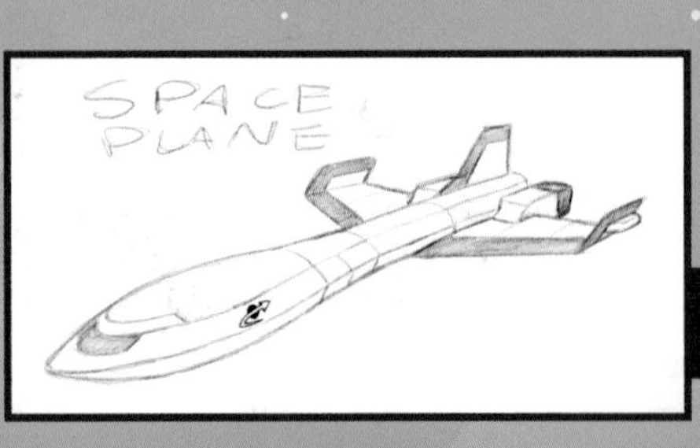
SPACE PLANE

Max's Space Plane design by Tracy Yardley

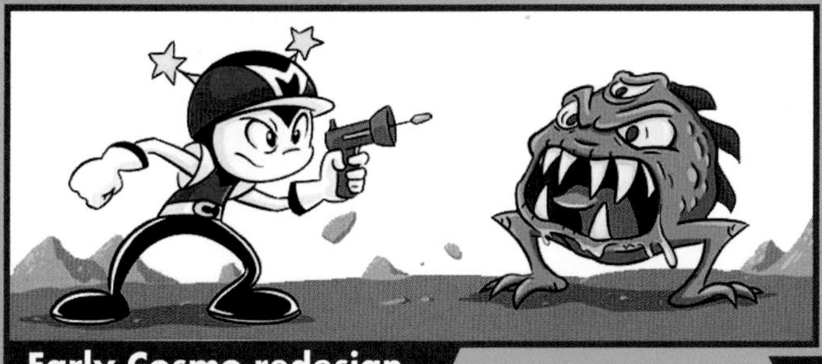

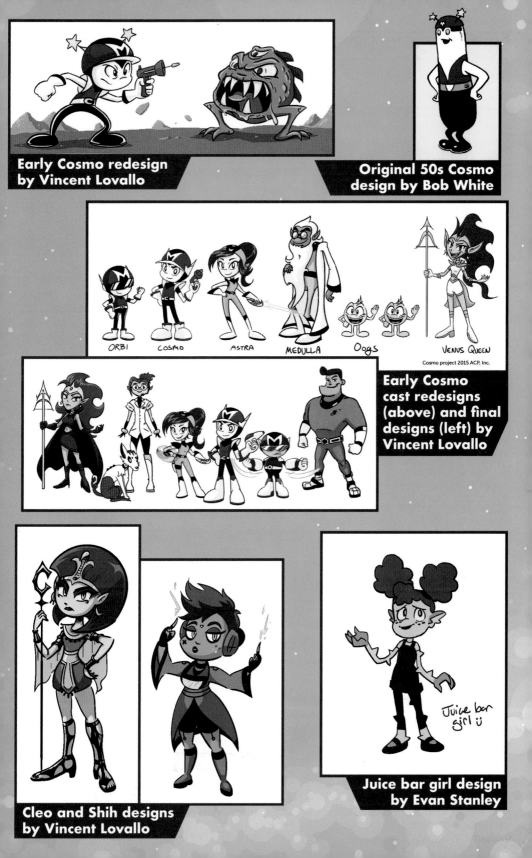

Early Cosmo redesign by Vincent Lovallo

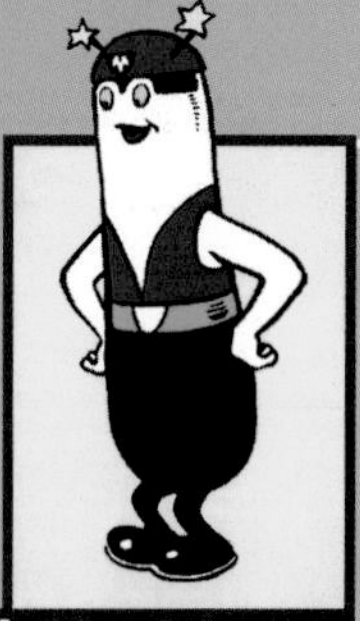

Original 50s Cosmo design by Bob White

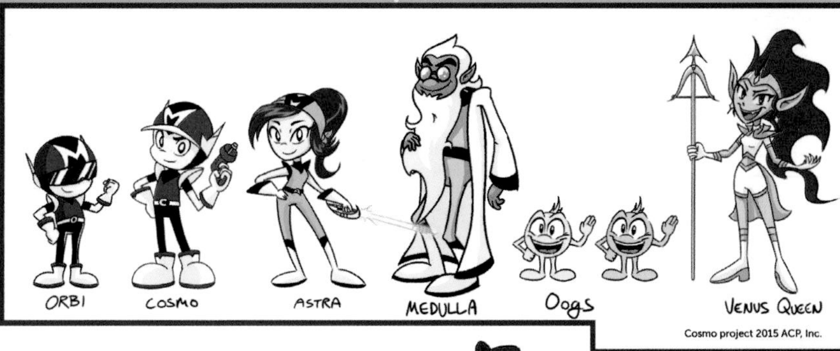
ORBI
COSMO
ASTRA
MEDULLA
Oogs
VENUS QUEEN
Cosmo project 2015 ACP, Inc.

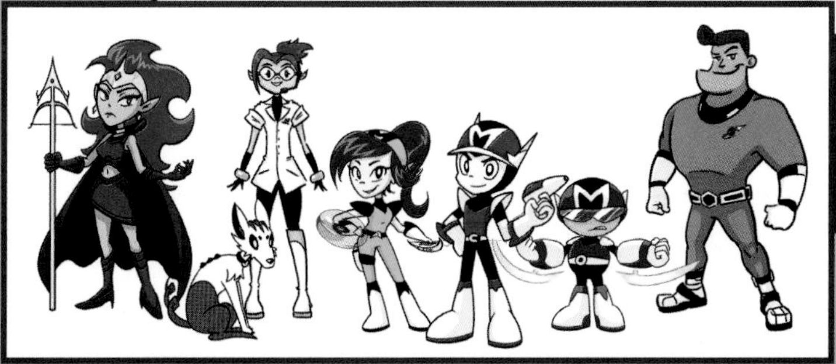

Early Cosmo cast redesigns (above) and final designs (left) by Vincent Lovallo

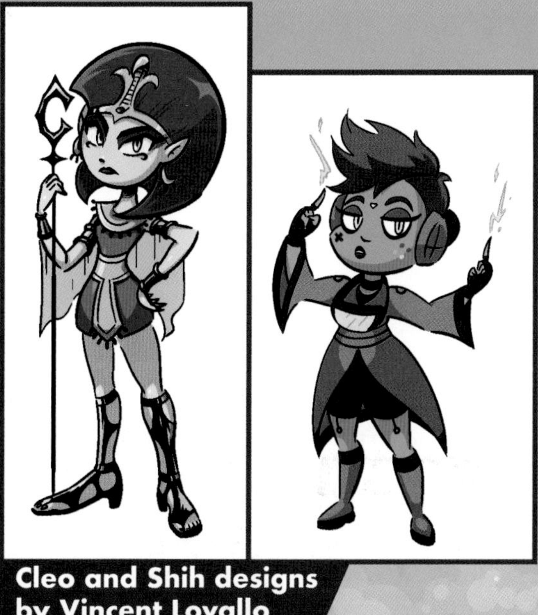

Cleo and Shih designs by Vincent Lovallo

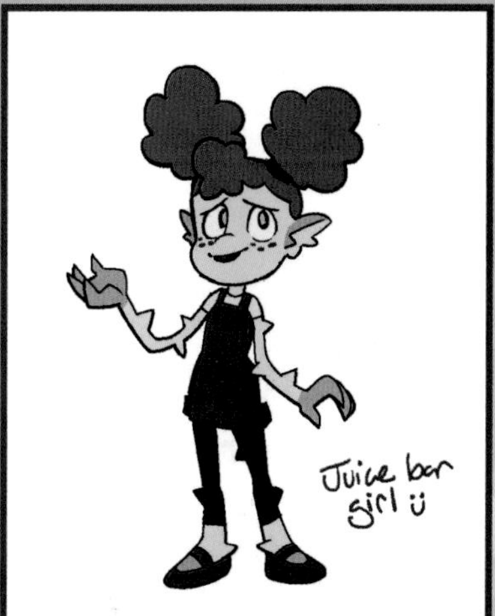
Juice bar girl

Juice bar girl design by Evan Stanley